No
Holding
Back

Center Point
Large Print

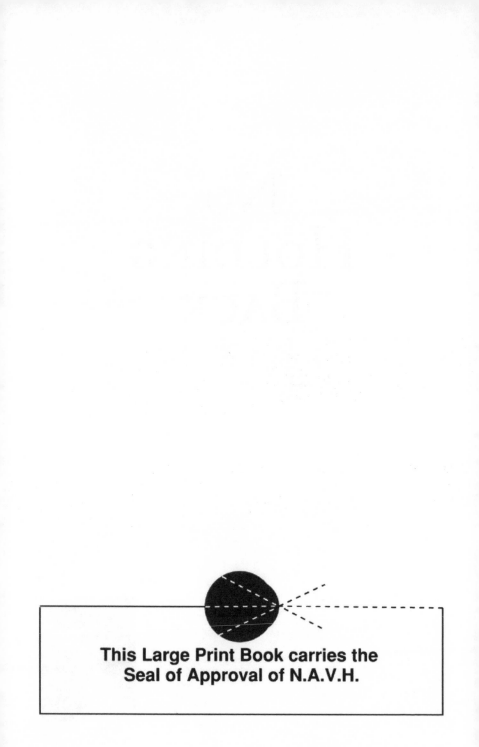

**This Large Print Book carries the
Seal of Approval of N.A.V.H.**

No Holding Back

The McKenzies of Ridge Trail

Lori Foster

CENTER POINT LARGE PRINT
THORNDIKE, MAINE

This Center Point Large Print edition
is published in the year 2021 by arrangement with
Harlequin Books S.A.

The text of this Large Print edition is unabridged.
In other aspects, this book may vary
from the original edition.
Printed in the United States of America
on permanent paper.
Set in 16-point Times New Roman type.

ISBN: 978-1-64358-859-9

The Library of Congress has cataloged this record
under Library of Congress Control Number: 2020952803

Very special thanks to Army Ranger Master Sergeant Shayne Laflin for answering the million and one questions I had on army rangers.

To amazing author Pamela Clare, and wonderful reader Kim Potts, thank you for sharing info on the Colorado landscape, highways, the front range and small towns along the Rockies.

I also want to share my heartfelt gratitude and deep respect to all who serve in our armed forces, and the families who love and support them.

And to the special police task forces fighting daily against human trafficking and forced labor, thank you. I know you see things no one should have to, and that your job is incredibly difficult on so many levels. Thank you for still doing it. You're making the world a better place.

Any and all errors, either on Colorado, rangers or task forces, are entirely my own!

CHAPTER ONE

Shivers racked her body as she watched him drink. Curled in the corner, waiting, dreading the inevitable—even breathing was difficult with so much fear crowding in around her. She wanted to cry but knew it wouldn't help. She wanted to let in the hysteria, but she hadn't quite accepted her fate . . . not yet.

She couldn't.

Outside the room, two other men stood guard. They'd told her she'd be forced to do this up to ten times a night, and she wasn't sure she'd even survive this first time.

She wanted to go home.

She wanted to curl up and die.

Mostly she wanted to fight—but how?

Amused by her fear, the man watched her while tossing back another shot. He enjoyed her terror— and that amplified everything she felt.

What to do, what to do, what to do?

Her gaze frantically searched the second-story room. One small window, opened to let in a breeze, led to a sheer drop onto a gravel lot. Would she survive going out that window? At the moment, did it really matter?

The man stood near the door. He'd slid a metal

bar into place, locking her in, ensuring she couldn't get past him. But also ensuring no one else could get in. Not until he'd finished.

He'd paid for two hours but now didn't seem in any rush to get started.

To the right of the door, a tiny table held a bottle of whiskey and a single glass. To the left, an empty wooden coat tree stood as a place for him to hang his clothes.

A bare mattress on a small bed occupied a wall. Nothing else.

Only her fear, the reality, the terror, her hatred, the cruelty . . . *her will to survive.*

When his loose lips stretched into a smug grin, she braced herself—and noticed that he stumbled a little as he stepped toward her.

Her heart punched painfully. Slowly, she slid up the wall to her feet. An invisible fist squeezed her throat, but she sidled sideways, toward that barred door.

Toward the little table.

From the hallway, loud music played. Whatever happened in this room, they didn't want to be bothered with it.

She kept her gaze locked on his, her hands clammy with sweat, so afraid that her limbs felt sluggish.

"Thinking to run?" he asked, his grin widening with anticipation.

"I . . . I was hoping I could have a drink, too?"

"You want to numb yourself? No, I don't think so."

He wanted her afraid. He wanted her to feel every awful second of this degradation. With a lot of effort, she tamped down the need to vomit and managed to ask, "Then . . . should I pour you another?"

Snorting, he propped a shoulder to the wall. "Want to get me drunk, huh? Sure, go ahead and try it, but you'll see, I know how to hold my liquor." Tipping his head, he narrowed his eyes and the grin turned into a sneer. "Alcohol makes me mean."

Refusing to dwell on that possibility, she forced a nod, reaching for the bottle anyway, letting him see how badly she trembled. She filled the small glass, then lifted it . . . while keeping the bottle in her other hand.

The obnoxious brute paid no attention; he focused on watching her quake as she came to him, the glass held out as a feeble offering.

Instead of taking it, he caught her wrist in a painful grip, jerking her toward him, laughing as she cried out.

She swung the bottle with all her might.

Sterling jerked awake with a start, her heart racing and her throat aching with the need to scream.

She didn't. She never did—no matter what.

9

Silence kept her safer than a scream ever could.

In just seconds, she absorbed the low light of the bar, the ancient rock and roll playing on the jukebox, the clamor of a few dozen voices talking low to one another.

God. She swallowed heavily, looking around at the familiar sights. Her gaze landed on the bartender.

He watched her. *Always.*

Nothing got by that man.

He could pretend to be an average guy, he could wear the trappings of a simple bar owner, but she knew better. He hid something, maybe something as monumental as her own secrets, but she wouldn't ask. The Tipsy Wolverine bar was her haven from the road. She could sleep in her truck, and sometimes did, but she didn't truly rest.

Here, in the little Podunk bar in the small mountain town of Ridge Trail, Colorado, she knew no one would bother her.

Because of *him*.

Again her eyes sought him out. She guessed him at six feet five. *Really* big, but solid head to toes. Posture erect. Awareness keen. He wore his glossy dark hair neatly trimmed, precisely styled . . . but it was those piercing blue eyes that really caught and held her attention.

His gaze had veered away from her, but that didn't make him unaware. Sterling pegged him as ex-military, or maybe something deadlier. He was too damn physically fit to be anyone ordinary.

Her nostrils flared a little as she looked him over. In the seedy area of town where locals slumped in their seats and laughed too loudly, he was always . . . mannered. Contained. Professional but not in the way of a suited businessman.

More like a guy who knew he could handle himself in any situation. A guy who easily kicked ass, took names and did so without a scratch. Those thick shoulders . . . Studying his body left a funny warmth in Sterling's stomach, sending her interested gaze to his pronounced biceps, watching the fluid bunch and flex of them with the smallest movement. His pullover shirt fit his wide chest perfectly, showing sculpted pecs and, letting her attention drift downward, a flat, firm middle.

Lord, the man was put together fine. Add in a lean jaw, a strong but straight nose, and those cool blue eyes fringed by dark lashes, and she assumed he broke hearts on a daily basis.

Not *her* heart. She wasn't susceptible to that kind of stuff. She could take in the exceptional view and stay detached. *She could.*

Only . . . this time she had to really concentrate to make it true.

His gaze locked to hers, catching her perusal, and his firm lips quirked in a small "you're not immune" smile.

It made her mouth go dry.

He couldn't know that, could he? Yet he looked as if he'd just read her every admiring thought.

Feeling oddly exposed, she held up her glass, realized it was still full and hastily mouthed, "Coffee?"

With a nod, he moved away to a service counter behind the bar. Less than half a minute later, he strode over in his casual yet confident way with a steaming cup.

He knew how she took it, with one sugar and a splash of creamer. He knew because he missed nothing. Ever.

Setting it before her, he asked, "Done with this?" indicating the shot she'd ordered—and hadn't touched.

Usually, to justify her lengthy naps, she bought a couple of drinks. This time, exhausted to the bone, she hadn't lasted long enough.

"Thanks." Sterling sipped her coffee.

That he didn't move away set her heart tripping. Defiant, she glanced up and caught a slight frown carved from what appeared to be concern. She was good at reading people—except for him. Most of the time she didn't know what he was thinking, and she didn't like that.

Suspicion prickled. "What?"

Heavy lashes lowering, he thought a moment before meeting her gaze again. "I'm worried that anything I say might put you off."

Sterling stiffened with accusation. "What do you have to say?"

"Such a lethal tone," he teased—as if they knew each other well. "You don't have to order drinks just to be in here. You want a place to kick up your feet—"

Abruptly, she dropped her feet from the seat of the chair across from her. She unconsciously braced herself—to act, to react, to protect herself if necessary.

"Or to rest without being disturbed," he continued, ignoring her tension. "You're always welcome." As if he knew her innate worry, as if he could see her automatic response to his nearness, he took a step back. "No questions asked, and no drink order necessary."

Before she could come up with a reply, he walked away.

For twenty minutes, Sterling remained, but he didn't look at her again.

Not until she walked out. He watched her then. Hell yeah, he did. She felt his gaze burning over her like a physical touch. Like *interest*. It left her with heightened awareness.

Of him.

Damn, damn, damn.

Cade wanted to kick his own ass.

She'd been coming into the bar for months now. She hadn't yet given her name, but he knew it all the same. He made a point of knowing everyone in the bar, whether they were important to his operation or not.

Sterling Parson. Star for short.

Privately, he called her Trouble.

At a few inches shy of six feet, her body toned, she walked with a self-possessed air that he recognized as more attitude than ability. She wore that swagger like a warning that all but shouted *Back off.*

Her long wavy brown hair was usually in a ponytail, occasionally in a braid and sometimes stuffed under a trucker's cap.

Despite the loose shirts she wore with straight-legged jeans and mean lace-up black boots in an effort to disguise her body, she'd be hard to miss. For sure no one in his bar had missed her.

The woman was unique in so many ways. Bold but somehow vulnerable. Composed, yet temperate. Beautiful . . . but only to a discerning eye, because she did all she could to blend in.

The big rig she drove had SP Trucking emblazoned on the side, yet she was far from the usual trucker they got as customers.

The day she'd first walked in, heads had swiveled, eyes had widened and interest had perked—but after Cade swept his gaze around the room, everyone had gotten the message.

The lady was off-limits.

Cade hadn't bothered to explain to anyone. He

never did . . . except occasionally to family. Then only when pressed.

From the moment he'd first spotted Sterling, he'd sensed the emotional wounds she hid, knew she had secrets galore and understood she needed a place to rest.

She needed *him*.

Star didn't know that yet, but no problem. In his bar, in this shit neighborhood, he'd look out for her anyway—same as he did for anyone in need.

Moving to the window, he watched her leave. Her long stride carried her across the well-lit gravel lot, not in haste but with an excess of energy. He couldn't imagine her meandering. The woman knew one speed: full steam ahead.

After unlocking the door, she climbed into her rig with practiced ease. Head tipped back, she rested a moment before squaring her shoulders and firing the engine. She idled for a bit, maybe checking her gauges, then eased off the clutch and smoothly rolled out to the road. Cade watched until he couldn't see her taillights anymore.

Where she'd go, he didn't yet know—but he wanted to. He wanted to introduce himself, ask questions, maybe offer assistance.

Her preferences on that were obvious.

Except that tonight she'd watched him a little more.

Actually, she often noticed him, in a cautious,

distrustful way. And she always came back.

Sometimes she'd sleep for an hour, sometimes longer. Tonight, she'd dozed for two hours before jerking awake in alarm.

A bad dream?

Or a bad memory?

If she kept to her usual pattern, she'd be back tomorrow night on her return trip. Maybe, just maybe, he'd find a chink in her armor. He glanced at the little table she always chose.

Tomorrow, he'd offer her something different.

After too much driving, sitting through endless traffic in Colorado's summer heat and going without enough rest, Sterling returned to the bar. Aching from her eyebrows to her toes, it was a relief to pull in to the lot a littler earlier than usual.

She'd thought about finding another place to rest. Bars and truck stops riddled this side of the Rockies. Before discovering the Tipsy Wolverine, she'd often crashed in a different location each time, but here . . . For some reason she was mostly comfortable here. *Mostly.*

It was the bartender, she knew. He didn't say much, didn't thump his chest like an ape—because he didn't have to. His commanding presence let everyone know that he was the one in charge.

She knew it. In that bar, no one could hurt her because he wouldn't let them.

Sterling shook her head. It was a crazy conclusion, but she trusted her instincts. So far, they'd served her well.

Grabbing her discarded jacket, she climbed out of the truck. Higher in the mountains, the chill could seep into her bones, but here in the valley, it had to be in the midnineties. The temperature in Colorado was all about elevation. The higher you went, the colder it got. She'd learned that her button-up shirt would be fine in the valley, but if the road climbed—and it sometimes did—she needed warmer clothes. The air-conditioning in the bar often chilled her, too, especially when she napped.

Her long sloppy ponytail bounced and her heavy boots crunched on gravel when she strode across the lot. Some strange sensation sizzled inside her.

She refused to acknowledge it as anticipation.

The minute she walked through the door, she knew something was different. Two men, regulars that she recognized, sat at her customary table. That hadn't happened since her third visit months ago. The table was usually saved for her. Without pausing, she continued into the dim room, giving a casual glance around.

No, it wasn't extra crowded.

Yes, there were other tables available.

So why, then . . .

The bartender stepped in front of her, his nearly

six and a half feet of muscle drawing her to a sudden stop. "Could I have a word?"

Almost plowing into him sent her heart shooting into her throat. She was tall enough that few men made her feel small, but this one towered over her.

Damn it, she hadn't even noticed him approach before he was just . . . there, standing too close, crowding her with his size and strength. In a nanosecond, her body jolted into defense mode.

She hid her unease even as she considered her options of fight or flight.

And damn him, he *knew* it. She saw it in the way his gaze sharpened, how his mouth softened.

In sympathy?

Screw that. Sterling took a step back, ready to retreat. Not like fighting was an actual option.

Raising his hands, his expression impassive, he said, "At the bar would be fine, if you have just a minute. I'm still on the clock."

Her gaze skipped to her table, and seconds ago she'd anticipated resting her bones in that well-worn seat. Now some of her exhaustion had lifted.

"I can move them if you want me to," he offered quietly. "After I've explained."

She had no interest in conversing with him, being drawn to him in any way. Familiarity worried her, yet curiosity won out. To cover her caution, she offered a casual shrug and indicated he should lead the way.

No way did she want him at her back.

He gifted her with that brief smile again.

Such a nice mouth, she couldn't help noticing. Not that she cared. Nice or not, she refused involvement.

He turned and headed for the bar.

Drawing in a bracing breath, she followed. Nice back, too. And forearms. And his backside in those jeans . . .

Sterling frowned at herself and vowed none of it mattered.

No one else sat at the far end of the scarred, polished wood counter, and once she'd taken the last stool, he circled around.

"Coffee? Cola?"

"Coke is fine."

"I can throw you together a sandwich if you want."

In most cases, she refused food when offered to her, but here, from him, it seemed okay— especially with her stomach grumbling. "Sure, thanks."

He went through a half door that led to the kitchen behind the bar and returned a minute later with a ham-and-cheese sandwich and chips. After setting the food before her, he filled a glass with ice and poured her a Coke.

Sterling realized he must have coordinated this little meet and greet, because one of his workers took over filling orders without being asked.

Obviously he was up to something—but what?

Watching her a little too closely, he leaned a hip against the bar. "You don't miss much, do you?"

Her gaze shot to his. She had a mouthful and had to chew and swallow before she could answer. "Should I?"

"No, but few people are as aware as you are." He opened his own cola, drinking straight from the bottle. "My name is Cade McKenzie, by the way."

"I didn't ask."

"I know. But I thought if you knew more about me, you'd—"

"What?" Panic, maybe anger, sharpened her tone. "Loosen up? Like you more? Get friendly?"

"Stop distrusting me."

Had her wariness been so noticeable? Apparently. "I'm eating your sandwich. What is that if not trust?"

Her reasoning made him grin, showing straight white teeth, and good God, when he did that, he was too damn gorgeous. The amusement softened his granite edge, made him feel approachable.

And damn it, it sparked something deep inside her.

She concentrated on her sandwich.

"My brother owns a gym in town," he continued. "You've probably noticed him in here a few times."

Of course she had. The family resemblance was

unmistakable. "He's younger, different-colored eyes."

Nodding at this additional sign of her awareness, he explained, "Different mothers, but we were raised together. I have a sister, too. She's the baby at twenty-six."

"Does she look like you, as well?" She hadn't seen any women at the bar that she'd have pegged as a relation.

"Similar features, only more feminine. Same-colored eyes as my brother, but her hair is lighter than ours."

It struck Sterling that she was chatting. Casually, easily. When had she last done that? The shock of it put her on edge. "I didn't ask for a family rundown."

"I know. Other than your usual table and an occasional drink, all you ask for is to be left alone."

"Yet here we are." Not that she could entirely blame him for that. She'd chosen to accept the food, the conversation. Nothing would come of it, though. Not more familiarity. Not friendship.

Definitely nothing beyond that.

He leveled that electric-blue stare on her. "I wanted to show you that I have roots here, that I'm not a threat in any way."

Refusing to lower her guard, she asked, "But *why?*" She didn't trust goodwill. A motive generally followed close behind.

"Because you're a good customer, a regular, and I get that you want your space—no problem with that—but I thought I could help."

Slowly, she ate another bite of the sandwich while considering him. The urge to walk away was strong.

Oddly enough, an equally compelling urge had her asking, "Help how?" Then she thought to add, "With *what?*"

He propped his elbows on the bar, leaning toward her as he eased into his topic. "So your table . . . I can keep it open for you if that's what you want. That isn't a problem. But since you usually catch a nap, I wanted to offer my office."

One of the chips caught in her throat, making her cough.

Thankfully, he didn't reach around to pat her on the back. He seemed to know touching her would be a very bad move.

Instead, he nudged her glass toward her.

It took three gulps before she could catch her breath. Then she gasped, "Your office?"

A big old *no* to that. Not in a million years.

"It locks from the inside, so you wouldn't have to worry about customers stumbling in on you."

Would she have to worry about him?

"I have a key," he said, using his uncanny mind-reading superpower. "But you could hold on to it while you're in there."

The offer so surprised her that she couldn't

find the right words to refuse him. She settled on shaking her head. "No thanks." She preferred to be out in the open. Not that the public option always equaled safety—she'd learned that the hard way. But at least this space was familiar to her. She'd memorized it in detail and knew the exits, the number of tables to the door, that the big front window was tempered glass and that Cade McKenzie kept a few weapons behind the bar—but generally wouldn't need them to restore order if it came to that.

That line of thinking took her attention to his hands. Big hands. Hands that would feel like sledgehammers if he made a fist.

No, he didn't need a weapon. He *was* a weapon.

Not deterred by her refusal, he continued explaining. "I only use the office before we open and after we close. Besides my desk and chair, there's a love seat, a few throw pillows. A private landline." His gaze searched hers. "You'd be more comfortable."

Suddenly, it struck Sterling as funny. Here they were, tiptoeing around the obvious: she *knew* he wasn't just a bartender. And somehow he *knew* she wasn't just a trucker.

Grinning, she sat back and studied him.

"That's nice," he said.

Taken off guard, she asked, "What?"

"Your smile."

Stymied by that, it took her a second to regroup.

"Look, I haven't even given you my name."

"I'm aware."

"But you know it anyway, don't you?" She expected him to lie, and when he did, she'd have solid reason not to trust him. She'd pay for her food, walk out and drive away—never to return.

Doing his own thorough study, he let his gaze move over her face as if cataloging each feature . . . and liking what he saw. "I can't go into details, or explain, but yes, I know your name."

Her heart skipped a beat. He'd admitted it! What did that mean for their association? Part of her shivered with alarm, but another part, a part she'd like to deny, suffered the strangest sort of . . . relief.

If someone actually knew her, then she was no longer alone. She existed. She *mattered*.

Sterling shook her head. Maybe he wasn't as good as she assumed.

Caught between conflicting emotions, she narrowed her eyes. "Fine. Let's hear it."

Straightening, Cade did a quick check to ensure no one listened to them, then casually dropped his research bombshell. "Sterling Parson, but you used to go by Star. You're twenty-nine, got your commercial driver's license when you were barely twenty-two, worked for Brown Transportation for a while, then bought your own rig when you were twenty-six."

Her jaw literally dropped. Dear God, he knew

24

so much. *Too* much. She'd been right to fear him—no, damn it. *Not* fear. Just good old caution, the same caution she used with everyone. The caution that kept her alive. He wasn't different, wasn't special, and she couldn't—

"My sister," he offered with grave seriousness, interrupting her private castigation. "She's a research whiz, and I was curious."

"About me?"

"About you," he concurred.

No apology, but an explanation? "You had no right," she whispered through stiff lips.

For a moment he looked away while using one long, blunt finger to trace a bead of condensation on his cola bottle. "You can call it second nature." He rolled a thick shoulder. "Or instinct." Tension ratcheted up when he looked into her eyes, making them both a little breathless. His voice sounded like a soft growl when he added, "I felt it was important to know."

Dazed, confused and, damn him, disappointed, Sterling shook her head. "Now I have to find a new place to go."

His focus never wavered from hers. "Whatever you're up to, Star, you'll be safer here. Give yourself a minute to think before you react, and you'll admit it."

"What?" she asked with a sneer. "You don't know what I'm doing? You don't know why? How . . . incomplete of you."

"I tried not to overstep too much."

That made her laugh, but not with any humor.

"You're drawing attention when I assume you'd rather not. No," he said when alarm stiffened her neck, "not from anyone dangerous. Actually, all the customers have been curious about you at one time or another. I don't think any of us have ever heard you laugh."

"You can't know who's dangerous and who isn't." More than most, she'd learned that it was sometimes impossible to tell.

Softly, he insisted, "Yes, I can. I know everyone who comes here. You can trust me on that."

She snorted. She wouldn't trust anyone ever again.

"Right now there are only locals, a few truckers and a few vacationers, but it's still better not to be noticed, right? In case anyone comes around asking questions?"

Regret froze her to the spot, leaving her a little sick to her stomach, full of angst. And yearning.

God, she had so much yearning.

This bar had begun to feel like . . . home? How absurd. It wasn't in any way special, and it wasn't even in a good part of town. It was just a place where she could relax, and she hated to lose it.

The location was ideal for her, being only thirty minutes from I-25 with plenty of places to hide in between, and closer still to other venues known for seedier practices.

She didn't want to give it up, but what choice did she have now?

Cade made a small sound of frustration, there and gone. "Your table is empty now," he pointed out.

Yes, she was aware of that. Standing, she pulled out some cash to toss on the counter, but Cade stopped her with a shake of his head.

"This one was on the house. Go get some rest—and think about my offer."

She really didn't feel like leaving yet. Now that she'd eaten, lethargy gripped her. Finally she nodded. "All right, I'll think about it."

"Thanks, Star. I appreciate it."

"As you pointed out, I *used* to go by that name. Now I'm more comfortable with Sterling."

"I don't think you're ever really comfortable, so let's not nitpick on the name yet."

Teasing again? The man had a dimple. How unfair! He was always so attractive, but now with satisfaction in his gaze and his sexy mouth curved? Devastating.

She didn't understand him. She didn't understand herself with him, either. Rather than let him see her confusion, she headed to the table, ignoring the curious glances from the regulars who knew it was unusual for her to chat up anyone.

Despite her new caution, the feeling of security remained. Within minutes of sitting down, she dozed off.

. . .

Cade knew the second she nodded off. She sat facing the rest of the bar, her long legs stretched out to the chair opposite her, her arms folded over her chest. Uncaring what anyone thought, she slumped in the seat, more reclining than otherwise, let her head rest back against the wall and closed her eyes. Long lashes sent feathery shadows over her cheekbones.

He admired her nose, narrow with the slightest arch in the bridge; he considered it perfect for her face. Not too cute, not too big or small. Like her attitude, each feature of her face and body was unique.

Her breathing deepened and slowed, but she didn't snore. Didn't go completely lax, either. Hell, he doubted she ever did.

So much churning wariness probably kept her constantly on edge. He knew it affected him that way. He rarely slept soundly, but then, he didn't need much sleep.

With any luck, she'd doze right up until closing time at midnight. Since being a bartender wasn't really his vocation, he didn't keep usual hours for the bar. Most in the area were open until 2:00 a.m., but he shut down at midnight and didn't open again until 4:00 p.m. That gave him plenty of time for other pursuits, and when the two overlapped, he had reliable staff to cover for him at the bar.

They were only an hour from closing when two strangers entered. The frisson of awareness that settled in his gut told him they were about to have problems.

Instinctively, his gaze shifted to Star.

He found her sitting upright, alert, her eyes narrowed dangerously. Well, hell.

He'd never known a woman so acutely aware of her surroundings. In that, she matched him.

Didn't mean he wanted her getting elbow deep in danger, especially not when that danger just walked into his bar.

Subtly, he drifted his gaze between her and the men—hoping she'd ignore them, that she'd go back to sleep.

Should have known better.

While he watched in frustration, she pulled the tie from her hair and let it tumble down over one shoulder.

Fuck me sideways.

He'd always known the difference a woman's hair could make to her appearance. But on Star? This softer look had a near-physical impact on him. The woman had gorgeous hair. Longer than he'd realized, and a rich brown streaked with gold by the sun. He watched as she tunneled her fingers in close to her scalp and fluffed it.

He would have liked to do that for her. Hands curled loosely, he could almost feel that silky mass.

When her slender fingers flicked open three buttons on her shirt, he locked his jaw—not that she noticed. Keeping her focus on the newcomers, she parted the shirt until a fair amount of cleavage showed, then tied the shirttails at her waist.

It took her less than thirty seconds to go from plain and reserved to a total bombshell. The "hands off" signals were gone, and instead her demeanor screamed "up for grabs."

Why? What the hell was she planning?

When she stood, he cursed silently, reading her intent.

She didn't spare him a glance. No, she'd forgotten all about him, and that nettled, because she'd been his first thought when he saw the two men.

The second she stood, she caught their attention. Wearing a flirty smile, she sauntered toward them.

Cade seriously wanted to demolish them both simply for the way they looked at her.

When she reached the bigger of the two men, she asked, "Got a cigarette?"

The guy sized her up in an insultingly thorough way, then pulled the pack from his front T-shirt pocket, shook one loose and offered it to her.

Maintaining eye contact, she leaned down and slowly slipped a cigarette free.

Both men looked down her shirt.

The second guy asked, "Light?"

"I have my own outside, but thank you." She sashayed out the door, and it wasn't just the two new guys watching her. Every man in the place had his fascinated gaze glued to her ass.

Shit. Cade quickly, but casually, directed others to cover the bar. Pretending he needed a break, he went down the hall and into the private office he'd offered for her use. After relocking the door, he went to the single window in the room, opened it and hoisted himself up and out. It was an awkward fit for a man his size, but he'd practiced before, ensuring he had multiple exits if it ever became necessary.

He considered watching Star's back very necessary.

Circling around the bar on silent feet, he listened. Her boots crunched on the gravel, guiding him. She didn't go to her rig, but then, maybe she didn't want them to know which truck was hers.

Smart—except that they could ask anyone in the bar about her, and that would be one of the first things they learned.

Cade leaned around the corner, still hidden by shadows but able to see her. She hadn't lit the cigarette, but she kept it dangling between her lips.

What are you up to?

She glanced several times at the entrance, and

when the doors finally opened, she made a show of frustration.

The one who'd offered a light smiled. "Couldn't find your lighter after all?"

She shook her head, sending that wealth of thick hair to move around her breasts. Wearing a sexy pout, she asked, "Did you bring one out with you?"

He produced the lighter, then teased her with, "Say please."

Taking the cigarette from her lips, she gave him a tight smile. "Really? Because there are twenty men inside who would be glad to give me a light—without stipulations."

"Seems to me you don't like them, or you'd have gone to them for the cigarette."

Her lips curled. "You think you know what I like?"

"I know you'd like more than a smoke."

At that, she laughed, a rich, husky sound that set Cade's teeth on edge. She played a dangerous game, and he hoped like hell she didn't push too hard.

"Maybe you're right." The finger she stroked along her cleavage drew the man's heated stare. "What's your name?"

"You can call me Smith."

She laughed. "Well, Smith, how much are you willing to give?"

Not for a second did Cade believe she meant to

sell herself. No, she had a bigger game in mind, and it made him scared for her.

Cade knew Smith—*what a crock*—because he and his brother had kept tabs on the man for more than a month. They knew Smith was involved in plenty of shady deals, but he was just muscle, not brains. Someone else called the shots. Someone with more power.

Cade wanted them all.

With her impetuous rush to get involved, Star jeopardized his well-made plans. Never mind that she didn't know he had plans . . .

"Tell you what." The guy reached to a back pocket and pulled out his wallet.

Finally, she looked a little nervous, but still, she didn't back down. Honest to God, she raised her chin.

Luckily—because Cade didn't want to blow his cover—the guy offered a card instead of cash. "You want to make a big score, come by Misfits tomorrow night. I have a buddy in need of cheering up and you'd be just the ticket."

Restoring that cocky attitude, she glanced at the card, then shoved it into her own pocket. "What time?"

"Ah, so you don't mind the idea of being his . . . entertainment?"

She shrugged but asked, "Is he a total pig?"

"Most of the women don't complain."

Most of the women don't complain. Meaning

some did . . . but it didn't matter? When Smith's friend finished with them, were they even able to complain?

Breathing slow and deep kept Cade from reacting. Somehow he'd ensure Star's safety, and eventually he'd bury Smith.

For a split second, she went blank—fear? anger?—before curling her mouth in another credible smile. "I take it you've given him other *gifts?*"

"He's partial to those with long legs and big tits."

With every beat of his heart, Cade wanted her away from the bastard, but he didn't intrude. Not yet.

Toying with a long curl, Star pretended the crude language and dark insinuation didn't bother her. "How much are we talking?"

Taken by surprise, Smith reached out, wrapping his fingers in her hair. "Enough, okay? Don't push me. Just be there at nine."

She didn't flinch, didn't show any pain and didn't back down. She actually moved closer to Smith. Too damn close. "Oh, I'll be there. And I'll expect you to make it worth my while."

He leaned forward, clearly intending to kiss her, and suddenly she freed herself—minus a few dozen strands of hair. "You pay first, sugar. I don't give out freebies." Before Smith could figure out what to do, she walked away.

To her credit, she went back into the bar and relative safety. But how safe would she be when she left?

Keeping an eye on the door she went through, Smith dug out his cell phone and pressed in a number. The light from the screen emphasized his twisted smile. "Hey," Smith said, when the call was answered. "Prep the back room, okay? I have a new one coming out tomorrow." He laughed. "Yeah, you'll like her. She fits your preferences to a tee." He listened, shook his head. "No, I'm sure she's not, but I'll follow her tonight just to be safe. One thing, and it's nonnegotiable." He waited, then said, "Once you're done with her, I'm next in line."

CHAPTER TWO

Sterling didn't see Cade when she walked back in, and it left her even more rattled. He made her feel safer, and right now, with her skin crawling and her heart jumping, she needed that. Whether it made sense or not, whether he wanted to protect her or not, she wanted him near.

Ignoring all the interested stares, chin up, eyes straight ahead, she went to her table. Belatedly, she remembered the stupid cigarette in her hand.

She never had gotten that light.

Just as well. She'd never smoked and would probably have choked on the thing.

Suddenly Cade was there, brushing past her, making physical contact for a single heartbeat before he went back to the bar.

The touch shook her, and settled her. How the hell was that possible?

Sterling watched him, but then caught herself and looked away. Trying to appear casual, she pulled out her phone and pretended to check messages, just to give herself something to do. Her hands shook, but hopefully no one noticed. She worked up a smile just in case.

The two men hung around, making no bones about watching her. So . . . now what? If she'd thought ahead, she'd have realized she needed an exit plan. But no, she'd seen them and, knowing what they were, simply reacted. The desire to destroy them had encompassed her.

Uber. That's what she'd do. And her truck?

Damn.

Cade slid another drink in front of her. So low she barely heard him, he said, "My brother is picking you up. Dark gray newer-model Ram truck. I'll take care of your rig. Leave the keys on your chair when you're ready to go."

Sterling blinked at him, but he'd already turned away. Aware of the two goons keeping her in their sights, she caught herself. Smiling like she didn't have a care, she backed up her ruse of a fun-loving girl without caution and tossed back the drink.

Because of her life choices, choices that often put her in dive bars, she'd learned to hold her liquor. This time she didn't have to. Cade must have anticipated her cooperation because he'd watered down the shot.

Just how well did he know her?

And how the hell did he plan to take care of her truck?

So far he'd made a lot of assumptions, including that she'd accept a ride from his brother. She should refuse, but . . . Her gaze strayed to the scumbags watching her. Yeah, they'd be a problem.

How was Cade's plan any worse than taking a ride from a stranger in an Uber?

Keeping the frown off her face wasn't easy, not

while being in such a pickle, but she'd thought fast on her feet before.

Okay, so he had a decent plan. Long as his brother didn't try anything funny, it could work.

Another glance at Cade and she saw him texting on his phone. When he finished, he murmured something to his employee—a medium-height, wiry fellow he referred to as Rob—and then went into the kitchen area.

Because she felt safe doing so, Sterling looked at Rob again. On her first visit she'd noticed his eyes. They were as black as Satan's, but somehow still kind. Or maybe, considering the overpowering presence of Cade, Rob's gaze only seemed kind in comparison.

When he announced the last call, she realized it was nearly midnight. Within the next few minutes, the bar began to clear. Even the two goons headed out. Or pretended to. She didn't trust them not to hang around outside in the hopes of catching her alone.

Cade reappeared under the guise of picking up her empty shot glass. "My brother is out front. Go straight to his truck, even if Smith tries to talk to you."

In the same easy tone he'd used, she replied, "Who put you in charge? Just so we're clear, you're not my boss."

That gave him pause. Clearly he was used to issuing orders and having them followed!

"Star—"

She ignored the use of her old name—for now. In some ways, it was even nice to hear. Familiar from a lifetime ago, before her whole world had upended. "I've survived on my own since I was seventeen. I'm not an idiot, either. So I accept the help—but if your brother tries anything, I'll kill him."

Another hesitation, and then Cade nodded. "Fair enough."

He wouldn't argue in his brother's defense? What insanity was that? Or maybe he didn't consider her a serious threat, which meant he didn't know her that well after all.

Less than reassured, Sterling asked, "You're sure my truck will be safe?"

"Guaranteed. We shouldn't talk too long, though, so tell my brother when and where you want it, and we'll get it there."

Her brows went up. "Just like that?"

Instead of explaining how he'd accomplish it, he said, "You started this. Do you have a better option?"

Sadly, no, she didn't. Standing, she scooped up her jacket—leaving her keys on the seat as he'd requested—and then pushed in her chair. "I suppose I should thank you?"

His eyes narrowed. "Not necessary. But you might consider that trust we discussed earlier."

Before she could reply, he walked away.

It was with a lot of trepidation and heightened awareness that Sterling exited the bar. Bright security lights lit the front but left murky shadows in the surrounding area. Immediately she spotted his brother. He didn't leave the driver's seat, but he did lean over and push open the passenger door.

With every crunch of her boots on the gravel, she felt eyes on her. She didn't see the goons, but she didn't doubt they were there somewhere, watching her and speculating.

Pasting on a false smile, she waved to Cade's brother as if happy to see him. She wished she at least knew his name, but Cade hadn't seen fit to tell her.

From seeing him before in the bar, she already knew his brother was a good-looking guy—not quite as tall as Cade, but close, and his body was every bit as muscular, maybe even a little more ripped. She recalled that he owned a gym and figured he'd gotten that bod as a natural result of working with customers.

"Let's go," he said when Sterling got close, as if she'd been holding him up.

Fine. She didn't want to be a nuisance, but her recklessness was over for the night. She quickly checked the door, ensuring she wouldn't get locked in, before sliding onto the seat.

She barely had the door closed when he said, "Buckle up," and put the truck in gear.

Annoyance brought her teeth together. Did he have to be as bossy as his brother? "I was planning to, so save the orders for someone else."

That made him grin. "Touchy, huh? Cade warned me, so no worries. Where we headed?"

Cade had warned him? "I'm not *touchy,* it's just—"

"Yeah, yeah. I insulted your independence. Don't chew it to death." He glanced in the rearview mirror, then back to the road. "Your place? If so, I'm going to take the long way around to lose our tail. Cool?"

Startled, she asked, "We have a tail?"

"Yeah—don't look! Damn." He scowled in annoyance. "Cade said you could handle yourself, so don't act like a rookie, 'kay?"

How infuriating! Slumping back in her seat, she snapped, "I *can* handle myself—you just caught me by surprise, that's all."

He snorted. "Sounds like a lot of shit caught you by surprise tonight. Hang on." He took a sharp turn, then accelerated until she had no choice but to grab the door handle with one hand, the dash with the other.

These were not straight, flat roads.

Even though he'd explained why, it alarmed her that he was speeding away from where she needed to go. "Look, you can drop me off at the mall—"

"Not a chance. Cade would have my head." His

gaze ran over her, then returned to the road. "For whatever reason, he's decided to focus on you."

Now, that felt incredibly insulting! His "For whatever reason" made it clear he didn't see the draw.

But damn it, she was *not* going to be offended over it. She didn't want either of them to find her attractive. She really didn't.

Through her teeth, she said, "He can just un-focus."

"Yeah, right." With a snort, he replied, "Try telling him that, because he sure as hell never listens to me."

It seemed Cade had coerced his brother into this impromptu rescue, and he clearly didn't like it any more than she did. "Damn right, I'll tell him."

Judging by his grin, he found that amusing. "Yeah, you do that. Can't wait to hear how it goes. But tonight I'm dropping you at your front door—after I lose them."

She grew more irritated by the second. "If you think I'll tell you where I live—"

"You don't need to. Now shush a sec while I concentrate on driving."

Shush? *Shush!* The urge to blast him bubbled up, but she still didn't see anyone following them, and actually, a tingle of new alarm climbed her spine. What if he was just a good liar using a story to get her out of town?

She'd gut him, that's what.

Slowly, she reached for her ankle and the knife she kept strapped there, but no sooner did her fingers touch the hilt than headlights appeared behind them.

"Determined SOBs, aren't they?" He searched the road ahead of them, then the rearview mirror again. "If you want to get out of this, I'd suggest you not stab me."

Guilty heat flushed her face.

Especially when he added, "Not that I'd let you."

"You—"

In a long-suffering voice, he said, "The mall it is."

Now that she knew the threat was real, Sterling didn't much like that idea. She'd be a sitting duck until she could find a ride. Sure, she was good at hiding, but it was past midnight, the air had cooled, and at this hour the mall was deserted. How hard would it be for the goons to find her— and then what?

Except that Cade's brother pulled in to a small, recently completed outlet mall instead of the larger mall she'd referred to. Turning off his head-lights, he quietly rolled away from the security lights, circled around the back and stopped, facing the main road.

So he wasn't dropping her off after all, just lying low for a few. She could handle that.

"Where do you want your truck?" he asked casually, as if they weren't hiding from danger. He half turned to face her. "I disabled the interior lights, but I can't use my phone yet. We don't want to tip our hand, right? But as soon as it's clear, I'll let Cade know. No reason he should have to stay out any later than necessary."

His ease afforded her some of her own. Getting comfortable in the corner of the door and the seat, as far from him as possible, Sterling considered him. "Cade knows how to drive a rig?"

"Big brother knows how to do a great many things. Ask him to jump out of a plane? No problem. Run five miles without breaking a sweat? Piece of cake. Swim underwater—"

"Do I detect some hero worship?"

"Hell yeah. Big-time." He turned back to the road, listened a second, then nodded in satisfaction. "There they go."

A car sped past them at an impossible speed, given the winding mountain roads. Subtly, Sterling let out a relieved breath. "We can head out now."

"We'll give it another thirty seconds. We don't want them to notice us, but neither do we want them to double back and find us, right?" He smiled at her. "Timing is everything."

Cade's brother was a little too cocky for her taste. She started to tell him so, but then he put the truck in gear and gradually moved forward again until he was at the edge of the road. From either direction, all they could see were streetlamps, but no traffic.

"So," he said, once they were on their way again, this time headed toward where she lived. "You and Cade?"

Denial rushed forward and she shook her head. "No." There wasn't a scenario of her with . . . anyone. Never had been and never would be.

"No?"

Did he have to sound so disbelieving? "I frequent his bar, that's it."

"Uh-huh. Cade overreacted because those were just Good Samaritans hoping to find you alone on a mountain road. Got it." He drove more leisurely now. "So where do you want your truck?"

This time the question didn't take her by surprise. "I have an office."

"Makes sense." He handed over his phone. "You can text Cade so I can keep my hands on the wheel."

He'd handed her his phone? For a few seconds there, she just stared at it with the same fascination she'd give a snake. But this could be her opportunity to learn more about Cade McKenzie. Past messages with his brother could tell her a lot.

Unfortunately, when she got around to looking at the phone, all she saw was one message: Pick her up out front.

She scrolled, but that was it. Nothing else. No other numbers in the phone, no other communication, at least none readily available. If she could dig around a little . . .

Glancing at Cade's brother disabused her of that notion. The jerk was grinning again.

Giving up, she texted, Take the rig to her office, and she put in the address. But her curiosity didn't wane, so she asked, "What is this exactly? Some supersecret cell phone communication?"

"Sure, let's call it that. It makes us sound cool, right?"

His good humor wore on her—then the phone dinged and she looked down to see a reply from Cade. Is she behaving?

Of all the . . . Without alerting Cade's brother, Sterling texted back, No. She kicked my ass n took over. Bitch is hard-core. Pretty sure she never needed our help.

To which Cade replied, Star? That you?

Damn it, her lips twitched. She curled a little more in her seat, the phone held close, and almost forgot about his insufferable brother humming beside her. Yeah, it's me. How'd you know?

Brother would never call u a bitch.

So the goofball driving had some redeeming qualities? Good to know.

She tried to figure out what to say next.

Cade beat her to it. You okay?

She wasn't but wouldn't admit it to anyone but

herself. Yup, NP. That is, no problems other than his brother, but she saw no reason to go into that. It'd only make her sound petty. My truck?

Getting it there now. Be safe tonight.

Did he have to treat her like a teenager? She knew how to take care of herself, and seriously, she would have been fine on her own.

Somehow.

Narrowing her eyes, Sterling texted, You 2. She waited, hoping that might offend him, but he didn't reply back.

She refused to acknowledge the disappointment she felt. After a few more seconds, she handed the phone back to his brother. "Do you have a name?"

"Course I do. It's on my birth certificate, all legal-like."

Such a frustrating man! "Care to share it?"

"No can do. After tonight, I hope to never see you again. In fact, tonight shouldn't have happened. Cade knows better." His gaze slanted her way. "You sure you two aren't boning?"

Good God, he was so ridiculous; it almost softened her mood. Instead of smiling, she dryly replied, "Pretty sure I would have noticed if we were."

"Ha!" He had no problem grinning. "See, you're getting the hang of it now."

"Meaning?"

"All that turbulent animosity is a waste of

good energy. You were over there crackling with hatred, on the edge of imploding, when snarky comebacks are easier, and more effective anyway."

"Effective?" Getting used to him and his odd insults, Sterling let her spine relax against the seat back and stretched out her legs. "When you're just laughing at me?"

"Not *at* you," he denied. "Jesus. *With* you. Lighten up, already."

"One thing—I wasn't *crackling with hatred.*" What a stupid way to put it.

"Then what?"

"Confusion? You haven't exactly been forthcoming, and I'm not sure what's going on."

"I'm rescuing you, that's what—but only because Cade asked me to."

"And I can't know your name because it's top secret?"

"Exactly. Consider me an enigma." He bobbed his eyebrows. "You intrigue me, though, because Cade is a hard nut to crack."

"So he wouldn't normally have offered his help?" Did that mean he considered her special— or was she in more trouble than he could ignore? Not a good thought.

"He would have helped you without you ever knowing. That he made it personal is downright fascinating."

Yeah, she had to admit, she found it rather

fascinating, too. "Will my truck truly be there when I check in the morning?"

"Yup. It'll probably be there in another twenty minutes, but I hope you'll pack away some of that prickly pride and go inside for the night. Lock everything up nice and tight and don't go anywhere alone for a while."

She'd already planned to stay in for the night, but she wouldn't share that with him. Enigmas didn't deserve full disclosure.

"Ah, you've clammed up again? I get it. I wouldn't like someone saving my ass, either."

She rolled her eyes. "You haven't saved my ass—"

"Beg to differ."

"But with every word out of your mouth, my curiosity expands. So tell me, what makes you think I'll still be in danger even after I'm home?"

"You kidding? For Cade to get involved, I'm sure it was life and death, right? Dude is usually so cool. And that means, despite my excellent driving, someone could figure out where you live."

Her place was secure, so she wasn't worried about that. "Cade is cool, but you're not?"

"I'm learning." He shrugged. "See, I used to be a hothead, but big brother has a way of tamping that shit down, ya know?"

He made it sound like he'd been a hothead in younger days, but then Cade showed up and gave

50

him a guiding hand. Did that mean Cade hadn't always been around?

"Now, don't start speculating," he warned. "My lips are sealed."

"Is that a joke? Your lips haven't stop flapping since I got in your truck."

"Flapping? I have several lady friends who would object to that description. *Flapping,*" he repeated with a snort.

Extreme exasperation had her huffing. "Might be a good idea for you to work on that sarcasm next?"

"Was I sarcastic?" He was on the verge of laughing as he turned down her street. "Guess your chipper personality just brings it out of me."

"You don't have to sound so cheerful about it."

He barely managed to bank his grin. "Look, my point is that anything you want to know about Cade you'll have to get from him, not that he'll tell you anything."

"Except that he's a bartender?"

"See, you've got it." He pulled in to her apartment complex. "Is this place protected?"

"It's safe enough." Two could play the close-mouthed game. "Don't worry your pretty head about it."

Showing no reaction to the insult, he said, "Wasn't planning to." He forestalled her getting out of the truck by adding, "Here. Cade said to give you this." Opening the glove box, he pulled out a cell phone.

She didn't take it. "Have one, but thanks anyway."

"Yeah, sure, I figured that. But this one has his number already programmed in."

It could also have a tracker or something on it. She forced a snarky smile. "If I took that, I'd just ditch it."

Nonplussed, he stared at her, followed by a laugh. "You're something else—let's not speculate on what. Okay then, how about this." Pulling a small notepad and pen from the center console, he jotted down a number. "Now you have it, but it's just paper, right?" He held it up, flipping it back and forth. "Not a threat. Does that work?"

"Why not?" Quickly pocketing it, she slid out of the car. "Thanks for the ride."

"You sure you don't want me to walk you up?"

"Positive."

"Suit yourself, but I'm waiting right here until I see your kitchen light come on."

Sterling spun around to frown at him. How did he know the kitchen window was the only one facing this lot?

Still being a goof, he wiggled his fingers in the air and said, "Woo-ooo, we enigmas are so mysterious."

And damn it, there was no way she could hold in her chuckle.

Course, the humor ended the minute she

entered the apartment building. She liked the place because it was spacious and open, without a lot of nooks or corners for anyone to lurk. Still, it was a nice feeling to know Cade's brother was there, waiting to ensure no one bothered her.

Keys already in her hand, she went up the carpeted stairs to the second floor and unlocked her door. Soon as she stepped inside, she pulled the knife from her boot and locked up again, not just the doorknob lock but also the dead bolt she'd installed. Crossing the living room, she checked inside the closet, then strode through the kitchen and dining area to the bathroom, where she peeked inside, even glancing into the bathroom cabinet and the glass-enclosed shower, then into the bedroom. This was the only room where someone could adequately hide, so she looked first under the bed—easy enough because she didn't use a bed skirt. The closet here was bigger with more clothes, so she took a few seconds to move them around before heading back to the dining room to check the patio door, which was thankfully still locked, the additional bar in place.

Stepping into the kitchen, she couldn't resist peering out the window to where she saw Cade's brother leaning against the front fender of his truck, arms folded, staring up at her window.

Damn it, she smiled . . . and stepped back to flip on the light. Seconds later he drove away.

Huh. Actual, bona fide protection courtesy of Cade and his crazy-ass brother. She couldn't trust it—no really, she couldn't.

Enigma? He had that right. There was far too much she didn't know about Cade, and that made his concern suspect.

But . . . it didn't feel suspect. It felt genuine.

Blast it all, it felt *good*.

Cade waited as long as he could, then called his brother. Soon as Reyes answered, he asked, "She's settled?"

"Far as I can tell," Reyes said, and then, "What the hell have you gotten yourself into?"

"It's complicated."

"If you mean the lady, no, she's not. In fact, I thought she was pretty clear. She means to demolish someone and doesn't want our help."

True enough—with one problem. "She zeroed in on Thacker, who told her his name was Smith."

A long pause preceded Reyes's explosive *"No fucking way."*

" 'Fraid so." It enraged Cade. "From what I could pick up, she's meeting him tomorrow."

"She's to be the entertainment?"

Base entertainment was the only use Thacker and his ilk had for women. "That's what it sounded like."

"You realize your girlfriend is going to fuck up a month's worth of work."

"Not my girlfriend," Cade corrected. "But yeah. Somehow we need to escalate things."

"Dad is going to blow a gasket."

"I'm aware." Cade resented that his father still tried to pull all the strings, as if they were mere puppets. "He'll get over it."

Laughing, Reyes accused, "You're not going to tell him, are you?"

"I'll tell him—a few hours before it all goes down."

With a low whistle, Reyes let him know what he thought of that plan. "And Madison? You plan to clue her in?"

Their sister, the home base of their surveillance, was absolutely necessary. "Yeah, I'll talk to her in the morning. Go get some rest. Tomorrow is going to be—"

"An unadulterated clusterfuck."

"You don't have to sound so cheerful about it."

Reyes laughed. "Funny—your girlfriend told me the same thing. Later, bro."

Girlfriend, Cade thought with a shake of his head. As if he had room in his life for anything that frivolous.

CHAPTER THREE

Hell of a position to be in, on the outside looking in, but Cade knew he had no one but himself to blame. As predicted, his father went quietly ballistic, but there was nothing new in that, at least whenever he dealt with Cade.

Reyes, of course, treated the whole thing like a lark. And his no-nonsense sister was as pragmatic as ever. For her, this was business as usual.

None of that made it easier for him to accept that Star mingled with human traffickers while he waited in the most disreputable of their vehicles, an aging, rusted white van with darkly tinted windows.

He'd parked across the street from the property in a run-down business district. Part bar, part hookup, a 100-percent members-only establishment, Misfits was, as they'd learned through meticulous research, a place for acquiring women and girls—against their will.

If Cade had his way, he'd go in, rip apart every bastard involved, then demolish the building so nothing was left but the blood of the abusers . . . and maybe a little dust. Unfortunately, he'd gotten voted down on that solution. He understood why, but that didn't make it any easier to bear.

Using binoculars, he watched through the front

window of the squat brick building as Star was shown in. Currently the atmosphere inside the bar was all about music and dancing, but two burly guards stood just outside the door.

Not to keep people from entering, but to ensure no one left without permission.

The original plan had been to keep tabs until they could nail the one in charge, but Star's involvement changed that.

For as long as he lived, Cade would remember the horror on the faces of the five women they'd already rescued from Misfits. Kept in the back of an airless truck, ages varying from seventeen to thirty-three, they'd been to hell and back before his sister had ferreted out the transfer and they'd arranged to intercept en route.

Because they worked with anonymity, he and Reyes had merely pulverized the drivers— instead of killing them—and then left them for local authorities to pick up after a hot tip.

They'd ensured the freedom of the traumatized women. His sister had followed updates about them and knew three of them had returned to family, one moved far away and another was in the women's shelter his father funded.

He had to believe they'd recover, but still they visited him in his nightmares.

If only he could find a way to shut down these fucking enterprises *before* they abused anyone. His father, who ran the operation, had no qualms about them using deadly force when absolutely necessary. Anyone who thought to enslave another deserved nothing less than death.

Cade believed that clear down to his soul. When he killed the heartless pricks, he did the world a favor.

Just then, he spotted Star dancing in the middle of several guys. Damn, the lady had nice moves.

Had Star noticed Reyes sitting at a booth? Not much got past her, but Reyes had subterfuge down to a fine art. Without Cade's military training, Reyes could fit in with the coarsest street toughs.

His brother was there as fast backup if it became necessary. With any luck, though, this was a trial of sorts, where they only wanted to see how far they could push Star, instead of imprisoning her tonight.

For once, Cade was glad he'd joined his father's family-based enterprise, though their reasons were different. Cade had resisted as long as he could, to the point that he'd enlisted with the army at eighteen in an effort to put distance between him and his only parent.

Unlike some of the new recruits, he'd taken to basic training, liking the structure enough that he went on to airborne school, and RIP— the Ranger Indoctrination Program—and finally, he'd served with the Seventy-Fifth Ranger Regiment. Military life suited him, and he would have made it his career, but after a lot of deployments carrying heavy weight, along with hard landings from jumping out of planes, his multiple leg issues had forced him into a medical discharge.

That didn't mean his no-fail mentality had changed, or that he didn't stay in top-notch shape. In a pinch, he could even sky jump from another plane.

He just couldn't do it on a regular basis.

Teaming up with the family in their effort to combat human trafficking was the only means he had to continue using his skill set.

Star danced past the front window again. She smiled, but he could already tell she was nervous. Dressed in a black breast-hugging T-shirt with an open gray button-up shirt over that, and skinny jeans that outlined her ass and legs, she looked like a wet dream—at a time when Cade wished she was a little less noticeable. His keen interest moved down her body from her sparkling eyes to her feet—and he grinned when he saw that she wore her shit-kicker boots. He'd bet those clunky things had steel toes, perfect for causing damage.

Sterling Parson had her own unique style, and he liked it. A lot. He liked her attitude. Her perseverance. Her bravery.

All good qualities, but did she also have what it took to weather the upcoming interview?

While he watched, she danced past a booth, stumbled and practically landed in Reyes's lap.

His brother looked surprised, but Star did not. She laughingly said something to him, patted his cheek a little harder than necessary, then danced away with a different guy.

Shit.

Seconds later his phone dinged with a text message. He hated to take his gaze off her, but he already knew it would be from Reyes.

Sure enough, the message read: She said to back off.

Like hell he would. Cade returned: Stay put.

Through the binoculars, he saw Reyes laugh and stow his phone again.

For another hour, things seemed to go okay. She was handed one drink after another, though he couldn't tell whether or not she actually drank any of them. She dodged grabby hands while keeping her grin in place.

When a guard led her off down a hallway, Cade tensed.

Showtime.

They knew the layout of the building, and Cade easily guessed that they were moving her to the back room, where they could privately intimidate her.

Reyes staggered like a drunk, following after them, but he'd be forced to veer off into the john. Closer, but not close enough to shield her.

It took a precious three minutes for Cade to drive around the back, staying far enough away to remain inconspicuous. Another goon guarded the back door, but luckily side-by-side windows gave him an adequate view inside of the room.

Two women were there with her now, one laughing uncontrollably while the other, with a few bruises, looked very shell-shocked. There were also three men: the two guys she'd met at his bar and another hulk of a guy who'd just walked in.

Up to that point Star had stuck to her role of a carefree, unsuspecting party girl, not overcome with giggles like the one girl, and not fatalistic like the other.

Whatever was said just then got her tight-lipped with some strong emotion that resembled part fear, part rage. Cade couldn't tell for sure.

In fact, the only thing he knew for certain was that he had to get her out of there. *Now.*

Sterling hadn't been prepared for the double whammy. First, she was introduced to a woman who'd been clearly abused. She appeared to be in her early twenties, either drunk or doped up, with an underlying fear that kept her breathless with panic.

That smack of reality was bad enough, really driving home her precarious position, locked in with monsters and little hope for escape. It reminded her too much of another time when she'd been locked in a room.

She'd been young and helpless then.

This time, she wasn't.

Knowing the danger and hoping to spare someone else the things she'd suffered, she'd gone into this with eyes wide-open—though admittedly with no solid plan or exit strategy.

On the heels of that first surprise was the second shocker, the one that really did her in.

Mattox Symmes. Twelve years had passed since she'd had to see the cruel sneer on his wet lips. Twelve years since he'd looked at her with those dead brown eyes as if she weren't a flesh-and-blood person.

Twelve years that she'd used to grow stronger, braver, to bury the past and give purpose to her present. She'd never thought to see him again, though she'd often thought of killing him, *dreamed* of killing him.

Still built like a freezer with legs and arms, and just as brutish as she remembered. His shoulders stretched the seams of his dress shirt, his neck too thick for the collar. The receding silver hair made his forehead seem more prominent. His gut was more prominent, too.

And he still looked at her like merchandise. *But* . . . he didn't seem to recognize her!

Needing to know for sure, she held out a limp hand and summoned up a careless smile. "Hello, there. I'm Francis." She waited for him to correct her, to say he knew the name was a lie.

Instead, he took her hand and smiled. "Now, aren't you a nice present."

Oh. Dear. God. Mattox was the man she was supposed to cheer up?

No. *Hell* no. She couldn't do it.

Entertaining him was not on her agenda. Cutting his throat, yes. Cheering him up, not so much.

She knew she had to come up with a real plan— fast.

The effort to retrieve her hand only got her fingers crushed. He tugged her closer. "Have we met before?"

Her heart lodged in her throat, making her short laugh sound borderline hysterical. "Pretty sure we haven't. I think I would have remembered you."

"Hmm." He continued to study her, his dead eyes appraising. "How long have you been in the area?"

"My whole life." Another lie, since she'd moved here after escaping. When had *he* relocated? Or did he have contacts all over the country? A morbid thought.

Sterling told herself that she'd changed, not just emotionally, but physically, too. At seventeen she'd been skinny, with dyed purple hair, a ring in her lip and an excess of dramatic makeup.

Her rebellious stage, as her drug-addicted mother had called it when she was clearheaded enough to notice what her daughter looked like, which wasn't often.

"I think I would have remembered, as well," Mattox finally said, before towing her over to a chair so he could sit. The chair groaned under his weight. Sprawling out his tree-trunk thighs, he freed her fingers, yet she didn't dare move.

In the locked room, where could she go? The windows behind her were accessible, but too high for her to get through quickly, even if she managed to break one before getting grabbed. Smith and his crony stood there grinning by the door. The bruised girl silently wept while the other couldn't stop snickering over everything. It was almost more than Sterling could take.

Besides, if she tried to move away, he'd react as all predators did, by capturing, subduing. Devouring. He would enjoy her fear. It would probably provide the entertainment he wanted.

"Goddamn," Mattox suddenly complained. "We have one too many in here." He gestured at Smith.

Smith roughly grabbed the laughing woman and put her on the other side of the door, where a guard all but dragged her away. Only then did the woman start to protest.

Her humor wouldn't last. Not for a second did Sterling think they'd let the woman go, and eventually the drugs would wear off. Best chance of her survival? If Sterling managed to kill these three men and whoever else was involved.

As Smith again closed and locked the door, her tension coiled with familiar emotions. The sense of helplessness. The burning hatred.

"Now." Mattox sat back and laced his fingers over his gut. "You two can strip down. Make it quick, because I'm short on time."

The other girl openly sobbed as she hurriedly stripped off her sandals and pants, tripping herself twice and making the men laugh. Fucking pigs. Sterling contemplated kicking Mattox in the nuts—but that would only get her killed.

Did Cade's brother have a plan? Or was he just visiting the bar for his own hookup? He hadn't left when she'd told him to, so did he know this was a location for buying and selling women? He'd seemed sharp, and Cade was most definitely more than a mere bartender.

"Jesus, Adela. Quit that caterwauling," Smith ordered, giving her a shove that sent her into the wall.

Adela. It was the first time Sterling had heard her name. How long had she been here?

Long enough to be scared witless, obviously.

Somehow, someway, she'd get herself and the other girl out of this. Until a genius plan occurred to her, she'd just have to play along. If she could distract them, maybe they'd leave Adela alone.

"So," she said, shrugging the unbuttoned shirt off one shoulder and shimmying so her boobs bounced. "How about I do this slow, like a tease? Would you like that?" It might give her an opportunity to get the knife from her boot. If nothing else, she could straddle Mattox's lap and use her necklace blade to slit his throat.

She'd tucked the necklace inside her T-shirt, but even if he saw it, he wouldn't recognize it as a weapon. It looked like nothing more than a decorative metal medallion on a long chain, but by the push of a small button, the disk opened to reveal a curved, razor-sharp blade that when used correctly would be deadly.

She knew how to use it, and here, in this moment, she wouldn't bat an eye at ending Mattox.

The impatient bastard showed his teeth in an evil smile. "No, I don't think I want to wait. Take off both tops." He stared into her eyes, the smile vanishing. "Now."

Well, hell. She tried to tease, but a tremor had entered her voice when she said, "Anxious for the goods, huh? Fine by me, but when do I get my money? I was told I'd be paid for this little performance, and I prefer cash up front."

Smith snorted. "Let's wait and see if you're worth it." Softer, he complained, "Adela sure as fuck wasn't, were you, doll?" He reached for the girl, who screamed. Sterling turned, prepared to attack him despite the consequences—and suddenly a chunk of concrete crashed through one of the windows, sending glass everywhere. A second later, the lights went out.

Chaos erupted with Adela shrieking and the men cursing as they lumbered around, but Sterling seized the opportunity. In a practiced move, she swiped the knife from her boot and stabbed toward the chair where Mattox had been sitting.

Her knife sank deep . . . into chair padding. How the hell had such a big man moved so quickly? Putting herself behind that chair, Sterling listened to the sounds of a vicious fight ensuing, trying to place bodies.

She couldn't see dick and wasn't about to use the flashlight on her phone, knowing that'd only draw attention to her. Hearing Adela's whimpers, she felt her way along the wall until she reached the girl.

Someone hit the floor in front of them, and what sounded like another body crashed into the wall where she'd just been. Whoever did the demolishing did so silently, efficiently.

Oh, she heard the grunts and groans of the men going down, but from the big shadow doing the damage? Not a peep.

Her hand closed around Adela's arm. The door behind her opened to let two more men charge in. Out in the bar, she heard pandemonium break out with panicked shouts and a lot of scrambling bodies, probably in a rush for the exit.

"Come on," Sterling said, dragging Adela

with her. It surprised her that the girl didn't fight her, didn't resist in any way, and she'd stopped sobbing. Maybe because escape seemed imminent.

Someone ran into them, almost knocking Sterling over, but she managed to keep her feet. She dragged Adela along until she felt the doorknob for the men's room that she'd noted when they'd led her down the hallway. Inside, the room was dark and foul, but Sterling didn't slow. On the opposite wall, the light of a streetlamp filtered through a grungy window.

"Let's get out of here, okay?" She didn't wait for Adela to answer.

The window was narrow, and it opened out instead of up, but she'd figure it out. She released Adela, then shoved the knife back into her boot to use both hands to force the rusted knob to turn. Knowing they could be found at any moment, her heart thundered and her palms sweat.

"I can't go," Adela whispered.

"What?" The window creaked ominously, like a special effect in a horror movie, opening inch by inch. "It'll be fine. You'll see. I can hoist you up first."

"No, I can't. They'll kill me."

Why did she have to get stubborn now? "They can't kill you when we're gone," Sterling reasoned. "I promise, I'll get you someplace safe."

"Your house?"

What? Since she wasn't about to reveal her own private location, she said, "No. I know another place—"

"I can't risk it." Adela drew a breath. "I should stay. We both should."

Terror did strange things to people, sometimes paralyzing them with the worry of repercussions. Sterling understood that, but she wasn't quite sure how to overcome it.

At least Adela wasn't sobbing anymore. Wasn't hysterical, either.

Someone shouted from the hallway. A flashlight shone from beneath the door.

"We have to go *now,*" Sterling whispered, reaching for the vague outline of Adela's body.

The girl backed away. "No. No, I can't."

"At least take this." Sterling fished a card from her pocket and thrust it toward Adela. "It's my number—in case you change your mind." The card had a phone number but nothing else. It wouldn't lead anyone to her, but it could be a link to freedom for a victim.

She'd handed out those cards a dozen times in recent years.

Adela took it, then opened the door and yelled, "I'm here!"

Hating herself for failing, mired in regret that she couldn't help Adela, Sterling turned and, with one boot on the edge of the sink, hoisted herself up and through the partially opened window.

She scraped her spine along the edge of the casing, her hip and thigh, too, before kicking and wiggling to land hard on her side on the rough gravel drive. Something cut through her jeans. Her palm cracked on a solid surface, and one of her fingers bent unnaturally.

For a moment, in her crumpled position, her body couldn't assimilate the pain. Then feeling rushed in, and with it a welcoming wave of adrenaline.

Too bad she didn't know where Reyes had gone. She had to admit to herself she wouldn't mind some muscle right about now. Unfortunately, in the dark chaos, she couldn't attempt to find him. She was on her own, so she had to get to it.

Teeth locked, she lumbered to her feet and took off awkwardly, running as fast as she could down an alley, behind two abandoned buildings, through a parking lot and finally to the main thoroughfare. A stitch in her side kept her half doubled over—and then she noticed the blood.

Ignore that for now. Ignore the people gawking, too.

Focused only on escape, Sterling hobbled toward the lot where she'd parked her car several blocks away from Misfits. She hadn't wanted to risk being followed, but she hadn't planned on leaving battered, either. Despite the expanding pain, she walked a wide path around the car, ensuring no one paid her undue attention, before taking the key from her boot and unlocking the driver's door.

As always, she checked the back seat, saw it remained empty and dropped behind the wheel. She hit the door locks first and then, with shaking hands, started the black Fiesta she drove when she wasn't in her rig.

What had happened with Cade's brother? Was he still in the bar? Was he the one who'd caused the ruckus?

For only a second, she considered circling back to make sure he was okay, but when she raised her hand to the steering wheel and saw her unnaturally bent finger, another slice of pain jolted her. Right now, she couldn't help anyone.

She stepped on the gas and hoped that Cade was there, watching out for his brother.

She had his number at home, and once she recovered, she'd call him. She had so many unanswered questions . . . .

But for now, she only wanted to put distance between her and Misfits. A couple of miles out, she pulled in to a well-lit Walmart parking lot and slowly worked off her loose shirt to tie it around her bleeding thigh. God, with her mangled finger, getting it done really hurt, but even without tightening much, it'd stem some of the bleeding.

By the time she got home, she felt like one giant pulsing bruise. She still used extreme caution in going up to her place, every step a trial of determination.

As usual, the apartment building was quiet and she didn't run into anyone. Severely limping now, she forced herself to keep to her routine, checking the doors, beneath the bed and in the closets, before staggering into the bathroom.

Under the bright fluorescent lights, she freed the shirt from around her thigh and winced. A chunk of glass embedded in her skin left an inch-wide puncture. Seeing the mess she'd already made on the floor, she more or less collapsed into the bathtub.

With a harsh groan, she caught the edge of the protruding glass with blood-slick fingers and, gritting her teeth, slowly pulled it free. Swamped with self-pity, she tossed it toward the garbage can. More blood blossomed on her jeans.

Two slow, deep breaths helped, as did her lame pep talk. *You're okay. Everything will heal.*

For now, you're safe.

She needed to clean the wound or she'd be facing bigger problems, like infection or even blood poisoning. There was no one to do it for her, hadn't been anyone for too many years to count—if ever.

Stripping off her clothes caused more than a few guttural groans, as well as a light sheen of sweat. Her lace-up boots and tight jeans especially proved difficult. Stupid skinny jeans.

She hadn't been skinny in a very long time, and it took a major incentive to get her to wear anything that uncomfortable.

Killing a human trafficker topped her list, but still . . .

It took every ounce of agonizing grit she possessed to get naked. Panting with the effort, her clothes in a heap on the other side of the tub, Sterling inspected the damage.

Black-and-blue swelling bruises marred her skin from her waist to her ankle. Christ, no wonder she hurt. If only Adela hadn't balked, if only she'd gotten that window open a little more. Failure left a bitter taste in her mouth.

She didn't want to move, but what choice did she have? It hurt like hell, but she could bend her leg, so she assumed it wasn't broken.

Slowly sitting upright, she turned on the shower and, once the water warmed, inched forward to sit under the spray, her forehead resting on her knees. At some point she must have zoned out. She didn't know how long she'd sat there, but the lack of hot water revived her. Teeth clenched, she carefully washed her thigh. When she reached to turn off the water, renewed pain seized her.

Her finger. With so many aches to choose from, she'd all but forgotten about the ring finger on her right hand. Looking at it now, she knew she'd dislocated it in her fall.

Switching to her left hand, keeping her right

tucked close to her body, she shut off the shower and, leaning heavily on the wall, managed to get upright. Her thigh continued to ooze blood, so she dried it as best she could and applied several butterfly bandages, then wrapped it in gauze.

Rather than get her bed wet, she eased her injured hand through the sleeve of her big terry robe, wrapped it around her and gimped her way to the couch, where she curled up. Exhausted, she thankfully slept.

CHAPTER FOUR

Cade tried calling her. He even tried tapping quietly on her door. It was two in the morning, far from a decent hour to call on someone, but he was surprised he'd lasted this long without getting hold of her.

He and Reyes had rounded up several women, as well as Smith and his cohort, but they'd lost sight of both Star and the young woman who'd been with her. That bastard Mattox had gotten away, too, and it tortured Cade thinking he might have Star. His sister was on it, and she'd locate Mattox eventually—when it might be too late.

No, he couldn't accept that, so here he was, checking Star's apartment and praying she was safely inside.

He knocked again, hard enough that a neighbor stuck her head out and cursed him.

Somewhere between eighty and ninety, eyeglasses askew, hair frazzled, cranky and nowhere near properly dressed, the woman snapped, "What the hell are you doing?"

Great. Not what he needed right now. "My apologies, ma'am."

"Just keep it down," she barked, then slammed

her door loudly enough to wake up the rest of the building.

Cade gave serious thought to breaking into Star's apartment. If she wasn't in there, he'd start scouring the area to find her—

"Who is it?" Her weak voice came through the closed door.

Fresh alarm mingled with relief, because at least he'd found her . . . unless she wasn't alone?

His gaze shot up to the peek hole in the door. Stepping back so she could see him, he said, "It's Cade. Let me in."

Nothing happened.

He leaned closer to the door. "Swear to God, Star, I'm about two seconds from knocking down the—"

The lock clicked and the door opened.

One look at her and uncontrollable rage returned. That was something that never happened to him. He worked best in cold deliberation, detached, proficient . . . but this was Star, and somehow she'd always jacked his control.

Stepping in and quietly securing the door again, he asked, "Who did this to you?" She looked like she'd been through a war.

With a pronounced limp, her face taut with pain, she went back to the couch and gingerly lowered herself. Instead of answering his question, she asked one of her own. "Why are you here?"

Several lights were on in the apartment. "Are you alone?"

She sat back. "Yes." Her robe parted and he saw her right leg.

Locking his jaw, he came to kneel in front of her. "Ah, babe, how the hell did this happen?"

Trembling, she swallowed heavily and closed her eyes. "Babe?"

Seriously, an endearment was what she wanted to talk about now? "You can gut me later. Tell me what happened."

Though she didn't actually shrug, he heard it in her tone. "I landed hard when I went out the window in the guys' john. I'm okay, though."

No, she most definitely was not. The bruising started dark red at the top of her thigh and down the middle, but then spread outward to blue, green and black. Actually, he couldn't see how high it went because the robe didn't part any higher. He lightly touched his fingers to her skin, especially over the bandages that covered a blood-encrusted cut.

Lethargic, Sterling said, "It looks terrible, doesn't it?"

He'd seen similar bruising, just never on a woman. "My guess is a pulled hammy. I don't know how you managed to get home."

"Adrenaline, I think. *Not* getting home wasn't an option, right? But yeah, now it hurts like crazy."

He noticed she held her arm, too—which drew his gaze to her fingers. *Shit.* He winced for her, but first things first. Gesturing at her leg, he asked, "Mind if I take a look?"

Those velvety brown eyes of hers stared at him. "Actually, since I'm buck-ass under the robe, yeah, I mind."

He hadn't needed her confirmation on that. His body already knew it, and conflicting needs were bombarding him. He wanted to help her. Protect her. Touch her.

Look at her.

Stop being an asshole. He drew in a deep breath and tried to be businesslike. "You need to see a doctor."

"Nope. If that's why you came here, you can run along back to wherever you live."

"Star." He braced his hand on the couch. "You can't think I'd leave you like this."

Her eyes narrowed. "Why not? I'm not your *babe,* and I didn't ask you to—"

"Let me rephrase that." He hardened his own gaze. "I'm not leaving you like this."

They stared at each other, a battle of wills, until she relented with ill grace. Hell, she looked too spent to do otherwise.

"Fine," she groused. "Suit yourself. Not sure I could fend off anyone if you led them here, so if nothing else, you can be backup."

"I didn't, but in case *you* did, you're right. I

make excellent backup." Now with a purpose, Cade stood. "We're going to handle this step by step, okay? First, have you taken anything?"

Eyes closed, body tight with pain, she asked, "Like . . . ?"

"Pain meds? And you should have that leg elevated, under ice packs, or you won't be able to walk tomorrow."

She gave a short laugh. "Walk? I'm not sure I could crawl." She lifted her head, and her eyes barely opened. "I probably shouldn't admit this, but just showering took it out of me. All I want to do now is sleep."

His heart softened. "You can do that soon, okay? After I get you more comfortable. So you need something for pain."

"I have aspirin in my medicine cabinet."

"And a first aid kit, apparently." She hadn't done a terrible job, but he could do better. "I'll properly clean and dress that cut, too. You know how you did it?"

"Chunk of glass." Again she put her head back as if any effort at being alert was too much. "It's in or near the trash can in my bathroom."

To know what he was dealing with, Cade went to retrieve it. Discarded clothes littered the floor, including bloodied jeans and her boots. She'd left a knife and a necklace on the counter. No, not a necklace. Though he recognized it as a hidden weapon, it took him a second to figure it out. With the press of a small mechanism built into the medallion, a claw blade opened out.

Jesus, what had she planned? Just how deep was she into her vigilante crusade?

Worrying about that would have to wait until he'd seen to her injuries. He found the chunk of glass. It appeared to be part of a broken bottle, still covered in Sterling's blood. In fact, she'd gotten blood everywhere—the floor, the tub, the edge of the sink . . .

The first aid kit was left open on the counter. Since the rest of her apartment was tidy, he'd pick up the mess for her once he had her better settled.

Next he detoured into the kitchen to find a bottle of water. Her fridge was almost barren, her cabinets cluttered with packaged food but nothing healthy. Figuring out something for her to eat would take a trick.

When he returned with the kit, three store-brand pain tablets and the water, she appeared to be sleeping. "Star?" he asked quietly.

"Hmm?" She sounded lethargic.

"Can you take these?" He touched her lips, and that got her more alert, her dark eyes watchful. He badly wanted to kiss that soft mouth, but all he said was, "Open."

She did, and he dropped them in, then handed her the water.

After swallowing the pills, she took several more drinks until she'd downed half the bottle. "No one's ever taken care of me."

No one? *Ever?* "Then let me show you how it's done."

Contemplative, she frowned at him, then gave up. "Fine. I'm starving, too. I don't suppose you know how to cook?"

"Better than you, apparently." He knelt down again and gently peeled away the butterfly bandages that had helped, but not enough. With the condition of her leg, it had to hurt like crazy.

"I didn't sleep at all last night," she explained, a mixture of pain and exhaustion running the words together. "I haven't eaten since early this morning, either. Add in tonight's . . . *excitement,* and yeah, I'm shot."

"Excitement. Right." Cade let that slide to silently concentrate on the job at hand. "I'm sorry," he said, dampening a cotton ball in antiseptic. "This is going to sting."

"I know." She clutched the couch cushion with her left hand. "Go ahead."

Her breath hissed out as he worked, so he tried to distract her. "Do you often go all day without eating?"

"Do I look like I'm starving?"

Definitely not. Sterling had a strong and shapely body that had caught his attention the moment he first saw her. Broad shoulders for a woman, hefty breasts and an ass he wanted to grasp with both hands. She didn't play up her assets in any way, and Cade thought she was sexy as hell because of it.

"So you skipped food out of nervousness?"

"I don't get nervous," she denied—then caught her breath as he cleaned a spot of debris from the edge of the cut.

"So why didn't you eat?"

"I was busy prepping." She scowled at him. "Are you about done?"

He'd take her annoyance over the sight of her pain any day. "Almost. You could really use a few stitches, but since the bleeding has almost stopped, we'll stick with bandages." The robe barely preserved her modesty, not that she seemed concerned. The woman was utterly unaffected by his nearness and her own nakedness—or else she hid it well.

Whichever, he appreciated how well she handled it. Any show of shyness now would have made it that much more difficult.

When he finished, he lightly covered her again with the edges of the robe. "Now." He sat beside her.

Making it clear she didn't like his nearness, she gave him another scowl.

"That finger is dislocated." She'd either need a trip to the ER after all . . . or he'd need to set it for her.

Looking away from her injured hand, she whispered, "I know."

Very gently, Cade took her hand, then trailed his fingertips over the swollen knuckle. "Does anything else on this arm hurt? Your wrist, elbow?" She was guarding it pretty good.

Lips pressed together, she shook her head.

"Are you sure?" He held her wrist firmly in one hand, the dislocated finger in the other. "Have you tried moving it?"

"Yes. I was reaching for the faucet when— *Ngahhh!*"

Before she could finish, he'd tugged the finger back into place and now gently held her hand in his, trying to soothe her. "Shh, I know. It's damn painful. Take some deep breaths."

"Go to hell!" she snapped, but she curled closer to him and moaned.

Cade had trouble swallowing. He'd set fingers before, his own included, but this was different. One arm around her, his other hand still holding hers, he kept her close. "I'm sorry, babe."

Her breath shuddered in. "Don't be." Still a little shaky, she said, "You fixed it for me."

"You should really see a doctor—"

She inhaled deeply, let it out slowly and eased away from him. "I'm sure it'll be fine."

The stubbornness started to grate on him. "Does anything else hurt?"

Her choking laugh sounded with pain. "What

doesn't hurt? It was a stupid idea to go out that window."

Since he'd been there to get her out, Cade agreed. But she hadn't known that. "I think it showed a lot of initiative."

She huffed a breath. "It was better than staying, I guess."

Before he could think better of it, he had his hand on her tangled hair, smoothing it down. "Can you tell me what you were doing there?"

"You first."

He looked up in surprise. "So you knew it was me?"

"I thought you might be around somewhere."

Talking seemed to help her collect herself, so Cade settled back beside her. "I was keeping an eye on you." He could tell her that much. He wanted her to know . . . what? That he cared, yes. That whatever she was up to, he could handle it for her. "What did you hope to accomplish, Star?"

Hand trembling, she swiped a tear off her lashes as if it offended her. "I was offered money, remember? What's your excuse?"

She had to be the most maddening person he'd ever encountered. "I can't go into it."

"Yeah? Well, ditto for me. Guess we can both keep our little secrets, okay?"

Cade tried a different tack. "You said you're hungry. Let's get the rest of the injuries looked at and then I'll see what I can put together."

"You already covered it, and I can rustle up a bowl of cereal or something."

He doubted she could rustle herself to bed, but he refrained from saying so. "Nothing else hurts on your arm? Your shoulder, back?"

"My back's a little sore, but hey, I scraped my spine on the window casing, then damn near landed on my head and shoulders, so . . . Guess I'm lucky I didn't break my neck."

The thought of that leveled him, made his heart thump and his lungs constrict. "Let me take a look."

Eyes narrowing, she curled a little away from him. "Don't tell me you're a doctor?"

"No, but I have some field experience—"

"Aha. Military." Pouncing on that, she said with triumph, "I knew it."

"And since you refuse to get actual medical attention, at least let me see what I can do." Seconds ticked by while she considered it.

"Yeah, all right." She struggled to sit up.

Carefully, he helped lever her more upright.

"I need panties," she said. "And maybe a button-up shirt. Then you can do all the doctoring you want."

The timing was all wrong, yet he teased, "Promise?"

"Get cute and you can get out."

Pleased to see her attitude back in full force,

Cade murmured, "Sorry," and helped her to her feet. "Can I help you dress?"

"You might have to. It took all I had just to get my robe on."

He hadn't expected her agreement, but he went along without a word, letting her lean on him as they made their way to her bedroom. Once there, she settled cautiously at the foot of the bed. "Panties are in the top middle drawer."

A new experience—helping a woman *into* her panties. Reyes would find it funny as fuck, but Cade was an eon away from humor.

He opened the drawer to a jumble of colors and fabrics all stuffed in together. Most were cotton, some with lacy trim, others nylon or ultra-sheer. Such a selection. He glanced over his shoulder. "You have a preference on full coverage or barely there?"

She smirked. "If by full coverage you mean granny panties, you won't find any there. But nothing too skimpy, and preferably cotton."

"Color matter?"

"Not to me."

Meaning it could matter to him? *Hmm . . .*

His hand looked too big sifting through her delicate underthings. Did her bras match her panties? Somehow he didn't think so, not unless it was a special occasion for her.

Did she consider sex a special occasion?

He'd like to find out. *Don't be an asshole.*

Deciding on hot pink with little yellow flowers, he turned and found her barely awake, her shoulders slumped, her head hanging. It wasn't a look he'd ever expected to see on Sterling Parson.

It bothered him. Too much. Somehow she'd already burrowed under his skin. When had that ever happened? Never.

Kneeling in front of her, he said, "Here," and helped to get the pretty panties over her feet and up to the knees she had pressed tightly together.

Standing, her uninjured hand braced on his shoulder, she said, "Not a word."

His face was level with her stomach, his hands bracketed outside her knees, her hand warm on his shoulder. Scenarios winged through his mind, heating his blood, tensing his muscles.

If she hadn't been hurt, he would have leaned forward, pressed his face against her, breathed in her heated scent . . .

One day soon, he'd be back in this position— once she'd fully recovered. *Not being an asshole, remember?*

Steeling himself, Cade looked up at her face.

Her gaze avoided his. "I mean it."

"I know." Watching her expression kept him from looking at her body, at the warm, silky flesh teasing his fingers and wrists as he tugged the panties up, under her robe, and smoothed them onto her hips.

It took a lot of iron control, but Cade stood. "Shirt?"

"No, I've decided to keep the robe, but you can look at my back if you want." Turning, she opened the belt and let the shoulders droop down.

More bruises, of course. He hadn't expected anything else, but at least these weren't as bad as her leg. Lifting her thick mass of hair with one hand, he touched, lightly prodded, but she barely flinched. "I think the worst of it is your leg and that finger."

"My finger feels better already, but yeah, my leg is crazy stiff."

He had a hot tub at his place, but inviting her there would cause more problems than he wanted to deal with. That is, if she'd even accept, which he doubted.

"How about we get you comfortable on the couch with an ice pack on your leg? I'll tape your fingers, then get food together."

"Wow, this whole 'being waited on' thing is nice. I had no idea what I've been missing."

The sarcasm made it easier for her, Cade knew, so he didn't reply as he helped her back to the living room.

Maybe if she'd had a different background, having Cade see so much of her under such crummy circumstances might have been more embarrassing. Truth? Her biggest issue wasn't nudity. It was being dependent on him.

That sucked rocks big-time, though she had to admit he made it easier than it could have been. He was so blasted matter-of-fact about it, like he did this sort of thing all the time.

Did he? No, somehow she knew he wasn't anyone's toady. Nice that, for right now, he'd be hers. Besides all the pampering, the view was pretty sweet. And stirring.

Yup, even though she felt like the walking dead, her hormones took notice of him. When he'd been on his knees? Downright fantasy inspiring.

Sterling wondered if he could really cook. Probably, given he did everything else with ease. Maybe someday she'd find out for sure, but right now she didn't have any basic ingredients for him to work with. Instead they dined on pizza rolls—fresh from freezer to microwave—with colas. It was the best she had since he'd discounted cold cereal and packaged cookies.

She felt better being clean, her finger straightened and taped to the one next to it, her thigh, resting on pillows to elevate it, numb from the ice he kept rotating, and food in her belly. Not good—good was nowhere on the horizon—but definitely less annihilated.

Less alone in the world.

Not that she'd start to depend on Cade. Hell no.

The man was far too secretive about every single thing.

"So." She idly rubbed an area of her leg not covered by ice. "What happened at Misfits? Was that your brother's plan, to cause pandemonium? I saw him, you know, before I got taken to that back room."

"Actually, that was all my doing, with only a short warning to my brother." He leaned forward over her injured leg to readjust the ice, then explained, "The other night when you left my bar to draw out Smith—who is actually Thacker, by the way—I listened in, so I knew he'd propositioned you."

What? No way. "I didn't see you."

With a shrug, he explained, "Neither did he, because I went out the office window and hung in the shadows. I knew right away you'd be walking into a trap, so I set up a hasty plan."

"You could have told me."

"So you could tell me to butt out? Not a chance."

Yeah, she probably would have. Far too often, pride overrode common sense. "I knew his name wasn't Smith."

"I figured."

So at least he credited her with some sense. "Were you in Misfits, too?"

"Outside, watching through a window. I knew what that bastard was likely expecting, and whether you were agreeable or not, I wasn't about to let you go through with it."

"Let me?" she asked quietly, with a fair amount of menace.

"Figure of speech, but accurate. I had the ability to stop it, so I did. Are you really going to protest now? Would you have handled it better on your own?"

Handle it? Ha. She'd been stuck with no way out, and he'd basically saved her. Unable to meet his direct gaze, she looked down, feeling cornered.

Damn it, she wasn't good at gratitude, at even recognizing it when she felt it, but she knew that had to be the emotion sitting heavy on her chest. "So . . . *surly* is generally my default mood, ya know?"

Instead of being insulted, he gave a small laugh. "I've noticed."

Peeking up at him, seeing the actual smile on his mouth had a strange effect on Sterling. They sat close, alone together in her apartment, and she wasn't exactly immune to his personal brand of attention. "Anyway," she said, reining in her unruly thoughts, "yeah, I appreciate the help you gave."

Trying to see her face, Cade tipped his head. "No problem."

For him, it hadn't been. In the darkness of the bar, she hadn't been able to see the ass kicker versus the ones getting their asses kicked, but somehow she knew Cade was the first. She remembered the silence from him, how he hadn't even breathed heavily while taking apart everyone in the room—except her and . . .

Adela! Sterling jerked her head up. "The woman who was in that room with me? Do you know what happened to her? Is she okay?"

With a small, regretful shake of his head, Cade said, "No idea, sorry."

Deflated, she decided it was past time for some truths. "Okay, enough. You were there with your brother. I was there. We don't trust each other—I get that. But I seriously need to know what happened."

Cade gave her a silent scrutiny.

Desperation wavered in her voice. "Please?"

It took him too damn long to nod, and he still didn't give in completely. "I'll share a truth, then you share. Deal?"

Dirty pool! She had reason for needing to know, but what reason could he have for not wanting to tell her?

Unaffected by her scowl, he said, "Take it or leave it, Star."

Ha! He knew she wouldn't refuse. "Fine. But you tell me what happened to Adela first."

"I can't. I told you that. But," he said before she could interrupt, "we nabbed Thacker—that is, Smith—and his buddy Jay, the two bozos who showed up at my bar. My brother also found several women locked in different rooms."

Her heart dropped hard. She grabbed his wrist. "You got them out?"

His gaze went to her hand, making her acutely aware of what she'd done. His wrist was so thick her fingers couldn't encircle it. Hot, rock-solid and dusted with soft hair—now that he'd drawn her attention to it, her palm tingled . . . and that tingle seemed to travel up her arm and on to places better forgotten.

"Sorry." She hastily withdrew.

"You can touch me anytime you want."

Such a thrilling offer! "I don't—"

He cut off her protest. "Those women are safe now, but we couldn't locate you, the other woman or . . ." He paused.

"Mattox?"

Cade's brows shot up. "He actually introduced himself?"

She understood his surprise. Mattox tended to keep a low profile, leaving it to his lackeys to do his dirty work, except for when it came to procuring women. Then the slimy bastard insisted on taking part.

Even more telling, though, was the fact that Cade obviously knew Mattox, or knew of him. So, she'd nailed it: being a sexy bartender wasn't his main vocation. Plus she now knew he had military experience. What, exactly, were he and his brother up to?

She wasn't sure how to answer him without giving away her own secrets. After considering it, she said, "No introductions were necessary."

"You already knew Mattox?"

"Yup." Knew him, despised him, badly wanted to see him suffer. "You did, too, right?"

He bypassed that to ask, "How? You'd met him before?"

"No, you don't. One question at a time. So tell me. What exactly was your plan at Misfits?"

"Keep you safe, period," he replied without hesitation. "Your turn."

"Bull! You already knew the place and the players, so don't try to tell me—"

"I've been aware of Misfits and what they do for a while. But I was there last night because that's where you went. Otherwise, I would have continued to . . ." He fell silent.

"Surveil?" she offered helpfully. "Investigate?" Damn it, what exactly was his role in all this?

One steely shoulder lifted.

Not good enough. Throwing caution to the wind, she looked him over. "So this is what you do? You find and expose human-trafficking rings?"

Nothing, not even a blink.

"And then what?" Were they actually on the same mission? That'd be cool. More and more, she liked Cade. She *mostly* trusted him. It'd be great to have her own personal badass around when she needed him, and the man was certainly easy on the eyes. Win-win.

"It's my turn to ask questions." He rubbed her foot through the blanket.

Almost stopping her heart.

Yeah, a foot rub was definitely not in her repertoire of experiences. Had to admit, though, it felt downright heavenly.

"So tell me, Star—"

"Sterling."

He gave a brief nod of acknowledgment. "What were you hoping to accomplish with that stunt?"

She supposed someone had to make the first move, right? Might as well be her. If she gave a little, surely he'd do the same, and maybe they could clear out the secrets between them.

Normally, she'd never consider such a thing. The less people knew her and what drove her, the safer she felt. But of all the men in all the world, she actually *liked* Cade—especially now that she realized they had a common goal: to bust up sex trafficking, free the women captured and punish the ones responsible.

With that decision made, she pondered where to start. "I hadn't figured on Thacker showing up at the bar." It was her haven . . . probably not anymore. "He never had before, at least not that I know of?"

Since she posed it as a question, Cade confirmed it for her. "It was his first time in."

Sterling nodded. "I've been aware of him for a while."

"How?"

"Mmm . . . I've talked with a few women who knew him. Yeah, vague, I know, but that's all you're getting on that." Unless he shared a few nuggets, too. This had to be an even exchange. "I kept wondering how I was going to get to him—"

"Jesus." Raking a hand over his short hair, Cade sat back and frowned.

There went her foot rub. Bummer.

"Then I saw him at the bar. Poof, he was within my reach. I saw it as an opportunity I couldn't resist."

"An opportunity for *what?* To get mauled? Raped? Sold?"

Having her worst fears thrown at her brought back her scowl. "Sheesh, what a downer. Have a little faith, why don't you?"

"Star," he warned.

"Sterling," she automatically corrected. When she'd started her new, empowered life, she'd changed everything—locale, appearance and nickname. "I thought I'd get a feel for Misfits, see how they ran it, you know? Getting in without an invite isn't easy, so this was the only way."

"No, it wasn't."

Right. Evidently he'd already been in there.

His brother, too. They saw Misfits for what it was. Not that either of them had bothered to tell her that, even though they knew she'd planned to go.

Seeing yet another opportunity, Sterling rethought her argument. Since Cade seemed determined to keep her safe, she could use that to her advantage. It wasn't like she wanted to tackle Mattox and his perverted pals on her own. That path led to failure, as she'd already discovered.

But with Cade's help? His brother's assistance?

She just might be able to get somewhere.

Smiling with her new intent, she stared into Cade's stunning blue eyes and suggested, "If you would share with me, we could coordinate." His entire expression hardened. If she hadn't already decided not to fear him, that look alone would have set off her alarm bells. Funny that she somehow knew Cade was different.

Now she had to convince him that she was different, too.

CHAPTER FIVE

Gauging his reaction, Sterling prompted, "You could do that, right? Get in, same as your brother?"

Voice dropping to a quiet but firm whisper, he warned, "This is not a game you should be playing."

"Says you. I feel differently." For the last few years, it was the only game she played, and she called it revenge, atonement, even satisfaction.

"You still haven't told me why."

Was that worry—for *her*—putting that particular dire expression on his face? Interesting. "Why doesn't matter. You see—"

"It matters a lot."

"Anyway," she said, stressing the word to make it clear she didn't appreciate his interruption. "If all had gone well, I might've ended a few monsters and freed a few women."

Incredulous, he stared at her as if she'd grown two heads. "Things did not go well."

A reminder she didn't need. Trying to sound cavalier, she returned, "No, but you saved the day."

Too quick for her to stop him, he flipped the ice packs and blanket aside. Indicating the deepening bruises on her leg, he said, "You call this saving the day?" Catching her wrist, he lifted her hand with the two fingers taped together. "Does this look like I'm some kind of hero?"

Whoa. That was a lot of anger, but oddly, it didn't concern her since he seemed to be angry on her behalf.

Given that Adela wasn't free and Mattox wasn't dead, Sterling considered her efforts a big old failure—and maybe, because she'd gotten injured, Cade felt the same.

Did he already feel responsible for her, just as she felt responsible for Adela? That possibility warmed her, but it also set off alarm bells. She'd been on her own too long to let anyone, especially a guy with secrets as big as her own, sidle in and take over.

Hopefully she hid her mixed reactions under sarcasm. "I'm here, alive, not mauled or raped or sold, so yeah. All in all, your diversion saved . . . well, at least me." She drew a breath. "That's something, right?"

Shoving to his feet, Cade paced the small area of her living room. Hers wasn't a tiny apartment, but with him prowling around it felt minuscule, as if his size and presence had shrunk the space. Looking at him was easy. All that fluid strength, tightly contained but ready when he needed it. She envied him that physical power.

He stopped to face her. "I do not want you hurt."

It fascinated Sterling, witnessing his protective instinct. Not something she was used to. "That makes two of us."

And actually, she didn't want him hurt, either, but she had a feeling he wouldn't appreciate her concern quite so much. "You said your brother got hold of Thacker and the other dude, and some women. What'd he do with them?"

He relented enough to explain, "The women were transported to a secure shelter. They'll get whatever help they need."

Nice. It's what she would have done, too. "And the scumbags?"

The look he sent her said it all.

Sterling whistled. "They're dead?"

He answered her question with one of his own. "Isn't that what you intended?"

"Yeah, but somehow I think you might have contacts that I don't."

"I have a lot of things you don't."

Was that supposed to be an insult? She laughed. "No kidding. Want me to name a few? How about big biceps and bigger fists? Muscled legs and granite shoulders. I'm tall, but you've got me on height, strength and ability." His irritation amused her. "My legs aren't short, but I know they're not as strong as yours. And while I'm not a weakling, I'm not on a par with you, either. Ability? I mean, I try. I have a lot of determination. But I'm self-taught, so I'm sure I don't have the same skill set you have."

"This is . . ." He turned away again, the set of his shoulders showing his tension as he paced. "I'm not sure how to handle you."

Handle her? She snorted. "You can't, so don't tax yourself. But can I make a suggestion? Try answering my questions and let's see if we find some common ground."

"We can't. Not on this."

Rolling her eyes, Sterling asked her questions anyway. "What shelter did you take them to? And how were you surveilling Misfits?"

He shook his head.

"All right, try these on for size." He had to tell her *something,* or their conversation was at an end. "How'd you know where I live? And where'd you learn to fight?"

Stubbornly silent, Cade rubbed his jaw, his gaze piercing as he stared at her. "It's almost morning. You should get some sleep."

Jerk. Extreme disappointment sharpened her anger. He didn't want to team up? Fine. She'd managed on her own so far. She didn't need him.

She didn't need anyone.

"Yeah, I am tired." She faked a widemouthed yawn. "Go on, run back to wherever you came from. Maybe I'll see you at the bar again sometime." She was just irked enough to add, "Or maybe not."

Cade went still, his nostrils flaring. Tone dark

and deadly, he asked, "What's that supposed to mean?"

"It means I don't like you much anymore."

His eye twitched. "I didn't know liking had anything to do with it." Dangerously on edge, he stalked closer to her, braced one broad hand on the back of the couch, the other on the arm, and leaned down close. "You always stop at the bar after a haul."

Even showing signs of anger, his nearness fired her engines. Too bad she was out of commission. "So we're sticking with me as a trucker and you as a bartender? Fine by me." With mock innocence, she said, "I don't have deliveries for at least a week. Good thing, since I'm not sure I could manage it until my leg heals."

"Your leg is going to need more than a week, and if you're not a trucker—"

"Oh, but I am. Just like you're a bartender." Her sugary smile snapped him upright again.

"You know I am. You see me there often enough."

Sterling sighed. God, he was impossible. Also sexy and fit, and so blasted competent, how could she stay resistant? "You've seen me driving my rig. Done and done. All is as it seems."

Anger seemed to emanate off him in waves.

Oh, poor baby. Was she getting to him? More like driving him nuts, but whatever. "Did you like me better when I mostly ignored you? Well, too bad. You're the one who forced this . . . whatever it is. Odd friendship."

His gaze drilled into hers. "Sexual attraction."

Was he trying to shock her? Not happening. Since there was no point in ignoring him anymore, she grinned. "That, too."

His eyes narrowed. "Mutual respect."

Unwilling to give up too much ground, she looked away. "Possibly." She definitely respected his ability, but she didn't think he returned the favor.

"It's a beneficial relationship."

"How so?" Curious now, she took her own turn glaring daggers. "How do you benefit? Because I haven't agreed to anything."

"You will."

Anger stirred. "Are you talking sex?"

"I'm talking shared confidences."

"I'm the only one sharing!"

Acknowledging that with a nod, he straightened. "I need to clear a few things." He picked up her displaced ice packs and carried them back to the kitchen but continued to talk. "I don't have autonomy, so it's better if I don't act alone."

Now, that was a tidbit she could dig into. Her heart started pumping double time, and she carefully turned so her legs were off the side of the couch.

Hurt. Like. Hell.

But once he left, she'd have to get herself to the

bathroom and bed, so she may as well start now. The longer she sat, the harder she knew it'd be.

She clenched her teeth and concentrated on bending her knee. Fire burned up her thigh. How was she supposed to stand or walk?

Needing a distraction and fast, she asked, "So you work with your brother?" Did he need to consult him before confiding in her?

She could hear him in the kitchen, emptying the ice packs in the sink, the clinking of ice cubes as he refilled them. The man was entirely too at ease in her apartment, but then, she imagined he took control everywhere he went.

He returned and, without answering her question, asked, "Could we make a few agreements? I'll let you know if I find Adela or Mattox, and you don't do anything else without letting me know."

Talk about a one-sided contract. "I don't answer to you."

He took in her strained expression, then moved forward to set the ice packs on the table. Slipping an arm around her, he helped her up. "Probably better if I don't tell anything more about them anyway."

"Wait, that's not what I meant." Leaning against him, with his arm around her back to support her and her hand clutching his shoulder, really drove home the differences in their sizes. Yes, she was tall, but he stood a head taller.

For too long they just looked at each other. When her gaze dropped to his mouth, he shook his head. "You're in no shape to start anything."

Of course he was right. If he let go, she'd probably fall on her face. A kiss, though . . . She could handle that.

He tipped up her chin. "Where are we going?"

Guess that settled that. "You're leaving." Pretty sure that was his plan, anyway. "And I'm making my way to the bedroom. Maybe the bathroom first, but . . ."

He waited. "But?"

"I need to know if Adela is found, if she's safe—"

"Then agree."

If she weren't so banged up, she'd . . . what? Her unique set of skills wouldn't get her anywhere with a guy like Cade, and she knew it. That was part of his draw, actually. A big part. Most guys just didn't appeal to her, especially when she knew she was stronger—emotionally, mentally and sometimes physically. She was definitely more ruthless than most.

But Cade wasn't the type of guy she could dismiss on any level. He proved that with his newest tactic. "Blackmail?"

"Negotiations," he countered, never fazed, never out of control.

What could she do but agree? There, it wasn't even in her hands. He'd removed all options for her, so she didn't have to feel guilty for the little thrill that came with her capitulation.

"All right, fine." To ensure he didn't know how she really felt, she added in a grumble, "Not like I'll be doing much for a week or two anyway."

Now that he'd gotten his way, Cade relaxed even more. It was subtle, the slight smoothing of his brows, the softening of his mouth, tension ebbing from his shoulders. He somehow felt closer, gentler . . . warmer.

"Bathroom first?" And then with concern, "Do you need any help?"

Not on her life. "You're pushing your luck, dude."

That earned her a small smile. "I don't count on luck anyway. I use good, sound calculation. But if you think you can handle it, I'll wait right out here. If you run into a problem, though, just let me know. I'm not squeamish."

She almost growled that she wasn't, either, but he might take that as an invitation. The day she couldn't pee on her own was the day she'd truly give up.

He left her leaning against the sink. She noticed that he'd tidied up for her. Her clothes were now in the hamper and the blood had been wiped up before it could stain. Nice. God only knew when she'd be able to get on her knees to scrub the floor.

The first aid kit was stowed under the sink, and her necklace hung over the knob of the medicine cabinet.

He'd opened it to expose the curved blade. Had he left it that way to show her he recognized it for a weapon—or because he hadn't known how to close it again? She'd bet on the first.

Cade McKenzie was a handy man to have around—in more ways than one.

While she was in there, she brushed her teeth. She gave her hair a cursory glance but didn't really care enough to mess with it. Stiff legged and limping, she opened the door and found Cade leaning against the wall, his arms folded over his chest.

He looked lost in thought, but he immediately stepped forward to put that steel band normally called an arm around her again. "Bed?"

"Yeah, but I need to lock up behind you first." She couldn't accomplish much tonight, so she might as well get some sleep. But she sort of hated to see their time together end, and she sucked at subtlety, so she asked, "When will I see you again?"

Standing there together, her more or less in his embrace, he asked, "What time do you get up?"

When she could walk? Usually by five. Now? She had no idea. "Maybe eight or so?"

"I'll have coffee ready."

He said that so casually she almost fell over.

"You'll be here first thing in the morning?"

With the light of challenge in his eyes, he said, "Figured I'd stay over, actually."

"Stay over?" And she squeaked, *"Here?"*

Apparently an unheard-of occasion, if the expression on her face was any indication. That didn't surprise Cade. Everything she did screamed *loner*.

If he had his way, that would end.

"You might need me." Rather than give her too much time to think about it, Cade steered her toward the bedroom. "Don't worry about the doors. I'll lock up."

Holding his breath, he waited for her refusal, for her sharp stubbornness to kick in.

Instead she grumbled, "Fine. I suppose I wouldn't mind the help."

His eyes widened, but he kept his face averted so she wouldn't notice. On the heels of that shocker, renewed concern followed. Her quick acceptance meant she had to be in total misery. Tomorrow would be worse before things started to get better.

Getting her from the living room to the bathroom had been the longest walk for her, but her bedroom was only a few steps away now. "Let me turn down the bed."

From what he could see, she didn't use a bedspread, but she'd smoothed the bedding into place. Leaving her to hold on to the dresser, he pulled back the sheet and quilt, then plumped her pillow.

"So." Voice strained, she asked, "Where will you sleep? Pretty sure my couch isn't long enough to accommodate a guy your size."

He'd slept in worse cramped places but didn't say so. Turning to her, he took her arm and urged her to the bed. "Where I sleep is up to you. I can crash beside you without bumping your leg—or make do on the couch. Even the floor is fine."

On her back, her dark hair fanned out on the pillow and her hands clutching the quilt, she looked younger.

And a lot more wary.

"I've never slept with anyone before."

Cade felt the bottom drop out of his stomach. "You . . . ?"

Annoyed now, she waved away his surprise. "I don't mean that. I've had sex. I've just never spent the night with anyone."

Way to stop his heart. "The night is almost over, so it wouldn't be more than a few hours anyway."

Looking to the side of the bed, maybe judging whether or not he'd fit, she said, "You're not clingy, are you?"

"If you're asking if I'd want to hold you, yeah, I would. But that's your decision." Trying to tease the worry from her expression, he promised, "I won't cuddle you in your sleep if you'd rather I didn't."

Disgruntled for only a second more, she

scoffed. "All right, let's not chew it to death." Going all brisk, she levered carefully to her side—facing away from where he'd sleep. "Get the doors locked and do whatever you have to do. I can't keep my eyes open any longer."

An hour later, enveloped by darkness, Cade silently called her a fibber. She was faking sleep, but he wasn't fooled. Maybe being in here with her wasn't such a good idea if his nearness was going to keep her awake.

Kept him awake, too, but he knew his problem. Despite her injuries, despite her wariness, he wanted her. Didn't matter that it couldn't happen, didn't matter that he wouldn't let it happen even if she felt up for it—which she didn't.

At the very least, he wanted to curve his body around hers, but she was so stiff beside him he thought she might startle if he reached for her.

Suddenly she made a small agonizing sound, breaking the spell.

Immediately he rolled toward her. "What's wrong? Leg hurting? I can get you more aspirin."

In reply, she snapped, "Just do it already."

His turn to go perfectly still. "It?"

"This cuddle stuff you mentioned. We're both awake, so you might as well—"

Not giving her a chance to change her mind, Cade carefully scooted closer until his body molded to hers, his legs fitting behind hers, his arm curving over the dip of her waist. Placing a soft kiss to the side of her neck, he asked, "Okay?"

Audibly breathing, she croaked, "Sure."

So warm, and surprisingly soft for such an attitude. He laced his fingers with hers over her stomach. "Relax."

Turning her head toward him, she asked incredulously, "Can you?"

"Eventually." He tugged her a little closer. "Close your eyes and take slow, deep breaths. If that doesn't work, I'm moving to the couch so you *can* sleep." When she said nothing, he directed again, "Breathe slow and easy."

Nodding, she sucked in a quick breath but did blow it out slowly, then repeated it . . . again and again, finding a smooth rhythm that lasted until her body went lax.

Cade knew the moment she nodded off, and then finally, he dozed off, too. Expecting her to stir off and on all night with discomfort, he was disconcerted to wake with sunshine filtering in through the window. Overall, they were in the same position they'd started in. Their fingers were no longer entwined, since she now had her uninjured hand tucked under her cheek, and his hand rested over her bruised thigh. Leaning up, he checked the clock on the nightstand.

Huh. He couldn't remember the last time he'd slept after nine, but it was damn near nine thirty.

On a soft groan, Sterling shifted—and went

still. She jerked her head around, then winced in pain.

"Easy. Let me disengage first. Then I can help. You're probably going to be twice as stiff now." He tried not to jar the bed as he got up and pulled on his jeans, leaving them unsnapped. He didn't bother with his shirt or shoes yet. "Can you sit up?"

"No choice," she said, teeth clenched as she let him help her upright.

Her robe had come open, so he got an eyeful, one that'd stick with him for . . . oh, the rest of his life, probably. Injured or not, she had a killer body. He didn't mean to, but his attention snagged on soft white breasts, tipped with rosy nipples.

Morning wood settled in real fast.

Without saying a word, he pulled the lapels together and retied the belt.

"You go ahead and use the bathroom," she said. "I need a minute."

"You won't move?"

She snorted. "Might as well warn you now, I'm not at my best in the morning, so mosey on while I concentrate on becoming human."

Grinning, Cade smoothed her hair. "Be right back."

A half hour later, he managed to get his unruly gonads under control, and she managed to make it to the bathroom and then the couch. They ended up positioned the same way as last night, with ice packs on her elevated leg, but now with coffee in hand.

He waited until she'd almost finished her first cup and then said, "I'll need to head out soon, but I want to make sure you're settled first."

Over the rim of her mug, those dark velvet eyes zeroed in on his face, before drifting down his body.

Several times she'd done that, her attention starting in one place and ending up on his bare chest or his stomach. Each appreciative study left him a little warmer. At one point she'd even stared at the crotch of his jeans until he worried he'd get hard again.

With the memory of her bare breasts at the forefront of his mind, it wouldn't take much.

When he cleared his throat, her gaze lifted lazily back to his. "Hey, you don't want me looking, don't show so much."

The things she said—hell, even her reactions, all of it—were entirely unexpected. "No way am I the first shirtless man you've seen."

Brows going up, she saluted him with her coffee. "No, but most don't look like you, do they? You've got some serious hotness going on. Work out often?"

Every day, but he wouldn't boast about it. "I like to stay fit."

"Because you routinely tangle with bad guys?"

Cade knew she casually slipped that in hoping

he'd automatically answer, maybe tell her more than he meant to. She was slick about it, but he wasn't that easy. "Habit. Lifestyle. Discipline."

"Yup, definitely military. And I guess that explains the tats?" She waited, but he only sipped his coffee. "You don't want to share yet? Bummer. I mean, we slept together, right? That should count for something."

"You think so? Then tell me—how often have you interfered with traffickers?"

"I'd rather know what the tattoos mean."

"I'll tell you—someday."

Turning away, she finished off her coffee and plunked the mug down on the table.

Disappointed, but not surprised, Cade strode back into her bedroom to pull on his shirt and grab his shoes and socks. He returned to the living room and took the chair adjacent to the couch to finish dressing.

She was still silent when he stood, provoking his impatience.

"I started," she whispered, "by picking up a girl on the highway."

Going still, Cade took in her expression, her carefully blanked mask that said so much, surely more than she meant to. Slowly, he reseated himself. "She was trafficked?"

Sterling nodded. "I knew the signs as soon as I saw her. Or suspected, anyway, but it didn't take me long to have it confirmed." Absently, she rubbed her leg. "It was cold, dark, and there she was, without a coat, her eyes . . . haunted. The second I pulled over, she got in and begged me to drive. She didn't care where as long as it was away. There were bruises on her arms, a few on her neck."

Getting up, Cade moved closer, sitting by her feet on the couch and curving a hand over her calf. "You got her somewhere safe?"

"She refused the police station. Airport was out without ID. Bus station was too shady, and the hospital would be too obvious, she said, because they'd know to find her there."

"They who?"

Sterling shook her head. "She didn't want to say." Her eyes met his. "But I talked her around."

Reading the vindication in her hard gaze unsettled him. "You went after them, didn't you?"

Bypassing that, she said, "There's a woman . . . I knew her years ago when I relocated. I trusted her." Sterling tucked back her hair with fidgeting fingers. "I got hold of her, and she helped me figure out what to do."

"Like what?"

"The thing is, knowing I made a difference, helping someone—it's empowering. Almost addictive." Flexing her toes, she winced, then shifted to get comfortable. "I couldn't give that up, so I've educated myself more."

Cade couldn't believe what he was hearing, but God help him, he knew this was her grand confession. It was truth, and somehow he had to bend his brain around it. "And so now you go trolling for victims?"

Insult sharpened her gaze. "There's no *trolling* involved. I'm on the most trafficked route in Colorado anyway, I'm in and out of truck stops, so yeah, I keep my eyes open, and when appropriate, I act."

A headache started at the base of his skull. "It's dangerous."

"Duh. But I can handle it."

He shot right back, "Like you did at Misfits?"

Pain forgotten, she sat forward and poked at his chest. "If you hadn't interfered, yeah, I'd have figured it out somehow. But you mucked it all up, didn't you? Now Adela is missing and Mattox is out there somewhere, so if anything, I'm in more danger now after your *assistance* than I'd be if I'd handled it on my own."

Cade nearly threw up his hands, but that wouldn't solve anything. He knew better than to let his temper take control. A man had to have a cool head to deal with most situations. Dealing with someone like Star? He'd let his anger fuck that royally.

Time to retrench, before she expected reciprocal confessions from him. Nothing had changed there. He still couldn't confide in her without implicating his family, and that was something he wouldn't do.

Getting up, he headed to the kitchen and rummaged through a few junk drawers before he found a pen and piece of paper. It gave him a second to collect himself and hopefully allowed her a minute to lose steam.

On his way back in, he preempted any angry outbursts by saying, "You're right. I'm sorry."

Mouth open—probably to blast him—Sterling paused, then clicked her teeth together. "I don't know if I accept your apology. It'll depend on what you tell me in return."

And there it was, the expectation of tit for tat. "We have a lot to discuss, but I really am running short on time, so how about giving me a list of groceries you want?"

She knew an evasion when she heard one. "Go. I don't need anything. My plan is to veg right here and watch TV."

"And what do you plan to do about food?"

That stymied her for a second. "Cereal is still in there."

"But your milk is bad."

Wrinkling her nose, she said, "Yeah, that happens a lot. Not your problem."

It bothered him that she'd seriously sit at home, hurt and without food, before she'd ask for help. Not that she had to ask, but it'd help if she didn't fight him every inch of the way. Now, of course, she had more reason than ever to be difficult.

"I do go after traffickers, with the end goal to take them out."

Eyes widening with an *aha* expression, she sat forward. "I *knew* it."

"We can compare notes soon, okay?" Maybe. Probably.

Probably not.

"But right now I want to run to the store before I have to get home and then to work. If you tell me your preferences, I can get some meals figured out, stuff that you can just nuke or eat cold, like sandwiches. What do you think?"

"I think you're a real mother hen."

"My family would disagree with you, but I am realistic enough to know you aren't in any shape to go out, your cabinets are all but empty, and I doubt you'd open the door to fast-food delivery."

Without denying or confirming any of that, she narrowed her eyes. "Why does it matter to you?"

"Why do you fight me?"

Her mouth twitched to the side. "Maybe because you confuse me and I'm not sure of your motives."

Something he could sink his teeth into. Hopefully it wouldn't make her more resistant. "I like you. I'm sure you've figured out that I want you." He held up a hand. "Not that I'm trading favors—"

"I *know* that." Color, both embarrassment and

irritation, warmed her face. "Give me some credit."

"Whether you and I ever get together, we're friends now, right? I'd help a stranger if I could, so of course I want to lend you a hand."

When she still didn't agree, he growled, "You like being disagreeable, don't you?"

Her mouth twitched the other way. "I don't want to be beholden."

"For food? You're telling me that once you're up and running again, you won't return the favor?"

Guarded, she asked, "Return it how?"

"Dinner? If you don't cook, we could go out."

"I cook." Touchy about it, she said, "I'm not helpless or dumb."

"Far from both," he agreed. "So we're on the same page here?"

"I'm not keen on going hungry, so feel free to play maid and chef."

God forbid she give an inch. Tamping down irritation, Cade asked, "Preferences?"

"I'll eat pretty much anything other than seafood, so get whatever's convenient. But I want the receipt so I can pay you back."

Knowing she'd insist, he nodded. "Fine."

She countered back with her own version of "Fine," loading the word with a lot of annoyance.

He picked up her keys so he'd be able to get back in and was almost to the door when she stopped him.

"One thing, Cade, and it's nonnegotiable."

Bracing himself, he waited.

"If you don't trust me with some details, you won't be welcome back, and I won't return to the bar. Maybe keep that in mind before you insist on doing my shopping."

Driven by her inflexible tone, Cade strode back to the couch, bent down and took her mouth in a quick, warm kiss—that really got to him. Her lips were soft, parted in surprise, allowing his tongue a brief foray. She tasted good and felt even better. He wanted to learn about that mouth. About all of her.

Before he got carried away, he stepped back but took in her bemused expression. She touched her lips, her gaze seeking his. First time he'd ever seen her speechless.

Next time she started haranguing him, he'd remember what worked. "I won't be long."

This time when he left, she didn't stop him.

CHAPTER SIX

Three flippin' days of laziness and Sterling was about to climb the walls. Sure, Cade continued to spend the night, getting in late after the bar closed and leaving late the next morning. But he still hadn't told her anything substantial. He answered her questions with questions of his own, to the point they were at a stalemate. The way he dodged getting to the meat of issues, she hadn't realized how little he'd shared until she started piecing it together.

Okay, so his buff bod distracted her. He slept in his boxers and didn't bother to dress until he was ready to go. What red-blooded woman wouldn't focus on that?

A couple of times now she'd wondered if he did it on purpose, just to keep her suitably dazed and on the edge of lust. If so, she didn't want him to stop.

She enjoyed it all too much.

The way he waited on her was sweet, too, but now she realized he'd sidestepped questions by cooking, tidying up the apartment, ensuring she had everything within easy reach before he left each day.

Finally, the bruising started to fade a bit and she could bear more weight on her injured leg.

No, she wouldn't be doing any deep knee bends yet, and driving her rig was still out, but she was pretty sure she could handle her car—and her own shopping.

Which meant it was time for him to fess up, or she'd have to send him packing. It didn't make sense for her to share anything more with a man who so obviously didn't trust her.

She'd just finished putting a compression wrap on her thigh when Cade asked, "How often do you actually transport or deliver?"

"Often enough to be legit," she replied, standing to test her leg. "Seldom enough that I can use my truck for other purposes."

He stood close in case she needed his help but didn't yet touch her. "Like searching for women along trucking routes?"

"Bingo." Satisfied that she could manage on her own, she took a small trip around the apartment. Her leg remained stiff and achy, but she moved on her own steam. "Mostly I pick up freight overload from bigger trucking companies, which lets me be pretty footloose with my schedule. When I have other leads to follow, I can pass on the job offer, and I never have to book myself too far in advance."

Sounding impressed, he said, "That's genius."

"I know, right?" She stopped to rest, one hand on the divider wall that separated the kitchen from the living room. "Now it's your turn, so—"

Her phone rang.

Disgusted by the interruption, she warned, "Don't go anywhere," and returned to the coffee table, grabbed up her cell and glanced at the screen. "An unlisted number." She answered, "Hello?"

"Francis?"

Oh, hell. Knees going weak, she lowered herself to sit on the edge of the couch. Already guessing the answer, she asked, "Who's this?"

"Adela."

Her gaze shot to Cade's. As if he'd picked up on the sense of danger, he came to sit beside her.

"How are you, Adela?" Sterling used her name to let Cade know the identity of her caller. "I hope you got out okay?"

"I need help."

Not exactly a direct answer. "Okay. Where are you?"

"I'm afraid to tell you—but I thought maybe I could meet you somewhere safe? You . . . well, it seemed you wanted to help, right? I'm sorry I wasn't as brave as you, but you can't imagine . . ." Her breath shuddered. "The things they've done to me, I couldn't risk it."

"I understand." Feeling Cade's gaze burning over her, Sterling tried to think. "What happened after I left?"

"I . . . I thought we'd stay at the bar, but they stuffed me in a car and drove to a different place."

"Where?"

"It doesn't matter. I got away, but now I don't know what to do. Please say you'll meet me."

Stalling for time, Sterling chewed her bottom lip.

"Francis?"

"It's okay. I'm here." Some anomalous emotion squeezed her lungs. Terror, likely. But also . . . uncertainty? Something here felt very, very wrong.

Cade shook his head at her.

The man dared to give her orders when he wouldn't tell her a damn thing? Screw that. She could make her own plans. "I hope you're somewhere secure, Adela, because I can't meet you for a few days."

"*Please!* I can't stay here. I'll get caught again, I just know it. They use horrible drugs and . . . and *violence,* and it scares me so badly—"

"Shh," Sterling whispered, hoping to calm her. "We'll get it figured out, I promise. You just need to stay safe a little longer."

After some heavy breathing, Adela asked, "Then you'll come for me?"

Heart clenching, Sterling vowed, "Of course I will, just not today. I hurt my . . . shoulder, when I went out the window." She couldn't say what prompted the lie, except that she'd learned extreme caution whenever dealing with traffickers or victims. "I'm sorry, but I can't drive yet. Another day or two and I should be better." Not giving Adela time to start crying again, Sterling asked, "How far do I need to go to meet you?"

After a lengthy hesitation, Adela blew out a shaky breath. "I'm off I-25. That's all I can say for now."

"But that covers a lot of ground."

"I'll be more specific when I know you're on your way."

With no other choice to take, Sterling nodded. "Okay, but give me a number so I can contact you tomorrow. We'll set something up for the next evening."

"No. I'll call you back." Agonized, Adela added, "I'm counting on you, Francis. Please, don't forget about me."

Hearing the finality in that small plea, Sterling said, "Wait—" but it was too late. She'd already ended the call.

The urge to throw the phone made it extra difficult for Sterling to gently place it on the coffee table, but that's what she did.

Then she ignored Cade as she concentrated on organizing her thoughts.

"You did well."

Adela stayed silent. His moods could be unpredictable at the best of times, and this wasn't a good time. He detested having his plans upset, but she'd tried her best. It wasn't her fault the woman wouldn't cooperate.

"We'll give her a day to stew on it," he decided. "Then you'll call her in a panic to make the arrangements."

"A panic?" That suggestion didn't bode well.

Eyes full of malice pinned her to the spot. He smiled, reaching out with one hand to finger the shorter wisps of her hair over her temple.

She tried not to flinch, but she couldn't help it.

"When she sees you, she needs to know you're in trouble. She needs to be completely horrified by your condition." His meaty hand opened to cup her cheek. "Do you understand what I'm telling you?"

Unfortunately, she did. She shouldn't have been cold, but the chill of the inevitable seeped into her bones, making her shiver.

His thick hand slid down her neck and gripped tightly—seconds before his other hand made sharp contact with her jaw. Stars erupted and she would have collapsed, except that he held her by the neck.

Standing, Sterling made her way to the patio doors and stared out at the mountains in the distance. It was a sight that used to soothe her. The vastness of the Rockies meant she could hide—but now it also meant she might disappear, and who would know?

Who would *care?*

This was the first time someone had contacted her directly. Usually when she helped a young woman, it was because she'd found her on the road or in the act of being traded. Truck stops were hotbeds of trafficking, which was the main reason she'd gotten her CDL.

Promising safety, she could usually talk a woman into getting into her truck. When conditions warranted it, when sleazeballs were keeping watch, she performed hasty kidnappings.

In her seven years as a truck driver, she hadn't made as much impact as she would have liked— but for the women she'd rescued, she'd made a big difference. They'd been given a second chance.

And in doing so, she'd given herself another chance, as well. A chance to add worth to her life. A chance to—

"How'd she get your number?"

The intrusion of Cade's voice disrupted her maudlin thoughts. A good thing, really. She couldn't afford too much introspection right now or she'd chicken out of what had to be done.

Glancing at him, she said, "I gave her a card the night we were at Misfits."

Fury and disbelief brought Cade slowly to his feet. "You did *what?*"

She curled her lip in disdain. Sure, she recognized his temper as concern, but the facts remained: *he didn't trust her.*

Whatever. She was done trusting him, too.

"Don't sweat it. All the card had on it was my number, nothing else, and I don't use GPS or public Wi-Fi on my phone. No one is going to track me down."

"I did."

Her brows climbed high. "Using my cell phone? No, I don't think so." Sterling turned back to the view, but she didn't really see it. Damn it, she had hopes of her and Cade teaming up, but he'd dashed them, and now she had to accept it wouldn't happen. "More likely you followed me home—or had someone else do it. Either way, it was a breach of privacy that I don't appreciate."

She hadn't heard his approach, so it took her off guard when his hard hands settled on her shoulders. Her senses stirred, awareness spiking.

His reflection in the glass showed his resolve.

Against her back, she felt the heat of him.

Odd, but his nearness calmed her rioting thoughts. Since she couldn't rely on him, that wasn't necessarily a good thing. To put them back on track, she said, "I'll have to go after her."

Cade pulled her against his body, his arms folding over her chest, enveloping her in his strength. "No, you won't. I can handle it for you."

"Oh, for sure, you look enough like me to fool her." Rolling her eyes, she twisted around to face him. "She'll be looking for *me,* an unassuming woman—"

Cade snorted.

"Not an imposing man. If she sees you, she'll bolt."

"You don't know that."

"I've handled it enough times that I can guarantee it. Men will not be high on her trustworthy list."

"Is that the voice of experience?" Appearing far too solemn, he cupped his hands around her neck, his thumbs keeping her chin lifted. "It'd help if you told me how you got started with all this."

It saddened her far more than it should have, but Sterling shook her head. "I don't think so. Interesting as this has been, it's going nowhere. I got that message loud and clear." She pulled away from him and hobbled toward the front door. "Time for you to go."

Cade didn't move. "I'm not going anywhere."

She spun back to face him and nearly lost her balance when her bum leg gave way. "Yes, you are."

"You can so easily dismiss this?" He gestured between them.

"I don't even know what this is. You said you needed to talk to others, to see what you could share. Well, you've had four days and still nada. I'm done. I have things to do, and they don't include dumping my past on you."

As she spoke, Cade seemed to get bigger, harder, maybe even a little menacing. In comparison, his tone was soft—and somehow more lethal because of it. "I kept putting off talking to my family because it's going to raise a lot of speculation. And I know how they'll react."

Family, meaning not just his brother? Was his sis involved, too? "Secrecy all the way, huh?"

"It's what we've lived by for many years. You know it, too. The best way to keep private info private is not to share it with anyone."

Her heart sank. Had she really held out hope that her ultimatum would change things? Stupidly, yes.

He'd done the unthinkable, dangling the carrot of shared experiences . . . only to yank it away. "Leave."

Instead, he scrubbed a hand over his face. "I never knew my mother."

In the process of heading to the door, Sterling froze. Afraid that he'd say no more, she kept her back to him and stayed perfectly still.

"My father raised me from birth. I'm thirty-two now and not once has my mother ever tried to contact me."

When she got light-headed, Sterling realized she was holding her breath. She let it out softly, then sucked in fresh oxygen. "Maybe she didn't know how to find you."

"No, that wouldn't have been a problem."

She heard him moving and chanced a peek back.

He now sat on the couch, legs sprawled, hands braced on his thighs. "My father never married, but he did have a life partner." He shrugged. "She was like a stepmother to me. They loved each other, and when she was taken, it leveled him in a way I've never seen before. He was . . . crazed."

Cautiously, Sterling approached, her heart beating double time, and eased down beside him. "She was never found?"

"Oh, she was. Dad has the kind of money that can hire the best and hire the worst."

"I don't understand."

"They turned the state upside down. He observed it all, the interrogations—and the vengeance. Finally, he found her. It's bullshit, the way Hollywood paints human trafficking as some high-style wealthy man's sport. It can be, but that's not the norm. It's what exists in our own backyards."

Unable to resist, Sterling put her hand over his. "I know."

"She was found in a shitty little hotel room, drugged to the gills and . . ." He swallowed heavily.

Again, with emotion making her throat feel thick, Sterling whispered, "I know."

Turning his hand, Cade clasped her fingers. "One year to the day that she returned home, she swallowed a bottle of pills."

Seeing his pain made it fresh for Sterling. Tears

burned her eyes, but a crying woman wouldn't help him.

A strong woman would. "I'm sorry."

"She'd left a note, a plea for Dad to do *something* so other women wouldn't have to go through that." His gaze locked on hers. "And that's all I can tell you for now. Don't ask me names or details, because I can't give them."

She was quick to nod. This was a moment, one she could cherish, one she could build on—and God, she wanted that. She wanted more than the emptiness her life had been.

It took her a second to decide on her next step, but it was instinct that brought her forward so she could sink against his big solid chest. Wrapping her arms around his waist, she squeezed him tight. "Thank you for telling me."

"Is it enough, Star?"

Damn it, she was starting to like the way he said her name.

He nuzzled against her hair. "Will you promise me you won't go after Adela alone?"

Feeling the weight lifted from her shoulders, she nodded. "Yes. I promise."

That got her crushed against him. "Let's go over what we know."

This. This was what she'd wanted. Someone to collaborate with, to help her with her plans. A sounding board that'd give her a new perspective.

Nodding, Sterling forced herself past the

satisfaction of having a cohort to address the business at hand. "Adela said she was staying off I-25, which doesn't tell us much."

"Except that it's known as a trafficking route."

Sterling knew that well. "Along the front range, drivers can easily travel from city to city and into other states. Here's the thing." With one last squeeze, Sterling straightened. "I've picked up three women along that interstate, all of them about an hour south of Colorado Springs in the same general area."

"You think it could be related?"

"Makes sense, right? It's how I knew about Misfits and—Thacker. But only if it's a widely spread organization. One of the women was from a spa that later got busted."

"Thanks to a tip from you?"

Pleased that he'd give her credit, she blushed. "Yeah, sure. I mean, I couldn't just charge in there with guns blazing, right? So I anonymously clued in some people, luckily the right people, and it turned into a big sting."

"I actually remember that. Around eighteen months ago, right?"

So *he* kept track of such things? Interesting. "That's right. Eight men were arrested and the spa was shut down."

His phone dinged with a message. Impatient, he glanced at it and didn't look pleased. "The other women you mentioned?"

Of course, now she wondered who'd sent him a message, but he'd just started opening up and she didn't want to pressure him, so she let it go.

For now.

"One had been held in a prostitution ring that operated out of this nasty little hotel. They thought they had her too intimidated to run, but she'd only been waiting for an opportunity, and that happened during a severe rainstorm that knocked out power over a wide swath. Plus the downpour made it tougher for them to search for her."

"But you found her?"

"At a truck stop, hiding behind a building. Being female, she trusted me more than the male truck drivers."

He nodded. "And the third?"

"She'd only recently been abducted. She was able to get away by jumping out of a moving car while they were transporting her, so she was pretty banged up. It was cold and she didn't have the right clothes. I think it was desperation that brought her near the road. Good thing I found her before anyone else did."

His admiring gaze moved over her face. "You're pretty remarkable, you know that, right?"

Again his words warmed her. "Just doing my part."

"Above and beyond."

"Like you?"

"There are definite similarities, and I'd love to compare notes, but that was a summons from my father and it's never a good idea to keep him waiting." As he stood, he asked, "You'll be okay until I get back after work?"

Since he'd stocked the fridge with chicken salad and pickles and left croissants and chips on the counter, canned soup in the cabinets, he didn't need to worry about her going hungry. "I'm better every day. In case you didn't notice, I can get around on my own now."

"I noticed." Intense emotion darkened his eyes. "I'm looking forward to you being one hundred percent again."

She couldn't hold back the silly smile. "Yeah? Why's that?"

For an answer, he leaned in and took her mouth again, longer, hotter this time, his tongue teasing against hers, his breath warm on her cheek. He lingered—until his phone buzzed once more.

On a low growl, he moved away, but not far, just enough to separate their lips. His hand tunneled into her hair to curve around her skull. "Make no mistake. We've come to an agreement. You'll stay in today, and tomorrow we'll make plans together?"

"Tomorrow we can discuss plans," she clarified. "But I won't go out. I'm not quite ready for that anyway. I thought instead I'd do some additional research on the area where I found the other women."

"Good thinking. I'll see you tonight after I've closed up the bar." With one last, sizzling kiss, he left her apartment.

Sterling would like to know more about his father. His brother and sister, too. Hopefully tomorrow he'd share details.

Would she share, as well? She *did* trust him, she realized, so what would be the harm? Yet caution was her constant companion, so she'd consider all the angles before making up her mind.

Crazy, but she already anticipated his return— and more than that, the day when she'd be healed enough to make him live up to the promise behind those kisses.

Dogged by his father's assistant, who also served as a butler and chef, pretty much everything, Cade went through the opulent mountain home toward the back deck, where he knew he'd find his family. "I know the way, Bernard."

"Yes, sir," he acknowledged, while continuing to be Cade's shadow.

Cade glanced back at him. "I thought we agreed you'd quit with the *sir* nonsense."

"You requested," Bernard said in his grating monotone, "and I declined."

Knowing Bernard to be as stubborn as Star, Cade let it go as he continued on through the massive great room and out to the three-tier deck that offered an amazing view of the mountains, as well as his father's man-made lake. Sitting on fifty-two acres, surrounded by wilderness, guaranteed a level of privacy not found in the skiing towns.

Cade loved the house and the surrounding land—not so much these visits.

It was cooler up here, so his sister, immersed in reading something on her laptop, had a colorful shawl around her shoulders. Reyes sprawled in a chair, one leg over the arm, his expression pensive—until he spotted Cade.

" 'Bout time you got here."

Curious over what that meant, Cade glanced at his father. Parrish McKenzie looked younger than his fifty-three years. Almost as tall as Cade, still fit thanks to the well-equipped gym on his lower level and a love of the outdoors, his father always made an imposing figure.

Sipping hot tea from a dainty cup and working a crossword puzzle, he looked nothing like a hard-core vigilante. Without looking up, he said, "You have some explaining to do."

At the same time, Bernard asked, "Something to drink, sir?"

"I'll take a beer."

"This early?" Bernard questioned, with disapproval.

"Not like I'll drink at the bar, so yeah. This

early." Hell, it had to be noon. Not like he was having it for breakfast.

"Yeah," Reyes said, perking up at that suggestion. "Grab me one, too, will you, Bernard?"

His sister never stirred, but then, when she got immersed in research, she tuned out everything else.

The second Bernard left, Reyes sang, "Cade has a girlfriend."

Cutting his gaze to his brother, Cade warned, "Knock it off." He dropped into an empty chair at the table.

Reyes only grinned. "But that's why we're here. I just figured I'd throw it out there rather than keep you waiting."

Shit. It had been too much to ask that his father might not yet know about Star.

Finally Parrish put down his pencil and sent an enigmatic gaze at Cade. "This won't do, you know."

"Not up to you, so save the dictates." Cade accommodated his father whenever possible. This wasn't one of those times.

"If you want her," Parrish said baldly, "just have her and be done with it."

Reyes snorted.

Madison glanced up, brows lifted.

It struck Cade that he had to have the strangest family in God's creation. Keeping his expression bland, he asked Parrish, "Does she get a say in it?"

Hot color rushed into his father's face. As a champion of women, it was an insult that cut deep. "You know I wasn't suggesting—"

"So you just assumed she'd be on board if I'm interested? I appreciate the vote of confidence."

"Logical conclusion." Shifting his gaze to Reyes, Parrish asked, "What's so special about this woman?"

"No freaking idea."

Cade thought about tossing his brother over the railing. He could roll downhill until he hit the lake.

"Is she beautiful?" Expounding on that, Parrish said, "Describe her."

Uneasy now, Reyes glanced at Cade, then shrugged. "Tall, strong figure, average face. Nice hair. Definite lack of fashion sense."

Frowning in confusion, Parrish turned back to Cade for enlightenment.

It was almost laughable. Almost. "Looks aren't everything, Dad." And then to Reyes, "Though you have to admit there's something about her."

"She's sexy," Reyes agreed. "But that's not what Dad asked."

"It's the attitude." Cade didn't mean to offer up details, but the words came out anyway. "If you got to know her, you'd understand what I mean."

"Yeah, uh . . . I got a small taste of that attitude, enough to neuter me, so no thanks." To their dad, he said, "It'd take someone like Cade to go toe-to-toe with her. She's what you'd call *challenging*."

"Challenging how?"

"Let's just say she's not a 'polished nails and styled hair' kind of gal—more like 'I'll gut you and walk away smiling if you get in my way' type."

Appalled, Parrish asked Cade, "Is that something you want?"

Even Madison put aside her work to hear the answer to that.

Their reactions left him grinning. Was it so unheard of for him to be interested? All right, so he never let his personal life cross paths with his work—until now.

It wasn't like he set out to find a balls-to-the-walls woman. Nope. Had he been looking for someone to match his strength? Not likely, since he usually was attracted to ultrafeminine women. Actually, he hadn't been looking for anything.

Then Sterling Parson had walked into his bar one night and he hadn't been able to put her from his mind since then.

That was his business, though, no one else's, and he wouldn't sit here while they dissected her. "Maybe you all missed it, but I'm thirty-two, too old to explain myself, so leave it alone."

"But you need our help," Madison said, then fell silent as Bernard returned with beers, little sandwiches and some type of individual cakes on a round tray.

"Bernard!" she exclaimed, already snatching up two of the small cakes. "You know these are my favorites."

"Yes, I do. That's why I made them." He handed her a napkin, then refilled her tea before offering the contents of the tray to Cade and Reyes.

Glad for the reprieve, Cade took two sandwiches, popping one into his mouth right away. Good. Some kind of specialty bread, with a tangy sauce, sliced roast beef and fresh tomatoes. "Not bad, Bernard."

"You'll make me blush with that type of praise."

Laughing, Reyes grabbed a few sandwiches for himself. "We all know you're invaluable, Bernard, so don't go fishing for compliments."

"Can't imagine what I was thinking." After setting the half-empty tray on the table, he turned to Parrish. "If you need anything else, let me know."

Parrish waved him off. "Go take a break. Maybe grab a swim. Put one of the pools to use."

"The indoor pool is heated just right," Reyes said, "but fair warning, the outside pool is cold enough to shrivel your . . ."

"Ahem." Bernard censured Reyes with a single withering look, then said to Parrish, "Thank you, but I need to start preparations for dinner."

With a sniff, he added, "The meat must marinate. Perhaps I'll indulge a swim later this evening."

After the French doors closed behind him, Reyes burst out laughing. "I do love shocking him."

Parrish shook his head. "For twenty years I've been telling that man not to be so formal."

"He enjoys the pomp," Madison said. "Let him have his fun." Her eyes, the same bright hazel color as Reyes's, narrowed on Cade. "Now, as I was saying—"

"I don't want your help."

She smiled. "Sorry, but you're getting it anyway."

CHAPTER SEVEN

Cade turned his ire on Reyes. "Felt like you had to confess all, huh?"

Unfazed, Reyes shook his head. "Wrong tree you're barking up, there. I didn't say jackola." He gestured toward Madison. "Did you really think *she* wouldn't find out?"

No, it would have been more surprising if she hadn't. His baby sister didn't miss much. By accessing street cameras and security cameras on businesses, and with the help of good old-fashioned bugs, she had surveillance everywhere.

No problem when it came to work, but apparently she knew he hadn't been home the last few days, either.

Because he'd been staying with Star.

Cade shifted his attention to his sister.

Defiant, Madison elevated her chin. "Of course I told Dad. When you risk yourself, you risk the rest of us."

An insult he couldn't ignore. "You think I'd let harm come to you?"

She winced in apology. "No, not really. I didn't mean that."

"So you think what? That Star will hold me hostage until I tell her all about you?"

Parrish scowled at Cade. "Don't put your sister

in an untenable position with divided loyalties. We work as a family. You know that." Admonishing, he added, "And she wouldn't have had to tell me if you'd done so instead."

"I planned to tell you soon."

"Why wait?"

Reyes started to speak up, likely with another joke.

He shut down when Cade turned on him. "I wouldn't if I was you."

Hands up, Reyes said, "Take it easy. Here on the balcony isn't the right place, but if you want a go at me, the gym is available downstairs."

Parrish slammed a fist to the table. "I didn't teach you to fight so you could maul each other."

For too many years, Parrish had been fanatical about his children learning both defensive and offensive moves. While he trained with one expert after another, always with the intent of one day getting the men who'd kidnapped his companion, he included his children so that they were trained, as well.

From the day his stepmother committed suicide, Cade was told his purpose in life was to seek justice for those who couldn't defend themselves. He, Reyes and Madison couldn't just be good—they had to be the best.

Once Reyes had stopped grieving his mother, he'd loved the discipline and had embraced the vigilante purpose with enthusiasm.

Madison, too, accepted her role as tech genius, falling into place from the age of nine.

Cade was different. He'd balked at having his purpose predestined by his overbearing father. Oh, he'd learned what he could. Training was a satisfying outlet for his sorrow at losing the only mother he knew, and having siblings he'd wanted to protect.

Fifteen at the time and already rebellious, he'd butted heads with his father at every opportunity—right up until he'd joined the military in defiance of his father's dictates.

"If you want to spar," Parrish said, "you'll do so when neither of you is angry."

Smirking, Reyes asked, "When is he *not* angry?"

Cade rolled his eyes. True, he used to stay at some level of rage day in and day out. But that was a decade ago, before the military had helped him tamp down the emotion under firm control. Reyes knew that, but Bernard wasn't the only one he liked to heckle.

"I'm not angry now," Cade said, "but I'd still be happy to kick your ass."

"Nah. I think I'll wait and take you by surprise." He grinned. "Ups my odds, ya know?"

Getting back to the matter at hand, Madison shared one of her gentlest smiles. "For what it's worth, I admire Sterling a great deal." She turned her laptop so Cade could see the screen . . . where she'd expanded her research to include a history of Star's life.

He didn't want to read it here, under his family's scrutiny, but he knew how proprietary Madison could be about her investigations. She preferred to keep everything in-house—literally—and under her own impenetrable security protocols.

If he wanted to learn about Star, he needed to read everything now. And there was the rub. "This feels like a huge invasion of her privacy."

Madison's smile quirked. "You don't think she'd read everything she could about you if she had access?"

Actually . . . he knew she would, if for no other reason than that she didn't fully trust him.

Aware of Parrish, Reyes and Madison all watching him, Cade pulled the laptop closer. At first he merely skimmed the details. Abducted at seventeen from her high school. Escaped at some point between then and her eighteenth birthday, because new photos of her emerged after that—driver's license, concealed carry permit (now, why wasn't he surprised that she'd carry a gun?), her CDL for driving. She'd used different names, lied about her age a few times and moved around a lot, all the way from Ohio to Colorado.

"Last page," Madison said. "Child protection services had been to her home multiple times before she was abducted. That probably explains why she didn't return for her mother's funeral, even though she was apparently free by then."

Various photos from different ages, some of them grainy, others clear, filled the file. Damn, she'd changed.

At one point she'd been more colorful, more dramatic, likely outgoing. Now she was usually so contained she was like a different person. Quiet, intense, focused on a single purpose . . .

No wonder she didn't want him to call her Star anymore. She'd reshaped her life, her appearance, her entire persona. She'd made herself into a different person altogether.

The reach of his sister's abilities never failed to amaze him. "How did you do all this?"

"Facial recognition software, mostly. It's easy once you have access to various databases. Biometrics map out features and match them up. I wasn't sure about a few of the photos, so I had to do some cross-referencing to be positive they were really her."

Parrish sat back, his hands laced over his stomach. "In case you didn't realize, she's a vigilante, same as us."

"But without our connections," Reyes said.

"Or our financial means," Madison added.

Were they championing her now? Cade didn't know what to think of that. Until Parrish wrapped it up for him.

"All of which means she could bring us down

with her blunders." Parrish watched him closely. "You understand that?"

They all waited, while Cade's calm chipped away. He met his father's gaze. "You may as well save your breath, because I'll do whatever I can to keep her safe."

"I'd like to know how." Parrish picked up his tea. "It seems keeping her out of trouble is going to be a full-time job."

"Put our stuff away."

She would, but . . . "It's cold." Arms wrapped around herself, Adela listened to the hollowness of her footsteps on the warped wooden floorboards. Drafts circled her legs. Cobwebs hung in every corner. It smelled damp, as if moisture had seeped in.

The mountain cabin—more like a shack—offered only minimum comfort. A rickety cot, a small generator to run the coffee machine and the mini refrigerator, and a private cell tower so making a call wouldn't be a problem.

Nervousness sank into every pore of her body. Already the cabin looked dark. How bad would it be when the sun set behind the mountains?

She swallowed hard. "What if someone finds us here?"

"We'll claim we were lost and needed shelter." Mattox rolled a massive shoulder. "If that doesn't work, offer yourself up." He went to a dirty window to look out. "No matter what, don't leave the cabin tonight."

As if she would.

When she didn't answer, he turned to face her, his gaze piercing enough to make her tremble. "You heard me?"

"Yes." She looked around again, dreading the next few days. Hopefully Francis wouldn't make her wait long.

"You wouldn't make it to the road, not in the dark," he warned, "and you could run into a snake, a mountain lion or a black bear—"

"I won't step outside." God no, she wouldn't. The mention of snakes made other threats unnecessary.

She shouldn't ask. She knew better, but she heard herself say, "I don't see why we have to stay here."

His gaze went icy. "Don't you?" Stalking toward her, he growled, "You fucked up, Adela. That's why Misfits is temporarily shut down. That's why fucking Francis got away. That's why we're losing money as we speak, and that, my little idiot, is why we're stuck in this fucking cabin."

A spark of anger ignited, but she kept it under control. "I played my part. How was I to know someone would kill the lights or launch an attack, or that she'd be so quick at finding a way out?"

Disgusted, he said, "You didn't stop her, did you?"

"I called out!" God, she hated getting blamed—even if what he said was true. She should have found a way to stop Francis, but she'd drawn a blank at the woman's lack of fear and her daring, plus it had been so damn dark she couldn't see her hand in front of her face. "You'll get her back."

For the longest time he studied her, his expression unreadable. Then he touched the bruise on her face as if fascinated. "Yes, I will—although I'm starting to wonder if she's worth the trouble."

Her eyes widened. "You think she'll stop now? That she'll just go away?"

"No, but it might be better, easier, to put a bullet in her skull and be done with it."

Adela was sure he didn't mean that. "So you've given up on making her pay?"

"No. We'll stick with the set plan." With a shrug, he added, "It'll work—if you play your part."

Glad that he'd relented, Adela promised, "I will."

Mattox tipped her face one way, then the other. "You look very much like a battered woman."

Which was the point, the very reason he'd struck her like he did. She held his gaze.

As if she stumped him, Mattox shook his head, then looked around the cabin. "For this insult alone, I'll make her beg for death. You can count on that."

Now that he was back to normal, Adela went about fixing them a light meal. Silence settled in, other than the occasional creak of an evergreen swaying or the whistle of wind.

Soon she'd contact Francis again—and then hopefully this would all be over.

Cade's brooding silence was starting to get on Sterling's nerves.

They sat at the small dinette table sharing the country breakfast they'd prepared together. He'd handled the bacon, eggs and toast. Mostly one-handed, she'd done the fried potatoes.

Impossible to remember the last time she'd cooked so much food for the start of her day. Her normal practice was to grab a protein bar and a cup of coffee. Because she didn't have it often, the food tasted extra delicious.

It felt good to be functioning again, to be off the couch and properly dressed. Okay, so she wore only a big T-shirt and yoga pants—her typical at-home clothes. She'd even gotten her hair into a ponytail, no small feat with her fingers still taped together.

An hour ago she'd awakened with his arm around her, his breath warm on her neck, excited by the possibilities of their new relationship.

Shortly after that he'd gone all silent and introspective. He hadn't even commented on her getting dressed, the jerk.

Tired of waiting for him to perk up, she demanded, "What's wrong?"

That got his gaze up from his plate. "Nothing."

So he'd make her drag it out of him? Fine. Not like she had anything more pressing this morning. "Couldn't sleep?"

"I slept fine. You?"

She ignored the question to ask another of her own. "Trouble at the bar last night?"

"No." Frowning, he set aside his fork. "Why?"

Well, that left only one other possibility. "Daddy get on your nerves? Or was it that annoying brother of yours? Don't tell me you got a cease and desist on sharing, because we already agreed."

His mouth quirked at her wording.

She did love his mouth, the shape of his lips, the crooked way he smiled . . . how he'd tasted. And that strong jaw, now covered in dark, sexy stubble.

Oh, and those electric-blue eyes—which were now trying to peer into her soul. "Uh-uh, no you don't." She pointed a crispy piece of bacon at him. "I see what you're doing, but you have some explaining to do first."

"As I recall, I did all the explaining last night— and today was to be your turn."

"Actually . . ." She thought about it, but if she told him a few select details, would he further reciprocate? She'd never been this curious about a guy, so the lure of learning more tempted her into agreement. "Okay."

"Okay?"

Ha. She'd caught him off guard. Always a good thing. Spreading out her arms, she said, "What do you want to know?"

Taking that question far too seriously, he pushed aside his empty plate and folded his arms on the table. "You're too passionate about helping others, so I assume you have personal reasons?"

Something in his tone . . . Why did this feel like a test? Did he already know the answers and he wanted to see if she'd be up-front? Irritation sharpened her tone. "Why can't I just be a Good Samaritan?"

"You can. You *are*. The way you tried to help Adela, how you're worried about her still, is commendable."

"Yeah, someone should pin a medal to my T-shirt. At least give me a gold star sticker, right?"

His shoulders flexed—and he ignored her sarcasm. "But it's more than that, isn't it?"

So. Much. More.

She'd never really had a chance to talk about that awful time. Her mother . . . no, she hadn't been clearheaded enough to listen, and there'd been no guarantees she wouldn't blab to the wrong person.

With Cade sitting there waiting, his expression warm, open and caring, the timing felt right to get it off her chest.

Sterling stared at the remains of egg yolk on her plate. "So . . . I killed a dude."

She waited for a gasp, for questions, maybe even accusations.

Nothing. No reaction, definitely no outrage or shock.

When she worked up the nerve to look at his face, all she found was honest empathy etched there. It almost choked her up.

Screw that. Making her tone as dispassionate as she could, she quipped, "He had it coming, though, you know?"

"Then I'm glad he's gone." Reaching across the table, his hand palm up, he offered her something new.

Understanding.

Theirs needed to be a business relationship . . . preferably with benefits. Getting emotionally involved with him could pose a problem.

But even knowing that, she couldn't resist lacing the fingers of her left hand with his. Unlike any other man she'd known, Cade made her feel delicate in comparison to his strength.

With him, it wasn't an unpleasant feeling.

Brushing his thumb over her knuckles, he asked, "Will you tell me about it?"

Telling him would be better than getting all

maudlin. "Yeah, sure. Not much to tell, really. I got snatched during my junior year, right after I left school. Two guys. They were flirting and I stupidly fell for it."

"Got too close to them?"

"Yup. I made it so damn easy." She blew out a breath. Self-recriminations got her nowhere. She'd lived through it, learned from it and would never again make that mistake. "I was in a van going . . . somewhere, before I could even figure out what had happened. For the rest of the day they transferred me around from one place to another, moving me farther from home each time. Then I killed the dick who paid to use me, and got away."

His hand tightened around hers, not painfully but in reaction to that stark recounting. "How did you kill him?"

"I'm not sure I want to talk about this." But when she tried to pull her hand away, he held on.

"I told you about my stepmother."

True, he had. "You didn't force the pills on her, though."

Both his hands held hers now. His nails were short and clean, his fingers long. Slightly calloused. Very warm.

Very masculine, and they made her think of things that involved his hands and long fingers—

"I'm not going to judge you, Star, and I swear to you, your secrets are safe with me."

159

Jostled from her inappropriately timed sexual thoughts, she used her bandaged fingers to trace along his knuckles, up to his thick wrist and then over the downy hair on his forearms. "You know, it's the oddest damn thing. I was aware of you all that time at the bar, and then we started talking and I felt like I could trust you."

"Because you, lady, have good instincts. Same as me."

Sterling eyed him. "You saying you trust me?"

"I wouldn't be here if I didn't."

Hell of a compliment there. He did that a lot, heaping little bits of praise on her and making her almost glow with it. Could she do this? Could she repay his understanding with a brief, glossed-over version of what had happened that night?

Sensing her uncertainty, he asked, "Have you ever told anyone?"

No, she hadn't. "Never seemed like a good idea."

"But now? With me?"

Would it make her feel better? She sort of figured it might. "All right, fine. I got put with several other girls. Some of them had already been . . ." She swallowed hard. "It was awful, Cade. Seeing them, knowing what they'd been through, made it all the more real. They hadn't gotten away, so how could I?" The guilt swamped her again, strong enough to choke a horse, because she *had* escaped.

And in doing so, she'd left others behind.

Cade said nothing, but he held her hand steady in his and somehow it felt protective. If only she'd had someone like him back when she'd needed him most.

All she'd had was an addict for a mother, and a society that barely knew she existed.

"Like I said, they shuffled us from one place to another, as if we were cattle. Or even . . . boxed goods, you know? Not people. Not humans with a heartbeat, or girls who felt fear and pain. They didn't acknowledge any of that. They didn't care." This detailed stuff was for the birds. It made her tremble like that long-ago girl who'd been so terrorized. "So anyway," she said, more brisk now, "we ended up at this big old house that was mostly bedrooms, with a small sitting room, one upstairs john and a tiny kitchen. Each bedroom had a lock on the outside of the door. They somehow advertised us and people put in orders, like . . . pizza. Except instead of thick crust, they wanted a heavier girl. Red hair, black, like pepperoni or sausage. Fresh . . ." She swallowed hard. "Or a little more seasoned."

Cade briefly closed his eyes. Yeah, if he thought it was hard to hear, he should have tried going through it—No. No, she wouldn't wish that hell on anyone. She'd gladly kill those who instigated or added to the misery, but she wouldn't make them suffer the same humiliations and abuse that she had.

"Guess I got ordered up. Gullible teen with purple hair and a pierced lip who cried a lot. Sounds delicious, right?"

"Don't." His voice turned to rough, broken gravel. "Please don't downplay what you suffered."

Suffered, an apt word. Looking away, Sterling nodded. He didn't need to know that downplaying it was the only way she kept it from taking over her life. "The guy was disgusting, old with a beer gut and jowls, and he literally savored every second of my shock. But he showed up half-drunk, and after that door was locked on the outside, he locked it on the inside, too. Just to intimidate me more, I think, but turned out that was his biggest mistake."

Cade's eyes turned steely. "With the door locked, no one else could get in?"

"I figured it would slow them down, at least—if they even heard the scuffle and bothered to investigate. They were used to hearing screams and cries and . . . rough stuff, so they played loud music in the hall."

Mouth tightening, he growled, "I wish they were all dead."

"You and me both." And if she had her way, eventually they would be. "So like I said, he had a bottle with him and I offered to pour him another drink. Just desperate to buy some time at first, but the idiot agreed, and when I got close to him, I smashed the bottle in his face." Bile seemed to clog her throat, cutting off her air.

Cade waited, gently stroking her palm . . . letting her know she wasn't alone.

It helped, enough for her to continue.

"It stunned him, but he was still upright, looking at me like he couldn't believe my audacity. That really set me off—that he'd be surprised because I fought back, that I wouldn't just meekly be raped—and since I had the broken neck of the bottle in my hand, I . . . I jammed it into his throat and twisted it deep."

Without hesitation, Cade said, "Good for you."

Trying a smile that felt a little sick, Sterling skipped past the massive amount of blood that had gone everywhere, the god-awful gurgling sounds the man had made. "That was the start of my great window caper. It was a hell of a drop, and I was afraid I'd break my legs, or maybe my neck, but I figured it was worth the risk."

"Jesus. You were on the second floor?"

"Yeah, but the ground broke my fall." This smile was a little more genuine. She'd gotten past the worst of it and Cade hadn't rained down judgments, so she guessed he was okay with it. Or at least he got it, that she'd done what she had to. "Knocked the wind out of me, and you should have seen the bruises I got then."

As if he couldn't quite believe it, Cade slowly

shook his head. "That was exceptionally brave and resourceful."

She wrinkled her nose. "I should be honest and say I had second thoughts once I was hanging out the window, but my grip slipped and I didn't really have any choice. Luckily that room faced the back, not far from an alley. I had no idea where I was, but I knew where I didn't want to be."

"So you ran."

"Down alleys, through buildings, across backyards. I think I ran that entire day, weaving my way as far from them as I could get." She shrugged. "In fact, I pretty much ran for a whole year."

"You didn't go home?"

"Mom wasn't really into helping anyone but herself, and most times she couldn't even manage that."

"How did you survive?"

"Halfway houses, soup kitchens. A little thievery. There was a woman at one halfway house who worked with battered women. I've contacted her since, when I first helped another woman. She's the one who told me what to do."

"I'm glad you could trust her."

"Trust her? No. But I liked her, and she was good for info." It seemed one memory churned up another, until it felt like she was living it again. "This elderly guy busted me stealing some of his laundry." That particular memory lightened her mood. "Know what he did?"

"I'm guessing he didn't call the cops?"

"He gave me more clothes, including some that had belonged to his deceased wife. He fed me, too, and didn't complain when I insisted on staying outside so he couldn't trap me. He told me I was smart for being cautious, but that if I was going to hang around, I might as well earn some money."

Cade stiffened.

She quickly said, "He offered me a job working on his lawn."

Relaxing again, Cade asked, "Cutting grass and stuff?"

"And trimming bushes, edging the lawn, picking up old tree branches. He kept that place pristine."

Cade actually smiled. "I like him."

"One day after this big storm had made a mess of things, he came out and started helping me work. We didn't talk or anything, we were just there together, getting the job done. After a while he insisted I take a break, and we sat together on a bench drinking colas." At the time, it had seemed the most normal, most domestic thing she'd ever done. "Finally he asked where I went when I left his place. At that time, I used to crash in the park, or I'd catch a snooze in an all-night diner."

"Not safe."

"Eh, it feels fine when you don't have any other options. But then he showed me his garage. Said he had a sleeping bag and I could lock the doors so at least I could rest without worrying. He didn't ask me to sleep in his house, but I think it's because he knew I wouldn't." Remembering brought a sense of melancholy that left her eyes glazed with tears. "He was so brusque about everything, real no-nonsense attitude, but he showed me that as bad as those bastards were who'd tried to use me, there were equally good, kindhearted people in the world."

Lifting her uninjured hand to his mouth, Cade kissed her knuckles. "Was he a truck driver?"

"Retired, but he had been, so yeah, the trucking company was his idea once he knew what I wanted to do. I stayed with him for years. We cleaned out the garage, and he put an actual room in there for me, with my own toilet and tiny shower. I had a chair and a TV, a cot to sleep on." She realized how lame that sounded, but for her, it had been a real home.

"It sounds comfortable."

"I swear," she whispered, "he was like my grandpa."

"Did neighbors assume that relationship?"

"Not likely, with him being Black." She grinned. "But he didn't have any close neighbors anyway. Didn't have any family left, either, since he and his wife had never had kids."

"You loved him."

The tears spilled over, so all she could do was nod.

Cade reached out to gently brush her cheeks. "I'm so glad you found him."

It took her a minute to regain her composure. Normally she would have been more embarrassed for the pitiful show of emotion, but as he'd said, Cade was different. With a sniffle and a clearing of her throat, she whispered, "When I was twenty-two, he helped me get my CDL, even gave me a reference for Brown Transportation. I worked there until I was twenty-six."

"Why didn't you stay there?"

"Gus passed away in his sleep. I knew we'd gotten close, but it stunned me to find out he'd left me his house. Isn't that crazy?"

"Sounds like you were as important to him as he was to you."

"Not even close, but God love that man, he made me feel . . . valued." More tears fell, and this time she angrily swiped them away. "There was a note with the will. He kept it vague, I guess in case anyone else read it, but he said to sell the house and use the money, with what he had in his accounts, to do what I needed to do."

Cade still held her left hand, but now he gripped it as if he couldn't let go. "You didn't want to stay in his house? Find a regular job?"

"Me? No way. I'm not cut out for that, you

know? Gus had provided a lifeline and I grabbed it. When he said he knew what I needed to do, he was right. I *need* to do this." That god-awful guilt shortened her breath and compressed her lungs, but she admitted her greatest sin. "When I escaped, I left other girls behind."

"You alone couldn't have helped them."

No, she wouldn't accept that, wouldn't take the easy out. She'd let her fear run her. All she could do now was own the truth. "I could have led police there. I did try calling it in once, but it was a week later before I thought of it, and I'm guessing after what happened, they'd moved on."

Cade sat quiet for far too long. He kissed her knuckles again, started to speak but didn't. Finally he said, "Hearing all this . . . it occurs to me that I might have been too pushy."

"No denying that." He'd pushed his way right into her life, but she enjoyed having him there. More than she'd ever thought possible. "Too late to take it back now."

As if magnetized, his gaze caught hers. "I'm guessing some things might be . . . difficult for you."

Not liking the way he verbally danced around it, she said, "A lot of stuff is difficult, so what? If you mean something specific, spit it out already."

"Sex."

"Oh." He was concerned that she was trauma-tized still? Well, yeah, in some ways she was—

but that wasn't one of them. "You know me now, right?"

"I hope so. I'd like to know you even better, but yes, we're getting there."

"So do you *really* think I wouldn't have fixed that?"

Skeptical, and obviously a bit confused by her wording, he repeated, "*Fixed* it?"

"With what I do, I knew I had to overcome some things. Getting caught would be bad enough, but if the thought of regular sex with a non-psychopathic guy left me paralyzed, how would I deal with a freaking monster who treated women like trained dogs?"

Finally he released her hand. He looked steady enough, but she saw the fire in his eyes and the acceleration of his breathing. "And you fixed that . . . how?"

He looked so intense right now that she could guess how he'd looked when he broke into Misfits. "Cool your jets. It's nothing bad."

"Define *bad*."

"I had sex," she said with a shrug. "Few different guys, few different occasions. Until it wasn't so scary anymore."

Sitting back hard, Cade studied her. "Did you like it?"

"I didn't hate it." Not the last few times. "That was the important part. Now I'm in the camp of take it or leave it."

Seconds ticked by. "Except with me."

The man did not lack confidence. "Yup. There you go again, standing out from the pack. I liked kissing you, so I'm guessing the rest will be fun."

Slowly, he pushed back his chair and stood.

Sterling held her breath, but when he reached for her, he only stroked her ponytail, down and over her shoulder, until his fingers cupped her chin. "When we get together, it'll be more than fun. I'm going to make damn sure you love every second."

Wow, now she could hardly wait.

CHAPTER EIGHT

Cade was patient, always, but two additional days passed without a word from Adela. He knew the waiting wore on Star. He understood that. With a woman in need, every day—hell, every hour—could mean life or death.

Using the time to get closer to Star, he'd kissed her a few more times, each a little longer, a little hotter, easing into her life. She was so open about what she liked, and she clearly liked intimate contact. It astounded him that she hadn't been more sexually active, but it made sense, given what she'd been through.

He wanted to be the one to show her just how hot sex could be—with the right person. So far she was on board with that plan.

She was recovering quickly but still had a limp to her walk, and she couldn't yet make a fist with her injured finger. Until she was 100 percent, he wouldn't let it go beyond kissing. For now, it worked as extended foreplay, wearing her down, softening her attitude. Not that he wanted to change her.

It was the hard-core woman who'd drawn him.

But when they came together, he wanted her totally involved, as ready as he was, maybe even more anxious for the ultimate release he'd give her, though how that was possible when he wanted her nonstop, he didn't know.

For now, sleeping with her each night was enough. Torture, yes, but he wouldn't be giving it up anytime soon.

He knew eventually he'd have all of her.

And then what?

His life wasn't set up for a significant other. Any day now his father could send him off on a mission. Reyes might hear something at his gym that required follow-up. Madison might uncover a lead.

He hadn't yet told Star that the main reason he ran a bar, besides fitting into the neighborhood, was because conversations from seedy characters could be overheard. More than a few times he'd gotten information he needed because too many drinks lowered caution. He could subtly ask the right questions and get good information that he then followed up on.

There'd been a man who bragged about the internet arrangements that had gotten him a few hours of pleasure. Another who'd laughed about how cheaply he'd bought time with a girl.

Keeping his hands off them was difficult, but when it led to bigger stings, Cade could hold it together.

Same with Reyes and his gym. All different types came in to bulk up. Even if they didn't talk about personal involvement, word from the street was usually sound. Reyes would hear enough to know when a new crew moved into an abandoned house or if a different guy was suddenly offering services from the corner.

Parrish had planned it all well. He'd purchased the bar and gym at opposite ends of the same downtrodden area, instructed each of them on what they'd do—and then he'd fully expected to be obeyed.

That part of the equation still annoyed Cade, but he couldn't deny they were effective. Not just in Ridge Trail, Colorado, but all over the US, since many of the roads here were used to transport women, kids and sometimes men in and out of various states. A local lead often branched out to different headquarters. Not all traffickers were on a grand scale, but some were—and they all deserved to be eliminated.

"I need to get back to work soon." Star didn't look up to make that announcement. At the dining table, her laptop open, she said, "I've had a few requests for deliveries."

Cade understood, but he didn't like it. When he had to take off to follow a lead, would Star understand? He might not see her for a day or two, or more. Would she demand answers that he couldn't give?

Unwilling to borrow trouble, he joined her at the table. "Local drives?"

"One is for an overnight, but two others are

local." Brows scrunched up, she studied the screen.

"Problem?"

"I keep thinking about Adela." She rubbed her temple wearily. "She was supposed to have called by now. If my stupid leg hadn't been hurt—"

"You still needed time to plan."

"I know. But it's been too long now. What if I'm gone on a job and she needs me?"

Knowing he had to be careful here, Cade tried for an offhand tone. "If you're away, you could call me with the details. I could follow up for you."

She slanted him a look. "We've been over that, right? You're a guy, so not trustworthy. She probably wouldn't let you get anywhere near her."

"She might if you told her that *you* trust me."

Slumping into her seat, she sighed. "I don't know. There are some things I prefer to do myself."

Right—like *most* things. That prickly attitude was a part of her personality, like her sarcasm and her inner strength. Altogether, they were . . . sometimes annoying, yes. But he also saw them as tools she'd used to survive, and for that he was profoundly grateful.

For now, she was safely ensconced at home, she slept with him every night, and each day a little more of her reserve melted away.

She had a strong will—but so did he. In the end, he'd convince her to see things his way.

When her phone buzzed, they both turned to look where she'd left it plugged in on the end table next to the couch.

"You rarely get calls," Cade noted.

"Rarely, as in never." She bolted out of the chair, limped hurriedly across the room and frowned at the screen. "Unlisted number again."

"Put it on speaker."

"Magic word?" she asked, but then did as he requested without making him say "please," answering on the fourth ring. "Hello?"

"Francis?"

Star gripped the phone tighter. "Adela? Hey. I thought you'd call before now. I'd about given up on you."

Voice choked, Adela said, "Please don't. Please don't give up on me."

Gently, Star said, "No, I won't."

"I'd have called sooner, but I couldn't."

Cade didn't move.

Star didn't appear to be breathing. "Why not?"

"I think he's found me, Francis." Softly weeping, she said, "I was in a cabin without cell service, and when I went into town, I saw him there. If I don't get away soon, I'm afraid he'll kill me."

Carefully sitting on the couch, Star said, "Tell me exactly where you are."

"I want to," she said in a small voice. "But you can't call the police. One of the cops is a regular. He'd lead Mattox right to me."

Eyes narrowing at that info, Star promised, "I won't tell the police, but I can't help you if I don't know where to find you."

"You'll come alone? You swear?"

Star's gaze met and held Cade's as she answered. "Yes, I swear."

Closing his eyes, Cade vowed that wouldn't happen. He wouldn't *let* it happen. If he had to dog her day and night to ensure she didn't try this on her own, that's what he'd do.

"All right." Adela sniffled. "I trust you."

"When should I come for you?" Star asked. "Right now?"

Like hell. Already Cade was reconfiguring his schedule, who he'd get to cover for him at the bar, how quickly he could arrange for Reyes to be backup.

He didn't doubt that his brother would do it. Come to that, Parrish would also extend all the protections he could. But that shit took time, and if she left right now—

"No!" Panic sharpened the single word. Then Adela immediately tried to explain. "Tonight. When it's dark. That way he . . . he won't be able to see us leaving."

"All right." Standing again, Star went into the kitchen and retrieved the pen and paper, then carried them back to hand to Cade. "Give me a number to reach you."

"No, it's too risky."

"I need *something,* Adela. At least an address or directions."

"Right." She breathed audibly, then asked, "You really won't say anything to anyone?"

Star rolled her eyes over the continued—frustrating—worry, but replied in a soothing tone, "I already gave you my word."

"You tried to save me that night. At Misfits."

"Yes, but I understand why you were too frightened to go then."

"He would have killed me," Adela claimed. "Right there on the spot. I didn't think you'd actually get away, but you did."

"We'll both get away this time, okay? Now quickly, tell me where to find you."

With only the briefest hesitation, Adela said, "There's a small town. Coalville. It's only five or six miles off I-25. As you enter the town, there's a stone church. Right after that, take the dirt road. It'll lead you up to the cabin where I'm staying. In case Mattox is watching the roads in that area, turn your headlights off."

It all sounded majorly fucked to Cade, even as he jotted it all down.

Star must've agreed, because she suggested, "Why don't you just meet me at the church? That'll be easier, right?"

"But if you don't show up, I'll be too exposed."

"I'll be there, and being close to the road will give us a better chance to escape." Not giving Adela a moment to change that plan, Star asked, "What time?"

"I guess . . . ten?"

"I'll be there. Adela? Try not to worry. I won't let you down."

"I can't thank you enough, really, but I should go." Nervously, she whispered, "I never know if Mattox has men watching the town looking for me. I'll go back to the cabin for now and wait."

"Until ten."

"Thank you, Francis. You're a lifesaver."

Deflated, Star returned the phone to the table, then just stood there.

It would be easier to have her cooperation, so Cade came up behind her, drew her back against his body and kissed her temple. "I'm going to help."

As if he hadn't spoken, she said, "Good thing my leg is so much better. I have a lot to get done now."

"Like what?"

Looking at him as if he were nuts, she said, "Like I need to rent a car. No way am I letting anyone track me down by my ride. And of course I want to go scope out that area. It could be a trap. Could be Mattox forced her to make the call."

He found no fault with her deductive reasoning. "It does seem a little too pat."

"She did agree to switch locations, and hopefully the church is more in the town than the cabin would've been. But . . . I don't know. Something doesn't feel right."

Turning her, Cade cupped her face in his hands. "You have incredible instincts, honey, so trust them."

"Yeah, I do." She frowned. "Those instincts are telling me something isn't right." She looked up at him. "But I still have to go."

"I know." Only she didn't need to go alone. "Will you trust me?"

Head cocked in challenge, she asked, "Trust you how?"

"I have . . . resources."

Her mouth twisted. "That you can't discuss."

A reality he couldn't get around. "Let me have the area checked. We'll be discreet. I can get you the alternate car, too. No need to use a dealer."

"Huh." Sounding impressed, she said, "No kidding? Just like that?"

"Yeah, just like that."

For several seconds, Star considered it. "The thing is . . ." She moistened her lips while carefully selecting her words. "I do trust you, because I know you. These other obscure peeps you talk about—they're big unknowns, and I just don't go there. So how about *you* trust *me* to get this job done without your interference?"

He didn't like having his assistance labeled as interference, but he got where she was coming from. He wouldn't trust the unknown, either. Still, he couldn't let her do this alone.

Looking past her, he checked the clock on the wall. He had only a few hours left if he wanted to accomplish all that needed to be done—with or without her approval.

He needed to accelerate their relationship—but would she see that as underhanded? Find it difficult to forgive—or insanely satisfying? Hard to say, and unfortunately, it was the only thing he could think of. His time to slowly win her over had abruptly run out.

"Is your leg healed enough?"

"I won't be running any races yet, but yeah, it's fine. Hardly sore anymore."

Yet she still limped—and he couldn't let that matter. Not now. "Good to know," he whispered as he bent to her mouth, kissing her softly at first, just moving his lips over hers until she leaned into him—which he took as a sign of agreement.

One hand at the back of her head, the other sliding down to her backside, he aligned her body with his. Hell if he wasn't already hard, but he'd wanted her for so long that giving himself permission was like flipping a switch. He was now *on* and only hoped he could get her there, too.

180

With all she'd suffered in her past, he planned to take it slow, to make use of the entire two hours he had. He could scramble last-minute with plans, but he wouldn't rush this.

He wouldn't rush her.

Her lips opened to the touch of his tongue, and the kiss quickly became hot. He turned his head for a better fit. She did the same. Her fingertips curled against his chest. Her hips nudged his.

Open mouths, lots of tongue play, heavy breathing. Now petting, too . . . Christ, she'd escalated things fast, but then, she was like that, a lit fuse waiting to explode.

He'd take a sexual explosion over her temper any day.

Urging her head back, he trailed his lips to the velvet skin of her neck, her warm throat, that sensitive spot beneath her ear. Tilting to give him better access, she gave a soft groan.

"Wow, I like that."

Had no one ever . . . ? No, he didn't want to think about her healing brand of sex, meant only to help her over an emotional hurdle, with no thought for pleasure.

He'd drown her in pleasure, and she'd never forget him.

The comfortable clothes she wore made touching her oh so easy. Liking the feel of her beneath the stretchy yoga pants, he opened his hand wide to enclose an entire cheek, then trailed his fingers down the cleft—then under, to touch her more intimately.

Gasping, she went to her tiptoes but didn't pull away.

Her tightened nipples, covered only by the soft cotton of her loose T-shirt, pressed against his chest. With a love bite, Cade encouraged another gasp . . . one that faded into a vibrating groan.

"Mmm," she whispered. "Do that again."

"Which part?"

"All of it?"

Even now, when he'd launched to the ragged edge, she made him smile. Star had substance, both emotionally and intellectually.

And in her curves. God yes, those curves.

She was as soft as a woman should be, but with core strength. She was bold enough to speak her mind, as she'd just done, and brave enough to travel to a remote area alone, without backup, to save a woman in need.

How the hell was he supposed to resist that enticing mix of attributes?

He couldn't.

With her active participation so obvious, he stroked her waist, then slipped his hand under her shirt and up to one heavy breast. He held back his own groan, but the warmth of her, the silkiness of her bare breast, made him forget his resolve.

"Cade?"

He came back to her mouth for another deep

kiss. She tangled the fingers of her left hand into his hair, and with the right, she cupped his face. He felt the roughness of the bandage on her fingers and turned to gently kiss those, too. "Hmm?"

"Is this your way of coercing me?"

Stark reality crashed onto his head. Had his motives been that base? That cold? Not with the way he'd always wanted her. Hell, he'd been looking for an excuse to rush his own self-imposed timeline.

Since he hadn't heard anger or accusation in her tone, just curiosity, he straightened to look into her eyes.

She gave him a smug, knowing smile.

Nothing got by her. He wouldn't have lied anyway, but now he knew she wouldn't have fallen for it no matter his reasons.

Before he could say anything, she grinned and cuddled close again. "Understand, I'm not complaining." Her uninjured hand traveled to his ass. "And if you live up to your promise, I might even be swayed to take you along."

Now, why that outrageous comment fired his lust, he couldn't say, but he crushed his mouth down on hers again. Full participation, that's what he got from her.

No reserve. No remnants of bad memories.

Such a remarkable woman in every way.

"So much enthusiasm."

God, she pushed his buttons. And humbled him. "Thank you for understanding."

"That you're not a user? No problem."

Her faith meant more than she knew, prompting him to another kiss, this one full of tenderness. And yeah, lust.

No way to dodge the lust.

"Bedroom?" she suggested, when he came up for air.

Cade smoothed her hair and cupped her cheek. Unique in so many ways. "No argument from me."

Smiling in satisfaction, she took his hand and led him through the kitchen-dining area, past the bathroom and into her room with the still-rumpled bed.

His conscience decided he needed one more confirmation, so he started to say, "Are you sure—"

But she pulled the T-shirt up and off, and he forgot he had a conscience. Shoulders back, spine straight, chin elevated. Her breasts were a handful, yet somehow she'd always downplayed that asset with her wardrobe choices. Her rib cage tapered into a smaller waist, then flared out for her shapely hips. His gaze lingered on the slight curve of her belly, exposed by the low-fitting yoga pants. Every inch of her fascinated him and made him want more.

"You're staring."

Without lifting his gaze from her body, Cade shrugged. "How could I not? You're perfect."

"Ha. I'm still bruised some, you know. It's all these hideous shades of green and yellow now. Really nasty."

Insecurity, from Star? That, more than anything, helped him gain a measure of control even though she stood there half-naked, tempting every basic instinct known to man. "I've seen bruises before, and I saw part of yours today before you dressed."

Wrinkling her nose, she tugged the band out of her hair so that it fell free. "Then you know what I mean."

Reyes was right. She did have incredible hair. Having it loose and tousled around her naked breasts added to the sensuality of the moment. "They're just bruises, babe, and they don't keep me from wanting you."

"Good thing, I guess, since I want you, too." She nodded at him. "Shirt off."

All too happy to oblige, Cade reached back for a handful of material and stripped it over his head.

"You still haven't told me about these tats." She moved closer, first trailing her fingers through his chest hair, then tracing the edges of one tattoo, a waving American flag that twined from his right shoulder to his elbow. Eyes dark with interest, she teased that soft touch to the eagle on his right pec.

185

He had another on the back of his left shoulder of a soldier drifting from a battlefield into heaven. All in all, pretty self-explanatory. "How about after?"

"After we do the nasty?"

She wanted to make it less than it was—but he wouldn't let her. "Nothing nasty about it. Not between us." He gathered a thick hank of hair in his fist, resisting her breasts for the moment. It felt cool in comparison to her hot skin. "Okay?"

"Another promise. You've got a lot to live up to."

"I'll do my best." And with that he cupped a breast, kneaded gently, then bent to circle the nipple with his tongue.

"Okay." Shakily, she drew in a breath. "Let me just get my pants off."

"Soon." He drew her in, sucking softly—then not so softly—while she moved her hands all over him. "Easy. Don't hurt your fingers."

"Worry about what you're doing."

The order amused him, especially since he understood it. "All right." He shifted his attention to her other breast, but at the same time he worked his hand inside the loose waistband of her pants, his hand cupping over her heat.

"You're a tease," she complained, her head tipped back, eyes closed. "Men aren't supposed to tease."

"Me and you, Star. I told you, we're different."

He kissed her slightly parted lips. "Quit trying to put us in a category."

Her heavy eyes opened. "Fine. But I've been waiting for this for too long, maybe even before I admitted I wanted you. So now is *not* the time for teasing."

God, he loved her forthright way of speaking. "You need to come?"

Her eyes flared, and a wash of color tinged her cheeks. "Well . . . I need *something,* okay? So stop playing around."

"All right." He went to his knees and reached for the waistband of her pants. "But one of these days you're going to like the way I play."

"One of these days—meaning you plan to stick around?"

Digging for future plans? What could he say? He wouldn't make promises until he knew he could keep them, so without answering, he tugged the pants and her panties down to her ankles. "Step out."

At first the only thing she did was breathe deeply.

He took his time looking at her body. And a hell of a body it was. Gorgeous legs, despite the bruising that drew his lips. He skimmed them over her skin as if he could heal the last remnants of her injury. The cut had closed nicely, but she'd have a small scar. He pressed a soft kiss to that, too.

The rest of her . . . so beautiful. He'd admired the length of her legs plenty of times, but seeing her like this, totally bared, ramped up the churning need. Sliding his hands to her hips, he leaned in—

"Wait." Sleek with muscle, her long thighs flexed as she balanced with a hand to his shoulder. Hastily, awkwardly, given the lingering stiffness of her injured leg, she kicked away her pants. Free of clothes, she straightened, nodded down at him and said, "Go ahead."

Cade actually laughed. Physical need consumed him, yet he'd never known anyone quite like her. In every way imaginable, she was incredibly special.

She was *his*.

She might not know that yet, but somehow he'd make it so, starting right now. "Anything you don't like—"

"Yeah, you'll hear about it." Again she threaded her fingers through his hair. "You curl my toes, Cade. I never knew that was a real thing."

He smiled again. "Let's see what else I can curl."

Oh. My. God. Over and over again, Sterling repeated that in her mind. She had Cade McKenzie, all six feet, five gorgeous inches of him, kneeling in front of her, touching her in incendiary ways while kissing her belly and thighs.

Now that she could play with it—and basically use it as an anchor—she found that his hair was thick and soft on top and in front, and she liked the way the shorter sides and back felt against her fingertips, like velvet almost.

Soon as he finished what he was doing—because she wasn't about to interrupt again—she planned to glut herself on his bod.

With his lips nibbling at her hip bone, he stroked over her sex. Yeah, she had to lock her knees for that—and then he pressed a finger into her, growling at finding her so wet. What did he expect? From the moment he started seducing her, she'd wanted to melt.

Didn't matter that he might have started this to get his way. It was as good a reason as any, right? Especially when it got her what she wanted most.

Him. Naked. With *her* naked. Full-body contact —and a big payoff in the way of pleasure.

Besides, he'd find she wasn't easily manipulated, awesome sex or not. If she invited Cade along, it'd be on her own terms, for her own reasons.

She had a feeling he'd meet her halfway, and until then, why not enjoy herself?

As he slowly fingered her, she not only heard but felt his groan. The pleasure built, coiling, heating . . . She wanted it bad. This, now, and more.

So much more.

She whispered that, *"More,"* aloud and got a second finger because of it. Much as she enjoyed watching the flex and roll of his broad shoulders, sensation compelled her eyes to close. Her head tipped back of its own accord, as if her neck offered no support.

Her knees were getting to the same point, especially when he used his other fingers to open her . . . and she felt his mouth.

Biting her lip to hold back the groan, she tightened. His tongue . . . yeah, that velvet tongue performed some magic, touching her just right, exactly *there,* over and over again, leisurely at first while he made sounds of enjoyment, then with more deliberate purpose.

She couldn't stay quiet any longer. Her nipples throbbed, needing him, but not enough to ask him to stop. The sweetest, almost painful ache curled in her lower belly. Despite the way she'd been pampering her leg, her thigh muscles tensed, a necessary adjustment to keep her upright so he could continue.

Shifting, he opened his hand on her behind and pressed her closer—then drew in her clit for a soft suckle and, good God, she cried out. Without restraint.

Who cared?

An incredibly powerful orgasm raged through her, leaving her one giant pulsing beat of sizzling sensation. Panting, a little sweaty, she realized she'd curled over him when he finally let up. Yup, that had pretty much wiped out her backbone. Maybe all her bones.

He shifted her so he could stand.

"Don't let go," she warned, unwilling to open her eyes. "I'll fall flat on my face."

Against her ear, he whispered, "Never," in a way that sounded like he meant more than this single moment. Her heart seized at the thought, but then in some crazy, gallant, straight-out-of-a-film move, he lifted her into his arms and placed her on the bed.

"Oh," she mumbled, stretching a little, snuggling into the bedding. "Well done. Very romantic."

Grinning, he opened his jeans. "You think so?"

"Yup." No way was she going to miss this. She managed to keep her eyes wide-open, didn't even blink. "Promises made, promises kept. I'm now a believer."

"And just think," he said, shoving down his jeans to stand there buck-ass and incredibly stunning, "we're not done, yet."

Wow, he was put together fine. Better than fine. It was as if someone had taken all things she considered masculine and expertly pieced them together. Dark chest hair, roped muscles over arms and legs, long bones and obvious power.

A big cock.

Sterling cleared her throat. "Looks like I won the lottery."

His smile went crooked. Pulling his wallet from his jeans, he dug out a condom. While she watched in fascination, he rolled it over a very rigid, pulsing erection.

Her mouth went dry. "What if I'd wanted to touch that?" When he glanced at her, she nodded at his crotch. Honestly, every inch of him fascinated her. She wanted to explore him— without a rubber in the way. In fact, she wouldn't mind stroking that firm butt, too, and those muscular, hair-dusted thighs, his flat abdomen with that sexy happy trail.

"It'd be over too quick," he said, stretching out atop her and pecking her mouth. "Next time, I promise, you can touch all you want."

"Hardly seems fair, considering."

Using his knee, he opened her legs and settled between her tingling thighs. "Complaining?"

On principle alone, she considered it, but he was already stroking her breasts, thumbing her nipples, and she felt that hard cock against her . . . "Nope. No complaints from me."

"Good." He sealed his mouth over hers—and thrust into her.

Holy cow. In sheer reaction, her hips lifted off the bed. He filled her up, the fit snug, the glide smooth, wet, pure pleasure, but it was so much more than that, too.

It was Cade's scent making her light-headed, the sleek feel of his taut skin under her hands, the provoking sound he made deep in his throat—a sound of pure, unadulterated lust.

Yes, she'd gotten used to sex.

Yes, there'd been times when she'd somewhat enjoyed it.

None of those times had anything in common with this.

She wrapped one leg around him, keeping him close, and lifted her other along his hip.

"Easy," Cade whispered against her throat. "I don't want to hurt you. Your leg—"

"Shut up, Cade." She grasped his butt in her uninjured hand and urged him to move, at the same time *she* was moving, rocking against him, twisting . . . exciting herself on the hard length of him.

He laughed roughly and took over.

It was a hard ride, one she encouraged however she could. Keeping him locked to her, she bit his shoulder, licked the spot, then sucked on his hot skin as another climax rocked her.

Grinding into her, Cade put his face to her neck and growled out a long, harsh release.

Huh. Hearing other guys come hadn't moved her at all. But Cade? She wanted to cuddle him— and how nuts was that? You didn't cuddle a tiger, right? But she couldn't let him go, couldn't stop putting soft kisses along his shoulder, couldn't stop stroking his hot skin.

It was a good ten minutes before she moved,

and even then, her limbs felt sluggish and uncooperative. Yes, her leg throbbed like a son of a bitch, but it was worth it.

"Good going," she whispered in a teasing grumble as she tried to adjust. "How am I supposed to deal with Adela or Mattox when my muscles have turned to noodles?"

An utter stillness settled over him, replaced seconds later by determination as he levered up, bracing his arms on either side of her shoulders. "You let me help."

He surrounded her with his size, his scent, his iron will. Didn't bother her at all. "Your muscles aren't limp?"

"I'll recover. Quickly." He pressed a firm kiss to her mouth. "This, what we just did, was a commitment."

What? No way. "Who says so?"

"I say so." Far too serious, his intense gaze drilled into her. "You're strong, Star. Strong enough to share the burden without worrying that I'll take over. I won't, you know."

She snorted at that. "You already are."

"No, babe. I want to share the plans, the setup and the risk. I'm guessing you don't know this yet, but it's easier that way."

"What's easier?"

His expression softened. "Everything." With extreme gentleness he smoothed back her hair. "Everything is easier when you're not alone."

"So . . ." Knowing she was out of her depth, Sterling tried to think, but it wasn't possible, not right now with his body all over her body, his gaze catching her every thought. Full honesty, then. "This wasn't a one-off?"

His smile was so tender that it turned her soft, too. "Once isn't near enough for me. Don't tell me it was for you."

"I want more." More of him, more of this. Maybe the sharing he mentioned, too.

"Good." He released a pent-up breath. "Difficult as it'll be, we have to get out of bed, shower—"

"Together?"

"*Alone,* because I have calls to make."

She pretended to pout, but seriously, showering with him would have been nice.

"We need to coordinate plans. I need to prove to you that having me along will be a good thing. But if we shower together . . . ?" He shook his head. "All my good intentions will go right out the window, because now that I've had you, I won't be able to keep from touching you." He cupped her breast. "Kissing you." He nuzzled her neck. Near her ear, he whispered, "Tasting you— again."

Sterling shivered. "You're promising a lot."

"Don't let it scare you." Laughing, he dodged her smack, caught her hand and pressed it down beside her head.

"I'm not *scared.*"

"Wary, then." He pushed off the bed but took the time to look her over as he picked up his boxers and jeans. "Take a few minutes more if you want. I'll shower first."

She watched him walk away with a sense of . . . peace? That, or something equally serene, invaded her very soul. It was a new, unfamiliar feeling, one of many thanks to Cade.

He was right, of course. He did scare her, mostly because she hadn't relied on anyone in a very long time. Maybe because she liked Cade so much, because she really wanted to rely on him, it made it somehow worse. More alarming.

But she wasn't a wimp, so she got out of bed and went for her laptop. She had a lot of research to do. Maybe that'd get her mind off the naked hunk currently in her shower.

Doubtful, but she'd give it a try.

CHAPTER NINE

After the explosive sex, Star finally agreed to let him take part in retrieving Adela. He would have assisted her anyway, but having her agreement simplified things.

He'd known they would be good together. After all, the chemistry was through the roof.

Yet the depth of what he'd felt, the extreme connection, had surprised him. He'd like nothing more than to spend an entire day in bed with her, exploring her incredible curves and enjoying her blunt, uninhibited way of responding.

Impossible when they had so much to do.

They'd already picked up the alternate vehicle from his family's private lot, a reinforced van with darkened windows that he and Reyes used when they expected gunplay. The black matte paint helped hide it in low light, plus it had incredible speed for a van.

He'd spent an hour trying to convince Star to let his family take part. Her protestations—that she didn't know his family, so how could he expect her to trust them?—made sense.

He understood and offered a compromise, suggesting, "Just my brother, then." Reyes made one hell of an ally. If there were ten men waiting to ambush Star, Cade could handle them. He had no doubts on his own ability. But a sniper bullet? Mattox was the type of cowardly abuser who might do anything, including lure her in for a fast death.

Making a woman suffer was more his speed, though, but Cade wouldn't take chances either way.

"You've already met him," he reminded Star. "He'll stay out of the way, but he'll be an extra set of eyes just in case something goes wrong."

"He's annoying," she announced, as if that settled it.

Laughing, Cade couldn't deny that she'd nailed Reyes. "It's true, my brother takes extreme pleasure in pushing people over the edge. But he's reliable, capable and loyal."

With ill grace, she growled, "Fine. So he's a sterling example of humanity."

"Let's don't go overboard." He knew and accepted his brother's faults—same as Reyes did for him.

With a frustrated growl, she said, "Involve him if you want." She gave him a hard glare. "But he's *your* responsibility."

Cade could just imagine Reyes's reaction if he heard that insult. Struggling not to smile, he said, "I appreciate the vote of confidence."

"Is that what it was? Felt more like me giving up because you wouldn't let it go."

That had been hours ago, and she was still

bristling about it as they prepped to take off.

In the back of the van, Cade reached out to touch her cheek. "I have to do what's necessary to keep you safe."

Mouth firming, she slid the Glock she'd just checked into a holster at her hip and stared up at him. "Long as you know I feel the same about you."

That declaration deserved a kiss, but he kept it soft and quick to say, "I assume you've practiced shooting left-handed?" Her injured finger wasn't taped now, but it was still swollen and no doubt painful.

"You're asking me now?" Grinning, she indicated the small arsenal they'd amassed by combining their weapons. She reached for a Smith & Wesson .38 revolver to put in her ankle holster. "I plan for all contingencies, including an injured right hand, so yeah, I've had plenty of practice. I'm more accurate right-handed, but I can make do with my left, especially if it's a target as big as Mattox."

As she tugged the leg of her jeans over the gun, Cade asked deadpan, "Packing anything else?"

"My knife," she said, turning to shake her booty at him so he'd notice the sheathed knife at the small of her back. "But I'd only use it if I got caught up close."

No way would he let that happen. Cade drew a breath.

Seeing her so heavily armed had a dual effect on him. He believed she was proficient at protecting herself; her ease with all the weapons reassured him of that. At the same time, he wished he could insist she hang behind and let him handle things. He'd get Adela, and kill Mattox if possible, but he knew Star well enough to know she'd never go for that.

If he suggested she sit this out, she'd not only refuse, she'd revert to handling things on her own.

"Let me help," he said when she lifted the bulletproof vest he'd brought for her. It was the one thing she seemed unfamiliar with. He dropped it over her head, then adjusted the Velcro straps so it properly fit her.

While she pulled on her button-up shirt, which was a tight fit now, he put on his own vest, and then the tactical belt that held more ammo, nylon cuffs, a Taser, knife, strobing flashlight, flash bang and two Glocks.

Brows up, Star nodded at the flash bang. "A grenade? Really?"

"Nonlethal, but good at disorienting people—in the case of a mob. There's no telling how Mattox might set this up."

"*If* he set it up," Star said, then asked, "You don't believe Adela?"

He stashed the first aid kit into a panel of the van, along with other emergency items. "I don't think I do," Cade admitted, "but mostly because I don't think you do, either. Want to tell me why?"

She appeared to like his answer. "There's something about her, right? I've dealt with traumatized women before. I *was* a traumatized woman. But this just feels a little . . . off. Not enough that I won't help her, but yeah, I've got my guard up, big-time."

"Do you know what triggered that feeling?"

"She knows Mattox. I know him, too." Casual as you please, she tossed out, "He's the bastard who had me kidnapped all those years ago. The one who was in charge, who ordered me into that room with a drunken rapist, who employed the goons who stood guard."

Completely floored with that last-minute disclosure, Cade stared at her in disbelief. Pretending it was nothing, Star pulled the cargo door closed and locked it. Gaze averted, she started past him for the driver's seat, but he caught her arm.

At first, no words came to mind. She looked at him in mild inquiry, but he wasn't buying it. She knew she'd just dropped a bombshell on him, and now she waited to see what he'd do.

Sensing there was a lot riding on his reaction, he forcibly tamped down the extreme annoyance trying to take precedence. "You have a history with Mattox?"

"Yeah, but the big lummox didn't recognize me. Remember, I looked way different back then."

That she'd kept this from him left him seething. "Is there a reason you didn't tell me before now?"

"Couple of reasons, actually. One, I figured you'd freak out."

Cade took a step closer to her. "I do not *freak out*."

"No?" She pointedly looked over his rigid posture. "What do you call this?"

"Furious?" He caught her shoulder before she could spin away. "Damn it, Star. You know you should have told me."

"Because we had sex? Get real." She pointed a finger at his chest. "That's one reason why I didn't. You're acting all territorial and stuff."

"How do you figure that?" Hell, he felt that way, sure. But he'd kept from showing it.

Or had he?

No, he definitely had. If he'd had his way, she wouldn't be in the back of a bulletproof van strapping weapons all over her lean, sexy body, making plans to charge into danger.

"It's the way you look at me now," she explained, as if it surprised her that he didn't know.

He pulled his chin back. "How do I look at you?"

Mouth turning down, she quipped, "Like you think you have me all wrapped up."

Yeah, right. "I'm not deluded." She was a loose cannon. God, he wished he had a little control over her . . . No, he didn't.

Part of what he admired most about Star were her guts and fortitude. She might bend, but she would never break.

He found that confidence sexy as hell.

And deep down, a small part of him thought she might be strong enough to handle the life he'd chosen.

Most weren't.

Tell other women that he eliminated human traffickers at any cost? They'd bail real fast.

Only Star saw it as an opportunity to team up.

"Maybe not deluded, but if I'd told you earlier, you'd have wanted me to stay behind—which isn't happening, so don't even go there."

He let his own anger show. "Don't assume my thoughts."

"I don't have to. It's right there on your face."

"Regardless of what you think you see, I know this is important to you. And you're important to me."

Her belligerent expression faltered. "I am?"

New irritation surfaced. "How the hell can you be surprised over that?" He cut her off when she started to speak. "I care enough that I'd like to stand with you, but I wouldn't stand in your way."

"Wow. Okay." A small smile formed, then went crooked. "Do I owe you an apology?"

"Damn right. You withheld info that I need to share with Reyes."

That took care of her softened mood. "I don't see why."

Cade already had his phone out. "Your past relationship with Mattox ups the chance that this is all a ruse to get to you."

Scoffing, she said, "I told you, he didn't recognize me."

"You can't be sure of that."

She threw up her hands. "Aren't you the one who said I have good instincts?"

The text he sent Reyes was brief and to the point. "You're giving me second thoughts on that." Given her gasp, Cade assumed the insult hit home.

"Well, too bad." Suddenly she moved against him, hugging him as tight as she could while they wore bulletproof vests.

Definitely not the reaction he'd expected. Automatically, his arms went around her. Without thinking about it, he rested his face against the top of her head, breathed in the warm musk of her skin and hair, and relished the feel of her.

How had she become so important to him so quickly?

Voice lower now, a little confused and a little worried, she said, "I watched Mattox's face at Misfits. It leveled me, seeing him again after so long. I don't mind telling you I was struck with a sort of blindsided panic."

Cade wished he could have spared her that. It

had to be rough, having her past just show up like that.

To reassure him, she pressed back to make eye contact. "There wasn't a speck of recognition. I swear, he had no idea who I am." Biting her lip, she added, "He didn't know that he'd ruined my life so long ago."

"Listen to me, babe, okay?" Here she stood, armed to the teeth, ready to take on the world—and her abuser. She'd suffered that recognition alone. She would have done this alone, too, if he hadn't found a way to talk her around. "You need to be ready to shoot. Shit goes sideways, don't think about it. Just protect yourself." Abusive assholes were expendable. She was not. "If anything at all sets off a warning, promise me you'll get out of there, okay?"

She nodded. "You betcha."

A returning text from Reyes dinged into the silence. Are you sure there won't be any other surprises?

No, he wasn't, but he replied: Just be ready for anything.

Reyes sent a thumbs-up emoji.

Putting the phone on vibrate and pocketing it, Cade said, "Time for us to go."

She nodded and got behind the wheel. He disabled the interior lights and then sat behind the passenger seat, where he'd have a view out the windshield and could also easily see Star.

There was no more talking as she drove out to the meeting place.

Coalville was a minuscule town, a population of around one hundred, give or take any recent deaths or births, with most of the residents being elderly. The quick research they'd done claimed it was a ghost town—a story that started back in the early 1900s when a mine explosion caused over fifty deaths and effectively destroyed the growing mining industry.

"If anyone lives here," Star murmured, "they must be up in the hills somewhere." She drove slowly over railroad tracks onto broken pavement that turned to gravel . . . that led to a dirt road.

The van's headlights bounced over scrubby bushes and boulders along the narrow sides of the road. They passed a couple of shacks that appeared abandoned, two mobile homes nearly rusted through and a small store with most of the windows boarded up.

"Should I kill the lights?"

"No." That's what Adela wanted them to do, and he wasn't in an accommodating mood. At the end of the bumpy, uneven road, Cade spotted the church. "Nice and slow. Reyes is already in place. If he's spotted anything shady, he hasn't said so."

"Where exactly is he?"

"Up in the hills somewhere, well hidden but with a good view."

"Wouldn't he have been noticed getting there?"

"Nah, he's good."

The van bounced roughly over deep ruts. Brittle branches from pinyon pines and junipers scraped against the roof. There were no streetlights and the moon wasn't bright this night, so heavy shadows lurked right outside the headlight beams.

Grime-darkened windows and dirty clapboard indicated the church had lost its congregation. It was the last building before the road climbed up the mountain.

"I don't like it," Cade muttered.

"Shh," she said in return. Without looking at him, she stopped the van several yards away. After a moment, a woman stepped out on the front stoop. "That's her."

"Let her come to you," Cade insisted.

"She's not. She's probably worried that I might be Mattox." Drawing a deep breath, Star opened the door and stepped out.

Cade swallowed his curse and did the same, sliding silently out the cargo door and hunkering down low, in a better position to defend her if necessary.

In a hushed voice, Star called, "Adela?"

"Who is it?" Adela gripped the railing and peered toward the van. "Francis?"

Star stepped out farther, moving to the front of the van so the lights hit her. "Quickly. Let's go."

Taking one step toward her, Adela asked, "Are you alone?"

"Yes," Star lied. "C'mon."

And suddenly Adela had company.

Sterling wasn't all that surprised when two men, dressed all in black, came out of the church around Adela, each of them armed, each of them aiming at her. Worse, she spotted movement in the scrub bushes to the right, and more to the left.

Surrounded? No, she wouldn't accept that.

They were all in the darkened shadows, but she stood in the light—an easy target. That got her feet moving.

Knowing she'd never get back in the van before they were on her, she ducked behind the open driver's door and glanced back for Cade.

The van was empty. How had he moved without her hearing it? He was like a damn wraith! A sound snapped her back around. In the three seconds she'd used to look for Cade, the dude had gotten far too close.

She smiled as she pointed her Glock. "Move and I'll put one in your forehead."

Laughing, he continued edging casually toward her. "You're lucky he wants you alive."

Screw that. She shot at his leg, but the bullet hit the dirt near his feet. Damn lousy left-handed aim—not that she'd wanted to kill him. Yet. And at least it made him dive off to the side for cover.

Since that had worked, she fired left and right, too. No one cried out, but she definitely heard some fast rustling.

Take cover, you goons. I won't go easy. She wouldn't go at all . . . not until she got what she'd come for. "Adela!"

"I'm so sorry," Adela wailed.

Sterling searched the darkness. Voices seemed to echo here, with the mountains around them, the night so still. Narrowing her eyes, she detected movement far ahead on the road.

It appeared someone—maybe Mattox?—was dragging Adela away.

How many men were there? So far she'd noticed four—if the men trying to close in around her were alone. There could be more. If they worked in pairs . . . insurmountable odds.

Mattox wasn't taking any chances, but then, he never did.

Was Adela in on it?

When a bullet zinged over her head, Sterling ducked—then looked back at the loud groan. A man was on the ground, clutching his leg and cursing a blue streak. Clearly he'd tried to sneak up behind her, but Cade's brother, wherever he was, must have spotted him.

Night-vision goggles? Seemed probable.

Just then, she saw Cade disable a different man with one vicious punch to the face. The man stiffened, then fell hard. Another launched at him, but in a very smooth move, he pivoted and elbowed the guy in the throat, sending him gagging and gasping to join his buddy on the dirt road. While he was down, Cade planted a boot in his face and the gagging stopped.

Huh.

She searched the immediate area but didn't see anyone else. "Is that it?"

His incredulous glare burned her. "There are now four bodies down around us, but a few of them might not stay that way, and I counted at least two more, so get in the van." With practiced ease, he disarmed the downed men. One of them groaned, but Cade ruthlessly punched him silent again.

"Wow." He had incredibly effective fists.

As he gathered up the weapons to dump in the cargo area, he repeated, "Get. In the. Van."

"Then what?" Before she took orders, she needed to know the plan. "More of them might be waiting on the road ahead." She should have already figured out a way to retreat, but instead she'd been focused on all the wrong things.

Like an unlikely alliance between Adela and Mattox.

And what Cade had said to her.

Could he really care that much? Given the way he'd protected her, he might.

She heard Adela scream again, but she couldn't see anything.

"Don't even think it," Cade ordered as he put nylon cuffs on the men. "You're staying here with me."

She knew that taking charge probably came naturally to him, and now wasn't the time to argue, especially since it was a good thing he'd come along.

If he hadn't, Mattox would already have her again, and her odds of getting away from him a second time wouldn't be favorable.

No, she wouldn't argue, but she did grumble, "I'm not an idiot." She wouldn't chase after Adela into unknown circumstances, but what to do about her?

It was only a small sound that alerted her, a soft-soled shoe crunching on the loose dirt and gravel road.

Swinging around, she managed to get off one shot before a big bruiser knotted a hand in her hair and jerked her around the door toward him.

"I'm done fucking around with you," he growled.

She nutted him as hard as she could. Using her injured leg for balance, she lacked some of her usual power, but she still connected solidly.

Groaning, he loosened his hold, just not enough, and with the way he pinned down her arms, she was as likely to shoot her own foot as his if she dared to fire.

So instead she headbutted him. Her aim was off

because she nailed him right in the nose. Blood sprayed.

"You little bitch—" he spit . . . just before a fist flew over her shoulder and knocked him out cold.

With his arms around her, she suddenly found herself crashing toward the ground.

Cade caught her, drawing her upright and pressing her back against the van. Face twisted with fury, he stomped the downed man, once, twice.

"He's out," Sterling whispered, awed by his violence. "Cade, he's out." She caught his arm. "Let's go while we can."

His jaw locked, but he did stop pulverizing the guy. Muscles pumped and expression deadly, he turned to her. "You're all right?"

She had that dude's blood on her face, but she nodded. "Fine."

"Stay put," he said, already moving away. "I'll be right back."

What the hell was that supposed to mean?

She got her answer a second later as the battle erupted behind her. Two men against Cade? Clearly not a problem for him.

How many more? A freaking army? She stayed alert, constantly looking around in case anyone else joined in, but she didn't see any others.

The man nearest her, the one Cade had stomped, stirred. Following Cade's cue, she kicked him in the face and put him out again.

She knew the dirt road continued on and then curved back to meet the paved street that would lead to an interstate on-ramp. Far ahead she saw the sudden glow of red taillights.

Whoever had Adela was getting away.

What to do? She couldn't give chase, not now.

Cade rejoined her, and together they watched the taillights fade away.

The eerie silence left behind seemed almost threatening. Neither of them spoke until his phone beeped.

"Your brother?" she whispered.

He ignored the question, saying, "In the van and lock the door," while half lifting her to do just that.

She quickly secured the lock but then stepped into the back to help him inside. He was already there, slamming the door and locking it.

"Stay down." He read the text. "My brother is giving chase on the car that took off."

They heard the roar of a motorcycle and briefly saw the lights flash over the road, and then he was gone. "That was him?"

"Yeah." He sent off a message, then shoved the phone in his pocket. "Are you hurt?"

A few hairs missing, but . . . "Not a scratch, thanks to you."

"Your leg? Your finger—"

"I'm fine, Cade." Just trembling from an adrenaline dump. "I heard Adela scream. Do you think your brother will be able to catch up?"

"He'll be in touch soon. Get behind the wheel, okay? Let's get out of here."

Through the windshield, she saw the long expanse of darkness. "It's safe?"

"Yes, as long as we don't linger." Gingerly he removed his vest.

That's when she realized . . . he'd been shot! Her legs seemed to give out and she dropped into a seat. "Oh my God."

"I'm fine," he said absently, lightly touching a wound near his collarbone. "Just a ricochet."

"But . . . you're bleeding!" Regaining her feet, she started toward him.

He caught her hand and kept her from touching his chest. "I need you to drive, babe. Can you do that?"

Filled with new purpose, she nodded fast and rushed to the driver's seat, putting the van in gear. "Hospital?"

For three seconds, he considered it, then growled out a breath. "No. I need to go to my dad's place."

"But . . ." She glanced back at him. "You could be seriously hurt."

"Dad is a surgeon. Or was, anyway. He's still the best option." Cade joined her in the passenger seat, not really moving like a mortally wounded man. With the first aid kit in his hand, he gave her directions.

Panicked fear tried to take over. "That's at least forty minutes from here."

"I know." Using a cotton pad, he covered the injury. "It'll be okay." His mouth tightened. "The bullet didn't go deep."

She started forward in the darkness, her gun in her lap. Actually, he had his with him, too. He was far too alert, one hand holding that makeshift bandage in place, the other holding his weapon as he constantly scanned the area.

They got to the highway without any trouble. Still . . .

Longest. Drive. Of her *life*.

She kept glancing at Cade. "How you holding up?"

His mouth quirked. "Worried about me?"

"Well . . . yeah." Her tone plainly conveyed what she thought of that stupid question. "I didn't know . . . When did it happen?"

His expression went dark and deadly again. "Right before that bastard grabbed you."

Reaching over, she patted his tensed thigh. "Down, boy. I told you, he didn't hurt me."

"It'd be a different story if I hadn't been there with you."

Yeah, he couldn't resist making that point. "Maybe." Most definitely. She'd been far outnumbered, and outmaneuvered, too. "I'm not one hundred percent yet. Usually when I nut a guy, he's out. That dude had brass balls or something."

215

She smirked. "I did smash his nose, though—I mean, before you completely rearranged his face. Pretty sure he's never going to look the same again."

Cade continually checked the mirrors. "It's not a joking matter." His glare burned over her. "I want another promise from you."

She almost groaned. She did give a quick roll of her eyes. "What now?"

"Whether Mattox recognized you or not, he's out to get you. That much is clear, yes?"

"He sent a small army, so yeah, not like I can deny it."

"Swear to me, until we have him locked away, or preferably dead, you won't try to deal with him or Adela on your own."

Her heart tripped, then settled into a fast, steady drumming. "You signing on for an extended period? Because there's no way to know how soon something like this could be wrapped up."

With no hesitation at all, he stated, "That's exactly what I'm doing. I don't care if it's a month, six months or a year." Tension poured off his big body, and he added in a hard, don't-argue voice, "We work together."

The warm glow started down deep in Sterling's jaded soul and fanned out until she couldn't keep the smile at bay. They were pretty crazy circumstances, and she was incredibly worried for Cade—despite his macho posturing—and still she couldn't repress a smile. "All right, you have my word." Urgency rushed back in on her. "Now no more talking. And don't you dare bleed to death!"

CHAPTER TEN

Getting shot was never a good thing. Cade didn't say it to Star, but it was his distraction with her that caused the mishap. The bastard had just grabbed her, and the man he'd been binding had managed to pull away. He didn't get in a clean shot, not with the way Cade broke his arm for the attempt, but the gun had discharged, the bullet ricocheted off the ground . . . and he got nicked.

Luckily below his face, but unluckily right above his vest. It hadn't slowed him down, not with Star being manhandled, but it sure as hell hadn't felt good, either.

His dad and Reyes would be worried. Then once they knew he'd be okay, Reyes would find it hilarious, and his dad . . . would have a fit. Not that Parrish McKenzie had ordinary fits. No, he'd condemn and harass and overall be a pain in Cade's ass.

He should have killed that prick who'd dared to lay hands on Star. Knowing what they had intended, he'd wanted to kill them all. If Star hadn't been involved, he probably would have, but that type of cleanup, with a witness around, would have really sent his father through the roof.

He'd have enough explaining to do already.

Chewing her bottom lip, Star's gaze repeatedly darted to him. It was almost endearing, seeing her fret, because he hadn't figured her for the type. If anything, he'd thought she'd take the same tack as his dad and bitch him out for it.

She needed a distraction, so he said, "I didn't see Mattox."

"Neither did I, unless he's the one who dragged Adela away."

Every bump in the road sent an echo of pain through him. "Might have been." A text dinged on his phone. Getting the damn thing out of his pocket wasn't easy this time. Knowing it would be Reyes, he locked his teeth, twisted, and finally pulled it free of his back pocket. He glanced at the screen.

"What?" she asked. "Is that your brother?"

"Yeah. He's caught up with them. It was definitely Mattox who took Adela."

Hands tightening on the wheel, Star asked, "Is she okay?"

"He says she is and that he'll explain soon." Reyes wanted to know where they could meet up. Given his injury, Cade had no choice but to text back: Home base.

The return text came fast. You shitting me?

Of course, his brother wouldn't just accept that when he knew home was the last place Cade wanted to be. He had to explain, but he kept it simple. I'm fine, but caught a ricochet.

On my way.

Damn. A full house. He glanced at Star. "Would it be pushing my luck to make one more request?"

"What's wrong?" Her gaze swept over him before returning to the road. "You won't pass out, will you?"

Cade snorted. "No, I won't fucking pass out. I told you, it's not that bad."

"You're still bleeding," she accused, her voice going a little high with stress. "And here we are, taking the long way to help."

He wished he could take her hand, but his were now smeared with blood. "Stay with me."

"I'm not budging."

That quick answer didn't reassure him one bit. "I mean it. No matter what."

Her brows climbed high. "Just what the hell does that mean? What are you expecting to happen?"

No help for it. He had to be up-front, if for no other reason than to prepare her. "I'm expecting you'll want to run once you meet my family. But don't."

"Bunch of scary ogres, huh?"

He wasn't about to go into detail. "Let's just say they can be overwhelming."

Softer now, more sincere, she vowed, "A pack of wild dogs couldn't chase me off, okay? We're sort of like partners now. And partners stick together."

They were a hell of a sight more than that, whether she wanted to admit it or not. But for now, partners would do. "I'm going to hold you to that." He indicated the next exit. "Get off here."

When the road quickly narrowed and climbed the mountainside, she asked, "Where are you leading me?"

"I told you, my father's place. It's home base for what I—*we*—do. And FYI, he's not going to be pleased."

She frowned. "With me or you?"

"Both—but mostly me."

Her neck stiffened. "Then why are we going there?"

For an answer, Cade lifted the pad and saw that the bleeding had almost stopped. "He can handle this—quietly." Taking in her profile with her brows now set in an obstinate line, he said, "Hospitals report gunshots, and that would bring up too many questions that we don't want to answer." She started to speak, probably to say something grouchy, judging by her frown, but he said, "Veer to the right."

"This isn't much of a road."

"That's the point."

Craning her neck, she looked up through the windshield. "Are those security cameras?"

"Two of the twenty scattered around the property."

Star fell silent. Awe? Intimidation? Or wariness?

They ascended a few more miles, and there in the distance, lights glowed. Day or night, the mountain retreat made quite an impressive sight. Stone columns climbed high to support a curved roof over a sprawling deck, backlit by floor-to-ceiling windows that overlooked the mountains.

Eyes rounded, Star pulled up to the gated entry.

"You need to enter the code to get through the gate." He shared the series of numbers and letters with her, and the wide iron gates opened.

Star paused. She looked as though she wanted to turn around and leave.

"It'll be fine," Cade told her. "If anyone can handle my family, it's you." At least, he hoped that was true. Before her, he'd never considered putting it to the test.

Incredulous, she blinked at him, then frowned at whatever she saw on his face. "You're ready to keel over, when you promised you wouldn't!" Misgivings gone, or buried under her worry for him, she stepped on the gas.

There'd be no keeling. It'd take more than the paltry injury he had to make him do that. But if it propelled her past her nervousness, he didn't mind the misconception.

And in fact, he did feel wretched. Loss of blood, maybe.

Well, that and the fact that he was about to

break a cardinal rule. He'd meant what he said, though. He didn't know another woman who could deal with what lay ahead. Star was the exception. Always. In everything.

With her, he believed it'd work out.

Driving past tall aspens and magnificent boulders, Sterling pulled up to . . . a freaking lodge. "That's not a house."

"It is."

"No." She shook her head and pointed at a different home off to the side. "That smaller place over there, *that's* a house." The place in front of her . . . she'd never seen anything like it, not even in a magazine.

"That's my sister's private cottage. Drive right up to the front door there and help me inside before I lose more blood."

That silenced her. But God, she was caught in conflicting emotions. Cade took precedence, most definitely, but this, all this grandeur and wealth? Not her cup of tea.

She put the van in Park, turned it off and rushed around to his side. He'd gotten out on his own steam, thankfully, because Cade was a huge guy and she wasn't sure she could bear his weight on her own, especially not with a bum leg. At the door, she leaned on a buzzer. "Didn't they see us driving up? What good are security cameras if you don't—"

A tall man jerked the door open, already glaring in fury. "What in God's name . . . !"

The only way to brazen through a situation was to really brazen it through. "Out of the way, man," she barked. "He's been shot."

Immediately the man tucked his own shoulder under Cade's other arm. "I'll take care of him. You may leave."

Leaning heavily on them both, Cade stated, "If she leaves, I leave."

That caused a visual standoff between the two men—until Sterling slugged the stranger in the ear. "He. Is. *Bleeding.*"

Impotent fury darkened the man's face. He looked like he wanted to say or do something—to her—but instead he bellowed, "Bernard!"

The sound echoed around a grand sky-high foyer.

"She follows us," Cade warned.

The man said nothing, but he didn't try to stop her. Another man—she assumed poor Bernard—came to a halt before them.

"What in the world."

"Get the door," the man said, but before Bernard could do that, Cade's brother came to a screeching halt on his motorcycle and bounded in.

"Run every red light?" Cade asked.

"And drove ninety," his brother said, moving her out of the way so he could take Cade's other arm. "But I'm here, so don't complain."

Securing the door, Bernard said, "I'll get things prepped," and then he rushed off.

"Can you walk?" his brother asked Cade.

"I'm fine—but I'd like to see you try to carry me."

The older man snapped, "Don't you two start."

They all ignored *her*. If she'd wanted to leave, now would be her chance.

Of course she didn't. She'd promised Cade, and besides that, she wanted to see with her own two peepers that he was okay.

So she meekly followed along.

A pretty young woman came out of a room, took in the scene before her and immediately set aside a laptop on a polished table to rush ahead of them. She now led the pack, while Sterling pulled up the rear.

They went across the great room, which really was great, before they veered off to the left and through the wide expanse of the kitchen, around a powder room, down a small flight of stairs, where the woman opened doors . . . into a lab?

Disbelief rounded Sterling's eyes and turned her in a circle as she took it all in. It looked like an honest-to-God operating room. Just what had she stepped into?

The men helped Cade to a white-sheeted bed that the handy Bernard had just finished making up with sheets from a metal cabinet.

Cade's brother neatly ripped open his shirt.

Blood was . . . everywhere, and Sterling felt her knees going weak. She reached out until her hand flattened on a wall, offering needed support.

Bernard set out a tray of stuff that looked too ominous for her peace of mind.

The older man, not Bernard, was busy scrubbing his hands and muttering, "You are the most stubborn, difficult—"

"Son. I know," Cade said, not really sounding like a man with a bullet in his chest. In fact, he was staring at Sterling, so she tried not to look so worried. "Reyes is the constant joker and Madison is the most obedient."

Reyes and Madison? Difficult *son?*

Her gaze slowly traveled to the sink where he washed. So that fire-breathing dragon was Cade's father? Yes, she saw the resemblance now, but . . .

Madison took offense at what he'd said. "Obedient? That's a lie."

Cade snorted. His brother did, too.

Madison folded her arms. "Don't take your temper out on me because you were foolish enough to get shot." Then to their father, who was now pulling on surgical gloves, Madison asked, "Is it serious, Dad?"

Sterling gaped at her. Serious? He'd caught a bullet! In his *chest*.

"No, it's not," Cade said, still not sounding all that wounded. "Damn bullet deflected off a rock and came back on me."

"You coulda shot your eye out," Reyes mused.

Madison reached out to swat him, but he ducked away.

They were all certifiably insane. From one to the other, Sterling stared—until she got snared again by Cade's gaze.

His father leaned over him, pressed . . . and announced, "It stopped at his collarbone, but luckily it doesn't appear to have broken anything."

Good news? At the moment, Sterling would take any she could get.

Utilizing scary surgical-type pincer thingies, his father poked and prodded while Cade gritted his teeth.

Madison stood stoic and Reyes was thankfully silent as he paced.

Bernard held a metal bowl . . . which clinked when the man dropped something into it. "Bullet's out. Let me make sure there's no other damage."

"X-ray?" Bernard asked.

Cade's father peered down at him. "Are you hurt anywhere else? And don't hold back."

Sounding disgusted, Cade said, "No."

"A few stitches, then." He turned to Sterling. "You're not sterile, so please remove yourself."

Of all the . . . ! That sounded like a truly terrible insult. Reyes and Madison—were *they* sterile? Or Bernard?

But he must have meant them all because Reyes

228

went to Madison and, with an arm around her shoulders, led her to the door. Bernard stepped away.

And that left only her.

"Bernard?" Cade called out, still looking at her.

"Yes?"

"Don't let her leave."

His father rolled his eyes, dismissed them all and began a thorough cleaning that, to Sterling, looked worse than what had come before it.

Feeling a little sick, she told Cade, "I'll be right outside the door."

"You'll wait in the kitchen," his father said without looking up. "Since my son has quite a bit of explaining to do, you may as well get something to drink."

"Come along," Bernard said gently. "I'll get you settled."

She didn't want to. But damn. These people were daunting, far more so than Mattox with a gun.

The second they were alone, his father gave up even the slightest pretense of politeness. "What the hell were you thinking?"

"That I make my own decisions? That I want her with me? That you don't run my life?"

A deep growl crawled up his throat, but his hands were steady and competent as he numbed the area. "You could have been killed."

Without Star to focus on, Cade stared up at his

father. "No more so than on any other job."

He paused. "We cover every possible scenario."

"Best we can, I know. I did the same tonight. That's why I convinced Reyes to tag along." He felt the tug of the first stitch going in, but no pain. "When you explode, don't include him. Against his better judgment, he did it for me."

Instead of doing some of that exploding that Cade expected, his father sighed. "Is the girl truly that important to you?"

Cade didn't doubt that his father had already surmised much of what had happened. Pesky details were only finer points of an overall view. "You already know the answer to that."

He finished stitching in silence. Once he was done, he treated the area with something and applied a light bandage. "You'll stay here tonight and tomorrow so I can keep an eye on this."

"Not without Star."

Moving away to wash his hands, his father remarked, "You shouldn't call her that. I've read your sister's report, you realize. Sterling Parson has good reason for having shed that name, and you endanger her by using it."

Cautiously, Cade sat up. His head swam a little, but he'd suffered worse injuries and he had a good grasp on what his body could and couldn't do. He took stock, flexed each arm and surmised that he'd walk out of the lab on his own. "I won't let anything happen to her."

With a sound of exasperation, Parrish turned back to him. His face was pinched. His eyes were narrowed. He looked pissed, but he said, "I suppose we should get to know her."

It was that concession more than anything else that allowed the residual aches and pains to swamp back in on Cade. Until he'd known if he had to fight his own family, which had been his presumption, he hadn't allowed himself to feel much of the discomfort.

The others would follow Parrish's lead, and he'd just offered an olive branch. Surprising, and very much appreciated.

Resigned, his father said, "I'll take you to your room so you can wash up and change clothes. Then we'll have a little talk with our guest."

Each of them had their own living quarters in the main house, for situations of this type. They were used when necessary, kept prepped otherwise.

Cade had his own house nearer to his bar, Reyes lived nearer to his gym and Madison had insisted on the separate cottage.

It was times like this that made having the quarters so convenient. He hated to admit to his own limitations, and he *could* make it back to Star's place if he needed to, but he didn't relish the idea of bouncing along the rough roads again.

Nodding, he carefully let his feet touch the

floor. His head spun, but not too badly. "It was Mattox," he admitted. "And he had Star once before. He's the one who started her on this path of vengeance."

"You don't say? Hmm." Again with his arm around Cade, Parrish started them forward.

His father was not known for an excess of sympathy, and he definitely didn't indulge coddling. Cade had never wanted or needed either, and Reyes pretended he didn't care. But Madison? He and Reyes tried to make up for his father's lacks, but Cade wasn't sure if they'd succeeded or not. He understood Reyes, but his sister was often a mystery to him.

Right now, though, Cade was glad his father didn't fuss with him, trying to insist that he rest. Not yet. Not until he convinced Star that she needed to spend a few days with him.

Here, where it would be safer.

Where they could come up with a better plan— to end Mattox, once and for all.

Sterling had left that home surgery center feeling pretty numb. Passing the powder room reminded her of the blood, and she detoured in there to wash her hands and face but couldn't do anything about her shirt. She still wore the bulletproof vest, but with Cade hurt, she hadn't even thought about it.

A knock at the door got her moving again.

"Hold on." She smoothed back her hair, made a face at herself and stepped out.

Bernard smiled gently. "Come to the kitchen and rest. I'll get you something to drink while I prepare food."

She didn't need rest; she needed Cade.

No, she didn't *need* anything. Certainly not a guy. But she would stick around for a bit just to talk to him again.

It wasn't until she sat down at the kitchen table that Sterling realized how badly her leg thumped and her finger throbbed. Even her scalp hurt now, from where the goon had pulled her hair. And that damn vest nearly suffocated her. With Cade safe in the bosom of his lunatic family, all the discomforts settled in and made themselves known.

She wasn't sure what to think about these people yet. Cade's father was obviously wealthy. His sister tall, slim and beautiful. His brother still a raging pain in the butt.

But anyone could see that they loved one another.

Even the stuffy Bernard, who was trying so hard to look unconcerned as he prepared food, couldn't adequately hide how much he cared.

They were a family in every way that mattered. Blood related. Loyal to one another. Comfortable with heckling—and confident in assistance when needed.

And here she was, stuck in the middle of them, feeling like a mutt Cade had dragged home.

It didn't help that Reyes hadn't stopped staring at her with the same fascination he'd give a cockroach.

She tried to ignore him, she really did, but waiting to know how Cade had fared sent her temper spiraling and she couldn't grapple it back under control. Glaring at Reyes, she snapped, *"What?"*

Lifting his chin, Reyes said, "Just trying to figure it out."

Honestly confused by that answer, Sterling asked again, this time with less animus, "What?"

"You got my brother shot."

Hands fisting, Sterling bolted to her feet and leaned over the table. "I've had just about enough of you."

He eyed her up and down without concern, still showing only curiosity.

It unnerved her, damn it. "In case you failed to notice, Cade is a big boy and he makes his own damn decisions. Do you honestly think I could've stopped him from going along? For your information, I tried."

"And failed," Reyes said.

"But don't you see?" Madison said. "That's the lure."

They planned to verbally dissect her? Screw that.

Sterling pivoted to Madison. At least this sibling was calm and apparently not that interested in provoking her. "What's that supposed to mean?"

It was Reyes who answered, "All that." He gestured at her rigid posture. "Apparently Cade likes them fiery."

Madison gave him a quelling look, saving Sterling the trouble. "I think Cade likes her because she's as strong as he is."

One side of Reyes's mouth quirked in a way that was so familiar to Cade's smile that Sterling's heart clenched.

Then he ruined it by saying, "Since she's standing while he's on a table bleeding, maybe she's even stronger?"

"You're an asshole," Sterling accused, choking out the words around the lump in her throat. She strode away before she did something truly appalling. Like cry.

Silence throbbed behind her, until Reyes ordered, "You can't leave. You heard what big brother said."

Like she would without first seeing that Cade was okay? She wouldn't, but she replied, "Don't plan to, but I don't have to stay in the same room with a jackass!"

She'd take a turn around this mausoleum and hopefully get herself in check before returning to the kitchen.

But first . . . she headed out the front door and to the van.

Madison came trotting behind her, then just fell into step with her. Pretending she wasn't there, Sterling opened the door of the van, yanked off her shirts, then ripped open the fastenings on the vest and tossed the heavy thing inside.

Madison said not a single word while Sterling stripped down to her bra. In fact, she got comfortable against the side of the van, watching as Sterling pulled back on her T-shirt. Madison held out her button-up shirt, her expression enigmatic.

Shrugging it on, Sterling slammed the van door and walked away without thanking her. She went back inside the open front door of the house, aware of Madison trailing her.

The silence dragged out until Sterling wanted to scream, but she clamped her lips together and managed to keep quiet. Where to go? She couldn't imagine traipsing through the house without an invite. Besides, it was so damn immense she might get lost. From the great room she spotted doors that led to a deck and darted that way.

Naturally, Madison followed.

Outside, gulping in the damp evening air, Sterling leaned on the railing. Being here like this, in the quiet night, the majestic mountains barely discernible in the moonlight, she felt incredibly small. Insignificant.

Then Madison shoulder-bumped her. "This is

better than leaving, right? You had me concerned for a minute there. I wasn't keen on tackling you."

Tackling her? Though her eyes narrowed, Sterling kept her gaze trained ahead, doing her utmost not to react.

"By the way, you shouldn't let Reyes rile you. He does it on purpose, you know, but if he doesn't get a reaction, he loses interest."

Damn it, that deserved a response, and she heard herself say, "What if I reacted with a fist to his face?"

Madison went still—then burst out laughing. "Oh, I'd love to see that. But you should be forewarned, we're all excellent at fighting. Dad made sure we studied a wide variety of disciplines. The only one I know who can best Reyes is Cade. My guess is that if you tried to punch him, you'd probably end up in some ridiculously undignified hold that would only infuriate you more, and then Cade would be angry with him and he'd pulverize Reyes, and then Dad would be upset. Me, too, I guess. I love my brothers, even though they're far too alpha and bossy. It's always distressing when they go at each other."

Very slowly, Sterling turned her head to stare in amazement at this particularly chatty sibling. "Maybe I should shoot him instead?"

"Well, as to that . . ." Grinning, Madison caught her hair in a fist to keep it from blowing in her face. "We're all pretty good at anticipating that sort of thing, too. Which makes it really curious that Cade allowed himself to be shot. Did you see how it happened?"

Sterling snapped her mouth shut and looked away. If Cade wanted to explain to his sister, then he could. Right now, she wanted to concentrate on ignoring the girl so she'd go away.

Turning to lean her back on the rail, Madison wrapped her arms around herself. "It's chilly out here."

"Feels good." Damn it, she hadn't meant to reply.

"Cade will be fine, you know. He's probably busy trying to order Dad around, and that never goes well. Neither of them seems to realize it, but they're just too much alike to always get along. Dad isn't a dummy, though. He'll see the situation for what it is and then it'll be fine."

Sterling wondered if her eyes had crossed yet. Had she really thought this sibling wasn't provoking? Unable to ignore everything Madison had just said, she gave up. "What, exactly, is that supposed to mean?"

"Dad knows when to cut his losses. He won't like it, but Cade brought you home, so he's obviously going to get his way."

"He didn't *bring me home*." Did Madison consider her a stray mutt, too? "He needed me to drive him here because he had a bullet in his chest."

"Oh, please. Cade could have driven—or even removed the bullet himself. He defines *tough guy,* you know."

Yeah, she did kind of know it.

Madison leaned closer, as if in confidence. "Personally, I think he saw it as a good excuse to push his own agenda."

"His agenda?"

Madison nudged her again. "You."

Bernard tapped at the doors, then stuck his head out. "I have food prepared, if you'd like to return to the kitchen now."

Before Sterling could decide what she wanted to do, Madison linked her arm through hers and pulled her along. "Thank you, Bernard. I'm suddenly famished."

Indulging her own whisper, Sterling asked, "Is he a butler?"

"Bernard? Oh, he's pretty much everything." Then louder, Madison added, "You take excellent care of us, don't you, Bernard?"

"I try."

And . . . that told Sterling nothing.

The only upside was finding Cade in the kitchen when she got there. His hair was wet and finger-combed back, he wore a clean dark T-shirt and fresh jeans, socks but no shoes, and in no way did he look like an injured man.

His gaze searched hers as she strode in, then moved to his sister with silent question.

Madison released her, saying, "We were just enjoying the view."

"Can't see much at night," Reyes pointed out.

Sterling shot back, "A black void is still more pleasant than you."

His mouth twitched. Then he said to Cade, "I like her."

Throwing up her hands, Sterling decided to stop wasting her time on that particular annoying brother so she could concentrate on Cade. Stopping before him, she took in the visible edges of a square white bandage at the base of his throat.

Maybe that's why her voice emerged all soft and feminine when she asked, "Are you okay?"

Enfolding her in his arms, Cade drew her close and asked, "Were you worrying about me? I told you I was fine."

Carefully, Sterling rested her cheek against his shoulder. Knowing for a fact that he was okay, seeing him hale and hearty, left her legs weak with relief. "I've never had to worry about anyone before."

"Baloney," he replied. "You worry about everyone."

Interrupting their moment, Reyes said, "You can stop worrying about Adela. That conniver is not a victim. In fact, from what I saw, she might be helping to run the show."

CHAPTER ELEVEN

Cade wanted to hear all about Adela and his brother's impressions, but a few other things took priority. Giving Star one last hug, he urged her to a chair.

Bernard had "thrown together" one of his incredible pasta dishes, and Cade wanted her to eat before she got more distracted.

Taking the seat next to her, he asked, "What do you want to drink?"

She stared at the angel-hair pasta smothered in a cream sauce that Bernard had pulled from his private stash for just such an occasion.

Bernard said, "I suggest sauvignon blanc—"

"Got a cola?" she asked instead, interrupting him. "Anything from a can is fine."

Smiling, Cade glanced at his family, daring them to say anything derogatory. "I'll have the same."

"I, as well," Madison said.

God bless his sister. Cade gave her a grateful smile.

Parrish said, "Pour me a glass, please," and took his seat at the head of the table.

Grinning, Reyes looked from one to the other. "Damn, this is fun. Guess as long as we're going with variety, I'll take a beer."

Appalled, Bernard stared at him. "With my pasta?"

"Yeah, but you're not the one driving me to drink, so don't sweat it."

Cade gave him a warning look, but Star smiled sweetly.

Once everyone was served, Bernard fixed his own plate and sat to Parrish's right. It was unusual for him to do so, but being unaware of the family dynamics, Star didn't seem to think anything of it.

No doubt about it, Bernard was curious about Star, and with good reason. Cade had never brought a woman home before. There were rules against such things, and he'd just crashed through them all.

Taking a bite of the pasta, Star gave a low groan that had each man staring at her. "Oh, Bernard." Another groan. "This is amazing."

Bernard actually flushed. "Thank you."

Pointing her fork at Reyes, she said, "So spill it. What do you know about Adela?"

That sounded so much like an order that Reyes took his time replying, and not with an answer but another question. "You're not surprised that she might be in cahoots with Mattox?"

"Nope, but I'd like details."

"We already suspected her," Cade explained.

"But naturally you rushed ahead anyway." Parrish made no bones about his disapproval.

"Hey, that was my fault." While twirling more pasta around her fork, Star said, "She contacted me, so I felt I had to be certain. Even tonight, it wasn't one hundred percent clear if she was a victim or helping to set a trap. And it *was* a trap, big-time. Dudes swarmed out of everywhere. I lost count. Six, maybe seven."

"Eight total," Reyes said, and Cade could see he was starting to relax. How could he not with Star being so casual?

"Night-vision goggles?" she asked. "Awesome. I need some of those."

"They come in handy," Reyes agreed. "I take it you couldn't see much?"

"Not in that darkness. Anything away from the headlight beam was more shadow than anything else."

"Yet you seemed to know when someone was moving in."

She shrugged. "Just sensed the movement, you know? Or heard a small sound."

"So astute," Madison enthused. "Dad, isn't she amazing?"

"Don't answer that," Star dared to order Parrish, then said to Madison, "I'm as far from amazing as a person can get, so don't fool yourself. I completely dicked up tonight. If it weren't for Cade—and actually, you, too, Reyes—I'd have been toast."

"You'd have been in Mattox's capture," Parrish stated with blunt insistence.

"Yup." She gave an exaggerated shudder. "Not

a place I want to be, so gratitude all around, guys. Thanks for saving my bacon. And, Cade, seriously, I am so damn sorry you got hurt."

Everyone fell silent again. Cade knew she wasn't what any of them had expected.

She was better. More refreshing.

Pride, that's what he felt. Star handled his family with more ease than he'd expected, mostly by just being her usual candid self.

Reyes raised a brow at Cade. "She must have been hangry before. She's much more agreeable now that she's fed her face."

"Food is always good," Star agreed with a wink at Bernard. "Especially when it's this delicious."

Heat crawled up Bernard's neck. "Again, thank you."

"And you," she said, playfully growling at Reyes. "You do like to push those buttons, don't you? I considered punching you in your face, but your sister warned me against it." She smirked. "Considered just shooting you, too, but Cade might not like that. For some reason I can't figure out, he seems fond of you."

Reyes burst out laughing, earning a look of censure from Parrish, which he pretended not to see. "You want to spar sometime, lady, just let me know. You're welcome to my gym any day."

"I might take you up on that." Plate empty, Star pushed it back. "But I'll wait until my leg and finger have completely healed. Now, enough of the pleasantries. Tell me what you saw with Adela before she decides to call me again. I need to know how to handle things."

Slumping comfortably into his seat, Reyes held his beer loosely in one hand. "Adela and some other guy got out at an empty lot. Mattox was there. I assumed they were going to meet up with anyone else who'd been able to crawl away."

"I left them bound," Cade said. "Unless some-one releases them, they'll be there awhile."

Parrish looked up from his plate. "You didn't kill them?"

Deadpan, Cade said, "You tend to frown over random murders that you haven't sanctioned. And at that point, I didn't know I'd be bringing Star back here."

"He was trying to tiptoe around the rules," Reyes offered. "Not all in, but not out, either."

Eyes wide, Star looked from father to son and back again. "Wish someone had told me the options. I wouldn't have had a problem sending a few of them to hell."

Realizing that he'd said so much, Parrish scowled. "This conversation didn't happen."

Star pretended to lock her lips and toss away a key.

Her antics had Reyes chuckling again. "No worries about anyone left behind. Mattox used the phone, so I assume he sent a lackey or two back for his men. If someone else finds them, it's not a worry. They won't say anything about us being there because that'd just expose their own agenda." He turned his attention to Star. "Your little victim gave Mattox hell."

"Seriously?" Star leaned forward, her arms crossed on the table. "You couldn't have misunderstood?"

"I know a female temper when I see it," he assured her. "Adela jabbed him in the chest, her mouth going the whole time. Mattox argued back, but she didn't look afraid. Mostly it looked like a lovers' quarrel."

"Euewww." Revulsion twisted Star's mouth. "Knowing what a disgusting ape Mattox is, I don't want to imagine that. It's too gross, but I suppose anything is possible. She did seem determined to hang back at Misfits, even though I could have gotten her out of there. And after that, when she claimed to want help escaping, she insisted that I come alone. You'd think she'd welcome an army, right? More rescuers would up her chances of getting away."

"If you knew all that," Parrish said, "then why did you go?"

"Because Mattox could have been forcing her." She shrugged. "You know he controls women, and most would do whatever he said to avoid the consequences."

"True enough." Reyes turned to Cade. "I followed them to another house. We can fetch her easily enough if that's what you want to do."

"Just like that?" Star asked.

"When we formulate an actual plan together, we're more successful than not," Reyes said.

Cade stroked her arm. "One of us could grab her while the other gives cover."

"And I can figure out the best time for it," Madison offered. "If Adela isn't under lock and key, it could be even easier. I'll sort that out."

"Not saying it'd be a piece of cake," Cade clarified, "but we can do it."

"With proper surveillance followed by careful planning," Parrish insisted. "Not this . . ." He flagged a hand at her. "Running off half-cocked business, like what happened tonight."

"Got it, but I don't think we should do that," Star said, thinking out loud. "With the extra info Reyes got, this could be a good opportunity to get all the players. Adela still thinks I consider her a victim, so it should be easy enough to set her up."

Overruling that idea, Cade shook his head. "Once we have her, we can question her."

"And she may or may not confide in us, right?" Star argued. "But if we use me as bait—"

Every muscle on his body clenched. "No."

Reyes, Parrish, Madison and Bernard all went still at his uncompromising tone.

Undaunted, Star continued as if he hadn't

refused. "I can pretend to let her capture me, with you guys all keeping track."

The hairs on Cade's nape stood on end. *"No."*

"You were all just boasting about your skill. Well, just think, we could uncover Mattox's whole operation."

Shoving back his chair, Cade rose to his feet to tower over her. "I said no."

Parrish sent him a look of disapproval for the outburst. "It's actually a sound plan."

"The hell it is," Cade shot back. "You know what could happen to her."

Slowly, Star stood to face him. "I'm aware of the risks. I'm also aware of the rewards."

"We'll come up with a different plan," Cade said with finality.

Trying to break the tension, Madison smiled. "And this time, we'll all work on it together."

Sterling looked around the suite of rooms with dread. Even this, Cade's private section of the mansion, was nicer than anything she'd ever known. Way more upscale than her cheap apartment—an apartment she actually liked and, until now, had thought was pretty spiffy. She should have headed home after dinner instead of letting them all bulldoze her into staying over.

Madison had acted like it was a done deal.

Reyes had told her not to be dumb.

Parrish had insisted, with a stiff smile, that she was welcome.

Even Bernard had promised an amazing breakfast in the morning.

But Cade was the deciding factor, saying it was her decision—and if she left, he'd go with her.

Tough as he might be, getting jostled along mountain roads wouldn't be good for him. How could she put him through that with her stubbornness? So here she was, looking around in amazement at his sitting room, kitchenette and bedroom.

The ceilings were high, tall windows everywhere, and it all looked like a designer's dream, like something she'd see in a magazine of the rich and famous.

"Bathroom is right through here," Cade prompted, opening a door to an opulently decorated retreat.

Smooth stone covered the floor and the walls of the shower, a vessel sink topped a carved but masculine cabinet, and a lit mirror and heated towel shelves polished off the decor.

"Wow."

He came to her, looping his arms around her waist. "Why don't you shower? I'll give those bloody clothes to Bernard to wash."

Appalled with that idea, she pushed him back. "Not happening."

"Bernard wouldn't mind."

"I mind." She looked around again. "I'll wash my shirt in the sink and hang it in the shower to dry."

A quiet knock on the entry door had them both looking that way. Madison stuck her head in and searched the couch and kitchenette before spotting them in the bedroom, then smiled. "Oh, good, I was afraid I might be . . . interrupting."

"And you opened the door anyway?" Cade teased. He released Sterling from his embrace but kept his arm around her waist as he led her into the sitting room. "We were just discussing Star's clothes."

"Then I have perfect timing." Madison held out a stack of shirts, a pair of loose cotton pants, a blow-dryer, a round brush and a bottle of lotion. "I noticed when she got rid of the vest that she could use a change of clothes."

Looking down at her shirt, Sterling groaned. "I'd forgotten about that jerk bleeding all over me or I'd have . . . figured out something before dinner." No idea what she could have done, but she scowled up at Cade anyway. "You let me sit at that table with your family looking like this. Why didn't you remind me?"

"Because no one cared."

"But . . . at dinner?" She wasn't stupid. She knew his family understood decorum better than she did, but even she knew you didn't share a meal with polite company while wearing some cretin's nose blood on your shirt. Her cheeks actually went hot with embarrassment.

Cade ran a hand over her head. "Bloody shirt or not, I wanted you to eat, relax and get to know everyone."

"And that's what we did," Madison said happily. "So mission accomplished."

Yeah, she'd tried. For the most part, she'd managed to get along, too. That is, until Cade blew up about her excellent plan—a plan she hadn't yet given up on. It would work; she believed that.

And the important thing was to stop Mattox once and for all.

"The shirts are stretchy," Madison was saying, "so they should fit okay. We're both tall, but I'm skinnier than you, so I grabbed cotton drawstring pants instead of jeans."

There was nothing skinny about Madison McKenzie. Cade's sister had a tall, willowy body with gentle curves that Sterling thought was far more appealing than her own sturdy figure.

"I figured you could sleep in one of Cade's shirts." Grinning at him, Madison added, "Didn't think you would mind."

"Thanks, hon." Cade drew his sister in for a one-armed hug, then took the stack from her.

"Yeah," Sterling said, a little overwhelmed with the generosity. "Appreciate it."

"We'll talk more at breakfast, okay? Bernard usually has everything ready by eight, but since we're up so late, I asked him to make it nine. Will that work for you?"

Sterling looked at Cade. His house, his schedule.

He nodded. "That's fine. We'll see you then." He followed Madison to the door.

Sterling saw them whispering but couldn't hear what was said. Probably something she wouldn't like anyway. This time when Cade closed the door, he locked it, then came past her in the bedroom to ensure the French doors leading to a patio were also locked. With that done, he set his sister's offerings in the bathroom.

"No more interruptions." Opening a dresser drawer, he pulled out a snowy white T-shirt and handed it to her. "Want some boxers, too? Or how about you go without?" He gathered her close, one large hand caressing her behind. "I won't mind."

Concerned for his injury, Sterling gently rested a hand to his shoulder. "Let me shower first, okay? You don't want to hug this mess."

He treated her to that crooked smile and, leaning in, kissed her without drawing her close. "Use whatever you need in the bathroom. Toothbrush, lotion, shampoo and conditioner. Make yourself at home, okay? I'll fold down the bed."

Standing there, Sterling looked past him at the king-size bed, then stupidly whispered, "We're sleeping together? In your dad's house, I mean?"

He actually laughed. "No one will know."

"Bull."

"Okay, so they'll all assume. We're adults, babe." His grin faded into a tender smile. "And I want to hold you."

She wanted that, too. "But you were shot. What if I bump you?"

"I'll keep you too close for that." He kissed her again, this time lingering until her toes curled in her boots.

It took her a second to regain her wits. Then she breathed, "All right." It had been an exhausting and disappointing day, and she was still worried about Cade. Snuggling close, reassuring herself that he was fine, sounded too nice to resist. "Be forewarned, though, if Reyes says anything tomorrow, I can't be held responsible for what I do."

"Whatever you do, I'll help." He steered her into the bathroom, leaving after a smack on her behind. "Let me know if you can't find something you need." He closed the door before she could come up with more objections.

Of course she knew her reservations were absurd. As he'd said, they were adults.

But she'd never before stayed over with a guy in his father's house. Cade had probably sneaked in a lot of girls, but their formative years were vastly different. Overall, there'd been no fathers for her to deal with, not even her own. A grandfatherly figure, yes, but that was different, since she'd lived in the garage and never, not once, had she considered inviting a guy to share that precious space with her.

She pampered herself for a bit, but not as much as she'd have liked with only Cade's masculine products at hand. At least the lotion Madison had brought smelled more feminine. She slathered it on, occasionally lifting her wrist to sniff it again. Lavender, maybe. Or something more exotic. Whatever the scent, she liked it.

Her hair was thick, and by the time she'd dried it, nearly an hour had passed.

Sterling glanced at herself in the mirror. If she weren't so tall, Cade's T-shirt would have covered more of her. Instead, it barely reached below her backside. Of course, that made her think of the affectionate smack he'd left there, and his comment . . .

He's injured, she reminded herself. *No sex, not tonight. Maybe not for a while.* Still, as she opened the door and stepped out, her nipples pulled tight.

Already stretched out in the bed, his big, gorgeous body bare except for snug boxers, his shoulders propped against the headboard, he looked relaxed, maybe even asleep.

Until his eyes opened.

"Sorry I took so long." She stood there, framed in the light from the bathroom.

His slumberous gaze traveled over her. "Feel better?"

"I didn't feel bad." Not really. Tired, frazzled, achy . . . but not bad. Feeling like a feast he wanted to devour, she tugged at the hem of the shirt.

A morbid thought occurred to her—how awful it would be if . . . *when* . . . they went their separate ways. No other man would be like Cade. And no other man could make her feel the way he did.

Standing here now, in this moment, seeing the naked desire on his face, it was easy to think they could carve out a real relationship, yet all she had to do was look around to be reminded that they came from very different worlds.

Because of the circumstances, his father and brother were tolerating her, and Madison was kind. If he hadn't gotten shot, he would never have brought her here. This was a one-off, because Cade's family loved him.

"What are you thinking?" He left the bed to stalk toward her. "I think you just wrote a book in your head, didn't you? Will you tell me about it?"

Not being a dummy, Sterling determined to enjoy it all while it lasted. She wouldn't waste a single second by moping about an uncertain future. Heck, there was a chance Mattox would kill her, so what did the future matter?

When Cade got close, she touched the bruising she could see around his bandage. "I was thinking that, even wounded, you are seriously sexy." Tilting into him, she lightly brushed her lips over the heated skin of his chest. His chest hair tickled, and he smelled indescribably good. "I hate that you got hurt because of me." He frowned, and she quickly corrected, "I mean, I hate that you got hurt, period. It's just extra sucky that it happened while you were helping me."

Taking her hand, he lifted it to cover the bandage. "I know better than to get distracted. That's not on you, okay? I was where I wanted to be."

"Because I was there. If I hadn't involved you—"

"Then I wouldn't have you here now." He stroked an open hand down her spine and over her rump to cup a bare cheek. Grinning, he bent to nuzzle her neck and whispered, "With your sweet ass available."

Sterling laughed. It was that sort of thing, the playful compliments and sexual teasing, that she enjoyed so much. "I'm putting my sweet ass in the bed. The bathroom is all yours."

"Give me five minutes. And don't you dare fall asleep."

The second the door closed behind him, Sterling hurried to the bed and got under the covers.

In only three minutes, Cade emerged. He'd

showered earlier but hadn't shaved. She liked him like this, his hair a little messy, not as precisely groomed, the beard shadow adding a rugged edge to his appeal.

It wasn't until he reached his side of the bed that she noticed the condoms on the nightstand. Her eyes flared, but he didn't notice as he clicked off the light and slid in beside her. In one smooth move he drew her against him and his mouth covered hers, stalling any protests she might have made over her concern for his injury.

Those large, rough hands slowly roamed everywhere, along her back, her shoulders, her thighs, yet they returned again and again to her behind. If she could have caught her breath, she might have laughed. He really did like her backside, when she'd never thought much about it.

He wasn't taking any chances on her using his wound as a reason to turn him down. How could he want her so much? It had to be magic, because no one else ever had.

Finally getting her mouth free, she whispered, "Slow down."

"Say yes, and then I will." He kissed a searing path along her throat to her ear.

He teased with his tongue, making her squirm. "Yes," she agreed. "With one condition."

"No conditions in bed, babe."

"I insist." Gently pushing him to his back, she crawled over him and sat on his abdomen. Her leg protested, but not enough to change her mind.

Staring up at her in the darkness, he held her waist and bent his knees so his thighs supported her back. "Lose the T-shirt."

It seemed second nature for Cade to give orders, but here in bed, she liked it. After whisking off her top, she said, "Now."

"Now," he agreed, shifting his hands to her breasts, lightly tugging at her nipples and obliterating her thoughts in the process. "Did I tell you how much I love these?"

She was starting to think he loved everything about her body. Dropping her head back, she let him have his way.

"So damn sweet."

He toyed with her nipples so long that she knew she was wet and beyond ready. "Cade . . ."

Leaning up while urging her down, he strongly sucked one nipple into the wet heat of his mouth.

Holy smokes. His tongue rasped over her, and she felt it in other places, especially between her legs. "That's enough." If he didn't ease up, she'd come before he ever got inside her.

He closed his teeth gently around her—and tugged insistently. Her breath shuddered in and released as a broken groan. She didn't mean to, but she rocked against his hard abs.

Humming his approval, he switched to the other breast.

"Whoa," she gasped, struggling for air.

"No."

Oh, what he did with mouth, lips, tongue and teeth . . . But he'd been shot, and she couldn't let this get out of control. *"Yes."*

With a last leisurely lick, he rested back on the bed. Her harsh breathing filled the air. His hands continued to stroke all over her.

Trying to regain control—as if she'd ever had it—Sterling braced her hands over his pecs, but that was a mistake. His skin burned, his muscles all knotted tight. He was closer to the ragged edge than he wanted to admit, and that turned her on even more.

"You're rushing it," she accused softly.

"You liked it."

"Yeah, course." She wasn't dead yet! One more cleansing breath helped to calm her racing heartbeat. "But seriously, Cade, you're hurt, regardless of how you want to minimize it." Getting words out wasn't easy, not with her nipples wet and aching. "To make this work—"

His fingers contracted on her hips. "It was working just fine."

"You need to let me take care of you."

He was silent a moment, just thinking. "Take care of me how?"

"You'll be still, and I'll do all the moving."

He snorted, and yeah, she got that. During sex, it was pretty damn hard to not move. "I mean it, Cade."

Lowering his arms to his sides, he said, "Go for it."

"I need you to relax."

"I'm relaxed."

She tsked. He felt like steel under her thighs. "Will you promise to tell me if I hurt you?"

"Hell no."

Such a *guy*. "Then I'll just have to be extra careful." Stretching out over him, she lightly teased her lips over his, dodging him when he tried to deepen the kiss. "Behave."

He choked on a laugh.

She trailed her tongue along his bristly jaw . . . to his ear. Closing her lips around his earlobe, she waited to see if he'd react the same as she had.

He did. Arms closing around her, he gave a vibrating groan and even turned his head a little for her.

Sterling ran her fingertips over the shorter hair at his temples, around to the back of his head to hold him still as she opened her mouth on his throat, grazed him with her teeth and sucked to give him a love bite.

His long fingers tangled in her hair, fisting gently.

Careful to keep pressure off his bandaged area, she rocked against him, deliberately teasing the hard cock straining beneath the material of his boxers.

A little roughly, he steered her mouth to his

and took over the kiss. She didn't mind that . . . but then, she couldn't think straight. In fact, she wanted him too much to think.

Right *now*.

Maybe it was the chaos of the day, the resulting fear from him being hurt, but she felt totally out of control—a novel thing for her. She'd never had a craving like this, but she craved Cade.

The kiss went on and on while she touched him everywhere, moved against him, drove them both to the brink.

Pulling her mouth away, she sat up and away from him, then began wrestling off his boxers. He lifted his hips to help . . . and there he was. Long, hard, throbbing.

Sterling didn't think about it, didn't plan it; she just gave in to her desires.

Taking him in her fist, she kissed his erection, tentatively at first, just brushing her lips over his velvety length. The heated, musky scent of him encouraged her. His choppy breathing did, too.

Wanting more of him, she licked—from the base up to the head—and felt him go rigid. She liked that enough that she growled low and drew him in for a soft, wet suck.

CHAPTER TWELVE

Cade had to grip the sheets to keep from taking over. He couldn't stop his hips from lifting. Or quiet the groan that rumbled from his chest. Her tongue . . . damn, her tongue kept lapping over the sensitive head of his cock, and he thought he might explode.

Star wasn't skilled, but she was damn sure enthusiastic, and that seemed to be all that mattered.

Her hot little mouth slid down his length, back up again, over and over while her hand squeezed and her wet tongue tasted him—no, he wouldn't last.

"Condom," he nearly gasped, reaching to the nightstand as he said it. "Babe, put the condom on me."

With a small, hungry sound, she took him deep again.

"Star . . . God." He squeezed his eyes shut and thought of everything under the sun except what she made him feel. That lasted five minutes, maybe, and then he knew he had to end the torture.

Tangling a hand in her hair, he gently tugged. "Let up, babe, or it's over for me."

Slowly, as if she hated to stop, she released

him. Breathing deeply, eyelids heavy, she licked her lips. "I liked that."

His eyes had adjusted and he could see her well enough to know she was every bit as stoked as he was. "I more than liked it." He decided to do the condom himself. Keeping his gaze locked with hers, he used his teeth to open the packet, then rolled it on. Even touching himself pushed his control.

"Stay on your back," she whispered, already climbing over him. "I like being able to see so much of you."

So her eyes had adjusted, as well? "No complaints from me." He held her waist as she positioned herself, rubbing her wet heat against him—before sliding down, taking all of him, in one steady move.

Christ, she was wet. And so hot. They both groaned.

Everything became fast and furious at that point.

Star had strong legs and she rode him hard, moving how she wanted, needed. With her hands braced on his biceps, he couldn't touch her as much as he'd like, but her breasts were right there, bouncing with each hard thrust, each roll of her hips. Her fingertips dug into him, and she tipped her head back on a low, throaty cry.

Lifting into her, Cade kept up the rhythm until she slumped forward, replete enough that she forgot about his wound and collapsed against him. Hell, he barely felt it with so much sensation pulsing in his erection.

Holding her hips tight to his, he easily rolled her to her back and hammered out his own mind-blowing release. Damn, she pleased him. Wrung him out, too.

In no hurry to move, he relaxed over her.

Long minutes passed like that, him resting on her warm, giving body, her sprawled legs around him.

Her choppy breathing had evened out, her thundering heartbeat slowed, and she lazily toyed with the hair at the back of his neck.

Soft and warm, she complained, "You ruined my plans."

Smiling, Cade lifted up to see her. And yeah, he felt it in his chest, around the bruised wound. But hell, it had totally been worth it. "How's that?"

"I didn't want you to exert yourself." She kissed his shoulder. "How are you? Okay?"

"Actually, I feel terrific." Tired, but also oddly satisfied. He turned to his back to take the pressure off his collarbone but gathered her close to his side.

To his surprise, she got out of the bed. "Hey." Catching her hand, he asked, "Where are you going?"

"I want to take care of you. Don't budge."

She pulled free, warning, "I mean it," before disappearing into the bathroom.

The sounds of running water reached him. Then she stepped from the bathroom, beautifully naked, not in the least shy. Because she left on the bathroom light, he saw that she held a tissue box and a damp cloth.

As she reached the bed, she said, "I'm getting rid of the condom and washing you."

What? Cade started to sit up, but she already had hold of his now flaccid dick. Leave it to Star to do something totally different. With every other woman, he'd had the honor of cleanup. Choking on an odd mix of embarrassment and tenderness, he said, "You don't need to—"

"Shush." She dropped the spent rubber into a tissue and then smoothed the damp rag over him. He twitched.

So maybe he wasn't so spent after all. How could he be when she concentrated on him like that?

Grinning, she glanced up at his face. "This is all so interesting."

"This, meaning my junk?"

"Yeah." Leaning forward, she pressed another kiss to him, then said, "Be right back," and strode off again, all sassy and without a care.

Of course, Cade watched her. She had *such* a fine ass.

He didn't know how he'd gotten so lucky, but

he knew she was worth fighting for, whether that meant fighting his family, fighting traffickers or fighting the lady herself.

Everyone looked up the second they stepped into the breakfast room. Surprised, Cade realized they'd kept them waiting. From the stove, where Bernard had been keeping the dishes warm, he began serving.

Star had assumed they'd eat in the kitchen again, but Cade explained that wasn't the norm, just something that seemed to happen during unusual occurrences.

The breakfast room was large and airy with windows that faced the mountains and the man-made lake below. There was no end of incredible views in his father's home.

Sipping from his coffee, Reyes glanced up, caught Star yawning and lifted a taunting brow. "Cade didn't let you sleep, huh?"

"Don't start," Cade ordered, unsure how she'd react. This morning she dragged a little, and yes, she kept yawning, but then, they'd had a trying day yesterday, and a satisfying night . . . that hadn't allowed for much sleep.

Today, he felt the activity in his collarbone but he wouldn't complain. No way did he want Star having any regrets, not when it was his own fault for waking her once in the middle of the night by nibbling on her shoulder. He hadn't been able to resist, but then, she'd come awake with her own intentions, completely on board in a nanosecond.

"What?" Reyes asked with mock innocence. "She looks . . . exhausted."

Taking a seat across from Reyes, Star picked up the silver knife at her place setting and studied it quietly. When she glanced at Reyes, Cade had to stifle a grin. He knew exactly what she was thinking.

Even sluggish, Star didn't disappoint, saying to his brother, "On top of all your other skills, are you good at dodging knives?"

Smile banked, Reyes sat back. "Depends. You planning to use it up close or throw it?"

"I'm thinking . . . throw it."

Reyes's amusement grew. "It's not really a throwing knife."

And, Cade recalled, Star had said she kept her knife for close contact.

"True," she agreed, placing the knife beside her plate—and reaching to the small of her back, where she kept a real blade strapped in a clip-on holster. She lifted it for Reyes to see and asked sweetly, "What about this one?"

Bursting out a big laugh, Reyes said, "Should I be ducking?"

"Not right now." She returned the lethal weapon to the sheath. "If I decide you deserve it, I'll wait until you least expect it."

Grinning ear to ear, Reyes flagged his napkin in

the air. "Then maybe I should call a truce. What do you think?"

"If you stop needling me . . . maybe."

Bernard handed her a glass of orange juice. "A hearty breakfast will improve dispositions all around."

Star inhaled the scents of breakfast meats, scrambled eggs, muffins and potatoes. "It certainly smells good enough to cause miracles."

Laughing, Madison loaded her plate. "This is fun, isn't it?"

That earned her a quelling frown from Parrish. "We have plans to make."

"I know, but usually we're all deadpan other than Reyes and Cade sniping at each other." She turned her smile on Star. "You're shaking things up, and I, for one, love it."

Bernard set fresh-cut fruit on the table. "I, as well."

Everyone looked at Reyes, but with one hand he just waved his napkin again while forking two sausage links with the other.

The ease with which Star dealt with his more bothersome sibling amazed Cade. Reyes didn't warm up to many people. Most never really knew him. He excelled at showing only what he wanted others to see, but with Star, he'd relaxed and opened up.

That may or may not be a good thing, considering Reyes's brand of humor could wear thin quickly, but so far Star didn't seem bothered.

Putting a hand to her back between her shoulder blades, Cade stroked her. He loved touching her, and he enjoyed the way she got up on his brother, how she didn't let Parrish intimidate her.

The urge to kiss her again nearly had him skipping breakfast, except that she was obviously hungry.

Parrish gave him a frown, making it clear he didn't condone the familiarity. Too bad. With Star near, keeping his hands to himself wasn't possible. Smiling, he let his father know what he could do with his judgment.

While helping himself to a slice of cantaloupe, Parrish said, "I assume Adela called you from an unlisted number."

"You assume correctly," Star said. "She's been very cagey about any details. It took some coaxing—or she wanted me to think I had to coax her—just to get a location on where to meet."

"She doesn't live in Coalville," Madison said. "I already checked. My guess would be that she's in another area altogether, that she chose Coalville because, one, it'd be easy to set a trap. Two, not many witnesses, since the town is so tiny. And three, it gave quick access to I-25, meaning she could make a hasty exit once she had you under wraps."

"Any idea why she wants you?" Reyes asked.

"I don't know her." Star shrugged while dishing up a bite of fresh pineapple. "I assume it's Mattox who wants me, and he's either forcing her to help, or she's a willing accomplice."

That careless attitude rubbed Cade the wrong way. "It occurs to me that you're in more danger now."

Brows lifting, Star asked, "How do you figure that?"

"They probably don't know where you live, but they do know that you frequent the bar. It'd be easy enough to ask around there and find out about your truck. You travel that way often. Some of the roads are long, lonely stretches."

"Perfect to shanghai me? You could be right." Star sipped her juice. "But you're in the same shape, right?"

Cade conceded the point. "If anyone at that church recognized me, then yes, they'll trace me back to the bar."

"And you travel back and forth, too," Madison pointed out.

Yes, and Cade hoped they'd come after him instead of Star. He could handle himself, but if they overwhelmed her . . .

No, he wouldn't consider the possibility of her being taken again. He'd kill them all before he let that happen.

Parrish held silent, watching, listening, allowing them to work it out. It was his way—not that he hesitated to interject whenever he chose to, but he considered discussion a learning opportunity. That he didn't object over Star's participation in what would normally be a family matter meant that he trusted Star, at least in part.

"Your trucking business is an issue," Reyes said. "It's too hard to monitor you if you go far."

Cade waited for her reaction to being monitored, but she skipped right past that.

"Thing is, it gives me legitimacy for what I do. No one questions a truck at a truck stop, right? And I have a reason to repeatedly hit the east-west expressway where long-haul trucks pass through."

Chiming in, Madison said, "That's why that area is ideal for human trafficking."

Glancing around the table, Star asked, "So you guys set up a bar and a gym for legit businesses, huh? Makes sense. I imagine both of you hear all the nitty-gritty, right?"

Reyes didn't answer, so Cade said, "That's the idea."

"You've rescued a lot of women?"

"Quite a few, yes." Parrish fidgeted with his napkin, then crumpled it in his fist. He asked Cade, "You completely trust her?"

Shocked, Cade knew exactly what his father was ready to do. It was unheard of, yet they'd all seen how concerned she'd been for him. And

Reyes had probably explained to Parrish just how hard Star had fought against those men trying to take her. Anyone could tell she had the right edge, a sharp intuition and a core strength that couldn't be faked.

Aware of Star looking at him, wanting clarification for what was happening, he nodded. "Yes, I do."

Bernard quickly pulled up a chair, expectant anticipation in his eyes as he took in each person at the table.

"Whoa," Star said, growing wary as tension thickened the air. "You're not planning to put me through a blood rite or anything, are you?"

Clasping her thigh beneath the table, Cade said, "I believe my dad is ready to tell you more about the task force he funds."

"A task force? No kidding?" Fascinated, Star folded her arms on the table. "That sounds pretty awesome."

"It is," Madison enthused. "It's at the heart of everything we do."

"But we keep our involvement quiet," Parrish explained. "It's always best to avoid obvious links to your private life."

"Probably easier to do if you have a lot of dough, right?"

"Yes," he allowed. "Wealth has its advantages."

"Benevolence being one of them?"

Parrish gave a slight nod.

Since no one else was jumping in to explain, Cade did the honors. "The task force is possible because of Dad's funds. It ensures victims get counseling, plus legal representation when needed."

Bernard took over. It wasn't often he got to brag on Parrish. "They also get financial assistance to start over, and guidance so that all legal avenues are used to convict the ones responsible."

"We make sure we have it all zipped up," Reyes said. "Dates, names, addresses, witnesses—the whole shebang."

"Wow." Impressed, Star asked, "I take it that's for the perps who don't die in the process?"

Bernard put his nose in the air. "There are, necessarily, a few who do."

She grinned at the way he said that with proper gravity. "You won't see me crying about it. I'd wipe them all out if I could."

"But you're just one woman," Reyes pointed out. "Unless you join us."

Eyes flaring, Star blinked at Reyes. Her gaze shifted to Parrish and Bernard, then to Madison, before she slowly pivoted to face Cade. "Is that a joke?"

"No." Cade squeezed her knee. "It'd be safer for you, and you'd have more effect."

As if they couldn't hear her, she leaned closer. "But I work alone."

"You work with me."

"Just that once!"

Cade considered her attitude, but he couldn't convince her here with his family all riveted. "I think maybe we need to talk privately. Are you done eating?"

"What? Oh, yeah." Standing, she picked up her plate and started for the kitchen.

"I'll do that." Bernard rushed around the table.

She kept going. So did Bernard.

Madison fretted. "She needs a minute, doesn't she?"

"She's been alone a very long time," Cade explained. He'd sway her, but he didn't delude himself that it'd be easy. Star was one of the most independent people he'd ever met, and with good reason, she didn't trust easily. Yes, she'd taken to him fast enough, once he'd introduced the idea, but he was one person, not a family unit.

And his family . . . Cade glanced at each of them. His father had initiated this, but he still didn't speak up. Cade pushed back his chair. "I'll convince her."

"I hope so." Rubbing his mouth, Reyes stated the obvious. "It's going to be a problem if she wants to walk away at this point."

"She won't." Cade picked up his own plate and went after her.

He stalled when he didn't find her in the kitchen, but Bernard said, "She went out the side door to the deck," as he took the plate from

Cade. "I had to wrestle the dishes from her. She's a very determined young lady, and she was most insistent that she 'pull her own weight,' even though I explained that this is part of *my* job." He made a rude sound. "But she's wonderful and I like her—as long as she understands the parameters of my domain."

Sounded about right. "I'll talk to her," he promised again and almost laughed. He had a growing list of things that required his skill at convincing. Usually not a daunting task, but with Star? She could be very bullheaded.

She wasn't in back, which would have put her in line with the windows where his family dined. Instead she'd taken up a corner of the wraparound deck, facing the side yard with tree-covered hills.

The second he stepped out behind her, she said, "Don't start," without turning to face him.

"Come on."

That got her attention. She glanced back with suspicion. "Where are we going?"

"I thought we'd take the trail down to the lake. One day we can fish there, if you'd like. Or take out kayaks. It's a private lake, so pretty damn peaceful."

Bracing her back on the railing, she smiled at him. "That sounds nice."

"Today, we'll just walk." And talk. He held out his hand.

She didn't take it right away. "Are we going to

have a fight? You want to get me alone so your family won't hear me yelling?"

So damn astute. He snagged her hand and pulled her forward into his arms. "I want you alone so you can speak freely."

She snuggled close. "Wasn't I already doing that?"

He couldn't help but laugh. "Do you need to be a hard-ass to the bitter end?" Pressing a kiss to the top of her head, he suggested, "Meet me halfway here, okay?"

"You're right," she said, surprising him. "Sorry."

Disbelief had him levering her back. "Do you ever say the expected?"

Her mouth opened, then snapped closed as she gave it thought. "I have no idea what the expected might be, so I don't know if I do or not. Other than brief exchanges with clients who want to hire me to carry a load, or when shopping or requesting food, I don't really have conversations with anyone."

"What about the women you've helped?"

Uncertainty darkened her eyes. "More like a question-and-answer deal. Like if they had a specific place to go, if they wanted cops involved or not, or if they needed a trip to the ER. Stuff like that."

He imagined she was a lot more compassionate than she made it sound, but he got her point.

"Come on. We'll go this way." With her smaller hand held securely in his, Cade tugged her to the spiral stairs that led down to the lawn. From there they circled around for the worn footpath to the lake.

"It's a long walk?" she asked.

Depended on the perspective. "It'll take us ten or fifteen minutes to get down there, but with a lot of nature to see along the way."

"I wasn't complaining, just curious." Tipping her head back, she peered up at the bright blue sky. "It smells different here."

"Fresh," he agreed. "All the trees and earth and the scents from the mountain . . ."

Smiling, she bumped him with her hip. "You love it here, don't you?"

"The land, yeah. Who wouldn't? There's something about being surrounded by the mountains, all the peace and quiet, immersed in nature. The scrub oak brush is something to see in the fall." Would he be able to show her? He hoped so, and that brought him around to the reason for their walk. "It was a huge concession for Dad to include you."

"I figured." Distracted by a boulder, she said, "Look at the size of that rock," and proceeded to climb atop it.

As agile as a mountain goat, she clambered up to the highest spot about six feet off the ground, then spread her arms wide. Cade moved around to the side of the boulder so he could catch her if she fell.

"I declare myself king of the mountain."

God, he loved seeing her like this. Playful. Relaxed. Mostly unguarded. "You might have to take that up with Bernard, since he claims he holds that title."

Laughter bubbled out. "No way! Stuffy Bernard does? Are you pulling my leg?"

"He loves it here, says it calls to his soul."

"I can believe it." She inhaled deeply. "It's awesome, for sure." Putting her head back and closing her eyes, she breathed deeply, but then abruptly looked down at him again. "What's up with Bernard? Does he live here? He's like a butler, right?"

"He and Dad have been best friends a long time, back before Reyes and Madison were born. As Dad's wealth grew, Bernard came along, working various jobs, though Dad swears he wasn't helping Bernard, that Bernard made his life easier because he could trust him. He moved in after Marian died—"

"Marian was his love? Mom to Reyes and Madison?"

Cade nodded. "Dad was a mess, and he was so consumed with grief, Bernard picked up the slack where he could. He loves to cook, though, and he's an organizational whiz, so that's mostly what he does."

"Huh. So he's part of the family?"

"Very much so." Tired of the distanced chatting, Cade held out his arms. "Jump."

"Ha! Not on your life." She looked around for an easy way down.

Cade knew she'd find that getting down was the hard part. "Chicken."

Her gaze clashed with his. "Take that back or I might just launch at you, and we both know I'm not a lightweight."

Cade mimicked her "Ha!" and left his arms up for her. No, she wasn't a delicate woman, but compared to him, she was still very female, smaller boned, curvy where he was straight, soft where he was hard. She needed to stop under-estimating his strength. "Trust me."

Her brows pinched together. "Have you forgotten you were injured?"

No, but he wished she would. "I'm fine." If he said it often enough, maybe she'd finally believe him.

Softer, with worry, she explained, "I don't want to hurt you."

"I promise you won't." He waited and knew the second she planned to prove him wrong. Using her strong legs to propel her forward, she did indeed launch at him.

He was grinning before she landed against his chest and was grinning still as he swung her around, going with the momentum until they stopped, body to body, her feet off the ground. Yes, that impact jarred him, but the pain was minimal and the reward made it worthwhile when she fit him so perfectly.

Not just physically, but in so many other ways, too.

Against her lips, he whispered, "Told you so."

Her laughter made it tough to kiss her, but he persisted until she slumped against him, her arms tight around his neck, her mouth open, her tongue greeting his.

It would be so easy to get carried away, but he didn't think she wanted to get naked on the mountainside. Plus, yeah, he wouldn't put it past his brother to break out the binoculars.

When Cade moved to kiss her throat, she whispered, "You are a certified stud."

"Don't forget it."

She laughed a little too hard over that, so he set her down and again got them walking toward the lake. It was ten minutes of peaceful quiet before they reached the edge of the water.

They had a dozen things to discuss, but Star's awe kept him quiet. Her eyes went soft and wide as she took in the reflection of junipers and fluffy clouds on the placid surface of the lake.

This early in the day, you could see to the rocky bottom. Rough boulders bordered one whole side of the large lake, with thick evergreens behind that. It was only this section that offered easy access to the water. Cleared per his father's instructions, a pebble-covered shoreline made it easy to fish.

Random wildflowers grew from between rocks, drawing hummingbirds that flitted here and there. Overhead, red-tailed hawks soared.

Silently, Star went to the water's edge and reached down to trail her fingers over the glassy surface, sending ripples to feather out. "Do you ever swim?"

"The water is always freezing."

She glanced back. "Is that a yes or no?"

"I have, yes. So has Reyes."

"But Madison has more sense?"

He grinned. "A nice way to put it."

"Women don't feel the need to prove things the way guys do."

"Oh, really?" He climbed up to sit on a flat sun-warmed rock, his arms resting over one bent leg as he stared out at the lake. "So that wasn't you who felt it necessary to challenge my brother?"

Joining him, she accepted the hand he offered to help her up. "Totally different," she said as she got settled. "Your brother needs to be knocked down a peg or two."

"I do that on a regular basis."

Leaning against him, she said, "I can't challenge your dad."

"No?" Cade had been wondering how to bring it up, but he should have known Star would beat him to it. She wasn't one to shy away—from a subject, danger or anything else. "Why not?"

Her shoulder lifted. "He's your dad. I don't know what to do with dads, but I do know I won't like being under his thumb. He's a dictator, isn't he?" Wrinkling her nose, she specified, "Super bossy, I bet. And if I go along with this whole . . . alliance, he'll expect me to toe the line. But that's not me."

As Reyes had said, there wasn't much choice at this point. That was Cade's doing. He'd brought her here, forcing the issue and putting his father in an untenable position.

But he didn't regret it.

After drawing her between his legs so he could wrap his arms around her, Cade propped his chin on top of her head. He relished the light breeze that blew over his face, and the way she rested her hands over his forearms. "You think I toe the line, babe?"

A sudden stillness settled over her. "Did I insult you?"

A little late for her to worry about that now, but he didn't want her to change, not when he already admired so much about her. "I butt heads with my dad plenty often enough."

"So how do you deal with him?"

"By listening when what he says makes sense." Which, much as it annoyed Cade, was most of the time. "When I disagree, I say so."

"Does he ever listen to you?"

Only when Cade wouldn't relent, but he didn't want to scare her off. "How about we put it this way—if you work with us, what's the worst that could happen?"

"I could lose my cool and . . ."

"What?"

"I don't know. I might make an ass of myself."

That candid confession had him barking a laugh, which had her turning on him. He kissed her before she could blast him.

"So what?" She looked like such a thundercloud that he kissed her again. "You're allowed to be human, honey. I am. Reyes and Madison are. My dad . . . well, he's more distant, very driven, but he's not bad. You *can* deal with him." One more kiss, this time teasing. "You know the best things that could happen? You'd be safer—and I'd know you were safer, so I wouldn't worry about you. You'd be able to help a lot more women."

"In more meaningful ways."

"Not what I said. I'm sure for any woman you've helped, it made a life-altering difference."

She stared out over the lake. "You think I can do this?"

Insecurity? From Sterling Parson? He hugged her. "I have faith in you."

Her scowl hadn't lightened up, but she grudgingly said, "Okay—on a trial basis."

That wouldn't do, but for now he'd accept it.

If nothing else, it'd give him time to talk her around.

And then what?

He didn't know for sure, but she fit so well into his life, he wasn't ready to let her go. Not today, not next week.

Not for the foreseeable future.

CHAPTER THIRTEEN

Cade would have been happier if he could have convinced Star to stay at his father's house, but he'd known that wouldn't happen, not without him there, and he had to go to work.

At least he'd talked her into coming to the bar with him instead of going to the apartment alone. Nothing unusual in her being at the bar. During deliveries, she'd often stopped in and stayed for hours. He doubted anyone would pay any attention.

She'd had to turn down two jobs for now, but for how long would she do that? If Adela didn't call back, then what?

He'd go after her, that's what. One way or another, this had to end. It was the only way to be fair to Star.

Tonight they'd go back to his father's—he'd used the excuse of Parrish checking his wound in the morning—but after that? Star made her own decisions, and she wasn't big on concessions. But then, she was also smart and she'd understand the need for extra security until Mattox was locked up or dead.

"I should check on my truck tomorrow. I never leave it to sit this long."

"We can do that, no problem." Cade pulled in

to the parking lot of the Tipsy Wolverine. His tendency was to park around the back and go in through that door, so when they left, it was likely no one would notice that they were together.

"Now that we're a thing . . ." She let that hang out there for a bit before continuing, maybe waiting for him to object.

Of course he didn't. Putting his SUV in Park, he asked, "What?"

Relief brought a brief smile to her mouth. "How did you come up with the name of this place?"

"Don't put that on me." He turned off the car. "The name was already on it when Dad bought the place. I came out of the military and got dropped into the Tipsy Wolverine practically in the same week." Pretty sure his dad had wanted to lock him down while he had the opportunity. "The name was already known, and I don't really care, so I never bothered to change it."

"What a disappointing answer." She opened her seat belt. "I was all set for a good story."

Laughing, Cade got out and started around to her side of the SUV. She didn't often let him open her door for her, but the instinct was there anyway.

Luckily he had amazing peripheral vision. He caught the rush of movement and automatically reacted, turning and kicking out at the same time.

He caught the tallest guy in the knee, watched it buckle awkwardly, but didn't have time to follow up as two more men charged him.

Dodging a short pipe aimed at his head, he buried a heavy fist into that fool's gut, followed by a head-snapping pop to the chin.

Something broke over Cade's back, almost taking him down as he staggered forward, but he caught himself and spun with another kick. He missed the man's face and only hit his shoulder. It was still effective enough to knock the guy on his ass, only he didn't stay down.

With only a quick glimpse, Cade realized all three men were young, probably no older than midtwenties. Had Mattox run out of muscle, or did he consider these boys expendable?

Willing Star to lock the car doors, he concentrated on ending the attack quickly.

They were definitely injured, but other than the one with a busted knee, they weren't yet out of the fight.

Handling that swiftly, Cade grabbed one by the throat, lifted and slammed him hard to the ground. Stunned, the breath knocked out of him, he didn't fight as Cade flipped him over to pin him down with a knee pressed between his shoulder blades. The rough gravel would cut into his face.

No more than he deserved.

The third fellow thought that'd be a good time to press his advantage, but Cade was using only one knee on the guy he held down, leaving both arms and a foot free.

"You're a dead man," the third guy said, then dived at him.

Cade flipped him, too—did they not learn? In a finishing blow, Cade punched him in the nuts.

An inhuman sound squeaked out of his gaping mouth, and pain curled him tight.

"Someone better start answering questions fast," Cade said. He got to his feet, pulled up the guy he'd been holding down and slammed his face into the wall of the bar. He crumpled backward without a sound.

Gaze locked on the goon with the badly mangled knee, Cade smiled. "Looks like you're it." Knowing the man he'd just nutted wouldn't function again anytime soon, he started forward.

The guy tried to crawl back but couldn't get more than a few inches before Cade hauled him up with a fist in his hair. "I'm going to ask questions, and you're going to give me answers. Got it?"

Face contorted in pain, he gasped, "Yeah, man, let up."

"Name."

"My name?" he asked, confused.

Tightening his hold, Cade lightly kicked his knee, earning a groan. "I'm only asking each question once."

"Right, yeah. I'm Paulie Wells."

"And the other two?"

"Brothers."

The one with crushed gonads growled, "Shut up, Paulie."

"You want another?" Cade asked him.

Wincing at the threat, he curled tighter to protect his jewels.

"That's . . . that's Ward Manton. You knocked out his bro, Kelly."

Cade dug a hand into Paulie's pocket and found a wallet but no cell phone. He checked for ID, saw Paulie had told the truth, then searched him for weapons before letting him fall into a whimpering heap.

He turned to Ward. "You like wielding pipes, my man?" Cade strode over to where it had fallen and picked it up, hefting it in his hand.

Ward amused him by looking both defiant and terrorized. "Just business, dude. Nothin' personal, I swear."

"Whose business is it?"

Shifty eyes darted around. "We, ah, we were just robbin' you, that's all. It's cool."

Cade spun the pipe in his hand, then rested it against Ward's temple. "That's your one and only lie. Tell me another and you won't be able to talk for a very long time." He paused to tell Paulie, "If you don't sit your ass down, I'll break the other knee."

Paulie promptly stopped looking for an avenue of escape and instead put both hands to his head, his expression lost.

Back to Ward, Cade tapped the pipe none too gently to his temple. "Do we understand each other?"

He heard *"Euewww"* and glanced back to see Star standing behind the open car door watching. Damn it, he would have preferred she stay hidden.

But of course, she did the opposite and stepped out. "If you're going to splatter what little brains he has, will you warn me first? I'd rather look away."

"Better yet," Cade said calmly, "why don't you get back in the car and—"

"Nope." She sauntered forward. "I'm not missing all the fun. In fact, I'll check this one while you do your brain splattering."

Ward eyed her warily, his gaze going from his still-unconscious brother to Star, then to Cade.

Kneeling down by Kelly, Star efficiently went through his pockets, tossing out a wallet, then a knife, brass knuckles and nylon hand ties. "Looks like they had a party planned." With the small collection in front of her, a look of icy rage on her face, Star said, "Maybe I want to watch you cave in his skull after all."

Kelly groaned, and without a blink, Star brought her elbow hard to his temple, knocking him out again. To Ward, she said, "You better start talking fast or neither of you will have any brains left."

Cade wasn't happy with her interference—the less low-life thugs knew about her, the better. Couldn't tell her that right now, though, not with their audience.

Glaring down at Ward, he whispered with tight control, "Were the brass knuckles for her or me?"

Properly terrified, Ward stammered, "For . . . for you, dude. You're big. We weren't gonna hurt her none. Mattox wants her in one piece."

"That answer is the only thing saving your ass." Cade shoved him over to his face. "Give me the cuffs."

Star lifted a brow at the order, then shrugged and carried everything to him. While he bound Ward's hands, she slipped on the brass knuckles. "I like these." Her feral gaze dropped to Ward. "Let's see how well they work."

Cade had to jump up to keep her from breaking Ward's jaw. Quietly wrestling her into submission, he said, "Not now. I have more questions for them."

"He was going to use these on *you*," she practically yelled in his face, the brass-enhanced fist almost touching his chin.

"Was never going to happen. They're children. You can see that."

"What I see is that they're a bunch of cowardly goons." She kicked past Cade's restraint, landing that steel-toed boot to Ward's shin.

Howling, Ward tried to scuttle away from her.

Fighting amusement as well as frustration, Cade urged her back more. "Hey," he whispered, "you're giving away too much. No need for them to know you care."

Nostrils flaring and expression red with antagonism, she said, "Well, I *do*."

Cade couldn't help it. He laughed. Leave it to Star to growl that declaration at him with murder in her eyes during a violent altercation. "Good to know."

She blinked, then shoved away from him. "You have a warped sense of humor."

"Maybe." He put his mouth to her ear so the downed goons wouldn't hear. "Now get it together, *Francis*."

It took her a second. Then she gave a stiff nod. Just as low, she said, "I want credit for letting you handle things."

His eyes flared.

Unconcerned, she pointed out, "I didn't jump to your defense right off since I saw you had it handled. You can thank me."

"Thank you."

She nodded and moved on. "No phones?"

"Let me check Ward. I have a feeling he's the head of this comic trio." Sure enough, once he'd roughly gone through Ward's pockets, he found an old burner phone, a slip of paper with the bar's name scrawled on it and a nearly empty wallet.

There were only three numbers saved in the

phone, none with contact info. He toed Ward with his boot. "Who's going to answer if I call these numbers?"

"Those two," Ward said, giving a slight nod toward his brother and Paulie. He didn't have much range of motion with his face in the gravel.

"And the third?"

Ward's face tightened.

"Need some incentive?" Cade asked. "I suppose I could turn her loose on you. Let her bloody up your face a bit, but I should warn you, she's damn strong and has a solid punch—"

"Mattox," he snapped. "It goes to Mattox." Then in a whine, "Dude, he's going to kill us."

"Mattox is the least of your worries right now." Cade wanted to ask about Adela, but the bar would open soon and customers would start showing up. He still had to clean up this mess. Besides, the clowns on the ground around him didn't look like the type to have any real info.

"What are we going to do with them?" Before he could answer, Star said, "FYI, I called for backup. Should be here any minute."

Renewed anger rushed through Cade. He said one word. "Who?" If she'd called the cops, that'd be a huge problem.

Cocking her head, she listened, then looked out at the road. "That's probably him now. Yup, it is."

Reyes pulled up and without a word joined them, his gaze going over each man. "From Mattox?"

"Yeah." Relieved that Star hadn't brought authorities in on things, Cade still said, "I could have handled it."

"Women," Reyes commiserated, just to rile her. "Guess she was worried about you."

And of course it worked. Star gave him a killing glare. "I still have my knife."

Hands in his back pockets, Reyes pursed his mouth, then shifted his gaze to Cade. "Gunning for her?"

"It's what they said."

Star jammed her fist at Reyes, showing off the brass knuckles. "They were going to use these on him."

His mouth twitched. "Pisses you off, huh? Well, no worries, doll. I'll handle them."

Her eyes narrowed. "By *handle them,* you better mean beating them to a bloody pulp!"

"If that's what it takes," Reyes promised, taking a pack of nylon cuffs from his pocket.

Snorting, Star said, "You're a little overprepared, aren't you?"

Shrugging, Reyes said, "You were all hysterical—"

"I was not!"

"So I thought there might be a mob or something." He grinned at her blustering indignation. "Now, why don't you wait in the bar? I'll handle this."

"Ugh." Face flushed, she snatched ties from

him and stomped over to Kelly to deftly bind his hands behind his back. It roused him, but Star was already working on his ankles, pushing up his jeans, dragging down his socks so the nylon was tight against his skin. He wasn't going anywhere.

"Ward?" Kelly struggled, twisting his head to try to see his brother. "What's going on?"

"We're done," Ward groaned. "Done."

"So much drama." Reyes was quick, and a little brutal, in how he bound Ward. Then he quickly gagged all three of them. Hoisting Ward over his shoulder, Reyes carried him to his truck and dumped him in the bed none too gently.

It took a little time to get them secured to grommets and concealed with a tonneau cover. It was a tight fit in the short bed, but bound and gagged as they were, no one would discover them.

Appearing a little worried, Star asked, "Where are you taking them?"

"Someplace private, where I can do a proper interrogation."

She bit her lip. "Will you kill them?"

Reyes slowly grinned. "Now you're worried about that? Just minutes ago you wanted them annihilated."

"Forget it." She started to stomp away.

Reyes caught her arm—then shocked her by pulling her into a hug. "Rest easy, hon. Once

I've found out what I can, I'll hand them over to someone else."

"Who?"

Arms folded, Cade leaned back against the truck and explained, "We have contacts who'll make sure they're off the street and that they're legally punished for their part in Mattox's plans." Interesting that Star allowed Reyes to hold her. Was it possible she didn't dislike his brother as much as she pretended? If they got along, it'd make things easier.

For Star.

"They won't die, though," Reyes assured her.

Shoulders relaxing, she glanced at Cade. "You said it yourself, they're boys. If anyone's going to die, I'd rather it be Mattox."

With another hug, Reyes said softly, "I'm glad you're not quite as bloodthirsty as you pretend." Not giving her a chance to blow up on him, he released her and headed around to the driver's side.

Cade put a hand to Star's back and together they followed. Lower, so the men wouldn't hear, he said to Reyes, "I took a cheap phone off one of them. I'll give you time to get well away from here before I call the three numbers."

"If you call now," Star mused, piecing it together, "they might realize their plan backfired. They could set a trap to attack—"

"Me on the road," Reyes finished. "I'd almost

like them to try." He looked back at the truck bed. "That is, if I didn't have cargo."

Nodding, Cade explained what he'd learned from Ward. "I think he's telling the truth about those numbers, that one will lead to Mattox, but I'll let you know."

Reyes nodded at Star's hand. "Plan to keep that little decoration?"

She curled her fingers around the thick brass knuckles. "Yup."

Shaking his head in a laughing way, Reyes got in the truck and drove off.

"Come on." Cade drew Star around to the bar door. He wanted her safe inside before he got more distracted with details. "We'll give it fifteen minutes so Reyes is off the worst of the winding roads. Then we'll call."

"We?" she repeated, as he relocked the door behind him. Strolling to a barstool, she took a seat, her long legs stretched out, one elbow resting on the counter.

She looked sexy as hell sitting there. Part of it was that she took the attack in stride. Star was unlike most people; she didn't fall apart under pressure, and in fact seemed to gain an edge.

Except when she'd lost it a little over those brass knuckles. He didn't want her worried about him, but he also enjoyed the show of concern.

Sidetracked for a moment, he asked, "What did you say to Reyes when you called him?"

Rolling her eyes, she gave a soft laugh. "He's a damn doofus—and a giant liar. I was *not* hysterical. Can you even imagine?"

No, he couldn't.

"I gave him the facts—maybe I gave them a little quickly, you know? I told him we'd pulled up to the bar and three guys tried to jump you."

"Just like that, huh?"

"Mostly like that. But yeah, I didn't know if there was a fourth or fifth around somewhere, or if Mattox was hiding nearby with a gun. So I told your brother to get his butt over there in case the tide turned." She rolled a shoulder. "Didn't take me long to realize you had it under control—which is kind of astounding, I have to say. Wimpy guys or not, it was three to one, with a pipe and a chunk of wood, but in no time, you had it all well in hand."

So it was a chunk of wood they'd broken over his back? He hadn't been sure. In the long run, it hadn't mattered. "Appreciate the vote of confidence." He went behind the bar to start prepping. Workers would show up shortly. They wouldn't have long alone.

"It's earned." She turned on the stool to keep him in her sights. "So the number we're going to call?"

"I assumed you'd want to be a part of it."

"Part of it? You do realize I'm the one who should call, right? I mean, in case Adela answers.

She'd hang up on you, but there's a chance she'll talk to me. And if she does, she might give something away. I might even be able to goad her into losing her pretense of being a victim. It's worth a shot."

Actually . . . "You're right." After he finished the bar prep, he checked the time, poured them each a cola over ice and set the cell phone on the counter between them. "On speaker."

"You betcha." Almost rubbing her hands together, she opened the screen, went to the first number and pressed to dial it.

"If any employees show up early, we can step into the office."

"Got it." With Cade leaning close, Sterling listened as the phone rang and rang . . . No answer.

"One down," she said, aware that her palms were a little sweaty. "Probably went to his brother or Paulie, as Ward said."

Cade lifted her chin. "You have great instinct, babe. I've told you that enough times. If anyone answers, just go with your gut. You've got this."

His confidence helped shore up her own. Yes, she could do this. If it was Adela, she'd play her part depending on what the other woman said or did.

Drawing a breath, Sterling moved on to the next number. Each ring caused her tension to notch up.

Again, no answer. Crazy that this was making her so nervous. They were away from the danger for now, and even better, she had the dynamic McKenzie family as backup. Whatever rolled out, it'd be fine.

But she knew, of course. Her frazzled nerves were based directly on one particular McKenzie. A specimen of the first order, impossibly strong, remarkably fast, unshakable and . . . He hadn't denied that they were "a thing." That made the risk about more than just her, because now it was about *them*.

That made it so much worse.

She'd already discovered firsthand that seeing him hurt sent her into a tailspin.

"Two strikes," Cade said, and he brushed his thumb over her cheek. "Third has to be a charm."

Sterling nodded and pressed the last button.

Immediately following the first ring, a deep voice growled, "Tell me you have her."

Ah. Mattox. Amazingly enough, her nervousness left and she settled in with a smile. This she could handle—as Cade predicted, her instincts kicked in with a vengeance.

"Hello, Mattox."

Silence, then a snarled, "You fucking bitch."

Sterling actually laughed. "What? You figured I'd be stuffed in a trunk by now or something?" That thought struck her, and she glanced up at Cade to mouth, "Car?" How had those three hoodlums arrived at the bar? In the middle of the chaos, she hadn't even considered that.

Cade shook his head and whispered, "Later."

Unaware of her sudden distraction, Mattox said, "I thought I'd have my hands on you any minute. It would have been such a pleasure—for me."

"So those boys you sent after me were planning to meet you somewhere?" She sat up a little straighter, all teasing gone from her tone. "Tell me where and I'll come to you right now, you miserable pig."

"I don't think so," he said with a laugh. "I'll get you soon enough."

"Really? How do you think to do that? You must be running out of lackeys by now. How many have I already brought down?"

Mattox snorted. "I doubt you've done any real damage, sweetheart. More likely your hulking bodyguard—but he won't be around forever."

The thought of him getting hold of Cade sent a wash of ice through her veins. Cade wouldn't appreciate her fear, and Mattox would try to use it against her, so she purred, "Oh, please. Please, underestimate me. It'll make gutting you so much more satisfying."

Cade shook his head. Apparently he didn't want her goading Mattox quite that much, but hey, too late to pull back now.

"So where's Adela?" Sterling asked. "Is she

standing right there, listening to our conversation?"

"Is that what this is?" Mattox replied. "A conversation? I thought it was me telling you how fucking bad you're going to suffer before I cut your throat and watch you bleed out. You want to hear details?"

Aware of Cade's hands curling into fists, she said, "Not particularly."

Of course, that didn't stop Mattox. "I have plenty of men left—and they'll each get a turn with you. Might have to make them draw straws to see who goes last, because by the end there won't be much of you left."

Though her stomach turned, Sterling laughed. "That's a lot of bold talk for a dead man." She hesitated, but the timing felt right, so she added, "Especially since you tried handing me out once already, and all you got for your troubles was a corpse."

Like the ticking of a bomb, the tension stretched taut—until it detonated. *"You fucking whore!"* Mattox roared. "You're the one who got away!"

"Ding-ding-ding!" All pretense of calm shredded away as she got to her feet and smirked down at the phone. "I recognized you right off, big disgusting ape that you are. But you had no idea, did you?"

He snarled something low, but then snapped,

"That was years ago, when I was still starting out. After all this time, the meat starts to look the same."

God, she wished she could kill him right now.

Cade took her hand and held it. Strong, steady, sexy Cade. He was counting on her, and she wouldn't let him down.

When she didn't reply, Mattox asked, "Do you have any idea of the trouble you caused me?"

Ah, it bothered him that he hadn't made her lose her temper. Good. Sterling smiled. "The upside is that when you're dead, your troubles will be over."

"You think you're smart?"

"Smart enough to get to you when you least expect it. There's not a hole deep enough for you to crawl in, not enough men to watch your back, to keep you safe. You better sleep with one eye open, because the second they both close, I'll end you."

He hung up and Sterling wanted to pitch the phone. Instead she peeked at Cade and asked, "Did I go overboard?"

Eyes like the center of a flame and jaw clenched tight, he drew her forward to lean over the bar. "I will never let him touch you."

Wow. She hadn't even realized his temper had risen. He'd seemed so cool during the call. He tried to act cool now, too, but yeah, she saw all that fierce rage in his eyes. "Er . . . thanks?"

Not amused, he put his mouth to hers. And proceeded to devour her. Holy smokes, possessiveness had really gotten his engine revving.

To soothe him, Sterling stroked the side of his face.

He let up but kept her close, his forehead to hers. "Sorry."

"No worries. Kind of turned me on."

He looked into her eyes—and laughed. "There can't be another woman like you in the entire universe."

And just like that, he lightened her mood. Unfortunately, a knock at the back door interrupted them, and shortly they were joined by employees, and then customers, too.

They had a lot of plans to make. Mattox would be coming for her—or rather, he'd send more men after her. Odds were, he'd try to take out Cade first. Obviously Mattox knew Cade, maybe even recognized him from the church.

She bit her lip, thinking about that. It was time to follow through on that trap, and if it required using her as bait, Cade would just have to get over it.

Talking him around wouldn't be easy, but she figured Parrish, Reyes and Madison would agree. They'd vote on it or something, she'd win, and finally she'd get the chance for her revenge. Now that Mattox had crossed her path again, she had to end him or die trying.

Once that was done, what would happen with her and Cade? She didn't know. For now she'd have to take their relationship one day at a time.

She glanced over at Cade as he served two pretty women sitting at the bar. The women flirted, their expressions showing awe, but then, Cade was such a big dude he had that effect on a lot of people.

He smiled at them, but it was his patented polite smile, not the kind he gave to her—the kind full of secrets and shared lust and so much more.

Over the next few hours, in between customers, Cade used the phone. Each time he held her gaze while quietly talking.

Strangers came in, putting her on guard, but no one that acted suspicious. They drank, talked and left.

She was starting to think it'd be a quiet night, and she even considered dozing like old times.

And then the call from Adela came in.

CHAPTER FOURTEEN

"Francis?"

She blinked, for once unsure what to say. "Yeah . . . Adela?"

"Oh, God, I was so afraid you'd be dead." Voice shaking, Adela whispered, "I knew he was trying to get you, and I'm so sorry. I couldn't figure out how to warn you."

Sterling caught Cade's eye to let him know what was happening, but he was stuck in a crowd. It'd take him a few seconds to get away, so she moved out of the main room of the bar and into the hallway where she could better hear.

"Are you still there?" Adela asked frantically.

"Yeah. So . . ." What to say? "I'm surprised to hear from you."

"I'm sorry, Francis, but listen to me. He's hiring men. A *lot* of men. He said he knows where to find you."

Sterling really didn't trust the woman. Not that she ever had completely, but now? She accepted Reyes's take on things, yet the thinnest doubt remained. Having been in captivity once herself, Sterling understood better than some how you said and did things that normally you would never consider.

Doing those things had allowed her to escape.

They'd allowed her to survive.

Was Adela trying to escape—or trying to entrap her? Sterling didn't want to believe that another woman would be so cruel, but too many things didn't add up. "How do you know all that?"

"I don't have much time. He'll be back in a minute, but I was able to listen through the door. He's . . . *enraged*. Francis, God, the things he's planning to do to you . . ." She started to cry.

Damn it, that sounded real enough.

"It's all my fault," Adela sobbed. "I shouldn't have involved you."

Twisting her mouth, Sterling considered things. It'd probably be best if she didn't question Adela's motives, so instead she asked, "How does he plan to get me?"

"He said he knows where you live. Or will know. I'm not sure. He plans to follow you, I think. Oh, Francis, you have to be careful. You should just go away—" Suddenly Adela screamed.

It sounded like the phone crashed to the floor. Sterling heard a man's voice. *"Stupid bitch."* Loud thumps. Slaps.

Worse.

With her heart caught in her throat, Sterling heard Mattox snarl, "When the hell will you learn?"

Frozen in horror, Sterling listened to Adela's hysterical, babbling voice, pleading, crying out . . . She winced at a louder crash, and then— deafening silence.

Her heart hammered in her chest.

There was rustling, and then, "Is that you, Francis?"

Sterling didn't reply. Anger roiled inside her, helping to settle the fear and upset.

"She's bleeding," he said, his tone taunting. "If she dies now, it's your fault."

The call ended.

Blindly, Sterling stared at the floor, trying to assimilate what she'd heard and what she knew.

"Hey." Joining her, Cade slipped both hands around her neck. "What's happened?"

"I don't know." She shook her head. "Something. Or maybe nothing." She gazed into his stunning blue eyes. "Either Mattox just beat Adela badly, or they're working together and want me to . . . I don't know. Act hastily? Or just feel bad, maybe."

"If you're mired in guilt, you can't think clearly." He drew her into his arms. "Whatever happened, none of it is in your control."

"But what if Adela is innocent? What if she really was trying to escape?"

"Reyes didn't think so."

She pushed him back. "Reyes could be wrong!"

"Could be, but probably isn't."

For once his calm, in-charge tone annoyed her. She was ready to lose it, and Cade was unaffected. "I still want to know for sure."

"I have some news that might help." He kissed

311

her forehead, then took her hand and led her to the office. Once inside, he closed the door and leaned back on it, his arms folded over his chest. "The three stooges gave up a few locations before Reyes handed them off."

"Locations for Mattox?" Finally, some good news! "Why are we still standing here? We should check them out."

"Reyes is doing that right now."

"He's one man! He can't be in three places at once."

"No, but my sister can. Remotely, that is. She's able to tell which buildings are occupied, which ones have activity."

Sterling didn't ask how. So far as she could tell, Madison had scary tech ability that'd be well over her head. "And?"

"An old house seems more likely than the other two. Mattox hasn't survived this long by being careless, so odds are he'll be relocating real fast. If Reyes gets lucky, he might be able to follow him, find out where he holes up."

That sounded beyond perilous. "What if he gets caught?"

"Worried about Reyes now, too?"

"You aren't?"

Taking mercy on her emotions, Cade admitted, "A little. He'll check back in soon."

How long was *soon?* Pacing, Sterling absently took in the room. Neat, of course. A solid but plain desk, comfortable chair—and the short sofa he'd offered her for napping. "We need to find out how the men got here today. There weren't any cars in the lot. Did they park somewhere close by?"

"Actually, they told Reyes they were dropped off so we wouldn't see a car and be alerted. They were to use my own SUV to bring you in."

Her mouth went dry. "You mean us, don't you? Bring *us* in?"

He looked away. "They don't want me, honey. I'd only be in the way."

No. Charging up to him, Sterling went on tiptoe to say, "Don't you dare act indifferent about someone trying to kill you."

For the longest time Cade just stared at her. "You understand the situation. You don't need me to tell you anything."

No and no again! Fear pushed her away from him. She needed distance to think, a way to lessen the awfulness of that possibility.

Cade caught her before she got far, pulling her into his arms and holding her when she tried to get away. "Why is it you can handle it if someone threatens you, but this is a problem?"

Her laugh sounded almost hysterical. "You, dead? No, I can't handle that at all."

His expression softened. "Did I look in danger of dying?"

No, he hadn't. He'd dealt with those men as

easily as he would have children. *But they won't all be that way.* "You're not invincible, you know."

She felt his smile against her temple. "I know. But I am highly trained for all situations, so the odds will always be in my favor."

Right up until they weren't. God, she felt sick.

"We need to stop and think now, okay?" He led her to the couch and sat down with her. "While I have Rob covering for me out front, tell me everything Adela said. We'll sort it out."

Because she wasn't sure what else to do, Sterling started at the beginning of the call and gave every grisly detail until she finished with what Mattox had said.

The calm retelling aided her, giving her a new perspective. "They might have wanted to panic me."

"If Adela is working with him."

She nodded and met his gaze. "I have to know for sure."

"We all do, okay? None of us takes chances with the lives of innocent people. That's first and foremost."

Yes, she'd realized that right off. Cade and his family were the good guys—and they were far better organized than she could ever hope to be on her own.

Calming even more, Sterling asked, "So do you have a plan?"

"I do, and it involves luring them in. Letting

them think they have the upper hand, when in fact we're the ones in control."

"Awesome." It sounded like they were thinking along the same lines. "It's like I said, right? Use me as bait, but I'll be safe because you guys will be on it."

His expression went blank. Then a second later he scowled. "Close, but I'll be the bait instead of you."

"What? *No.*" If he'd thought it through, he'd already know why that wouldn't work. "They want to *capture* me, but you they want *dead.*"

"They'll take me alive, hoping it'll help them get to you."

"You can't know that!"

He kissed her fast before she lost her cool all over again. "I have to get back out to the bar, but I promise you, Star. We'll go over every detail, and we'll all be in agreement before anything is put in motion. Does that work for you?"

What could she say? It worked for her only because she'd never agree to anything that dumb. But damn it, she had joined their little group, and what if she got outvoted, instead of the other way around?

Hand to her churning stomach, she gave a grudging nod, but deep in her heart, she had a very big problem.

She'd already fallen in love with Cade McKenzie—and nothing dicked up clear thought like an overblown emotional attachment. Well, hell.

Knocked to the floor, her jaw aching, her lip split, Adela scooted to sit against the wall. Thacker entered the room quietly, keeping a wide berth around Mattox, and handed her a cloth filled with ice.

Busy watching Mattox, she didn't thank Thacker. He looked nervously at Mattox, then sidled out of the room again, closing the door softly behind him. The cell phone, probably busted, lay on the floor between them.

Mattox was out of control in a big way. She hadn't lied about that. The floor shook beneath his stomping stride.

He'd made two turns around the room, knocking furniture out of his way, before he paused in front of her. "You okay?"

"Yes." Quickly, not trusting his feet, she stood but stayed against the wall.

"That shouldn't have happened."

"It was her fault, not yours." She tried to smile, but the swelling in her cheek made it difficult, and with him glowering at her . . . "She infuriates you. I understand."

Taking her wrist, Mattox lowered her hand to see her face. Whatever he saw tightened his mouth in disgust. "She's going to pay. For every-thing."

He said it like a promise, so she replied, "I . . . I know."

"We have to relocate, the sooner the better. Be ready in five minutes."

Adela watched him storm out. He had a mercurial temper, but his rages didn't last long, thank God. She'd probably be dead already if they did.

When she knew he was far enough away, she picked up the phone. The screen was cracked, but it seemed to work still. Not that she had anyone else to call.

"Sorry, sugar. My plans got changed." Sitting in yet another car, one of ten that Parrish had purchased for different occasions, Reyes stared through the windshield at the front of the old house. Patience might be his weak link. He detested downtime. If he had his druthers, he'd just plow into the house, find Mattox and beat the prick to death.

Unfortunately, no one wanted him to do that, least of all his father. The plan was to bring down the whole shebang, not just one man, but damn. Stakeouts were boring as shit.

"Reyes," she complained. "I already had dinner planned."

Seeing movement behind the front window, Reyes narrowed his eyes and said in distraction, "Sorry, Annette. I'd be there if I could."

"You could come over when you get done with . . . whatever you're doing."

"Family stuff." He lifted the binoculars and looked at those windows more closely. Yup, that was definitely shadows shifting. "I'll have to eat on the fly."

"So we won't do dinner first." Her voice went low and throaty. "I'll still be here all night."

"You're tempting me, doll." Unfortunately, he couldn't afford a distraction. "It could be late."

"So wake me when you get here." She added in a singsong voice, "I'll be naked."

A quick visual flitted through his mind. Annette's curly blond hair and sexy smiles, big boobs and shapely legs . . . "Sold." Yes, he was that easy when it came to sex. "If I can wrap it up before midnight, I'll be there. But if I'm a no-show, it won't be lack of interest for that intriguing offer, okay?"

"I'll make it worth your while."

The front door opened, and Reyes rushed to say, "I do enjoy how you tease. Gotta roll now, but keep the motor revving for me." He disconnected the call before Annette could say anything else.

Four people came out of the house. First was Thacker, the slimy worm, and he didn't even try for subtlety as he searched the area, a gun already in his hand.

Behind him was Mattox . . . *dragging* Adela along with a bruising grip on her wrist.

Well, hell. The binoculars gave him a very clear view of Adela's battered face. Someone had socked the lady, and none too gently. Head down, short brown hair tangled and shoulders slumped, she followed meekly to a clichéd black sedan, where Mattox shoved her into the back seat.

Frowning, Reyes wondered what had changed. Did he need to reevaluate the situation?

He rubbed his chin, sorting through it all as he'd been taught.

No, he wouldn't make up his mind, not yet. Not until he had more to go on.

With that thought, he tailed the car from a safe distance, checking constantly to ensure he hadn't picked up a tail himself. That's what he and Cade would have done. Switched it up. Let someone think they were following along, while they were actually being followed.

A short time later, he called Cade. Soon as his brother answered, Reyes said, "Best as I can tell, they're heading back to that cabin in the woods, near Coalville."

"Ballsy," Cade said, "since we're already aware of that area."

"Yeah, but it was a good hideout, and situated where it's easy to spot anyone coming or going. If it came to that, they could hide in the mountains, or in one of the old coal mines, plus I can't follow them there. They'd be onto me in no time."

"For now you're safe?"

"Yeah, just rode past. I'll circle around a few times, just so they don't catch on to me. Then I'll hang out an hour or so to make sure they're not moving again."

"I want you to be extra careful," Cade said. He explained about the call Sterling had gotten. "Mattox is unhinged, and I have no idea what's going on with him and Adela."

"Yeah, as to that . . . Someone knocked her around. The scene was total opposite of the other day. Fucker dragged her out of there and she looked cowed."

"Shit."

"Yeah, hard to read them, but I retract my earlier conclusions, at least until I can see more—which might be difficult with them hiding away. Doubt there's any electronic eyes there for Madison to pick up. Hell, might not be Wi-Fi, either."

Cade didn't answer, but Reyes knew the silence meant he was thinking. Cade was like that. Quietly methodical in all he did, whether it was plotting or kicking ass. Impressive stuff. He'd always admired his big brother, but no, he wasn't much like him.

Cade could handle a stakeout all day and never lose his edge. Sometimes it was eerie. He didn't know what the military had done to his brother—but then, Cade had always been somewhat remote. Deep. A loner.

Sad part was, he dealt with women the same way—or at least he had until Sterling charged in. He grinned, just thinking about it.

She was one hell of a surprise.

Not that his brother avoided female company. Hell no. But a relationship? That was the shocker. Anyone who knew Cade could see he'd staked a claim. The amusing part was that Sterling seemed every bit as possessive.

"Star is worried," Cade said, interrupting Reyes's thoughts. "Mostly because she's not sure of things, either. I trust her impressions on this, so I think it's more complicated than we first considered."

"I agree she's sharp." Reyes took an exit to circle back and make another loop. "I just got an idea. If Madison could come up with an eye of some sort, I could sneak in later tonight and hook it up. Maybe at the main entrance to the town. It's one dusty road, right? Should be easy enough to do, and then we'd at least get a heads-up if Mattox leaves there. If Madison has anything super high-tech, we might even be able to tell if he leaves alone or with Adela."

"Good idea, the sooner the better. You want me to get hold of her to ask?"

"Just so you can relay to me? No, I'm already bored to tears. I'll make the call."

Without comment on his complaint, Cade said, "Then keep me posted. And I mean, posted as in every hour or less. Star isn't used to worrying, but she's worried about you."

His brows shot up. "No shit?" The grin came slowly. "Now, ain't that sweet?"

"Check in," Cade ordered again, "and let me know what Madison has to say."

"You got it." As he drove past, he did see Thacker just departing, but Reyes was close enough to see he was alone. So he'd dumped Mattox and Adela somewhere inside the town or up in the mountain? Without transportation? Or was Thacker just running an errand?

He called his sister and explained the situation, adding with concern, "There's not a lot of light in this section—"

"I know just the thing," Madison said, and it sounded like she was on the go.

"I'm guessing we'll probably need three of them."

"Perfect," she enthused. "I've got it covered."

"It needs to be something I can install superfast."

"Won't take me more than a few minutes to get them each going."

"What—*Whoa.*" No way in hell did he want Madison getting physically involved. "You won't be installing them."

"Course I will. You can keep watch. I think you're forty-five minutes from me, but I'll leave within five. I'll call you when I'm close so we can meet up. No reason we can't sneak in there together."

Talking tech always excited Madison, but Reyes wasn't at all keen on her being in the same vicinity as Mattox. "We'll meet and you can talk me through how to do it."

"Byeeee," she said, and the call ended.

"Son of a . . ." Reyes cut short his discontent, knowing it wouldn't do him any good. If he could figure out exactly where the three cameras should go, he and Madison could get out of there quickly. Thinking of what they needed to know, and what would be least dangerous for his kid sister, he chose a post next to the railroad tracks—it would catch anyone attempting to arrive or exit that way. The second could go on a telephone pole but would require him standing on his car to get it high enough so it wouldn't be noticeable. That'd exclude Madison.

Under the overhang of the shabby church would be the perfect spot for the third camera because it would also catch anyone coming down the mountain on the narrower trail. But did he dare let Madison do that? Could he stop her?

Probably not.

He wouldn't let anything happen to her, though. They'd use extra care, which meant it'd take a little longer, but he'd deal with it, and Annette would just have to deal, too.

Once he had that worked out in his mind, he

drove south to the next exit, found a gas station a mile down on the right and called his sister.

"I'm on my way," she assured him. "Where do we meet?"

He gave her directions, then tried insisting again, "I'll put up the cameras."

"Reyes." Exasperated, she stretched out his name. "I have to be there anyway to ensure they're properly connected and that I can access them. The three I have are motion activated, but that could still mean an animal, a bird or even a tree branch moved by the wind would kick them on. I'll be able to remotely clear recordings, which will be on my server and impenetrable from outside, so that we don't have a cluttered feed."

Making a winding motion with his finger, Reyes said, "That's all over my head. I'm talking about actually getting them mounted—"

"I want them done a certain way. You can ensure no one sees me."

"You realize you sound as stubborn as Cade."

"Thank you." With laughter in her tone, she said, "Love you, brother. See you shortly." Again, she disconnected him.

Sisters, he grumbled to himself. Yes, he knew he was sexist—most especially when it came to a baby sister he loved. Did he know she was capable? Yup, he did. Was he confident she could do it with or without his help? No doubts.

But that didn't mean he wanted his sis in the line of fire. Not if he could help it.

Couldn't stop her, though. Madison was sweet, but she didn't put up with any macho crap. So he slumped in his seat, drummed his fingers on the steering wheel and waited.

She arrived sooner than he'd expected, which was good, since he'd already been away from the site too long. Typical of Madison, she immediately took charge, but at least she allowed him to drive. They rode to the site together, all the while with her chatting about the cameras and what they could do.

For the most part, Reyes tuned her out, uninterested in the technical details that fascinated her when he'd rather work out the logistics of getting her safely in and out of the area.

He just knew Cade was going to have his head, being he was ten times more protective than Reyes.

Fortunately for him, he was able to park down the tracks away from the small main road, close enough that they could sneak into Coalville on foot, unnoticed. Since she insisted on installing each one, he had to hoist Madison onto his shoulders to get two of the cameras in place, but she was incredibly efficient, as well as silent, in getting that completed. After only a few brief adjustments, she wrapped it up.

As he lowered her back to the ground, she

whispered, "Now I just need to connect them to my device so I can transfer it all back home and voilà—I'll have eyes here."

"You're so clever," Reyes murmured absently, while constantly scanning their darkened surroundings. So quiet, not even a rodent stirred.

Sort of electrified the small hairs on the back of his neck.

If he didn't have Madison with him, he'd creep around a little, see if he could figure out exactly where Mattox had hunkered down, maybe discover if Adela was okay.

But not with her along for the adventure. "Let's go." Reyes nudged her forward, considerate of her slower pace while she picked her way over the rocks and rubble.

When they reached the car, they both did a quick check around it, ensuring they hadn't been discovered. Madison flipped on her phone light just long enough to see that no one had hidden in the back seat. Then they went dark again.

Reyes drove slowly without headlights until they merged onto the interstate. He flipped them on and released a tight breath at the same time. "I'll take you to your car." And he'd follow her home, just to be extra safe.

Annette would keep, or not. He wouldn't leave his sister's safety to chance.

He checked in with Cade a few times, and yeah, big brother was all PO'd over Madison being involved at the site. Reyes listened, and since he didn't disagree, what could he say? "It wasn't *my* idea."

Cade still chewed his ass, but in that controlled way that sounded more like a disappointed father—as if he needed two of those. "Next time, I'll call you and you can try your hand at talking her around."

Cade exhaled sharply, but said, "Be safe tonight."

Rolling his eyes, Reyes said, "Yeah, same to you."

It was two long, grueling hours later before he got to Annette's front door. She'd left the outside lights on for him, making him smile. Since he had a key, he let himself in without a sound.

Unlike him, Annette was far too trusting.

Not in a million years would he give a key to anyone other than family.

Inside, he flipped on the foyer lamp. The house was quiet, and he didn't sense any threats—something he always checked—so he slipped off his shoes and started down the hall.

Her bedroom door was open, and with the light from the foyer barely filtering in, he saw her slender form in the bed, stretched out on her stomach . . . and naked as she'd promised.

Already getting hard, Reyes caught the edge of the sheet and slowly pulled it to the foot of the bed. Annette shifted to her side, curling her luscious bod to keep warm.

Yeah, he'd help her with that.

Without taking his gaze off her body, he removed his wallet and placed it on the nightstand. Quietly, he set his gun beside it. Then his knife. Annette knew not to touch his weapons, but he always put himself between her and them anyway.

He peeled off his shirt and tossed it to a chair, then opened his jeans and tugged down the zipper.

Annette opened her eyes, purring sleepily, "Reyes?"

"You expecting anyone else?" If so, he wouldn't stay.

Going to her back, she whispered, "Come here."

"Yes, ma'am." He finished stripping and climbed in beside her.

Out of the three women he currently visited, Annette was the most affectionate. Cathy, an exec in the business world, wanted her booty calls scheduled in advance, and he had to be prompt. Unlike Annette, Cathy wouldn't tell him to come by whenever.

Lili loved to call him when the mood struck her. If he was available, fine; if not, she moved on to the next guy.

Annette would do the same, but she always swore he was the best. And after sex, she wanted to laze around together. She wasn't clingy—none of them were, or he wouldn't visit them—but she did enjoy an extra closeness.

Tonight, he wouldn't mind that, either.

Her hand snaked down his chest and went straight to his dick. "Mmm, already ready for me?"

"I was ready the second I stepped in the door."

Laughing softly, she kissed his chest, his ribs . . . and slowly worked her way down.

Annette had an *amazing* mouth, meaning his night would definitely be more rewarding than his day had been.

CHAPTER FIFTEEN

Sterling was excited about seeing Reyes's gym this morning. It was yet another facet of the whole McKenzie operation, and she wanted to learn as much as she could.

It might give her a leg up in dealing with Parrish, because she was pretty sure their relationship would take some adjustment.

Relationship. With Cade. With his siblings and father. With the awesome Bernard. She wanted to hug it all to her chest and cherish it for however long it lasted.

She was always cautious when she went out, but Cade took it to a whole new level. Getting jumped last night hadn't helped. He'd been extra attentive in delicious ways, but she knew he'd also strained his injury. His father hadn't been pleased this morning when he insisted on checking things, but he wasn't really the doting sort, either. More like a sour general.

Getting from the bar to her apartment so she could get some things last night, and then back to his father's house, had taken twice as long as it should have just so Cade could backtrack twice, his way of guaranteeing no one followed them. By the time they'd actually gotten to bed, she'd been exhausted.

Not *too* exhausted, not when Cade had stripped down and curved around her, all hot and hard and keenly interested. She'd taken quick advantage of that and the incredible pleasure he offered.

But she felt the lack of sleep catching up with her today.

Good thing they were doing something fun.

A massive front window showed the interior of the gym where Reyes stood on a mat instructing two men. He wore only shorts and wrestling shoes, and she had to admit he was a good-looking guy.

"What's he teaching them?"

Cade shrugged. "I'm guessing basic defense."

Through the window, she watched as the guys went into a stance. Reyes continued to instruct, right up until both men charged him.

Her brows climbed up in delight as Reyes lowered a shoulder and tossed the heavier of the two men. Just as quickly, he tripped the other. While Cade's brother still stood there instructing, the other two men sucked wind from their backs.

Sterling laughed.

"Amusing, right?" Cade put an arm around her and steered her to the door. "We can watch for a while, or you're welcome to try out the equipment."

More interested in seeing than doing, Sterling shook her head. "I'm not dressed for it."

"There's not a dress code, babe." As he often

did, he stroked along her spine down to the small of her back over the soft cotton T-shirt she wore, then down to the seat of her faded jeans, where he lightly copped a feel of her backside. "Other than your boots, you're fine. You'd just need to remove them before you stepped on a mat."

One of these days she'd get used to all the familiar touching, but it was going to take a while. Trying not to show how deeply he affected her, Sterling asked, "You know all this stuff, too?"

"I do."

She leaned into him. "Then I'd rather you teach me."

His slow smile did crazy things to her. "It'll be my pleasure."

It was nice to know that his brain stayed centered on sex as often as hers did.

A sign on the door read "Walk-ins welcome, but we can't guarantee all equipment will be open."

Once she stepped inside, she knew why: the place was packed.

The interior was more spacious than she'd realized. Every inch utilized in one way or another by sweat-damp people ranging in age from late teens to early sixties, male and female alike.

In the back section, heavy bags hung from reinforced beams and, beyond that, speed bags. It appeared to be mostly younger males using those. Stationary bikes lined one wall, occupied by women and elders. Various racks of weights and bars, with a few benches, took up the opposite. One of the men doing bench presses had grotesquely huge arms . . . especially in comparison to his thin legs.

Cade whispered, "No balance. Reyes has tried to tell him, but he focuses on that one exercise and won't do anything else."

Sterling snorted, then glanced around at the women. A few of them seemed mostly concerned with looking stylish, standing around in their cute clothes and chatting. Others were clearly there to work out, their hair in ponytails or clips, sweat dampening T-shirts or sports bras.

One gal in baggy sweatpants, an oversize T-shirt, shoulder-length blond hair held back with a wide band and earbuds in her ears, popped her neck as she walked to a heavy bag. She wore fingerless gloves and shin guards.

She looked absurd in her getup but didn't seem to care—and that impressed Sterling.

"I'm going to talk to Reyes a few minutes," Cade said. "Want to join us?"

"I'd rather look around." Whatever they discussed, Cade would tell her later. Why risk letting Reyes provoke her temper when she didn't need to?

With a long look, Cade said, "Stay where I can see you." He touched her cheek. "Everyone in here is probably fine, but Reyes can't know each person, and I'm not willing to take chances right now."

"You don't think you'd notice someone dragging me out the front door?"

His fingers spread, threading into her hair and cupping her head. "There are two back doors, one out of a break room and another at the end of the hall near the bathrooms."

Ah, yeah. If she went to the bathroom, and someone was waiting . . . "I'll stay within range if you will, too," she promised, then sauntered off.

Something about that other lady drew her. As Cade had noted, she had good instincts. Something inside her screamed that the woman had trouble on her heels and could use a friendly face.

Often Sterling felt that way with the women she helped. She was good at reading them, at knowing what to say and when, whether to push or just wait.

Odd, but she hadn't quite felt that connection with Adela, or at least not consistently.

Finding one heavy bag unoccupied, she gave it a tentative push. The woman stood next to her, giving the bag hell—and ignoring Sterling. She seemed intent on abusing her legs. Even though she wore shin guards, Sterling winced.

With the earbuds in, she couldn't really give a

friendly "Hey" to break the ice, so she moseyed on. But her gaze repeatedly went back to glimpse the woman working. She was so intense, so focused that Sterling couldn't help but be impressed.

And worried.

Fifteen minutes later, while she idly examined a weird contraption that looked too complicated for her to figure out, Cade and Reyes joined her.

So much for avoiding the annoying brother.

And with him stripped down so much, ignoring his presence wouldn't be easy.

As if he'd read her thoughts, he said in a singsong voice, "Hi, Sterling."

With a roll of her eyes and a sigh, she turned to him. "What's up, troublemaker?"

Reyes grinned. "Let's head to the break room. I could use a cold drink."

"First . . ." Damn, Sterling really hated to involve him, but if he knew the woman, maybe he could put her worries to rest. "So, don't stare, but the lady back there, kicking the stuffing out of the heavy bag?"

Curious, both men glanced that way.

"You guys suck, you know that?" Hands on her hips, Sterling scowled at them. "I said don't stare, but you both did."

"There's staring, and then there's *staring*," Cade said. "Besides, you didn't specify it was anything like that."

She rolled her eyes.

With his gaze still on the woman, Reyes asked, "What about her?"

Already frowning, Cade gave her a longer look, too. "Something's off."

Sterling nodded. "Fear is working her hard."

After a lengthy perusal, Reyes cursed softly. "You're right."

It reassured Sterling that she wasn't imagining things. "Do you know her?"

Reyes shrugged. "She's been coming in for about a month but keeps to herself."

"So no?"

His mouth flattened. "No."

"Huh." She'd expected Reyes to have some snappy comeback, but instead he looked displeased. With her? No, with himself. Digging a little, she said, "Haven't hit on her, huh?"

That got his eyes narrowed. "This is my gym. Think what you want of me, but I take my pleasure elsewhere."

His sincerity made Sterling feel a little bad for deliberately provoking him—but *only* a little. "Scruples. Bravo." Aware of Cade grinning and Reyes growling, she turned to keep the woman in sight. "She's not here to stay in shape, or to bulk up or trim down. She wants to know how to hurt people."

Cade slanted a look at Reyes. "Told you she was astute."

"I never denied it." Propping his hands on his hips, Reyes asked, "If she wants to learn offensive moves, why didn't she ask for instruction?"

"Maybe because you look like that?" Sterling nodded at his body, and when she did so, she couldn't help eyeballing his sweaty, naked torso. Not out of interest, but because he really was a specimen.

She noticed him the same way she might a really nice pair of stilettos. She appreciated the style, but you'd never catch her wearing a pair.

Rocking back on his heels, Reyes asked, "What the hell is that supposed to mean?"

"You're intimidating." Much like Cade, Reyes had muscles everywhere. Not overblown, but very defined. His eyes were hazel, like Madison's, instead of electric blue like Cade's, but they were still nice.

He was almost as tall as Cade, too, but he wore his dark hair a little longer, and his attitude was a lot less restrained.

"I've never intimidated you," Reyes pointed out.

She grinned. "I'm not the average woman."

"True enough." Laughing, Cade drew her into his side. "You're above average."

Reyes groaned. "It's almost nauseating the way you two fawn all over each other."

"Oh?" Feeling devilish, Sterling asked, "So I know how to bug you, while getting awesome

338

benefits at the same time? Sweet." Even as she spoke, she cuddled closer to Cade and walked her fingers up his chest.

"Hey, I run a reputable business, you know," Reyes mock-complained. "Take that foreplay elsewhere."

Cade reached for him, but he ducked away, then asked, "So you think my size has put her off?"

Sterling wasn't sure if he threw that out there because of real interest or just to get her off molesting Cade. But whatever, she'd save the good stuff for when she had Cade alone.

"You are big," she admitted.

He and Cade both grinned, and she knew exactly what they were thinking.

Willing herself not to blush, she spoke before Reyes could. "But it's not just because you're tall and fit. You're . . . sexual?" Considering that, Sterling shook her head. "Yeah, not a great word, but you know what I mean."

Both brothers now stared at her, prompting her to roll her eyes again. "A woman who's unsure of men wouldn't want to approach someone as cocky as you."

More disgruntled by the minute, Reyes said, "I'll have you know, plenty of women like me just fine the way I am."

"I bet they do." She snickered. "The thing is, the same reason why those other women like you is probably why that one prefers to watch a video or something on her phone. At least, I think that's what she's doing. See how she keeps looking at the screen and repositioning her stance?"

Cade nodded. "Trying to mimic the moves . . . but not really doing them correctly. It's tough to figure out without in-person instruction."

While Reyes was distracted watching the woman, Sterling sent her elbow into his stomach. "You need to offer."

"Ow, damn." Scowling, he rubbed his side. "Maybe, but not now. She's heading out."

Without being obvious about it, they watched the woman walk to a duffel bag she'd left in the corner near a wooden bench. She dug out a bottle of water and took a long drink. After storing it away again, she located a small blue towel, which she used to dry the sweat from her face and arms. Then she removed her earbuds and unplugged them from her phone, stripped off the protective gear and stuffed everything into the bag, located keys in the front pocket, and started for the door.

Judging by the frowns the brothers wore, they didn't like having to wait any more than Sterling did, but Reyes was right—stopping her would seem too presumptuous, especially when she already seemed . . . well, not exactly skittish, but more like reserved. "You're sure she'll be back?"

"She's been here every day for a month," Reyes said. "So unless you scared her off with all that staring—" This time he dodged her elbow. Laughing, he predicted, "She'll be back. And yes, I'll see if I can figure out a way to offer."

"Thanks." Looking up at Cade, she asked, "You two finished your talk?"

With a nod, Cade took her hand. "You want a tour around the place, or would you rather head out?"

"A tour." She added to Reyes, "I'm impressed, by the way. Nice place you run here."

Grabbing his chest, Reyes pretended to stagger, but the second Sterling turned away, he mussed her hair and took the lead. Anxious to show her around? It seemed so. Little by little, she was starting to like Cade's brother—or at least she was learning to tolerate him.

Reyes strode ahead of them, and yup, the back view of him was impressive, too. Nowhere near as nice as Cade's, but she glanced around and saw many of the women looking their way. Sterling they didn't even see, because Cade and Reyes held all their attention.

And here she was, right in the middle of them.

Overall, not a bad place to be.

The next morning, wearing snug shorts, a clingy tank top and battered sneakers, Star looked entirely different—and downright edible. Cade watched as she twisted her long hair up onto her head. He couldn't take his eyes off her. No matter what she did, or how she dressed, he found her irresistible.

But like this? Her body clearly outlined under the close-fitting clothes, those long, toned legs on display . . . He wasn't a saint. Far from it. And right now, he'd rather take her back to his room, where they could both get naked.

The more he had her, the more he wanted her.

It was like an addiction—Cade's first, since he avoided vices. This vice, though, sating himself on Star's unique brand of sex appeal, he didn't mind at all.

The plan was to spar here in the privacy of his father's private gym so he could assess her ability, fine-tune what she already knew and teach her a few new tricks.

Most important, she had to be able to defend herself. If anything should happen to him, which was unlikely but still possible given his vocation, he needed to know Star would be okay.

"Quit primping," he finally said, knowing it would rile her. "If someone attacks, you won't have time to put up your hair."

She snorted and strode out to the middle of the mat. "You might have to pay for that."

Banking a grin, Cade joined her, then easily ducked the swing she threw and followed it by tripping her to her back.

Instead of being annoyed, she stared up at him with a smile and a droll "That was slick."

Little by little, he got used to her attitude. She got angry when someone tried to take over, him included, but she was always up to learn something new and didn't mind being instructed.

Or tripped to her back.

Cade held out a hand. "Your turn to try it." He showed her the moves, when to pull, how to use her feet in combination with her hands and body, and by the third try, she nailed it.

"Good job," he praised as he rolled back to his feet. "Especially since I'm a lot bigger."

Her mouth twisted to the side. "You *let* me do that."

"To see if you could, yes. While I'm coaching, that's the best way. We'll get to the hard-core stuff soon, I promise. One step at a time. Okay?"

"If you say so." She got into her stance. "Ready when you are."

For the next hour they practiced hard, and by the end, Star was a lot smoother. No matter how many times she hit the mat, she didn't get frustrated or angry.

She brushed herself off, asked pertinent questions and tried again.

She had so much moxie it made him want her even more. How was that possible?

Groaning, she rolled to her back. "I think I finally understand it. Thanks for not losing your patience."

Amazing. How many women—or men, for that

matter—would thank him for repeatedly tossing them to their backs? Star was unique because her motives were unique, and they aligned with his in a way he hadn't expected to find. Definitely not with a woman he desired.

She wanted to be highly trained to successfully attack, defend and rescue those in need, even against the most insurmountable odds. Her mettle impressed him, as did her dogged attitude.

"Hello," she teased. "Yoo-hoo, Cade. You still with me? You're just staring."

Shaking his head, he squatted down beside her and got back to the business at hand. "That's one move," he explained. "We'll work every day until you have a cache of ingrained responses. The idea is for it to be automatic. What one person does triggers what you do, preferably without you having to think about it."

"That's what you do, huh? The other night at the bar, it amazed me how easy you made it look."

Drawn by the way her sweat-dampened shirt stuck to her breasts, how the waistband of her shorts rode low to reveal a strip of her flat, damp stomach, he felt himself stirring.

"Bad example, because they weren't much challenge at all. With trained men, it'd be a little tougher."

Her lips quirked. Still breathless, she pushed a hank of hair off her temple and asked, "Tougher, but not impossible?"

344

Cade couldn't claim an ounce of modesty, not when it came to his ability. "I'm good."

Her voice dropped as she purred, "At many things."

That did it. He started to reach for her, but she utilized the move he'd taught her and lunged for him instead.

Laughing, he countered it by catching her to him, then rolling her to her back to come down over her, pelvis to pelvis, his hands holding her breasts but his elbows catching some of his weight.

Eyes gone heavy, she asked, "Is this a legit move?"

"Damn right," he said, devouring her mouth with a kiss that made him forget about further lessons. Star always tasted so good, and now her exertion had intensified her scent. As he breathed her in, it added to the sudden onslaught of lust.

When he moved to kiss her throat, she whispered, "Then I'm glad it's you teaching me instead of your brother."

Reyes? Jealousy slammed into Cade, and he reared back to scowl at her—only to see her barely repressed grin. He should tell her that joking like that wasn't allowed. He opened his mouth—

Taking swift advantage of his distraction, she bucked him to the side and straddled his hips.

Laughing in triumph, she said, "That was a joke, for crying out loud."

"I'm not sure it's funny."

She only laughed harder. "All's fair in love and war."

Thoughtful, Cade caught her waist to keep her still and asked, "Which are we?"

Her expression shut down at the question. "Um . . ."

Yeah, maybe he shouldn't have asked that. Star was still skittish about any references to their relationship. He knew he had to go slow, to give her plenty of room.

Every day that got a little harder.

For now, he slowly grinned, then flipped her again and said, "You're too easy."

"Jerk." She smacked his shoulder, then blanched and carefully pulled aside the neckline of his shirt. "I keep forgetting you're wounded. Maybe because you don't act like you are."

"I forget myself. It doesn't hurt anymore." When he was this close to Star, his physical need blunted everything else.

He started to kiss her again, but she protested. "No. I'm gross with sweat. Let's go shower first."

Clearly she was getting used to being in his father's house. One of these days he'd have to tell her that he had a place of his own. He hadn't yet because he didn't want her to insist on leaving.

If Star weren't with him, he'd be home alone right now, but Mattox's last threats had been extreme and they didn't yet know what was going on with Adela. He hadn't said it to Star, but they'd take care of that soon. Another reason to stay here. Being in his father's fortress during a sting was not only the safest place to be, but it also provided the quickest way to get info.

While they were still sprawled together on the floor, the door opened and Reyes and Madison stepped in.

Seeing them entwined, Reyes quipped, "Not sure that form of defense will be effective."

Maybe he needed to teach his brother a new lesson, Cade thought as he moved away from Star. She sat up but didn't yet say anything.

"Got any gas left in the tank?" Reyes asked her.

She rolled her shoulder. "Could be. Why?"

"I want to give it a go."

"Nope."

"Chicken?" Reyes asked.

Slowly, Star looked up. "If you persist, I'll agree. But I strongly advise you wear a cup, because I'll go after your vulnerable spots full force."

Scowling, Reyes tucked his hips back, his hands protectively folded over his junk. "That's not how you spar."

"That's how *I* spar—with you." Her smile looked evil. "I have wicked knees." She clenched a hand. "And my fist isn't too bad, either."

"Damn." Reyes turned his accusing gaze on Cade. "What the hell are you teaching her?"

Already grinning, Cade held up his hands. "I'd say the animosity was taught by *you*."

"Men and their precious jewels," Madison complained. She kicked off her shoes and stalked closer. "Come on. I'll go a round or two with you, and the boys can observe."

Star's smile slipped. "I don't think—"

"I'm trained," Madison promised. "But I'd prefer not to get my lady parts wounded, so how about we make this a teaching moment? Cade and Reyes can then offer suggestions. They are good at this sort of thing, you know."

Brows up, Star looked at him for confirmation. Cade nodded. "Madison knows what she's doing, and she is good, so why not?" He gave Reyes a shove that nearly took him off his feet. "Even my brother occasionally has valuable input."

Under her breath, Star grumbled, "It's the audience I object to," but she got to her feet and quickly tucked loose hairs into her topknot. With a glare at Reyes, she said, "No color commentary, got that? Just pertinent facts."

"Yes, ma'am." Then he said to Madison, "Go easy on her."

Star drew a big breath, got in a stance—and barely stopped Madison when she shot in on her.

Standing next to Reyes, Cade watched Star deflect one move after another. To his brother, he said, "She's actually better than I realized now that she's with someone closer to her own size."

"She's fast," Reyes agreed. Then with a sideways glance at Cade, he added, "But how often will she get attacked by someone smaller?"

True enough. Madison was shorter than Star, though both were tall, but she was probably thirty pounds lighter. Where Star was sturdy, Madison was delicate.

His sister compensated for that with speed and agility, and a refined skill in technique. He could see that both women had forgotten about the men watching while they enjoyed the combat.

Star, especially, looked invigorated. She even laughed a few times, either when she missed Madison, or when she caught a hit or kick.

Reyes stepped closer, calling out to their sister, "Wrong leg. Left . . . *now* the right."

"Block it," Cade countered to Star. "That's it. You have to immediately move."

"When she reaches for you, grab . . . Yeah, that's it."

Star had tried grabbing Madison's wrist, but Madison knew that move and how to counter it. She locked her own hand over Star's and pivoted, and Star ended up with her arm twisted behind her, forced to her knees.

Cade briefly stepped in to show Star how to avoid that trick. He encouraged them to go through the same scenario three more times before he was satisfied that Star had it down.

Once she'd nailed it, he had them reverse so

that Star knew how to use the move to subdue an attacker.

"She's a quick learner," Reyes said.

Without taking his eyes off the women, Cade nodded. "A natural survivor. Always has been."

"Didn't have a choice?" Reyes asked without his usual caustic humor.

"No, she didn't." Distracted, Cade said, "You're being defensive, Star, instead of offensive. Don't try to escape until you have control."

This time Reyes demonstrated, and with him in teacher mode, Star didn't seem to mind.

Life would be easier if those two got along. Ignoring him wouldn't do her much good, would in fact only encourage Reyes to ramp up the taunts. So far, Star had managed by giving as good as she got, and Cade had a feeling she'd earned Reyes's respect because of it.

More kicks were thrown, punches blocked.

"How about another lesson?" Cade asked. "That is, if you're both up for it?"

"Sure," Star immediately said, rolling her head to work out a kink in her neck, shaking her hands to loosen them up again. "I'm game."

"Fine by me," Madison agreed.

"This one might work better if Reyes takes part." He beckoned his brother to the mat.

Reyes stepped in with a grin, rubbing his hands together. "Which one is my victim?"

For that comment, Madison kicked his feet out

from under him. Since Reyes wasn't expecting the attack, he went down, but he shot right back up with a laugh, pointing at his sister and saying, "Sneaky. And you already know payback is hell."

While he shared that silly threat with Madison, Star got an impish look in her dark eyes—and copied his sister's move so that Reyes went down again. This time he sprawled out with a chuckling groan. "They're ganging up on me, Cade! Get control of this lesson already."

"You're a good sport," Star said, her wide smile proof that she was having fun.

As if requesting help, Reyes raised a hand to her, but she backed away shaking her head.

"We're not both fools," she laughed.

Loving the way Star fit right in, Cade drew her close for a quick kiss, then explained what he wanted them to do. "Reyes is going to behave himself for this demonstration, isn't that right, brother?"

"Me? Maybe you failed to notice that I'm the one on my back?" Saying that, he rolled to his feet and gave both women a *try me* look. They snickered but didn't engage.

"Reyes is going to invade your space."

"You got it," Reyes said, knowing the lesson and stepping in close to Star—at least until she leaped back. "Hey, I can't show you if you don't let me get hold of you."

Rife with suspicion, Star asked Cade, "Why can't you demonstrate?"

"You're too comfortable with me." He thought of the expression on her face after she'd joked that all's fair in love and war. And without thinking, he'd replied, *Which are we?*

She'd looked ready to bolt, and it bothered him, because Star didn't run from anyone or anything. Love? Yeah, he was there, but clearly she wasn't.

Not yet, anyway.

He'd sway her eventually by building on their shared inclinations and showing her how great they'd be together.

With that goal in mind, he gestured for Reyes to continue.

This time, Star went stiff, but she allowed him to put his arm around her and crush her close into his side—just like a creep would do.

"Now," Cade said, walking her through the process of freeing herself. It took a few tries, especially since Reyes wasn't making it easy for her. Then she nailed it, getting a firm grip on his brother's wrist, ducking under his arm and, in the process, twisting his hand up behind him. Immediately, she put her foot to Reyes's ass and shoved him forward, giving her the opportunity to flee . . . if she'd been in real danger.

Madison applauded.

Reyes did, too, actually, but Cade tried to keep it on point by saying, "If you try that move, be ready to race away as fast as you can, but keep in mind that it'd only work if you're in a congested area where you can quickly find help."

"Or if your attacker is severely out of shape," Madison added. "It's a disgusting reality that *just* fleeing isn't usually the best option."

"So let's give me a weapon," Reyes suggested, "and you can show her how to take it from me."

Intrigued by that, Star held up a hand while breathing hard. "Give me five. Then we can try that."

That's how they ended up working an hour more, with all of them involved in one way or another. Twice she'd successfully taken the dummy knife from Reyes. The concept was the same with a gun, and eventually they'd practice that, too.

But for now, before Star completely collapsed, Cade called a halt. He and Reyes were fine, but then, they took physical training to an extreme. The women, however, looked completely spent.

Hands on her knees, sucking in air, Star said, "That was invigorating."

"Right?" Madison agreed, gulping her own breaths. "I got more of a workout with you than I ever do with my brothers."

"You two are more evenly matched," Cade said. "That's a good thing, but also problematic."

Reyes stepped forward to offer them each water. "You did great, Sterling. You have a natural ability, but Cade's right. Next time we need to wear protective gear so we can really push it. You were both holding back. Cade and I sometimes do the same for simple sparring, but the best way to learn is to go full force."

"Sweet," Star said, accepting the water and chugging it down. "What kind of gear?"

"Headgear and face protector, for starters," Cade offered. "It'll ensure against broken noses or cracked jaws while you practice face strikes. Mouthpiece to protect teeth. Some pads would help, too." His family always took self-defense seriously.

"Sounds good." Star finally straightened, still breathing hard, yet smiling. "The better prepared I am, the more I like it."

Madison grinned, too. "My sentiments exactly." She tossed a towel to Star. "Give it a few days, and then we can work on marksmanship, as well."

And speaking of that . . . Cade took Star's hand. "You can shower in a minute, but first I want to show you one more thing."

As they crossed the length of the lower level, all the way to the other side, Reyes and Madison followed along. It made Cade wonder if Parrish knew they were congregated downstairs. No doubt he did, because not much slipped past his dad, but he wouldn't take part in giving Star the tour of their armory. Later, perhaps over lunch,

Parrish would weigh in with his thoughts—and no doubt judgments.

Didn't matter. Star would be working with Reyes and Madison, and that's what he'd wanted.

Things with Mattox would come to a head very soon. Madison kept a log of movement. They wouldn't stay hidden long, and they all needed to be prepared.

CHAPTER SIXTEEN

Never in a million years would Sterling have guessed that she'd one day be in a freaking mansion practicing lethal skills with three totally badass people. Talk about unbelievable things to happen . . . This one would top her list.

Reyes had actually been fun, and Cade was such an amazing teacher. Everything he did fascinated her even more.

Plus, she loved it that Madison was *so* incredibly proficient—which meant that, one day, Sterling could be that good, too. It gave her a rush, made her blood sing and had her eyeballing Cade hungrily, wondering when she might be able to get him alone.

How working herself into a sweaty mess and turning her limbs to noodles could make her hungry for sex, she didn't know, but then again, there'd been a lot of close contact with that big hunk she currently got to call her own. What red-blooded woman wouldn't react to all those warm, straining muscles, the incredible scent of his heated skin, his sexy take-charge attitude and bone-deep confidence? Cade was the whole, delicious package, and she wanted to gobble him up.

Reyes and Madison were still following along, and Sterling knew she needed a shower, but she figured if he wanted to show her one more thing, she may as well indulge him. He'd certainly indulged her long enough, teaching her so many valuable moves.

He led them all to a back room that appeared to be mostly empty, with a few crates and storage boxes stacked around. There was no drywall on the walls, only exposed studs.

Sterling wondered if there was something in one of the boxes that Cade wanted to show her—until he pressed a concealed lever on the floor and a section of wall swung open, exposing another room behind the insulation.

Eyes flaring wide, she slowly stepped inside to take it all in. Holy smokes. The hidden room was smallish, maybe eight by eight, and it was utilitarian in design—linoleum floor, concrete walls . . . and an astounding display of weaponry. "You have an arsenal."

"We're prepared," Cade countered.

"For your own private war?" She didn't say it as a criticism, more in awe. Strolling along the back wall, Sterling took in rifles, revolvers, handguns of every make and model. Grenades, smoke bombs, flash bombs. Long knives and switchblades. Tasers and batons. She also noted helmets, body armor, camo and utility belts. "This is remarkable." On another wall, ammo filled multiple shelves, surely enough to last them for a good long while.

Madison and Reyes stood aside, silent and watchful, apparently leaving this introduction to Cade.

That worked for her. In fact, she'd like it even better if they gave her some privacy with Cade, but she knew that wasn't going to happen. They might quibble with one another, but the siblings were close. Probably came from protecting one another.

"I'm fascinated," she said, to put them all at ease. "Impressed, too, and I'd love to try every one of them." She ended her circuit of the room in front of Cade. "Got some specific reason for showing me this?"

He put his hands on her shoulders. "We don't leave things to chance, so if Mattox doesn't make a move very soon, we'll go after Adela. I want to know that you can protect yourself—when I'm not available to do it."

Aw. That was sweet. Surprisingly, it didn't insult her. Facts were facts, and although she'd already known it, today's practice reinforced that Cade was far better trained for combat. Being military, that made sense. But of course, he'd taken it well beyond that. She'd never met another person so wholly equipped to handle danger of any sort.

He and his siblings were trained pros, and she was not.

Sterling accepted that she had a lot to learn.

One day she'd love to be on a par with them. Until then, she liked that Cade would look out for her—if it became necessary. Knowing he wouldn't let her be hurt made her feel better about being bait to lure in Mattox. Sure, Cade still thought he'd do the honors, but she'd talk him around somehow.

Her plan made more sense.

She smiled. "Thank you." *For so many things.* Getting close, she hugged him tight. "*Now* do you think we can get that shower? I'm ready to melt in my own sweat."

Reyes laughed, and a definite note of relief resonated in the sound.

Had they expected her to be shocked—in a bad way?

She wasn't. If anything, she loved that they were so well prepared to care for others. It was what she'd always wanted to do, had tried to do, but obviously they did it better.

"That's my cue to head out," Reyes announced. "I'm already running late for the gym."

"And I need my own quick shower before I get back to monitoring things," Madison added. "Bernard will only cover for me so long before he loses interest."

Once they were alone, Cade closed up the room and led the way to his suite.

Taking his hand, Sterling pulled him into the bathroom and clasped the hem of his clinging

T-shirt, tugging it up and over those scrumptious abs, broad chest and rock-hard shoulders. She paused at the sight of his injury. It didn't seem to bother him, but the skin around the stitches was now more discolored. "I hope you didn't overdo it."

Without replying, Cade finished tugging off his shirt, then returned the favor by removing hers and her sports bra, as well.

Breasts bared, Sterling trailed a finger over one of his tattoos. She wanted to trace the design with her tongue, and thinking about it sent a curl of desire through her. "I've been worrying about Adela. I'm glad we won't wait to save her."

"If she needs saving."

Yeah, there weren't any certainties yet. "Reyes said she was hurt. That's enough for me."

"I know." He opened his hand on her cheek. "As long as you don't try anything on your own, we can push it whenever you want."

Nice, so he'd leave it up to her instead of Parrish? That was an unsettling idea. After all, they had a smooth-running outfit. She ran more on emotion.

But thinking logically, she got the idea of throwing a wider net. That method would ultimately save more women . . . but could she sacrifice Adela for a possibility that may not pay off? "How do you feel about it all?"

Without hesitation, Cade said, "I don't like it

when things don't add up. Something is going on between them, I just don't know what."

And that made it riskier. If she had to worry only about herself . . .

"What?" he asked, his thumb brushing the corner of her mouth.

Guessing how he'd react to her thoughts, she smiled. "Every time I see you, I'm struck by how lucky I am."

That got him refocused real fast. "You think I'm any different?" In rapid order, he removed the rest of her clothes, even kneeling down to tug off her sneakers. "Every part of you, Star, this—" he ran his hands up her bare legs, around to her backside to draw her in for a kiss to her stomach "—but also the way you smile, your core strength, your occasional insecurity and your bold attitude—"

"Hey," she protested shakily. "I'm not insecure." *Liar.* She knew she sometimes was, and apparently he knew it, too. But he didn't disagree. Strong and bold, those were attributes she didn't mind.

"The way you argue," he added, with a nibble to her hip bone. "God, how you smell, how you feel—I love all of it, everything about you, inside and out."

Her lips parted. *Love.* Earlier, when he'd teased about love and war, she'd at first gone blank . . . and then accepted it as a joke, nothing more. But this? The way he looked at her now?

Honest to God, Sterling didn't know what to do, what to say. She knew how *she* felt, but him? She didn't have a clue. "You confuse me."

Smiling, Cade rose back to his feet. So tall. So damn strong. So freaking impressive in every way.

As he finished stripping, he said, "I don't know why you'd be confused. You're sexy, smart, quick-witted, strong, compassionate—"

Embarrassed heat flushed her face. "That's enough."

"Not even close." Taking her shoulders, Cade turned her away from him so he could free her hair. His fingers were gentle as he loosened the band and slid it free. "You're a remarkable person in so many ways. Do you honestly think I can be around you without wanting you?"

Wanting, sure. She wanted him nonstop, too. But he'd mentioned *love* again. Frowning, she turned to face him. "Instead of standing around talking, how about we make use of that warm shower? Together."

Cade pressed a soft kiss to her mouth. "Love the way you think."

Her eyes widened. Did he use that damn word on purpose now?

With a lazy smile, he turned on the water and got out two towels. A little numb, Sterling stepped under the spray to soak her face and hair. She needed to stop gawking over the things he said.

She also needed to know if he meant anything substantial by it, but she was too cowardly to ask.

Getting in behind her, Cade took the shampoo bottle from her. "Let me."

Why not? If she was going to stand there feeling stupid, she may as well let him take over.

And take over he did. In diabolical ways.

Massaging the shampoo through her hair was somehow very erotic, especially when she felt his powerful body behind her. Cade made her feel small—and very feminine. It was unique for her, and her hormones loved it.

After she'd rinsed her hair, he picked up the soap and, keeping her back to his chest, proceeded to clean her.

All over.

Slick fingers worked her nipples until she couldn't breathe. Her breasts felt heavy, so sensitive that she trembled all over. "Cade . . ."

"Shh." He kissed the side of her throat. "I love touching you."

She groaned at his insistent use of *love,* but she couldn't muster up a real protest. Trying to distract him, she moved her backside against his erection, but being the man he was, he lightly sank his teeth into her shoulder.

Delicious sensation prickled all over her body, every nerve ending electrified. Good God, she felt close to coming, and all he did was play with her breasts. "Let's go to bed," she pleaded.

Pleaded. It was both appalling and exciting that he'd reduced her to that needy voice.

"Not yet." He licked the spot where he'd given her a love bite, and those broad, slightly rough hands coasted down, over her stomach, her thighs, between them . . .

Pressing back against him, Sterling tipped her head to his strong shoulder.

"That's it, babe. Don't fight me."

Fight him? What a joke. He was bigger, stronger and currently far more in control.

"Feel how slick you are?"

Very aware of her body's response, she gave another small groan. He pressed a finger into her, worked her carefully, then pulled out only to add a second finger.

She clenched around him. It felt so good—but she wanted more than his fingers. Reaching back, she clamped a hand onto his thigh to ground herself. With her other hand, she covered his and pressed his fingers deeper, then moved sinuously against him.

She was close, so close, if he'd only—

Cade pulled away, then repositioned her. "Lean against the wall. That's it. Now open your legs."

Eyelashes spiked with the shower spray, Sterling looked at him through a haze of lust— and did as ordered.

Lowering to his knees, Cade touched her again. Her breasts, down to her belly, lower, exploring, and pressing his fingers in again. Nuzzling against her, he found her clit and licked.

"Oh, God." Sterling locked her knees, her eyes squeezed shut, her head back . . .

He drew her in, sucking, teasing rhythmically with his tongue while keeping those long fingers thrust deep—on and on it went until an incredible climax crashed through her. Like, literally *crashed*, stealing the strength from her limbs, wringing a harsh cry from her throat, putting tears in her eyes even.

Luckily the shower would hide that, but wow. She tunneled her fingers into his close-cropped hair and rode out the pleasure until she felt herself slipping down the wall.

Cade caught her hips and stood in a rush. His mouth on hers, his tongue delving, that solid erection pulsing against her belly.

She reached for it, but he caught her hand, lifted it to his mouth for a tender kiss and said, "Not this time, babe. I'm too close to acting stupid."

Gulping breaths, Sterling managed to get her eyes open. A tiny bit, but enough to see that the blue of his eyes had turned incendiary. Curious, she whispered, "Stupid . . . how?"

"Forgoing protection."

"Oh." He turned away before she admitted that she wouldn't mind. Actually, the idea of feeling him and only him sparked a new stirring deep inside her.

In extreme haste Cade washed and rinsed, then turned off the water, grabbed the towels and pressed one against Sterling's chest.

"I would do the honors, but I need you too damn much. Get dry, or close to it, and let's go to the bedroom where I can grab a rubber."

Her mouth twitched with a secret little smile of happiness. She'd never seen Cade so frazzled.

She'd never been wanted that much.

Her heart expanded, making her chest feel tight with emotion. Lazily, while watching him, she dried off, then flipped her hair forward and wrapped it in the towel.

She was still bent forward when Cade hoisted her over his shoulder, making her laugh.

"I like the way you lust for me," she admitted. "Especially since I lust for you so much."

"Good to know." He put her on the foot of the bed so that her legs hung off the end, then strode to the nightstand to grab a condom and quickly rolled it on. "Turn over."

Since she was already on her back, she blinked. "Do what?"

Without waiting for her to understand, he flipped her to her stomach and kneed her legs apart.

Curious, she lifted up on her arms to look back but went flat again as he gripped her hips and drove into her.

He filled her completely and was already

thrusting, lifting her up to meet him each time he sank deep. His thighs met the back of hers, his firm abdomen slapping against her softer backside. Another climax started to build, and she knotted her fingers in the bedding.

"Star," Cade growled low, the sound almost tortured. "Can't wait." Reaching around and under her, he found her clit again, did no more than lightly pinch, holding her like that as he continued the hard rhythm, and far too quickly they were both coming.

It was so deep this way, his thrusts more powerful, and she loved it. Every second of it.

Because she loved him.

This time the knowledge didn't frighten her. Heck, she was now too exhausted to be frightened. Her thoughts were blessedly free of any angst. Even long-buried fears seemed to have evaporated, leaving her utterly replete.

Resting over her, still in her, Cade murmured, "Every time."

"Hmm?"

"Every time . . . is somehow better."

In total agreement with that, she sighed. "Mmm."

She felt his smile on her shoulder, then the tender kiss he pressed there before he pulled away.

Sterling wasn't sure she could move, not even for an earthquake, but Cade took care of it, cleaning her with his towel, then scooping her up and placing her in the bed, even tucking her in. He kissed her forehead and whispered, "Be right back."

It was the last thing she heard . . . until he woke her sometime later.

After arriving at the gym an hour ago, Reyes had repeatedly lost his concentration.

It was her fault. That cute little mystery woman.

Even while listening in on a trio of knuckleheads talking about some underhanded business—one that could pertain to his family's pursuits—Reyes couldn't keep his eyes off her.

She appeared to be close to his age of thirty—maybe a little younger. Honey-blond hair swung loose to her shoulders, dipping and swaying each time she landed a kick or threw a punch.

Improperly.

He chewed his upper lip. She did okay, and she put plenty of effort into it, but her stance was off. To get the best impact with her strikes, and to avoid getting thrown off balance, she needed to lead off with the other leg. She also let her hands drop each time . . .

Why the hell was he still dwelling on her?

He heard one of the guys say, "Seriously, man, easy cash. Just gotta be ready to pull the trigger."

Ears perking up, Reyes listened more closely.

"I traded my hardware a month ago," another complained.

"Damn, G, they'll give ya the firepower to protect the deal."

"What kind of deal?"

"The fuck does that matter?"

Reyes silently sighed. *G?* As in *gangster?* What a misnomer for the strung-out, scrawny fool sporting very amateurish tattoos all up and down his skinny arms.

"I don't know, man. I got that bum beef already. Don't wanna be messin' around."

"There'll be four of us," the recruiter continued. "Meetin' out at some farm. I was gonna catch a ride with you."

While listening, Reyes studied the woman.

What curves she lacked up top, she made up for with a really stellar ass.

Suddenly her attention snagged on him with a nasty glare.

Oops. Busted.

Busted looking at her *butt*. Definitely not cool.

Even all narrowed with annoyance, her blue eyes were nice—a soft color, thickly lashed.

Dismissing him, she turned away, which made his gaze return to that premium part of her anatomy. She didn't get back to work, though; instead she stood there with her hands on her hips, her shoulders set in annoyance.

He hadn't meant to interrupt her workout . . .

but he also hated to miss anything else the knuckleheads said.

He heard "Aspen Creek," but the rest was indistinct, and now they were heading out, spines bowed, feet shuffling.

One of them glanced toward him. Reyes met his gaze. "Can I help you?"

"You seen Mort?"

Having no idea who Mort might be, Reyes lied, "He usually shows up later in the day."

"Tell him I was lookin' for him, yeah?"

"And you are . . . ?" For certain, they hadn't come to his gym to work out, but then again, it's why he had the place, so cretins like that could pass along info.

"Hoop."

Novel name. "You got it, Hoop. You want to leave a number?"

"He has it."

Reyes looked back at Will, who manned the desk. "You see Mort come in, tell him to call Hoop." Then he walked away from Will's confusion, because Will had no idea who Mort was, either.

Satisfied, the two-bit thugs left.

Reyes waited until they were out of sight before he went to Will. "If you see anyone named Mort, let me know."

Will had learned not to ask questions, so he just nodded. He was a good worker, always showed up, and because Reyes paid him extra, he knew to keep his mouth shut and his eyes open.

The mystery woman regained his attention.

Guessing that she wouldn't linger much longer, Reyes moved toward her through the crowd. Occasionally he answered a quick question for a patron, all the while keeping his gaze on her.

He was pretty sure she felt his attention, but she didn't look at him again, not until he reached her.

Lips tight—very plump lips, he couldn't help noticing—she pulled out her earbuds and draped the cord around her neck.

Damn it, he never hesitated to speak his mind with women, but with her being so unapproachable, he floundered.

With a resigned sigh, she looked up at him and asked politely, "What?"

"I'm Reyes McKenzie, owner of the gym—"

"I know who you are."

She did, huh? But he noticed she didn't introduce herself. He rubbed his neck, shifted his feet like a friggin' schoolboy and waited.

This time she rolled her eyes before saying, "Kennedy Brooks. I've signed up for a year, but if there's a problem with my membership—"

"There's no problem." Surprised him, though. Most didn't choose the yearly option. In this part of town, people sometimes didn't know from one week to the next if they'd have money or time.

Most of his clientele was fluid, which was how his father had planned it. Lots of people coming and going made it easier to catch information from the street.

He'd tell Will to let him know from now on whenever they sold a big membership.

"Kennedy." Somehow the name fit her. She probably stood five feet five, making her damn near a foot shorter than him. "You need any help?"

She shook her head. "No, thank you."

He should have walked away, but he didn't. With Sterling's certainty in his mind, Reyes said, "If you want to defend yourself—"

"Just getting in shape."

Complete BS. She'd said it too quickly, and she didn't meet his gaze. "I don't think so."

She'd just been ready to punch again but paused at his reply. Slowly, she turned to face him. Crossing her arms and cocking out a hip, she looked him over with mere curiosity.

No interest. Nope. Just like . . . she wondered why he was still bothering her.

Reyes sighed.

She half smiled. "Why do you say that?"

"I've been watching you," he explained, hoping that'd lead into more.

"I noticed you watching," she replied, with no invitation to extend the conversation.

Well, too bad for her.

"I was watching because I see the difference between getting in shape and learning how to fend off attackers."

"Huh." Very sexy lips curled. "Well, that confirms something for me."

For whatever reason, he found himself stepping a little closer to her. "What's that?"

Her chin lifted. "You're not a mere instructor."

Her insight nearly blew him over, but he quickly recovered. "I already told you, I own the gym."

"So?" She rolled a shoulder. "You're more than a mere gym owner, too."

He opened his mouth, then closed it. Her lips were *really* distracting, especially when curved in a superior smile.

"You think you're the only observant one here? No, Mr. McKenzie, I notice things, too."

"Reyes." Mr. McKenzie was his father, for Christ's sake.

"Like you listening in to those young toughs. I noticed that, as well. Did you hear anything insightful?"

Well, hell, this lady was dangerous. "I give my attention to everyone who comes in."

"Yes, there's attention, and then there's listening in on a conversation to ferret out info." She gave his own words back to him. "I see the difference. So, Mr. McKenzie, how about you mind your business and I'll mind mine, and we'll get along just fine."

Well . . . He really had no idea how to react to that, so he merely saluted, said, "Carry on," and stalked away. He wasn't running, but it did feel like a strategic retreat.

This time he felt her gaze drilling into his back.

Later, he'd give Sterling hell. For now, though . . . Kennedy intrigued him even more. He couldn't get her off his mind—and the fact that she didn't pack up and leave immediately, that she stuck around, glancing at him every so often, felt almost like a dare.

Or an invitation? Not likely.

He wouldn't act on it anyway, not yet. He didn't want to be a creeper who bothered the clients. But he wondered if she reconsidered her stance, maybe she'd approach him next time.

It was a nice little fantasy, one that included him getting his hands on that plump backside . . . Shaking his head, he retrieved his cell phone and sent Cade a message about what he'd heard. Four guys probably didn't mean anything, but a farm in Aspen Creek might. Never hurt to share the tidbits he heard.

He'd just finished when Will called out to him. "Hey, Reyes, you have a call."

As he headed to the desk, he decided it was time to get his mind off a certain prickly-but-somehow-sexy woman. He wasn't a glutton for punishment like his brother.

Yet even as he made that vow, his attention

wandered back to her. He needed things with Adela and Mattox to blow; that'd give him something else to focus on.

While speaking with the head of a youth group about sponsoring a field trip, he deliberately turned his back on Kennedy. When he heard the front door open, he jerked around and saw her walking through it, her gym bag in hand.

Even while keeping up with the phone conversation, Reyes tracked her movements through the big front window. She scanned the parked cars, up and down the street, her gaze watchful. Made sense for the neighborhood, but he sensed it was more with her, like an ingrained wariness.

Most people took safety for granted; clearly Kennedy did not.

Reyes saw the moment her attention snagged on something out of range of the front window. Frowning, she tossed her bag into a little red compact, relocked the car and headed slowly, cautiously along the sidewalk and out of view.

What the hell?

Too curious to ignore it, he wrapped up the call so quickly he bordered on rudeness, ending with, "Sorry, something's come up, but sure, I'd be glad to sponsor. Just give the details to Will. Thanks." He handed the phone to Will, then hurried out the door just in time to see Kennedy walk between the two buildings.

All kinds of shady shit happened in the alleys.

Never mind that it was the middle of the day, or that he wore only shorts.

Reyes went after her, his stride long and fast—until he spotted her kneeling next to some garbage cans. Behind a broken-down cardboard box was . . . a very mangy cat.

"Careful," he said softly, already moving forward to join her.

"Shh," she replied without looking up, as if she'd already known it was him. "He's scared."

Reyes could imagine. The cat, who had probably once been white but was now too messy to tell for sure, had very strange eyes, one pale gray, the other mustard yellow, and a little . . . googly. Mud and filth streaked his face, and part of his tail was missing.

He hunkered back, eyeing Reyes.

"Do you think we can catch him?"

Staring at her, Reyes asked stupidly, "Catch him?"

"He's hungry," she cooed.

Cooed.

For him, she'd been all snippy and smug, but for a mangy cat—And then he heard a softer, squeakier little sound. Ah, hell. Resigned, he let out a groan.

"Shh," Kennedy said again.

Her bossiness made him grin. "That's not a tomcat."

She didn't look at him, only asked, "No?"

"You don't hear it?"

"What?"

"Kittens." The tiny meows came again—very nearby, in fact.

Her eyes went wide, her mouth forming a soft O. Then she breathed, *"Kittens."*

Yeah, he knew exactly what that expression meant. Either way, he'd have helped the cat, but kittens changed the manner he would have used.

When she started to stand, he said, "No. Don't start looking for them yet. They're close by, but we might spook the mama if we disturb them before we've won her over."

Trusting him, at least on that, Kennedy nodded. "Right."

Reyes considered the situation. "If she's nursing, she needs to eat."

"I was trying to figure out how I'd sneak in a cat, but a cat with kittens?" Kennedy turned to him. "Where I'm staying, pets aren't allowed. What are we going to do?"

We? Minutes ago she'd told him to buzz off, but now they were working together? Okay, he'd take it. "If I can corral her, I can put her and the babies in my office for now." Responsibility for the cats would give them a neutral link, one that might bridge the divide so she'd tell him what she was up to, and whose ass he needed to kick for her.

"Would you really?" Excited now, she smiled

at him, a genuine smile that made him want to lick her mouth.

Down, he ordered himself. "Keep an eye on her while I go find a box. I packed food for later today—we might be able to use it to lure her in."

We. He used that word, reinforcing it for her.

And she didn't object.

But that was a little too easy, so he wanted it confirmed. As he stood, he asked, "You *will* be back to help me figure this out, right?"

"You know I come to the gym nearly every day. Of course I'll be back." Just then, the cat crept out enough to butt her head into Kennedy's extended hand. "Aw."

The lady looked very different when she was being all gentle and sweet. She looked a little too appealing, in fact.

Maybe seeing all that overblown chemistry between Sterling and Cade was starting to wear on him. Not that he wanted anything that substantial . . . but it did have him looking at Kennedy differently.

Before he said or did something stupid, he went inside to get what he needed. He returned with a nice-sized cardboard box, a plush towel in the bottom of it and half of his chicken salad croissant.

Kennedy had the cat nearly in her lap at that point. "After this, I'll pay for her food and whatever else she needs."

No way would he commit to that. "Let's just

see how far we get today, okay?" He held out the sandwich.

Kennedy gave him an incredulous look over his bait. "Croissant? You?"

What did she think, that he sustained himself on Cheez Whiz and beer? "It's delicious—but I didn't make it."

Her brows leveled out. "Ah, girlfriend?" Then on the heels of that, with a darkening frown, she asked, "Wife?"

That particular acerbic tone caused a laugh that startled the cat.

While she won the scraggly thing over again, Reyes said around a big grin, "No girlfriend, definitely not a *wife*."

Her jaw flexed over the way he stressed the word, but she said nothing. It took only seconds to locate the kittens in a torn bag of trash. Reyes carefully transferred them into the box. There were only three, thank God. He double-checked, looking everywhere. The mama, still on Kennedy's lap, went alert and immediately started fretting . . . until she found the food.

Making a sound somewhere between a purr and a growl, she devoured it but still kept her eyes on Reyes. She ate the entire sandwich, croissant roll and all, which made him realize just how hungry the poor thing had been.

When she finished, she went into the box with her kittens, circled once, then lay on her side to lick her paw while the kittens nursed.

Yeah, that melted even his own heart a little.

Standing close to his side, Kennedy whispered, "She was starving."

He glanced down at her, then had to look away again. He'd never seen a woman with quite that particular mix of tenderness and sympathy.

"She'll be fine now," he assured her, slowly closing the box so she couldn't leap out the minute he moved her. He was about to suggest that Kennedy walk with him, one hand on the cardboard flaps, until he got the animals inside, but his phone beeped, and when he checked the message, he saw it was go time.

CHAPTER SEVENTEEN

Watching Star stir awake from her nap was a distinct pleasure, one that Cade wanted to enjoy every day for the rest of his life.

She still had a towel, now lopsided, on her head, and a hickey on her shoulder. He lightly brushed his fingertips over the mark.

The core of his basic nature was to protect his own, and she *was* his now, whether she'd accepted that as fact or not. Eventually she would. He'd see to it. "Hey, sleepyhead."

On a sinuous stretch, she murmured . . . and settled again.

Knowing he'd caused her exhaustion with sexual excess left him aching with renewed lust—and love. The urge was to cradle her close, coddle her, spar with her, train her, make love to her and then start all over again. Conversations, meals, showers, danger, sex . . . Sharing with her made everything better.

It struck him that he needed a lifetime of that, a lifetime with her.

The emotional overload left him combustible, agitated and needing her again. He curved his hand around her shoulder, absorbing the satiny feel of her skin, the warmth.

Her lashes barely lifted. "Cade?"

Smiling at her, he said, "You taste so good I'd prefer to have *you* for lunch. But since everyone will wait on us . . ."

Eyes popping open wide, she stared at him in blank surprise. "Lunch?"

Damn, she was a sweetheart with that comical confusion on her face. "Bernard has outdone himself, and he's waiting for your praise."

"Bernard," she repeated, before coming up to one elbow and groaning. "It's time for lunch already?"

"You've been asleep awhile."

She reached up to keep the towel on her head. "But I *never* nap."

Leaning in, Cade whispered, "Guess the awesome sex tuckered you out. I gave you two big Os, if you recall."

The fog left her gaze and she grinned. "Of course I recall. Sex with you makes up my favorite memories."

Severely disliking how she worded that, he clarified, "Reality."

"What?"

"Us, together. That's reality, not a memory."

She softened, her lips curving. "You do like to say confusing things, but if everyone is waiting, I need to make myself presentable instead of trying to figure you out."

She made to get out of the bed, but with a kiss, Cade took her down to the mattress again, his chest against the soft cushion of her breasts, one leg thrown over hers to keep her still. He searched her gaze, determined to gain an admission. "Tell me you understand, babe. Say that you like our relationship."

"You kidding?" She ran her fingers along his jaw, around his ear to his nape. "Course I do. I'm not dumb."

That answer didn't really satisfy, either, but then, short of her telling him how much she cared, no answer would. Cade gave her a firm kiss. "Dad checked my stitches, bitched because I'd pulled one, and redressed it. If he says anything in front of you, ignore him."

Blanching, she whispered, "Your dad knows what we were doing?"

Cade almost choked on his humor. Because teasing her was so much fun, he used the same hushed tone she'd had. "Yes." Scorching heat rushed into her face, leaving her cheeks blotchy. The grin broke through. "He knows we were *sparring*."

Relief took away her starch. "Not nice, you butthead. You knew what I was thinking."

"I couldn't resist. Seems to happen a lot where you're concerned." With a last firm kiss to her mouth, he rolled out of the bed, then hauled her up. "Bernard has hot roast beef sandwiches with caramelized onions on crusty bread—that's the description he insisted I share, along with the warning that you'll want to enjoy it while it's hot, so hustle up. Lunch is in fifteen minutes."

"Ack." Beautifully naked, she darted around him, already whipping away the towel. "You should have told me all that five minutes ago!"

Sitting on the side of the bed, Cade listened to the blow-dryer and smiled with bone-deep satisfaction. Had he done this much smiling before Star? He didn't think so. For most of his life he'd been driven. Driven to buck his father's dictates, then to succeed in the army, and now to right wrongs for women and children exploited by traffickers.

Singular focus kept him on track, or at least it did before Star. Now he enjoyed thinking of her, seeing her, touching her. He'd always do the best he could, but responsibilities had moved aside to make room for pleasure.

To make room for Star.

When the noise quit, he found himself saying, "I have a decent place of my own."

The door jerked open and Star stood there, still naked but now with her hair loose the way he liked it. She stared at him a moment, then stalked forward to get clothes. "A place other than this apartment?"

He'd never really thought of these rooms as his apartment, but then, he knew he had a small home to call his own. Star didn't. "I bought it after I was medically discharged from the army while serving as a Ranger."

Pausing with her panties halfway up her legs, Star's gaze clashed with his. After a second, she pulled them up and came to sit by him. Breasts bared, eyes watchful.

Cade said nothing, leaving it to her to ask any questions she had.

"You were a Ranger?"

"Once a Ranger, always a Ranger, so I'm a Ranger still, medically retired."

Uncertainty trembled in her fingers as she tucked back her hair. "Medically retired, why?"

It felt good to share with her, to finally, completely open up. He laced his fingers with hers, moving her hand to his thigh. When with her, he couldn't touch her enough. "After a lot of deployments and hard landings when jumping from planes, I had multiple leg issues."

"You jumped from planes?" Surprise was immediately followed by concern. "You're hurt?"

"I'm in prime physical shape for the average man."

The concern shifted to amused interest. "Heck yeah, you are."

"But for a Ranger?" Keeping his attention off her breasts wasn't easy. "Not so much."

That statement left her disgruntled. "Who says so?"

His mouth twitched. "Don't act like you're sorry I'm here."

"What? No, course not." She stood again

and reached for her bra. "So tell me about your house—and how come we're not there instead of here?"

He'd known that would be her response. "Like I said, it's small. Two bedrooms, one I use for storage. Family room, eat-in kitchen, bathroom. A single-car garage. There's a nice big basement, though, so I have my workout gear down there. Nothing like Dad's downstairs setup, just bare concrete walls and floor, exposed pipes and all that."

She pulled up straight-leg jeans, tugging a little to get them over her perfect ass, and then pulled on a loose shirt. "And we're here because?"

"It's the safest place to be right now."

Brows pinching in thought, she sat beside him again to get on her socks and those shit-kicker boots of hers. "If I wasn't with you, would you feel the same?"

"You are with me." He trailed his fingers through her hair. "And you matter to me, Star. A lot."

Some turbulent emotion brought her gaze snapping to his. He saw her slender throat work, watched her lick her lips. Shooting for cockiness, she said, "Ditto."

He wasn't buying it. Her attitude was mostly uncertainty, not disinterest. What would she do if he said that he loved her? With everyone waiting, he decided not to put it to the test.

Bent at the waist to tie her boots, she said with nonchalance, "You're the only one who calls me that now."

"Star? It suits you."

"I thought Star had disappeared years ago."

Very softly, he said, "I found her again."

Denials hung in the air, but she didn't give them voice. Instead she stood and held out a hand. "Come on. I'm starved."

Knowing this was difficult for her, Cade let her lead him out. "Before I got to know you, I called you something else."

"Yeah? You called me Sterling?"

"No." They started up the steps.

"Then what?"

"Trouble." Catching her at the top of the stairwell, he pinned her to the wall. "Massive trouble—especially to my libido."

Her laugh sounded almost like a giggle, and damn, that pleased him. "Your libido is fine."

"It's in hyperdrive around you."

Dodging his mouth, she said, "Lunch is waiting."

"Then give me a kiss to carry me through the next hour or two."

Challenge sparked in her dark eyes and she focused on his mouth. Small but capable hands slid around his neck. "All right."

Damn. She leaned forward—and singed him.

He shouldn't have started this when he knew the others were waiting, but he wasn't about to end it, either. She nibbled on his bottom lip, licked the upper, sealed her lips to his and dueled with his tongue.

He had his hips pinned to hers, grinding against her, when he heard the door open.

Star freed her mouth and immediately used his shoulder as a shield. Cade concentrated on breathing.

Behind them, stunned silence reigned, and then Bernard stated, "Lunch will not keep, so I hope this will." He slammed the door again.

Shoulders shaking, Star held on to him.

"I have a boner."

The snickers turned into full-blown howls.

It was nice, hearing her laugh so freely. He wanted to hear it more often. "It's not that funny."

She tried to catch her breath, took one look at him and fell into another fit.

To get even, Cade moved his open palm over her breast, whispering against her ear, "Your nipples are also telling a tale."

That earned him a groan and a tight squeeze. "If I wasn't so hungry, I'd say to hell with lunch, but after all that exercise this morning, I think I need to eat."

"We have the rest of our lives," he said and tugged her through the doorway before she could stop sputtering.

Getting past her reserve was a challenge, but also strangely satisfying. And fun.

Especially since she liked the physical side of their relationship as much as he did. The rest? He didn't know yet, but he refused to believe he was the only one falling hard.

"Bernard, you outdid yourself." Sitting back, one hand to her full stomach, Sterling sighed. Much as she wanted to see Cade's home, she would definitely miss Bernard's cooking.

For the moment, she refused to dwell on why Cade hadn't yet shown her his place. There'd been opportunity, before the danger ramped up, so why hadn't he? Did he want to keep his personal life separate?

Even to her skeptical mind, that didn't make much sense, not with the careless way he threw around the *L* word. And what was that comment in the stairwell? *The rest of our lives.*

Like maybe he expected them to spend that life together?

Hoping for too much could lead to the biggest disappointment she'd ever known—and God knew, she'd known plenty. But she couldn't help herself. Her heart had already launched on a gleeful path of "what if?"

Was it possible?

If he had something to say, why didn't he just come out and say it already? All those verbal clues that she didn't know how to decipher were making her a little nuts.

"Oh, hey," Madison said, sitting forward to stare at her laptop. "We have movement."

Cade's sister had alternated between eating, joining in the casual conversation and scanning her screen. No one had commented on the laptop set on the table before her.

"What is it?" Out of his seat, Cade went behind Madison's chair, one hand braced on the back of it, to see for himself.

The expression on his face warned Sterling, apprehension instantly filling her.

Why? She wanted to get Mattox, so she needed to know the truth about Adela. It's what they'd been working for, what she wanted.

But she'd just been contemplating her future and now reality came crashing down around her.

"It's go time." Already with his cell out, Cade keyed in a message.

"Getting hold of Reyes?" Parrish asked.

"He'd messaged me earlier about some guys hanging out, talking about a job tonight. No idea if they're connected, but it's possible."

"My instincts are telling me this is it." Madison glanced up. "Tell Reyes to make arrangements to leave the gym."

Getting her gumption back—sort of—Sterling asked, "He has someone to cover for him?"

"Every eventuality has been prearranged," Parrish explained.

Of course it had. Clearing the sudden lump of

nervousness from her throat, Sterling asked, "Do you see Mattox? Is Adela with him?"

Already shaking her head, Madison used her mouse to take a few screenshots. "It's a ten-foot box truck and I'm willing to bet there are women inside. Here comes a car."

"Reyes said he'll be ready in five, just waiting for directions." Returning his phone to his pocket, Cade went back to looking at the screen with his sister. "That's Mattox getting out of the back seat. I can't see if Adela is in there."

Sterling sat still, listening as they coordinated around her. She felt like a useless lump, but she was out of her element and didn't want to slow anyone down.

"He's opening the back of the truck—I wish one of the cameras showed that view!"

Cade rested a hand on his sister's shoulder. "The three cameras are helping, hon. Will you be able to follow them?"

"Probably, or at least enough to get a fix on where they're going. Tell Reyes to get over to I-25 near there. He needs to be closer to pick up the tail once we know."

Almost at the same time, Sterling's phone rang. Startled, she gave an inelegant jump.

All eyes turned to her.

The lump in her throat expanded, but she managed a cavalier smile that carried over to a neutral tone. "Hello?"

"Francis?"

That panicked voice had her sitting forward. Was Adela not with Mattox?

Quickly, she put the phone on speaker and said, "Adela. I haven't heard from you in a—"

"You have to help. *Please.* He has new women, Francis. They'll be in the same shape as me, but if you can figure out a way to stop him . . . I didn't know who else to call!"

Knowing how the others would react, but wanting to gauge Adela's reaction, Sterling suggested, "The police?"

Parrish shook his head at her. Alarm raised Madison's brows.

Cade just held up a placating hand, indicating they should wait and let her do her thing.

So what was her thing? Somehow, while falling in love with Cade, she'd forgotten.

"Not a good idea. I told you, he's bought off some of the cops."

So Sterling hadn't tripped her up on that. Did Mattox have a few cops in his pocket? It'd be worth finding out. "How do you know?" It wasn't unheard of for a cop to be complicit, but it was rare, and she figured Cade and his family would have forewarned her if the problem was around here.

"I don't have much time! He could be back to the cabin any minute."

"What cabin?" Sterling asked, playing along— just in case. "Where?"

"It's a shack in the mountain, near Coalville."

Brows shot up everywhere. Adela admitted it? She was either truly desperate or riding out with Mattox right now.

"But that doesn't matter," Adela rushed on. "He has eight new girls. I overheard him talking about north on I-25, something about meeting at an abandoned farm near Aspen Creek."

Cade's entire demeanor changed. It was amazing to witness as he started texting Reyes again.

Gently, with understanding and sympathy, Sterling asked, "If you don't want cops, how do you expect me to handle it?"

All she heard was heavy breathing. "I thought . . . I thought you had that big guy with you. Mattox has been furious that he was able to fight off all the men he sent after him. He even said some of his guys are still missing."

Huh. Adela had managed to hear a lot. "He's one man, Adela. And I assume Mattox won't be alone."

"No. He doesn't go anywhere without personal protection, plus I think he hired on a few more."

Sterling waited.

"I'm sorry. You seemed so resourceful . . ." Adela caught her breath. "Guess I was wrong, so maybe you could go ahead and try the police? Just, please, don't tell anyone I tipped you off. He'd kill me if he ever found out."

"I can come get you from the cabin—"

"No, he's leaving people here to watch me. It'd be too dangerous. Besides, I don't matter right now. I just don't want those other women . . ." She drew a shaky breath. "I want them to have a chance, okay? But I have to go now. If I don't hide this phone, he'll know." The call died.

Just like her nerve. Just like her backbone.

Sterling looked up at Cade. Dear God, she wasn't sure what to do.

"I've got this," Cade said, his voice firm. "Did I tell you that Rangers are critical thinkers? We are, so let me handle things."

Relieved that this time she didn't have to sort it out alone, Sterling swallowed back her misgivings and came to her feet. "Okay. Right." She'd made her voice firm. She wasn't a wimp and she wouldn't start acting like one. "So what do we do first?"

Parrish's discerning gaze missed nothing. He turned to Cade. "You're good to go?"

"Glad things are finally in motion," he said. "The men Reyes overheard at the gym also mentioned Aspen Creek."

Madison frowned. "What else?"

"Four men, and Mattox is ensuring they're all strapped."

"You've devastated his organization," Parrish mused as he pushed back his chair and began to pace. "First getting Misfits shut down, then going through his men. He's afraid to operate until you're out of the picture. This is his Hail Mary, a last desperate attempt to try to regain his footing."

Desperate? Sterling wondered if Parrish was delusional. "Four men," she emphasized. "All armed."

Cade shook his head. "Bozos, Reyes said. Nothing to worry about."

Incredulity tensed her body. "You can't know that."

Perturbed by her tone, Parrish zeroed in on Cade. "Do we need to wait, to investigate more?"

"Forget the number of men. There may be eight women. Eight innocents."

"If she wasn't lying," Madison pointed out.

Resolute, Cade said, "I'm not willing to chance it."

Parrish's eyes narrowed, but he nodded.

Not good enough, not for Sterling. "If they're armed . . ."

"I'll disarm them."

Of all the idiotic—She couldn't believe he was that arrogant.

Cade held out a hand to her. "Come on. We'll need to leave quickly so we can rendezvous with Reyes on the way."

Knowing she had to find her own arrogance and fast, Sterling nodded.

"Bernard, would you please keep an eye on things here while I help them get ready?"

"I'll be diligent," Bernard announced while taking her seat. "If anyone moves, I'll alert you."

"Thank you." Madison jogged around and ahead of Cade.

Getting ready, Sterling found, meant donning body armor, strapping on guns, and stowing a sniper rifle and plenty of ammo. Much better stuff than the knife necklace she'd worn to Misfits. God, that felt like a lifetime ago.

When she'd been all alone in the world.

Shaking off those maudlin thoughts, Sterling put her knife in her boot, the brass knuckles in her rear pocket. With Madison's assistance, it was such seamless prep that within minutes she was seated in the passenger side of Cade's SUV while he had a few quiet words with his father. Madison had returned to the kitchen as command central.

Through the window, Sterling watched as Parrish put a fatherly hand on Cade's shoulder. Seeing that touched her heart. Cade's father was nearly as tall as him, still very fit, and for once she detected concern in his gaze. This, she realized, was how Cade would look as he aged. Distinguished, impressive and in control.

Maybe Cade had inherited his attitude from Parrish, too. With their cool command, the two of them were very different from Madison's joyful persona and Reyes's maddening personality.

The more she looked at Cade, the harder her heart pounded.

This could be it. She could die—worse, *Cade could get hurt*—and all her newfound happiness would mean absolutely nothing.

This caring stuff was awful. How simple her life used to be when she had no one, when even *she* didn't matter that much. Now she was crazy in love and worried sick because of it.

It changed everything.

Cade slid into the driver's seat and started the SUV.

Looking back at Parrish, she found him still standing there, his hands clasped behind his back, watching as they drove away.

Sterling lifted her hand in a wave. He returned the gesture. Parrish might be a dictator, but he obviously loved his kids.

How stressful must it be for him, having his sons in the field?

Facing forward again, she glanced at Cade. His hands rested on the steering wheel, his posture relaxed. It all felt surreal.

"Everything okay, honey?"

"Yes." *No.* She wasn't sure anything would ever again be okay.

"You're staring."

"Because you are devastating to my senses." *And I need to absorb more of you while I can.*

Smiling, Cade handed her his phone. "Here, Madison will send updates, in case they get too far ahead of us."

Her palms felt sweaty when she accepted the cell. Why? She'd done stuff like this before . . . Okay, *that* was a big lie. She'd never done *anything* this complex.

But she'd wanted to, right?

Apparently sensing her turmoil, Cade put a hand on her knee. "We'll pick up Reyes shortly."

Knowing Cade's brother was also effective in this crazy stuff, that he'd be good backup for Cade, made her feel a tiny bit better.

Again, anticipating her reaction, Cade drew a bottle of water from the door and handed it to her. "Hydrate."

Hydrate, she mocked silently, even as she took a quick drink. His "business as usual" attitude was really starting to irk. "What about you? Don't you need to drink some?"

"If I do, I have another bottle."

So calm, so matter-of-fact.

Get it together, Sterling ordered herself. Cade was smart enough to know if he couldn't handle the situation. She should take comfort in his confidence, not get annoyed by it.

Scenery passed in a blur, much like her thoughts. Madison texted once to say that she'd confirmed two men in the truck, and one in the front seat of the car chauffeuring Mattox.

Sterling read the message to Cade and sent back his simple acknowledgment, but her mind scrambled on the math. Four men hired, three accompanying Mattox, and Mattox himself . . . That was *eight* men.

Against the three of them.

And they still didn't know if Adela was along for the ride, complicit in everything, or cowering, possibly injured, back in an isolated cabin.

Not long after that, they turned down a narrow road off the highway and picked up Reyes. He'd parked his truck behind some trees and strode out with the same insouciance as Cade.

She was ready to chew her nails, and they acted like it was nothing.

Cade got out and walked around to meet his brother at the back of the SUV.

Twisting in her seat, Sterling watched as Reyes suited up, starting with a back holster that held two handguns. Unlike Cade, Reyes adjusted his bulletproof vest right over his T-shirt.

Too antsy to sit still, Sterling got out to join them.

Reyes glanced up with a smile. "Hey, girl. How's it hanging?"

"Hey."

Far too perceptive, Reyes did a double take, but wisely chose not to comment on the visible tension in her frame.

Instead, he picked up the semiauto precision rifle. "It's going to rain."

Cade shrugged. "Every afternoon, this time of year. You won't melt."

"I'd rather not calculate wind, though."

When Sterling frowned, Cade explained, "Reyes will cover us from farther away."

That was news to her. "He won't be with us?"

"I'll ensure no one sneaks up behind you."

Well . . . that was reassuring. "You're a crack shot, huh?"

Tugging on a lock of her hair, Reyes said, "Even with wind and rain." He closed the back of the car. "Let's go. I'll drive."

So that Cade could ride shotgun, Sterling took the back seat. Heavy clouds moved in and around the sun, one minute making it gloomy, the next leaving the day bright. She knew they were right. Rain was inevitable, and it fit her mood.

If they all got through this day unscathed, she'd reevaluate how she lived her life. Cade mattered. His family mattered.

And by God, that meant she mattered, too.

CHAPTER EIGHTEEN

They came into the farm from the side, skirting around scraggly woods, making their way over a neglected field. Given that dried stalks remained scattered about, she guessed someone had once grown corn.

Age and neglect had ravaged the farmhouse, the windows all broken, the roof half gone. Farther back, and to the right, an old weathered barn remained standing.

If not for the box truck and black sedan parked behind it, Sterling would have thought they had the wrong place. But no, the evidence was there. Had they come in through the front, they wouldn't have seen either vehicle parked in back.

Both men were quietly focused as they took in a big gnarled tree near a fence line, a massive boulder and an old trestle bridge over a creek.

"There," Reyes decided, nodding at the bridge. "I'll have a better line of sight from there."

Cade nodded. "I'll circle around and come in on that side of the barn. I'll be able to see what I'm up against and you'll be able to cover me."

"Should I pick a few off right away?"

"That would just announce us and might not be necessary anyway. Wait and see how it goes."

Sterling frowned at them as they went over plans. There were eight men out there, waiting, anxious to kill Cade and probably Reyes, too.

Anxious to get hold of her.

In no way did she feel equipped for this—but how could she say that when they were so freakishly calm?

Reyes lowered the binoculars. "I only counted five inside the barn. Think they're planning to stash the women there?"

"How secure could it be? Wouldn't take much to have the whole structure falling down around them."

"What if it's a trap?" When both men turned to her, Sterling curled her fingers until she felt her nails digging into her palms. "What if one of them has a sniper rifle of his own? He could pick us off as we close in."

"Not likely," Reyes said. "I'm not sure these buffoons can manage that much planning. The punks at the gym definitely don't have any talents beyond finding their way into trouble."

"Mattox is not a punk," she insisted. "He's a bloodthirsty, heartless bastard who would take pleasure in killing all of us."

Slowly, Reyes lowered the binoculars. Seconds passed before he spoke, and again he chose to overlook her trepidation. "A few of them have gone to the back of the truck. They don't appear to be aware of us."

"Mattox?" Sterling leaned forward, staring hard, but without binoculars of her own, she couldn't make out any people. "Did you see him?"

"Neither of them look thick enough. Besides, I can't imagine Mattox doing the grunt work."

"We've stripped him of his resources." Cade took another look. "He's here. I sense it."

Sterling whispered, "Me, too." Somehow she knew Mattox was there . . . and she knew everything about this was wrong.

Cade glanced back at her in sharpened awareness. Dissecting her. Analyzing her. Coming to conclusions.

How could eyes so cool be so scorching?

In defensive belligerence, she asked, "What?"

"Now isn't the time to hold back. If you have suspicions—"

"It feels *wrong*," she blurted. "All of it. In my gut, I know we're being set up." Sitting back, she waited for their derision. She waited for their doubt.

The brothers shared a look.

Reyes surprised her by saying, "Gut feelings have kept me alive more than once."

Cade nodded. "So this might not be the cakewalk I anticipated."

Now that she had their attention, Sterling started to relax.

Until Cade caught her hand. "I don't want to

piss you off, babe, but I have a favor to ask."

Reyes hummed a little, drummed his fingertips on the steering wheel and went back to surveying the barn.

With a terrible foreboding, Sterling lifted her chin.

"I think you're right. I think it's a setup of some sort—but it's nothing I can't handle."

Tension burrowed into her every muscle. "You've gotten through things like this before?"

"Many times."

Clearly he wasn't retrenching—and she wasn't willing to hold him up. "Okay, so let's go. The waiting is worse than the doing."

Cade didn't budge. His hold on her hand tightened. "Since it likely is a trap, we need someone at the wheel, ready to go, in case we have to bounce in a hurry."

Of course she knew where this was going. "You mean me?"

"You're good. I'd never say otherwise." His low voice seemed to brush over her skin like a reassuring caress. "Put to the test, I know you'd handle any situation. No doubts at all, I swear. But the truth is—"

"You and Reyes are better at this." A blatant truth.

"We're bigger. Stronger." His thumb rubbed over her clenched knuckles. "And yes, better trained for this."

It galled, knowing that Cade was giving her an out.

He must have known that, too, because he tacked on, "It's either you or Reyes—"

Reyes snorted but continued studying the barn. "Still only see five. No women."

Sterling knew she should have been gracious, should have accepted the excuse with gratitude, but instead she said, "I'm agreeing under duress."

His shoulders relaxed, telling her that her decision had mattered to him.

Before Cade, the concept of the future had no real meaning. Now she wanted to see what happened between them. She wanted to know what tomorrow, the next month, an entire year would bring. "You need to understand, Cade. I'm going to be very worried for you. *Very.*" It horrified her that her voice wavered with emotion. "Damn it, you've stolen my edge!"

"I'll go get in position." Taking the rifle from the floor near Cade's feet, Reyes left the SUV, then kept low as he cut across the field. He'd have to wade out into the creek to climb the trestle, but she didn't have a doubt he could do it.

With terrible timing, Sterling realized she liked Reyes now. Heck, in such a short time, the entire McKenzie family had become dear to her.

When Cade got out and circled around, she stepped out to meet him, oblivious to the light rain that immediately dampened her clothes and hair. Without missing a beat, he pressed her to the side of the SUV. His rough hand cradled her cheek. "The timing is fucked, but I need you to know something."

"Wha—"

"I love you."

Her heart shot into her throat and stuck there, feeling as big as a grapefruit. Unfair! *Now* he decided to make it all crystal clear, with her rowdy emotions flying out of control?

At her stunned silence, his mouth quirked. "I *love* you, Star."

It took a second, but she found herself smiling, as well. "Cade—"

"There's no way in hell I won't come back to you." He punctuated that with the briefest of kisses to her slightly parted lips but then wasted no more time talking. "Get behind the wheel, keep the doors locked and stay alert."

He took it one step further, practically putting her in the seat himself, locking the door and quietly closing it.

He hadn't given her a chance to tell him how she felt, and now she desperately wanted to. Did he not trust what she'd say? Was he uncertain of her?

A laughable idea. She was a complete nobody, without special talent, no family, nothing to recommend her, and he was . . .

He was everything to her.

Cade loves me. She hugged his confession to her heart, and in that moment, she believed it would be all right.

Had he known her misgivings? Course he had. Cade missed nothing. He'd deliberately saved her by saying they needed a driver. That hadn't been discussed in their prior plans, so she knew he'd come up with it on the fly.

Somehow, he truly knew her, well enough to understand her even when she had trouble understanding herself. Without the excuse he'd given her, she *would* have gone along. And she likely would have been up to the task.

She knew it. Cade knew it, too. And that's what mattered.

He'd been considerate . . . because he loved her.

More focused because of that, she stared ahead, already losing sight of Cade, still unable to spot Reyes. She picked up Cade's discarded binoculars. If it became necessary, she'd lend a hand.

Otherwise, she'd be right here—waiting.

Spotting Reyes on the bridge, positioned behind a beam, Cade stole low through the high weeds and cornstalks until he was on the other side of the barn, then crept forward. Once he got close enough, he could hear men talking. Not Mattox, not yet, but he sensed the bastard was near.

"Think they'll show?" someone asked. "Should have been here by now, right?"

"Have a look around. Take someone with you."

Cade flattened his back to the rough, weather-bleached boards and waited. The men murmured low, mostly complaints about the rain. Then one said, "You check around back. I'll go this way."

Perfect. He could take them on two at a time, but individually would be quieter, ensuring he didn't alert the others.

The first started around the corner. Slouched, one hand shoved in his pocket, the other hand holding a revolver at his side, he spotted Cade a second too late.

Snagging the much smaller man into a tight choke hold that both kept him silent and immobilized him, Cade torqued up the pressure until the man's skinny legs gave out and he slumped. Lowering him to the ground, Cade quickly wrapped his mouth with duct tape, then secured his hands and feet with nylon cuffs.

He stuck the guy's weapon into his waistband and in less than thirty seconds was at the back of the barn—where he caught the startled surprise of the second guy as he stepped into view. Hair in a ponytail and missing two front teeth made the sight pretty comical.

When the thug opened his mouth to scream, Cade slammed his fist into his face, putting him down, dazed, but not yet out.

Easy enough. Straddling him, Cade gripped his throat tight. "Make a sound, and you're dead."

Blinking fast in panic, the idiot went still. Cade released him but only to land another hard punch, and this time it put him to sleep. He trussed up that guy much like the first.

Reyes had spotted five, so he had three to go.

A twig snapped, and Cade looked back to see two more men standing there, and if their wild-eyed expressions meant anything, they were scared spitless. They each held guns but hadn't yet aimed them.

Even more reckless, they were within reach.

Slowly, Cade smiled—then spun, leg out, taking them off their feet. They crashed into each other.

Either Mattox was getting really desperate by using wannabe street toughs with no training, or he didn't care if they all died.

Not that Cade committed random murder, but still, he took them apart pretty easily, even while preparing for another threat to show. He bound their hands and feet, and when he heard the shot, he knew it was Reyes.

On the other side of the barn, someone howled in pain. The last man? Or maybe Mattox.

Back on his feet, Cade peered into the barn, saw it was empty and felt fury expand. Where the fuck was Mattox?

He had a few prisoners who might be able to tell him.

Turning back, he met the gaze of one of the punks.

Face bloodied and eyes wild, he watched as Cade strode toward him.

Trying to scuttle back, the panicked guy asked, "Who the fuck are you?"

Cade kicked him in the ribs. With his hands bound, he couldn't block the strike at all. "Where's Mattox?"

"Goddammit!" he yelled, trying to curl in on himself. "Fucking asshole!"

The outpouring of profanity didn't faze Cade. He aimed his Glock. "You have two seconds. One, t—"

"He's in the farmhouse!"

"Shut up, Mort," the other man growled. "Mattox'll cut your fuckin' throat."

"And this one will shoot me, man! Either way, I'm dead."

In the house . . . "Why?"

"Don't want his biz told, that's why."

Idiot. Ignoring Mort, Cade stepped on the other one's nuts, hard enough to make him scream. *"Why* is he in the house?" With the house barely standing, the barn would have been a better choice.

Urgency beat in Cade's brain. He needed to see Star, needed to touch her. Needed to know—

Mort stammered, "Some sort of setup, dude. We don't get details. Now let up 'fore you kill him."

Blinding rage coalesced. *Star.* It all became a blur at that point. He quickly gagged Mort and the other idiot. Then in a flat-out run, he headed for the house.

The gunshot scared Sterling, making it impossible for her to stay in the car. Heart rapping, she got out with the binoculars and stared, but everything must have been happening on the other side of the barn.

Had Reyes fired, or had one of Mattox's men?

Caught in indecision, she chewed her lip—and suddenly Adela slammed up to the fender of the SUV. Swinging around to face her, the gun already in her hand, Sterling gaped in shock.

Adela's mouth was swollen, crusted over with dried blood, and one of her eyes was blackened. A purpling bruise spread out on her jaw. "What in the world—"

"Francis . . ." Now half draped over the hood of the car, her legs unable to hold her, Adela groped her way around. "Please. Help me."

Empathy took over, sharpened by rage, and Sterling snapped to attention. "What happened?" After holstering the gun, she hurried over to put an arm around Adela. "Mattox did this to you?"

"Yes." Slumping against her, Adela held on for dear life. Her clothes were torn, a dirty T-shirt ripped from the hem halfway up her midriff. Jeans ragged and dirty. Hair tangled.

413

Struggling with the deadweight, Sterling tried to steer her to the side of the SUV so she could open the door and get her inside. "Easy. Take a few breaths." She reached for the handle . . .

Adela laughed as she pushed her back, taking her off guard. She had Sterling's gun in her hand.

Things clicked into place easy enough. "Huh. So I was right. You're part of the setup."

"Don't lie!" Adela raged. "You had no idea."

Curling her lip, Sterling said, "I suspected you all along."

Stymied, Adela's mouth firmed, her eyes narrowed and she looked ready for murder.

Sterling immediately considered how to react, what she'd do, when she'd do it. It'd be dicey, but she wouldn't go down without a fight.

Then Adela surprised her by smiling. "Did you know I arranged it all? Ah, I see that you didn't."

All? No, she wouldn't buy that. "Mattox doesn't take orders from a woman."

"Of course not. He's all man. He's all *mine*." As if gloating, Adela said, "I suggested how to get you, and he liked the idea. It's worked before."

Worked before? What the ever-loving hell.

"I don't want to kill you out here. Mattox would be disappointed, so turn around and walk."

At the moment all Sterling felt was stark anger and firm resolve. Cade was near, but she'd handle this without distracting him. He already had his hands full.

"Move!"

Smirking, Sterling asked, "And if I don't?"

Adela limped closer. "Mattox will shoot your boyfriend right in the face." Glee twisted her abused features. "He has him, you know."

Cade told her to trust him, so that's what she'd do. Keeping her expression impassive wasn't easy, but Sterling gave it her best shot. "You've already proven yourself to be a liar, so why should I believe you? If anything, Mattox is already dead."

"No!" Closer still, Adela's breath rasped harshly. "Mattox has him, and if you don't come along, I'll shoot you in the leg and drag you there."

If Adela got near enough, Sterling felt certain she could disarm her. But no, she stopped with too much distance still between them.

To goad her, Sterling snorted. "You can barely keep yourself upright."

"Fine. I'll shoot you in both legs and tell Mattox where to find you."

On the off chance Cade had been outmaneuvered, Sterling wanted to be near him to help, so going along suited her. "Fine. To the barn, then."

"No, not the barn." Adela stayed behind her. "The house."

The house? "You're kidding, right? There is no house."

"Two inner rooms are intact." Breathing

heavily, probably in pain, Adela snapped, "Hurry up. It's going to rain again."

Sure enough, lightning flickered in the distance, and the sky grew dark and menacing.

Outlined by the coming storm, the house looked like a specter of bad things to come.

It seemed a good idea to keep Adela talking. "Was taking a beating part of your grand plan? You look like you've been through hell and back."

"That's *your* fault! He can be more tempered, except when you've enraged him. You forced us into hiding, forced him to lose business." Adela laughed brokenly. "Now he's going to make you pay."

"Looks like you already did."

"Mattox can be very gentle. Once he's finished with you, he'll be gentle again."

It twisted Sterling's stomach to witness such madness. "You forgive his abuse that easily?"

With a shrug in her tone, Adela said, "It was necessary to reel you in. No, I didn't like it, but there's a lot of necessary things I don't like— especially the way Mattox obsesses about you." She made a giggling sound. "He'll be so thrilled to see you again."

"Somehow I don't think *thrilled* is the right word."

"Oh, but it is. He doesn't like hurting me, but you? He's going to take great pleasure in hearing you cry."

Sterling steeled her resolve. If she let it, fear would weaken her. She couldn't think about Mattox, about what he might do to her if things went wrong. She'd never again be a victim.

She wouldn't.

Adela prodded her hard in the spine, probably leaving bruises behind, before scuttling out of reach again. Perverse bitch. But even as Sterling thought it, she felt pity. It seemed pretty clear that Adela wasn't well. Whatever she'd gone through in her life had left her damaged enough to see Mattox as a hero.

She glanced back, but already Adela had put enough space between them to be out of reach. She might be insane, but she wasn't taking any chances on Sterling getting her hands on her.

"See the light in the house?" Adela gloated. "They're in there. Who knows? Your man might already be dead . . . or dying. So hurry it up if you want a chance to say goodbye."

Yes, she did hurry, going so fast that Adela had difficulty keeping up with her. Whatever motivation Mattox had for beating Adela, he'd overdone it, leaving her weakened and hurt.

Sterling went up the broken front steps, alert to any opportunity to turn the tables. So far there'd been none.

Missing boards in the porch forced her to pick her way cautiously before she stepped over the threshold. Rainwater puddled on the floor beneath an entirely collapsed section of roof.

Up ahead, in one contained room, Mattox stood, gun in hand, massive shoulder propped on a mold-covered wall, face twisted with cruel satisfaction. "Well, well, well. You actually did it, Adela."

"I told you I would." She shoved Sterling forward, almost making her fall.

Senses keenly attuned to the danger, Sterling noticed the eerie silence.

Mattox didn't have Cade.

Relieved, she breathed easy again. Cade was still out there with Reyes, and that meant she had a chance. They all did.

"Ah, I see the hope in your eyes," Mattox crooned. "It's lovely, truly it is."

"I told her there were women in the truck," Adela said with a sneer. "She doesn't yet know that you actually brought more men."

"Four more," Mattox explained. "They're already out there scouring the farm for your hulking friend."

Sterling leveled an unimpressed stare on Mattox. "You sent more sacrifices to be slaughtered?"

"I sent them fully armed."

"And you think that'll help them?" She scoffed. "So far no one you sent has even been a challenge."

Mattox didn't seem bothered by that. "It's true, I've been forced to use the dregs of society.

"Oh, he does," Adela bragged, regaining her attitude. "They'll replenish some of the profits *you* cost him."

Nope. Not a chance in hell of saving her. At that point, knowing other women were terrorized because of her, Sterling no longer cared.

Instead of speaking to Adela, she asked Mattox, "If they're not here, then where?"

"You think I'd tell you?" He evaluated her new posture against the wall but didn't seem to notice anything amiss. "No, I'll keep that information to myself, but I will tell you that they'll be transported soon." He eyed her distress with interest. "That bothers you? Well, it's partially your fault. I need cash, and they'll each earn a fair price. No daily rentals, as I had planned for you way back then. These women will be pets . . . Perhaps you'd like to be one, as well? Maybe even my own personal pet."

"Seriously, dude, I'm going to puke."

Mattox grinned. "When I'm done with you, you won't have such a smart mouth."

Adela scowled. "I thought we were going to kill her?"

Licking his thick lips, Mattox murmured, "Yes— *after* I've gotten my fill."

Trepidation kept her guts churning, but Sterling eyed him up and down with disdain. "You won't live long enough to make those threats a reality."

Fury brought Mattox forward. Stopping a few

feet from her, he demanded, "Call out to him."

"Him?" Sterling asked, pretending confusion.

"If she plays dumb again," Adela shouted, "shoot her in the leg!"

Mattox raised his brows at her ruthless suggestion.

Stalling for time, Sterling asked, "What do you want me to say?"

"Yell his name." Mattox grinned with satisfaction. "That should do it."

Drawing a slow, deep breath, Sterling called out, "Cade?"

No answer—not that she'd expected one. Cade wasn't stupid. She had no doubt that he already had a grasp of the situation and all the players. He had a plan, and he would come for her. She only prayed he didn't get hurt in the process.

"I think I need to make you scream." Adela started to move forward.

Again, Mattox pulled her back, this time with keen impatience. "Call him again, and you better make it good."

Trying to determine which way Cade would enter, Sterling quickly scanned the open areas of the half-demolished house. Mattox had his back protected by a wall, so Cade couldn't come in behind him. That probably meant he'd enter through the side of the house where much of the structure was missing, or the front doorway that Sterling had used.

Either way, they'd see him coming, and that would make him an easy target for Mattox.

Just then, three rapid shots rang out. They echoed over the barren fields, making it impossible to pinpoint a direction.

In her heart, Sterling knew it was Cade, doing what he did best—kicking ass.

Adela blanched. Equally rattled, Mattox swung his heavy Glock around and took aim at her chest. "Call him! Make sure he knows I have you."

If Mattox thought that would save him, he'd find out otherwise.

"Call him, call him," Adela sang, her eyes going vague with excitement. *"Call him."*

By the second, she became more unhinged.

Sterling filled her lungs. "Cade!" To appease Mattox, she added, "I'm in here, Cade."

Eyes glittering, Adela held her breath.

The silence dragged out while Mattox's flinty gaze bounced back and forth between the two entrances—and suddenly Cade dropped through the hole in the ceiling, landing on his feet right before them.

A sort of blindsided panic held them both enthralled, but not Cade. Incandescent rage seemed to emanate from him. He appeared bigger, as invincible as he claimed. Turning fast, he violently kicked the gun away from Mattox, likely breaking his forearm in the process. While Mattox flailed, Cade grabbed him by the throat, lifted him from the floor and slammed him into a crumbling wall. His boulder-sized fist connected with Mattox's crotch. Then a forearm to his face cut off the scream of pain. Last, a punch to his throat.

Mattox was done for, a heavy deadweight hanging limp from Cade's grip.

It all happened so fast that Sterling stood there staring, riveted by the fluid ease of his attack.

Adela's shrill, earsplitting scream of rage jolted her back into action. She watched Adela scrabble for the gun.

She's going to shoot Cade?

Like hell! Throwing everything she had into a tackle, Sterling took them both down hard. She was bigger than Adela, surely stronger . . . and yet she wasn't fast enough.

The gun discharged with a deafening explosion.

Fighting a rush of suffocating fear, Sterling managed to glance up. But no, Cade hadn't slowed at all. His heavy fist repeatedly hammered Mattox's face.

"No!" Insanity made Adela stronger. Despite Sterling's efforts, she forced the gun around again, snarling like an animal, consumed with hatred.

Sterling tried, but she couldn't wrest the gun from her. *No, no, no.*

She would not let Cade be shot.

Savage protective instincts surged up . . . and

424

her lessons kicked in. She reacted, fast, harsh. Brutal.

Just as Cade had taught her.

Her elbow slammed into Adela's already injured nose, crunching it and sending out a thick spray of blood. It dazed her long enough for Sterling to grab her knife and, without pause, drive the blade deep, once, twice, a third time.

Just as quickly, Sterling withdrew, moving back in horror.

Mouth going slack, eyes wide and sightless with shock, the gun slipped from Adela's hand. Blood pulsed and oozed from the wounds in her midriff.

Trembling with the aftereffects, Sterling saw her try to speak, then slump flat to the floor. Lifeless.

They weren't yet safe. Tamping down the horror of what she'd just done, she snatched up the gun and got back to her feet in time to see Cade release Mattox.

The floor shook as his body landed.

A big blackened hole gaped in his side. Adela had killed him.

Somehow that seemed fitting.

The queasiness returned in a rush, but before Sterling could assimilate all the sights and scents of death, Cade had her, crushing her close, his face in her hair.

God, he felt good. Warm, safe . . . *alive.*

425

"Are you hurt?" He thrust her back, his gaze searching over her, his hands examining her arms, her waist, down to her hips.

Sterling rested a trembling hand against his steeled shoulder. "I'm okay."

"You don't look it."

Maybe because her head was splitting now that the adrenaline waned. She made a lame gesture toward Adela's body. "She cracked me in the back of the head with the gun."

Immediately, Cade turned her. "Aw, babe, let me see."

"It's all right." It annoyed her that she'd gotten caught like that while he stood there without a scratch other than his knuckles.

Tenderly, Cade sifted his fingers through her hair, lightly prodding her skull. "Damn. You have a massive goose egg." He turned her again to look into her eyes.

"I'm fine, Cade. I promise." Shock settled in, making her shiver and shake. "You?"

For an answer, he pressed his mouth to hers. The kiss wasn't sexual but reassuring. Soft, lingering, comforting.

From behind them, Reyes asked, "Some new form of resuscitation? Because I *know* you're not making out when we have shit to do."

Cade ended the kiss but didn't step away. He gathered her to his chest and said to his brother, "Madison called it in?"

"Ambulance and cops will be here any minute." Looking past Sterling to the bodies, he asked, "Dead?"

Sterling didn't have an answer to that.

Stepping around them, bypassing Mattox, Reyes went to one knee and pressed his fingers to Adela's throat. "Light pulse. She might make it."

In a truly gallant move, Cade lifted Sterling into his arms and turned to leave the destruction behind. Once outside, he moved a good distance from the house—and didn't put her down.

"Do you think Adela will—"

"Either way," he said, "that's not on you."

Understanding that and accepting it were two different things. "I couldn't let her shoot you."

Jaw flexing, arms tightening, Cade struggled with himself, all while his vivid blue eyes held hers captive. "Just so you know," he rasped in a growl, "I'm never letting you out of my sight."

Liking the sound of that, Sterling rested her head against his shoulder and whispered, "Good."

CHAPTER NINETEEN

As soon as they'd gotten home, his dad checked Star, going over all the signs of a concussion. She did have a slight headache but otherwise seemed fine. Introspective, but not lethargic. Quiet, but responsive to questions asked. No blurry vision, and hungry enough to eat a few cookies.

Though she grumbled about it, Cade stayed with her while she showered and changed clothes. There were many things he wanted to say, but he could wait. He had her with him, she was safe and that's what mattered.

When she'd finished dressing warmly, they moved outside to the deck, where the cool mountain air revived her. She hadn't complained when he'd sat down and pulled her onto his lap. In fact, she'd been so silent it worried him.

With her attention on the mountain view, Star said, "It's a good thing that Mattox is gone."

"A very good thing."

"Even though she didn't mean to, I'm glad that it was Adela who killed him."

They knew that an ambulance had taken Adela away, but no one really thought she'd make it. Previous injuries from the sick games she'd played with Mattox had already worn her down.

Cade didn't know how many beatings she'd

taken, but Adela participated in hurting women and she'd wanted to hurt Star, too. She'd done her best to lure them into a trap.

If she died, he wouldn't lose sleep over it.

"Have you heard from Reyes yet?"

His brother had gone after the captive women, using the details Cade had gotten from one of the men hired to kill him. "He checked in."

"And?" Twisting around, Star faced him. "Were they there? Those men hadn't lied?"

Their loyalty to Mattox ended as soon as Cade had started wiping them out. "Once Reyes found the women, he allowed the task force to take over." Not everyone realized that his father founded the task force, and that they were, ultimately, answerable to him—which meant they could keep tabs on the women to know, without a doubt, that they were helped.

That, more than anything, was important to his father. To him, Reyes and Madison, too.

And now, obviously, to Star, as well.

She searched his gaze, and as understanding dawned, she again relaxed against him. "We need to know where Mattox got them."

"Working on it." In fact, that was the next step, and his sister was already chasing down leads. The thugs hadn't known much about the operation, but Mattox's driver, and the bastards who'd brought the truck, proved to be better informed—once they'd been persuaded to talk.

Luckily his father had great contacts in both law enforcement and politics. Within a few hours, Parrish had learned that the police had rounded up all the fucks involved. There were a few unavoidable fatalities beyond Mattox—and maybe Adela—but with any luck, there'd be nothing to trace the incident back to them. Not that they couldn't handle it, but it offered unnecessary complications.

If anyone did sniff in that direction, Parrish would handle it.

Star's small hand opened over his chest. "I want to be a part of that, okay?"

She could be a part of everything, as far as he was concerned. "That's a given, babe." But he added, "You can be involved as much, or as little, as you like."

"Good. They all need to be destroyed."

"Agreed." Cade knew she was working things out in her mind. Yes, she'd done some awesome work on her own, but the violence today was at a new level.

For him, it was routine. For her . . . not so much.

"Everything that happened today . . ."

Her voice trailed off, so Cade didn't push it. He just held her, his hand coasting up and down her arm, over her hip and back.

"When I was taken all those years ago, I was nothing but a victim."

A victim who had used her wits and bravery to

escape. Sadly, not every person in her position had a chance to do the same. "No, babe, you were a survivor."

She turned her face to kiss his throat. "I got away, but I was still . . . still a casualty. Helping other women helped *me,* too, because I felt useful, like I was making a difference."

"I understand."

"Today, leading up to things, I got so nervous I couldn't think straight. It was terrible."

Again Cade said nothing. He'd picked up on her growing anxiety and had tried to spare her. In that, he'd failed.

She drew in an audible breath, rubbed at her eyes and shivered again. "I learned that I can handle it, you know? I did okay today."

"You did amazing. I keep telling you, you have incredible instincts and you're a fighter. But it's more than that. You're a natural defender."

She kissed his throat again. "Why do you say that?"

A fresh wave of fury ran through his veins. Knowing Mattox had been *that close* to her, knowing that Adela had hoped to witness her murder, kept him teetering on the edge of rage. He wanted to secure her safety, he wanted her to let him care for her the way he wanted to—the way she deserved.

He wanted to spend his life with her. To share everything. Especially commitment.

He wanted marriage.

Tilting up her chin, Cade looked into her eyes, hoping she'd see everything he felt. "You protected me today."

A wry smile twisted her mouth. "Well, I tried, but I'm not sure it was necessary."

"If Adela's aim had been better?"

Wincing, she said, "Well, she did get off a shot."

"Just one, because you acted fast, ensuring she didn't get another. You were there, and I trust you, so I was able to focus solely on Mattox." But he'd lost his control, and that never happened. "Because of what he did to you in the past, because he dared to come after you again, I wanted to kill him with my bare hands. If Adela hadn't shot him, I would have beat him to death."

She swallowed heavily. "You almost did. I was . . . impressed. You moved like a very agile wrecking ball."

Cade wanted to give her time, but it wasn't easy, not when she looked at him with her heart in her eyes.

He wanted it all. Did she?

Just then, Parrish opened the door and stuck his head out. "You two might want to come see this."

They each looked up, but Parrish was smiling, so Cade wasn't concerned. "In a bit."

"You'll be sorry if you miss it."

433

"Well, now I'm intrigued." Scooting that sweet rump over his lap, Star got to her feet. Looking a little desperate for a change of topic, she took his hand and tugged. "Come on. I need a distraction."

Cade didn't, but he let her pull him to his feet, then held her back until his father went inside ahead of them. She might not have a concussion, thank God, but Cade could see that her head hurt. It was there in her pinched expression, the shadows under her eyes.

"Before we go in, I want you to know that I'm incredibly proud of you."

Her bottom lip trembled before she caught it in her teeth.

Not exactly the romantic declaration he wanted to make, but definitely something she needed to know.

"I don't think anyone's ever said that to me before."

No, probably not. Her life hadn't been an easy one. She'd conquered more hardships than any person should have to, and was still beautiful inside and out, strong and independent, caring and sexy. "What you did, how you handled yourself, was nothing short of remarkable."

Leaning into him, her forehead against his chest, she shivered. "I was afraid if I showed my fear, they'd just feed off it. That's what happened when Mattox first had me. They all loved fear, like it was a big joke." Her hands fisted in his shirt and she confessed, "But I was afraid, Cade. So afraid."

"God, me, too."

That got her gaze up to his real fast. "You?"

"Don't you dare be surprised by that." Tears filled her eyes, shredding his heart. "Please don't cry."

"I'm not," she denied, sniffling.

He brushed her cheeks, catching the tears on his fingertips before cupping her face. "I've never in my life been that afraid. If I'd lost you . . ." He couldn't finish that thought. Putting his arms around her, he gathered her close. "I *can't* lose you."

Swiping her eyes on his shirt, she swallowed, nodded. "I don't want to lose you, either."

Cade started to remark on that, but they heard the laughter from the great room and it drew Star's attention. She gave a tremulous smile. "Are they having a party?" Curiosity took her to the door, and since he wasn't about to leave her side, Cade followed along.

In the great room, they found the usually stuffy Bernard on the floor, long legs crossed, with a very grungy cat rubbing against his chest.

Star stalled. Cade stared.

"Yes, precious," Bernard crooned in a ridiculous voice while stroking the cat's back. "You're a beauty, aren't you, darling? Such a sweet little mama."

435

"Little?" Cade eyed the long, gangly cat currently getting white fur all over Bernard's dark slacks.

"Mama?" Star asked at the same time.

"Kittens." Sitting opposite Bernard, Madison gazed down into a cardboard box. "Three of them."

Star made a beeline for the box, dropped to her knees, and seconds later a beautiful smile bloomed on her face. Emotion bubbling over, she lifted a tiny ball of fur to her cheek.

God, he loved her. So goddamn much it was killing him. He thought of how she'd stood strong, how despite her fear she hadn't buckled. And now seeing this, that soft, tender side of her . . .

She smiled toward him. "Cade, isn't it adorable?"

Still holding her gaze, he whispered, "Very."

Arms folded, Parrish stood by the fireplace, watching it all with a slightly dazed expression. Reyes was there beside him, his stance aggressive.

Amused by that, Cade joined them. "Where did—"

"It's my cat," Reyes stated, his muscles bunching and his chin jutting.

Holding up his hands, Cade fought a grin. "Okay. No problem. So you got a cat. Makes perfect sense. Can't imagine a better time for it."

The blatant nonsense stole Reyes's angry edge, and with a roll of his eyes, he said, "It's not like I planned it. She was in the alley next to the gym. Starving, trying to care for those three little fur balls. What could I do?"

"You had to take her in," Cade agreed, clapping his brother on the shoulder. "I'd have done the same."

"That's all understandable," Parrish said. "You wouldn't be my sons if you could turn a blind eye to any suffering. The shocker is Bernard." Smiling in disbelief at his old friend, he said, "Just look at him. Have you ever seen anything like it?"

Now on his back, unconcerned with his usually impeccable clothes or his gawking audience, Bernard laughed as the cat walked over his chest to butt into his chin.

Cade shook his head. No, most definitely he hadn't. "I didn't know he liked animals."

"Neither did I," Parrish admitted. "I knew he was a loyal friend, that he loves you all like his own, that cooking is his passion and that he's a ladies' man—"

"He *what?*" Reyes asked.

Yeah, that was news to Cade, too. From what he'd observed, Bernard cared about many things—his appearance, his job . . . all of them. But sex? "Where the hell does he find the time?"

"Where there's a will, there's a way" was all

Parrish said. "But in all the time he's worked for us, he's never mentioned having a soft spot for animals."

Reyes stared in disgust as the older man sat up again, hugging the cat to his cheek, much as Star had hugged the kitten. The difference was that the cat hung from his arms, her crooked, mismatched eyes half-closed in bliss, her broken tail twined around Bernard's forearm.

"I didn't bring her home as a gift to him. I just . . ." Reyes ran a hand over his head. "I couldn't leave her alone at the gym, right? I mean, that was my intention at first. But I got the call to get moving, so I didn't have time to set her up as nicely as I meant to. After I wrapped up things today, I kept thinking about her, and it bothered me."

"Understandable," Cade said, while fighting a grin at his brother's discomfort.

"I stopped by the gym on my return. She was in the box with the kittens, but it was a tight fit. She needs a real bed, cat food, too, and—"

"A litter box," Star added as she joined them. She'd put the kitten back in the box, but that sweet little smile remained on her face. "You're keeping the cat?"

Reyes stared at Bernard. "Hell, I don't know if he'll give her back." Slanting his gaze at Star, he said, "And that's going to be a problem, because Kennedy will want to know where the cat went."

"Kennedy?" Parrish asked.

"Sterling pointed her out to me at the gym." Then to Cade, Reyes added, "The hedgehog teaching herself defense techniques?"

"You talked with her?" Star asked.

"I offered her help, but she wasn't receptive. In fact, she was downright insulting about it." Gaining steam, Reyes glared at Star again. "She'd already figured out that I'm more than a gym owner. Said if I didn't want her snooping in my life, I shouldn't butt into hers."

"Huh." Star fought a grin. "So she's not only cute, and maybe in danger, she's also shrewd. I like her already."

Aggrieved, Reyes rolled his eyes.

Madison stepped up. "Want me to look into her background? What's her last name?"

Succinct, Reyes said, "No."

"Why not?" Star asked. "You guys didn't hesitate to check up on me."

"Cade was interested in you." Denying it a little too strongly, Reyes said, "Totally different story with Kennedy."

"Uh-huh." Madison nudged Star, making it clear she wasn't buying Reyes's declarations. "I want her last name—just in case."

"Anyway," Reyes said with irritation, "she's the one who found the cat. I just followed her when she started down the alley."

Brows up, Star said, "You followed her?"

On the spot, Reyes flung a hand toward Bernard, then rounded on their father. "What am I supposed to do now? She expects to see the cat at the gym."

Parrish always had an answer. "Tell her you took it home to better care for it. It doesn't sound like she wants to get close to you, so that'll keep her from demanding a visit. But if she does want to see the cat again, invite her to join you on a trip to the vet."

Approving that plan, Cade stepped in with his own advice. "The cat and kittens will all need to be checked. You should get that scheduled right away."

When the kittens started mewling, the cat looked up, abandoned Bernard and hurried back to the box.

Covered in white fur, grinning ear to ear, Bernard strode over. "She'll need several things, but for now I can put together some food and better bedding. Tomorrow, I'll go to the store."

Madison gave him a hug. "I never knew you were such a big softy, Bernard."

That put his nose in the air. "I'm not."

Reaching out, Parrish plucked a clump of fur from his shirt. "You do an incredible impression."

Bernard shrugged. "I adore cats."

"Since when?" Cade asked.

"I was raised on a farm. My parents grew corn and soy, and we always had cats around." One thin hand smoothed his silver hair back into place, and in his usual lofty tone, he announced, "I've missed them."

Everyone stared at him.

Clearing his throat, Reyes took a step forward. "Look, the cat is my responsibility—"

Eyes narrowed and mean, Bernard took a step, too. "She's staying here." The challenge was clear—a first for Bernard.

Taken off guard, Reyes retreated, hands up in surrender. "Fine. No problem. I appreciate the help."

"Oh my," Star breathed.

Cade glanced at her, then followed her gaze to where the mother cat sat by Bernard's feet, a kitten in her mouth.

Bernard went comically mushy all over again. "You're bringing me your babies?" he asked in a high, silly voice. "Oh, you precious, precious thing." He sank down and accepted the little bundle. "I'm overwhelmed."

They all shared another look. Star couldn't hold back her grin, and it got to Cade. After the melancholy following the sting, she was happy again.

Relieved, aware of several strong urges, he pulled her to his side.

Madison leaned against Reyes, patting him in sympathy. After all, he'd gotten, and lost, a pet in record time. "I have some leads we can follow based on where the women were grabbed."

Jumping on that, Reyes asked, "All from the same area?"

"Very close. I've configured a map and I have a few ideas."

"It's getting late." Stressing that it was time to take a break and regroup, Parrish gave a pointed look at Star, which luckily she missed.

Knowing the toll it took to do their specific jobs, Parrish was keen on physical and emotional health.

Star, being new to it all, would especially be affected, so Cade gave his father a nod of appreciation for understanding and not pushing her.

"We can plan our next move tomorrow—" Looking down at Bernard, Parrish shook his head. "I was going to say over breakfast, but now I'm not sure."

"There will be breakfast." Bernard cuddled all three kittens in his arms, and he looked deliriously happy. "Just don't expect anything fancy."

Cade wasn't about to miss that perfect segue. "Star and I are heading downstairs. We'll see you all in the morning."

She was still trying to say her goodbyes when Cade led her from the room and to the stairs.

"Why are we rushing?"

"Because the way I need to kiss you, I figured you'd prefer we were alone."

Warmth entered her dark eyes and humor lifted the corners of her mouth. "Too impatient to wait?"

"Something like that."

She took the lead, passing him by, making him laugh out loud, until they reached his rooms. After securing the door, she started undressing—on her way to the bedroom.

"Wait up."

"Found your patience, huh?" Her T-shirt hit him in the chest and she kept going, her hands busy on her jeans. "Well, I don't want to wait."

With his longer stride, Cade caught her before she got her jeans down any farther than her knees.

Lord help him, how she looked bent over, her perfect ass on display, was enough to test his strongest convictions. But she'd been hurt, and whether or not she'd admit to the ache in her head, he wouldn't forget it.

Pulling her upright, he slid an arm under her hips, scooped her into his arms and went to the barrel chair adjacent to the dresser. Sitting with her again in his lap, he took her mouth.

He meant to be gentle, but she already had her slender fingers clasping his jaw, keeping him close while she consumed him. Her warm tongue stroked, her sharp little teeth nibbled and, yeah, he lost it.

"I want you," she groaned, shifting around so she could grab his shirt, peeling it up and over his head. Her scorching gaze traveled over his chest, and she leaned forward to lick a tattoo.

He wasn't made of steel. "Your head—"

"Is fine." Breathing hard, she leaned back to see him again. "It's my heart you need to worry about right now."

"Aw, babe." This time he kept the kiss short and sweet. "I will always protect your heart, I swear."

Emotion softened the lust, made her lips tremble. "My heart needs to feel you, around me, in me. Give me that. Please."

She'd easily outmaneuvered him, and Cade knew when to relent. Kissing her more deeply, he stood and carried her to the bed.

It felt good to have Cade hold her so easily, proof of his strength and his affection. Even better was how he carefully lowered her to the mattress, then stripped away her jeans and panties.

That compelling steel-blue gaze moved over her. "You'll tell me if your head—"

"Yes." She patted the bed beside her. "I'll tell you."

He stripped out of his own clothes, robbing her of breath with his remarkable body. Now, being turned on, his abs were tight above an impressive erection. Always, his body hair fascinated her, how it spread out over his chest, how that happy trail led down to his cock. Every single part of him, from his military haircut to his patrician features, his granite body down to his feet . . . She loved it all. So very, very much.

Not unaffected by her rapt attention, Cade

snagged a condom, opened the packet and rolled it on.

The second he stretched out over her, her hands went exploring, relishing the warmth of his taut flesh, the flex of firm muscle, his indescribable scent that both incited and soothed her. A little overcome, Sterling hugged him tight with her nose in his neck, breathing him in.

Cade said nothing—not with words, anyway. He used his hands and lips, the stroke of his tongue and the press of his body to tell her how much she meant to him.

Now, after everything, she believed him. This was real. Solid. A commitment she could count on. Security she'd never known she wanted but relished so very much.

He kissed her, teasing at first, just brushing over her lips, tracing with his tongue—until her breath caught and she arched up against him.

Angling his head, he let his tongue sink deep. Hot, wet. Possessive.

Sterling's fingertips gripped his shoulders, and that seemed to fire his blood even more.

"You're mine," he rasped, reaching down between their bodies to find her sex, to slide his fingers over her warm wetness . . . to press in, fill her, make her cry out with escalating sensations.

Marveling, Cade breathed, "Damn, you're close already."

In agreement, she pulled him into another

tongue-thrusting, molten kiss while tightening around his fingers, rolling her hips against him, needing and taking.

He pulled away, but only to readjust, and then it was his cock pressing into her. Braced on his forearms, his hands holding her head and his mouth eating at hers, he rode her hard.

And she loved it.

Their combined sounds of pleasure filled the room. Desperation grew. Pleasure coiled tighter and tighter.

The second the high, vibrating moan escaped her, Cade put his head back, jaw clenched in concentration, until she began to ease in the aftermath of her orgasm. Tucking his face to her neck, he growled out his own release.

For only a few moments, he gave her his weight. With limbs tangled, all aches and pains forgotten, misgivings shelved, Sterling felt entirely at peace.

When she sighed, he struggled up to his elbows again. "Hey. You okay?"

"Mmm. I think you've found a cure for head-aches. I'm blessedly numb."

The smile showed in his eyes, if not on his mouth. "Is that so?"

"Don't look so pleased. You already knew you excelled at *everything*."

Something else joined the humor in his eyes. Affection.

Love.

"Look who's talking." Rolling to his side while keeping her tucked close, Cade heaved a big breath. "We both need some sleep."

She did, but she didn't want to sleep yet.

As usual, he seemed to know her thoughts. While stroking her back, her hip, he asked, "Something on your mind?"

Never had she thought to be in this place—a place of satisfaction and contentment. Admitting to the fears that had always plagued her seemed incredibly easy, at least with Cade.

"Star?" He lifted his head. "What's wrong?"

"I've always assumed a normal life wasn't possible for me, and I was right."

"Hey." With the edge of his fist, he nudged up her face.

She pressed a finger to his lips and spoke around the choking emotion. "I was right, but this, with you, isn't normal."

The tension in his shoulders eased a little. "It's exceptional."

"Very much so. You've given me what I didn't think I could ever find. A place to fit in." The damn tears spilled over, but this was Cade, so she didn't mind. "I never used to cry."

"Not on the outside," he agreed, and his hand settled under her breast. "But here, in your heart, I think you were very sad."

How could he know her so well? Easy—he

loved her. Well, it was time she opened up, so she smiled and said, "I appreciate how you trust me, how you recognize what I can do . . . and what I can't."

His mouth touched hers. "You can do anything, babe."

Love swelled her heart until there were no hollow corners left in her soul. "No, I can't. And now I don't mind that. We complement each other, you and I. I feel safe with you when I'd forgotten what safe felt like."

His eyes went a little glassy, too. "I will always protect you."

"I know. Just as I'll protect you."

He smiled and said softly, "I know."

With her newfound freedom and confidence, Sterling said, "You love me."

"More than I knew was possible."

That seemed like enough. "I want to live with you," she stated.

"I want to marry you," he countered. "Naturally we'll live together."

Marriage. It had always sounded like the standard norm, a normal she'd never have.

Now it sounded like *them.*

Sterling hugged him, letting his scent surround her, his strength cradle her, and knew she'd found the most incredibly perfect man—for her. "I love you, too. So damn much."

"Will you marry me?"

"Yes, please." Giddy happiness consumed her. "As long as we don't live here—not permanently, anyway."

Cade grinned. "I think it's time I showed you my house."

"Tomorrow," she whispered, already comfortable against him. "You might not have noticed, but I had a trying day."

EPILOGUE

Everyone was in the breakfast room when they finally made it upstairs. Cade was surprised they'd waited on them, or so he assumed, until Bernard came in looking harried.

He carried a large tray of dishes . . . with his hair uncombed and his shirt untucked.

Cade shared a look with Star, who appeared equally boggled, then glanced at the others. Madison hid a smile. Parrish looked harassed.

"He's already been out," Reyes complained with a glare at Bernard. "Buying things for *my* cat."

Going rigid, Bernard paused by the table. "Her name is Chimera."

Left eye twitching, Reyes said in a soft, lethal tone, "You named my cat?"

Nose up, arrogance in full force, Bernard glared at him. "Better than calling that beautiful creature *Cat*."

"Beautiful?" Reyes leaned forward, his elbows on the table. "She has mismatched eyes and looks like she was run over by a mower."

"Her eyes are *stunning,* and now that I've bathed and brushed her, her fur is gorgeous, as well."

Astonishment dropped Reyes's mouth open. "You—"

At the head of the table, Parrish cleared his throat. "Enough on the . . ."

Bernard stabbed him with a look.

Parrish quickly amended, "Chimera. Food would be nice, preferably before it gets cold. Or did you only plan to stand there and let us smell it?"

The tray clattered to the table. In rapid order, Bernard set out scrambled eggs, muffins, fresh fruit and a plate of sausages.

Before he could leave, Star said, "Thank you, Bernard. I don't know how I got by so long without your cooking. You're a master."

Smug, Bernard sent Reyes a look. "Thank you. It's nice to be appreciated."

That earned a round of protests from everyone, but Bernard wasn't moved. For a moment there, Cade thought he'd flip them all off as he exited the room in his lofty way.

They dealt with a lot of crazy shit, but Bernard in that particular mood? Strangest of them all.

The stillness lasted all of three seconds before everyone started laughing. Madison pushed back her chair. "I'll go soothe the beast." She nudged her brother. "And you—stop needling him."

Reyes grinned. "No can do. The more I complain, the more determined he is to care for that . . . Chimera."

Cade snorted. "Good save. He did seem adamant about her having a name."

Even Parrish chuckled. "I've never seen him so rattled. He went out bright and early, buying everything from food and dishes, to catnip and toys, to bedding and brushes. He rushed back, afraid Chimera would miss him."

Star laughed. "She probably did."

"Didn't sound like it, given the racket she made while he bathed her. He had to change clothes, but then Madison came in, and shortly after that, Reyes showed up, so Bernard didn't have a chance to properly spiff up. You know he's fanatical about having food ready."

Plate already filled, Reyes settled in to eat. "I had no idea what I'd do with the cat, but Bernard has offered the perfect solution."

"There are still three kittens," Cade pointed out.

"And I have two siblings. Problem solved."

As if someone had just handed her a million dollars, Star squealed. "I get a kitten?"

"When they're old enough to be weaned—though I imagine Bernard will demand visitation rights."

Cade was smiling when Star turned a worried frown on him. "I'd love a kitten, but it's your house we're talking about, so I'll understand—"

"It'll be our house."

That got everyone quiet again. Reyes even paused in midchew with his mouth full.

Madison returned with Bernard in tow. He still

looked frazzled, but he'd at least smoothed his hair. Or maybe Madison had done that for him.

Now that they were all present, Cade decided to make an announcement, before Reyes stirred Bernard up again. "I asked Star to marry me."

All eyes turned to her. Wearing a cheek-splitting grin, Reyes said, "I'm guessing you said yes, or he wouldn't be looking so pleased."

"Of course I said yes. I'm not a dope."

In seconds, Madison was right back out of her seat, circling the table to grab Star in a hug. Appearing pleased, Bernard lifted his orange juice in a toast. "Welcome to the family."

Even Parrish smiled, saying to Cade, "Finding the right woman for you is the greatest gift you'll ever receive. I'm happy for you."

That sobered them all. It was a stark reminder that Parrish had found his love—and lost her to violence. That loss had determined how he'd raised his children, and how they lived their lives.

Seeking justice.

Because of that, he'd met Star.

Such a lifestyle shouldn't have been conducive to a prolonged relationship, much less love or marriage, yet if it wasn't for his sharpened insights, he might not have noticed Star right off.

Knowing he owed Parrish a debt of gratitude, Cade looked at him, an older version of himself, and said simply, "Thank you, Dad."

Star leaned into his side, smiling, happy.

"Yeah, thanks. For a bunch of stuff, but mostly for raising such an awesome son."

Being an ass, Reyes asked, "Do you mean me or Cade?"

Bernard threw a napkin at him, and Parrish protested the disruption. Ignoring them all, Madison opened her laptop while eating.

Star turned to Cade, grinning. "Don't tell them I said this, but your family is truly awesome."

As Cade looked at each of them, old resentments faded away. He'd been coerced to this life, but because of that he had Star. They were still nuts, but they were his. He hugged Star tight. "I agree."

Center Point Large Print
600 Brooks Road / PO Box 1
Thorndike, ME 04986-0001 USA

(207) 568-3717

US & Canada:
1 800 929-9108
www.centerpointlargeprint.com

GREAT PROGRAM MUSIC
How to Enjoy and Remember It

GREAT PROGRAM MUSIC

HOW TO ENJOY AND REMEMBER IT

By
SIGMUND SPAETH

GARDEN CITY PUBLISHING CO., INC.
New York

DEDICATION

THIS BOOK is dedicated to all those who have read *Great Symphonies: How to Recognize and Remember Them*, or *The Art of Enjoying Music*, or *Stories behind the World's Great Music*, or *The Common Sense of Music*, or *Music for Fun*, or any other volumes that might be considered logical preliminaries. Why not be generous and include all those who like music that tells a story or paints a picture in tones or implies a program of any kind? And why omit those who like music in general? Or even those who don't like music yet but will some day? Dedications are generally too personal. This one is as impersonal and universal as the publishers and booksellers can make it, with the full consent and co-operation of the author.

ACKNOWLEDGMENTS

Wʜɪʟᴇ most of the musical illustrations in this book are in the public domain, and even the quotations from copyrighted material represent what the law calls "fair usage," the author wishes to express his thanks to the various publishers who have co-operated in making this music available in a practical form. The kindness of the E. B. Marks Music Corporation is particularly appreciated in permitting the use of their complete text for *The Happy Farmer*. Special permissions were also kindly given by the Associated Music Publishers, representing a number of important contemporary foreign composers.

Acknowledgment is enthusiastically made of the helpfulness of the Music Department of the New York Public Library and of the employees of G. Schirmer, Inc., New York, whose unfailing courtesy and efficiency have continually softened and smoothed out the hard road of research. Miss Virginia Barker was of great assistance in preparing the list of phonograph records.

A valuable contribution to this book was made by Katharine Lane Spaeth in preparing the index and attending to other unpleasant but highly important details. The Editorial and Manufacturing Departments of the Garden City Publishing Company have functioned with their customary skill.

PREFACE

THIS BOOK is a compulsory sequel to *Great Symphonies: How to Recognize and Remember Them,* an experiment which proved surprisingly successful. The heresy in that book was to set words to symphonic melodies so that people could retain them in their memories and thus be able to follow the musical structure of a symphony from start to finish. It was heartily condemned by those who evidently prefer to keep most listeners entirely ignorant of what symphonies really are. But it has become increasingly popular with both children and adults who listen to symphonies over the radio or in the concert hall and would honestly like to get a clearer idea of what is going on than the average announcer or program note is likely to give them. Most of them did not mind the harmless little jingles, because they helped them to recognize and remember the music.

The use of words is far more legitimate in this

ix

book on the great program music of the world. For program music, by its very name, implies a music that has a definite meaning, clearly indicated by the composer. It promises by its title, or by some note or explanation, to tell a story or paint a picture in tones, possibly even to imitate sounds that would not ordinarily be called musical. Even if it merely suggests a mood or an emotion it may be called program music in the broadest sense. Technically it must have no words in its original form, but there is no reason on earth why words should not be added to the outstanding melodies, as the composers have generally made their meaning perfectly clear.

Since the author was not inclined to apologize for *Great Symphonies,* there is even less reason to be apologetic about *Great Program Music.* There is ground for believing also that it will find a far larger audience than the symphony book, merely because people love to read meanings into music, even when they are quite at variance with the composers' intentions. How much happier they should be, once they know that everything is entirely legal and that they are simply putting into words what the creator of the music actually wanted them to be thinking of.

Much has been written in the past about program music, and there is general agreement as to its boundaries, its peculiarities, its virtues and its limitations. The classic volume on the subject is by **Dr Frederick Niecks**.[1] There is an enlightening essay by Ernest Newman, and the American critic, Richard Aldrich, also wrote pleasantly on program music in his *Musical Discourse,* selected from the Music Department of the New York *Times.* This book does not pretend to be either exhaustive or argumentative. It accepts the findings of authoritative scholars, as well as the clearly expressed intentions of the composers themselves. It is addressed (as usual) primarily to the layman and aims to be a practical and comprehensive summary of what is best and most popular in the whole attractive category of program music, clarifying, analyzing and interpreting this material without intentional exaggeration or too vivid an imagination.

The quotations are for the most part given in singable keys, often corresponding with the originals, and they can be played by any home pianist of moderate ability, with one hand. At best the words are to be considered no more than a guide to the composer's expressed or implied meaning. If they make it easier to remember and interpret the tunes, that is all that can reasonably be expected of them.

There is no attempt at appraisal of the music itself. This can safely be left to the individual reader, especially after the repeated hearings that

[1]*Programme Music in the Last Four Centuries,* Novello & Co., London.

the author hopes this book will encourage. If it accomplishes no more than to stimulate such open-minded listening it will have justified itself.

Sigmund Spaeth

Westport, Connecticut

CONTENTS

CONTENTS

CONTENTS

CONTENTS

INTRODUCTORY

WHILE the term "program music" has become quite common in the literature of the art, its meaning still seems rather vague to a surprising number of people. An immediate and exact definition is therefore in order.

In its broadest sense all music that offers a definite program, in the way of telling a story, describing a picture, imitating the sounds of Nature, or even suggesting some specific mood or feeling comes under the head of "program music." Its opposite is generally known as "absolute" or "pure" music, consisting of a mere pattern or design of tones, treated for their own sake, without attempting anything more than an abstract musical expression, attained by the combination of technique and melodic invention.

Obviously all vocal music belongs automatically to the "program" class, for the words themselves are the clearest index to its meaning. The narrower and more accurate definition of program music, therefore, and the one generally applied by musical scholars is limited to *instrumental* music whose composer has announced a definite

1

meaning or program, either by the title or by some explanatory note.

Most symphonies, sonatas, string quartets, trios and quintets are *absolute* music, even though some people insist on reading hidden meanings and often whole slices of autobiography into them. Their titles give no hint of a story or a picture, or even a suggested emotion, much less an actual imitation of sounds in everyday life. They are known by their opus numbers (meaning simply "work" or "composition") and possibly their key signatures. If the public in time supplies them with titles (as in the case of Beethoven's popular *Moonlight Sonata*) they are still absolute music from the composer's standpoint. He is the only one who has a right to announce a program or to restrict the significance of his musical workmanship.

Real program music may be classified as narrative, descriptive, imitative or suggestive, and often the same piece belongs in more than one of these categories, perhaps in all of them.

It will be found that the composers of the classic style wrote mostly absolute music, while the romanticists and the moderns showed a marked preference for program music. There are at least two good reasons for this. The classic composers, notably Bach and Haydn, were primarily interested in dealing with the arrangement of tones for their own sake, with emphasis on form and technique rather than content or emotional significance. But they were also equipped with limited orchestral resources, so that they could not have created the dramatic and realistic effects of a later period even if they had wished. While the earlier composers (and particularly those of lesser talent) made frequent attempts at descriptive or even imitative music, they were not particularly successful, and to modern ears most of these experiments sound delightfully naïve and completely unconvincing.

It is a mistake, however, to argue that absolute music in general is superior to program music, nor is it fair to insist that great program music should make its meaning clear without any definite announcement on the part of the composer. Obviously, however, the finest program music is well able to stand on its own feet, regardless of any specific meaning, while the best of the world's absolute music can afford to be interpreted in any way that the individual listener chooses. The two opposite extremes therefore meet eventually on the same plane, which is purely musical.

The weakness of program music is that after an idea or a meaning has been definitely established almost any expression may satisfy the listener, who is entirely ready to believe what the composer has told him in advance. It is all too easy to burlesque program music, as in the familiar pianologue, *Three Trees,* in which the trees, the stream and the rabbit are all suggested in an equally ridiculous fashion. (There is also the story of the composer who set the Nelson column to music by simply making a growling trill far down on the keyboard to represent the lions at the base, then running a glissando upward for the column itself and finally adding a tinkling chord at the top for Nelson.)

But program music has its advantages, too, chief of which is the power to interest a listener in spite of his or her complete ignorance of music. The same thing is true of all art. A picture with attractive subject matter will appeal to the public regardless of its technical excellence or defects. A book may be badly written but win readers by the compelling power of its plot and characters. In the same way music, if it promises to tell a story or to express a definite meaning of some sort, will find plenty of listeners. Even if the execution is not particularly convincing there will be an audience quite ready to be fascinated. Inside information is always attractive, and the gushing lady who can interpret the whole piece before a note has been sounded is sure to have a wonderful time, even if she bores you to extinction.

Program music also faces the indisputable handicap of too great versatility. It is distinctly embarrassing to find the same sequence of notes given several different meanings. Motion pictures

4

have revealed this weakness over and over again. It is unfortunate but true that unless we are told in advance exactly what is intended the same agitated chords and chromatic runs may indicate a chase, a fire, a thunderstorm, a battle or a rushing stream. Similarly a quiet, sentimental passage may connote feminine virtue, faith in fundamental ethics, a reconciliation or the memory of past happiness, with an occasional hint of the propagation of the human race.

Honesty forces the admission that program music may be very cheap and obvious, yet effective because of the announced plot. But it has the unquestioned advantage of attracting quick and sincere attention, if only because the hearer wants to check up on the composer. When it surmounts the restrictions of its program and justifies itself as pure music, as is often the case, it is likely to find a far wider audience than the absolute type.

The following pages contain excerpts from what seems to the author the world's most important program music. The selections are of three kinds. Either they represent great music, regardless of the program, or the program is so clearly carried out that the composition deserves recognition for its dramatic and realistic integrity, aside from any musical value as such. Finally it is necessary to include music that has won a wide popularity, either because of its program or because of its melodic appeal or by a combination of both factors. In no case is there any attempt to glorify the music or exaggerate its importance.

The compositions are generally treated in chronological order, grouped according to their creators, and the aim is to sum up the musical structure of each piece, perhaps with its historical and biographical background, briefly but clearly. The themes are supplied with words, quite legitimately, since the intentions of the composers have generally been made entirely clear. But the words must be considered merely a reminder of the expressed meaning of the music, a practical aid to the memory and nothing more.

Approached in this rather naïvely straightforward fashion, program music becomes an endlessly entertaining subject, free from all abstruse argument and scholarly verbosity. There is a minimum of theorizing, for in practically every case the composer has clearly indicated what he meant his music to say. Operatic *Overtures* are included, and here the words, wherever possible, are based upon the libretto itself. In many cases the *Overture* is actually a miniature opera, summing up the entire plot of what is to come.

Program music is definitely the best introduction to music in general. A well-made *Overture* will create the desire to hear the entire opera. A symphonic poem paves the way to actual symphonies, with a casual acquaintance that may easily ripen into real friendship and understanding.

It is human nature to follow the line of least resistance, and program music represents that line in the musical field. Vocal music is the easiest of all for the average listener, for the words tell the story, and often the music is a negligible quantity. Next to actual words, possibly with the accompaniment of scenery, costumes and action, as in opera and the ballet, a definite program is the surest way to capture the attention. Dependence on pure pattern or design offers far more difficult problems.

Why not be honest about this normal human reaction and rejoice that so much good and even great program music has been written? If it brings new listeners to music in general so much the better. In any case, there is ample material in the following pages for the experienced student of music as well as the beginner in appreciation or enjoyment. Preliminaries will be kept down to a minimum, with a consistent concentration on the music itself in its most logical and significant aspects.

EARLY EXAMPLES OF PROGRAM MUSIC

Two ENGLISHMEN get credit for having written the earliest instrumental program music on record. The *Fitzwilliam Virginal Book* contains a *Fantasia* by John Mundy (who died in 1630) in which various sections of the music are labeled "Fair Weather," "Lightning," "Thunder," "Calm Weather" and "A Clear Day"! It is all very primitive and childlike, with rolling bass notes for expressing thunder, quick, disjointed figures for lightning and any quiet melody serving for the rest. Nobody would ever guess what the music meant without the composer's labels.

About the same time the greater and far better known William Byrd (1543–1623) wrote the first battle piece still in existence, appearing in *My Ladye Nevell's Booke*. Here is the composer's description of the contents: "The march before the battle; the soldiers' summons; the march of footmen; now followeth the trumpets; the Irish march; the bagpipe and the drone; the flute and the drum; the march to the fight; here the battle be joined; the retreat; now followeth a galliard for the victory." (A later copy,

8

in the British Museum, closes with "the burying of the dead," with a "Tarratantarra" inserted in the midst of the battle.)

Byrd was more successful than Mundy in carrying out his program realistically. His imitations of trumpets, fifes and drums are excellent, and the musical descriptions of fighting and of the gradual retreat ending in disordered flight carry conviction even to modern ears. Obviously a battle piece is the easiest kind of program music to write and the most likely to impress its hearers.

Early English program music might include a delightful series by John Dowland (1563–1626) with the melancholy title: *Lachrymae, or Seven Tears Figured in Seven Passionate Pavans, for Lute, Viols, or Violins, in Five Parts.* This fine composer, of whom it was said that "his heavenly touch on the lute doth ravish human sense," often used descriptive titles, but these generally referred to the original tunes on which they were based, like *The Carman's Whistle* and *The Hunt Is Up.*

Italy produced many examples of program music in the instrumental passages of seventeenth-century operas, particularly those of Claudio Monteverde (1567–1643), Francesco Cavalli (1600–1676) and Marc Antonio Cesti (1620–1669).

A very bad piece of imitative music was produced in 1627 by the Italian Carlo Farina, court violinist in Dresden, with the title *Capriccio Stravagante*. The "extravagance" is definitely an understatement, for the composer tried to express in his music the cackling of hens, the mewing of cats, the barking of dogs and such instruments as the flautino, fifferino della soldadesca and chitarra spagnola.

There is better workmanship in two *Sinfonie Boscareccie* ("Wood Symphonies," in 1669) by Marco Uccellini, one of which he called *La Suavissima* and the other *La Gran Battaglia*. Actually this battle was not very terrifying, being mostly limited to two violins snapping at each other.

The great organist, Frescobaldi, who died in 1644, also wrote a battle piece, *La Battaglia,* which is really a set of variations on a bugle call. He imitated the cuckoo call in one of his capriccios and the pifferari in another; but on the whole Frescobaldi composed absolute rather than program music.

Another Italian, Alessandro Poglietti (d. 1683) imitated the nightingale in two of his caprices and based another on the crowing of roosters and cackling of hens. In a set of variations written for the Emperor Leopold I, Poglietti made his organ music successfully suggest the Bohemian Bagpipe, Dutch Flageolet, Hungarian Fiddle and a Juggler's Rope-Dance, with one movement which he called "French Baiselmens" (i.e. "hand-kissings" or "compliments").

Germany's earliest composer of program music was Jacob Froberger (d. 1667), a pupil of Frescobaldi and a great player of the harpsichord and organ. He was credited with knowing how "to represent on the clavier alone whole stories, with the portraiture of the persons that had been present and taken part in them, together with their characters"—a fairly large order for the naïve music of the seventeenth century. Mattheson, in his *Ehrenpforte* (1740), describes a Froberger manuscript which tells in music "what he experienced between Paris and Calais, and from Calais to England, from robbers on land and sea, and how the English organist had abused him, taken him by the arm to the door and kicked him out." This may all be true, but it seems agreed that Froberger overdid it when in his *Lament on the Death of the Emperor Ferdinand IV* he finished with a C major glissando representing "the Jacob's ladder on which Ferdinand IV ascends to heaven." (Cf., the burlesque on the Nelson column above.)

Unquestionably the most important program music of the pioneering days was that of Johann Kuhnau (1660–1722) who preceded the great Bach as cantor in the Leipzig Church of St Thomas. In the year 1700 Kuhnau wrote six *Bible Sonatas* for the clavier, with the following titles: (1) *The Combat between David and Go-*

liath; (2) *David Curing Saul by Means of Music;* (3) *Jacob's Marriage;* (4) *Hezekiah Sick unto Death and Recovered of His Sickness;* (5) *The Saviour of Israel, Gideon;* (6) *Jacob's Death and Burial.* But Kuhnau added to these titles a detailed description of each sonata, leaving no doubt as to the meaning of practically every note of his music. Thus, for example, he summarizes the argument of the first sonata: "The boasting and defying of Goliath; the terror of the Israelites, and their prayers to God at sight of the terrible enemy; the courage of David, his desire to humble the pride of the giant, and his childlike trust in God; the contest of words between David and Goliath, and the contest itself, in which Goliath is wounded in the forehead by a stone so that he falls to the ground and is slain; the flight of the Philistines, and how they are pursued by the Israelites and slain by the sword; the exultation of the Israelites over their victory; the praise of David, sung by the women in alternate choirs; the general joy, expressing itself in hearty dancing and leaping."[1]

With the French composers of the seventeenth and eighteenth centuries program music may be considered firmly established and, on the whole, amply justified. With Couperin and Rameau sharing top honors, the lutenists and clavecinists

[1]Two of the Kuhnau sonatas have been published by Novello, London, and all six are reprinted in the *Denkmäler Deutscher Tonkust,* Vol. IV.

of France showed the world how artistically satisfactory program music could be, combining adequate realism with a high standard of purely musical values.

The founder of this French school of program music was Dennis Gaultier (d. about 1665) who wrote sixty-two pieces for the lute, under the title *La Rhetorique des Dieux,* many of which have descriptive titles, mostly relating to mythology. *Phaeton foudroyé* (Phaeton's Folly) "bears witness to Phaeton being, by his imprudence and ambition, the cause of the conflagration of the half of mankind, to the punishment meted out to the rash youth by Jupiter and to the sorrows of his father Apollo on account of his loss." Of a paradoxical piece called *La Coquette Virtuosa* it is written that "this fair one, who makes as many lovers as there are men that understand her, proves by her priceless discourse the sweetness she finds in the love of virtue, the great esteem she has for those who adore it and that she will give herself to him who will have first attained the title of the magnanimous."

François Couperin *le grand* (1688–1733) must be considered the first great master of program music, a tone painter of miniatures, yet a musical genius in the absolute sense, regardless of subject matter. His four books of harpsichord pieces contain many descriptive titles, sometimes sentimental, often humorous, suggesting states of feeling, even personal portraits. In his preface to the collection (1713) the composer wrote, "I have always had an object in composing all these pieces; different occasions have furnished me with it— thus the titles correspond to the ideas I have had."

Couperin's clavecin pieces range from such generalities as *Happy Ideas, Regrets* and *Tender Languors* to definite musical descriptions and even imitations of bees, butterflies, the nightingale, the mill, the clock, etc. He applies his musical imagination to *The Carillon of Cythera, Wandering Shades, Female Pilgrims Asking Alms, The Comic Performance of Buffoons on a Trestle-Stage, The Effects of Bacchus,* various phases of war and ages of childhood. Perhaps the most elaborate group of pieces is the one called *Records of the Grand and Ancient Minstrelsy,* composed of five "acts," which Couperin described thus: "Act I. The minstrel notables and jurymen; Act II. The hurdy-gurdy players and the beggar; Act III. The jugglers, tumblers and mountebanks with their bears and monkeys; Act IV. The invalids, or those crippled in the service of the grand minstrelsy; Act V. Disorder and defeat of the whole troop, caused by the drunkards, the bears and the monkeys." This is definitely a foretaste of such later program music as Schumann's. In fact, Couperin may have suggested the Schumann *Carnaval* by his *Folies Françaises ou les Dominos.* He de-

14

scribes these "follies" in detail, under twelve titles:
"(1) Virginity under the domino of the color of
the invisible; (2) Pudicity under the rose-color
domino; (3) Ardor under the carnation domino;
(4) Hope under the green domino; (5) Fidelity
under the blue domino; (6) Perseverance under
the drab domino; (7) Languor under the violet
domino; (8) Coquetry under different dominoes;
(9) The old gallants and the superannuated female treasurers under purple and withered-leaves
dominoes; (10) The kind cuckoos under yellow
dominoes; (11) Taciturn jealousy under the
mauve-gray domino; (12) Frenzy or despair under the black domino." There is an epilogue, also
Schumannesque, of "Lent repentance after carnival indiscretions."

Two of Couperin's most elaborate and fanciful
pieces of program music are the *Apotheoses,* referring to the composers Corelli and Lully, the
first bearing the additional title *Le Parnasse.*
This tribute to Corelli has seven movements, superscribed as follows: "1. Corelli, at the foot of
Parnassus, asks the Muses to receive him among
them. 2. Corelli, charmed by the good reception
given him on Parnassus, shows his joy thereat.
3. Corelli drinks at the fountain of Hippocrene;
his company continue. 4. Enthusiasm of Corelli
caused by the waters of Hippocrene. 5. Corelli,
after his enthusiasm, falls asleep and his companions play the following slumber music very

softly. 6. The Muses awaken Corelli and place him beside Apollo. 7. Thanks of Corelli." (It all sounds a little like those old Salvini stories.)

The *Apotheosis of Lully* is even more complicated, with this detailed program: "1. Lully in the Elysian Fields concerting with the lyrical shades. 2. Air for the same. 3. The flight of Mercury to the Elysian Fields to announce the descent of Apollo. 4. Descent of Apollo, who comes to offer to Lully his violin and his place on Parnassus. 5. Subterranean noise caused by the contemporaries of Lully. 6. Complaints of the same, for flutes and violins, very subdued. 7. The carrying off of Lully to Parnassus. 8. Reception given to Lully by Corelli and the Italian Muses. 9. Thanks of Lully to Apollo. 10. Apollo persuades Lully and Corelli that the union of the French and the Italian taste ought to make music perfect. 11. Lully playing the principal part and Corelli accompanying. 12. Corelli playing in his turn the principal part, while Lully accompanies. 13. The Peace of Parnassus made on the remonstrance of the French Muses, subject to the condition that in future, when their language was spoken there, sonade and cantade should be said, just as one says ballade, serenade, etc. 14. Sally (Epilogue)."

Some of this material is treated naïvely, almost childishly, and much of it does not lend itself naturally to musical interpretation. Yet one must

16

agree that the Couperin pieces show a wide variety of expressiveness and that they are musically significant, quite apart from their announced programs.

Almost equally important, and far better known today, is the program music of Jean Philippe Rameau (1683–1764). His *Tambourin,* suggesting the Provençal fife and drum, is often heard on the piano, as is *La Poule,* a striking imitation of the cackling of a hen. Rameau's clavecin (or harpsichord) pieces include such other titles as *The Call of the Birds, Sighs, Whirls of Dust, The Savages* and musical characterizations of indifferent, triumphant, timid, happy and indiscreet heroines.

Of other early French composers of program music Louis Claude Daquin (1694–1772) is remembered chiefly for his charming finger exercise, *Le Coucou,* which imitates the familiar cuckoo call throughout. But he also wrote musical descriptions of the swallow, the guitar, pleasures of the chase, etc., all in a very pleasing, melodious style.

Jean François Dandrieu (1684–1740) composed a book of clavecin pieces with elaborate titles relating to war, the hunt and a village festival. His chase music is mostly fanfares and imitations of horns, with galloping rhythms in six-eight time. War is also indicated by trumpet effects, and at one point the composer tells the player that he can imitate the report of a cannon by pounding the lower keys with the entire palm of the left hand! (How many modernists think they invented that trick?) Dandrieu's *Village Festival* is a series of rustic dances. The charm of his music is equalled by the disarming confession that he uses programs to "awaken simple ideas acquired by ordinary experience of common and natural sentiments," and he adds naïvely, "Perhaps I have not always succeeded."

The contemporary giants of music, Johann Sebastian Bach (1685–1750) and George Frederick Handel (1685–1759) wrote as a rule either absolute music or vocal compositions whose meaning was made entirely clear by the words. Yet both can be credited with a certain amount of instrumental program music of the highest type. Handel's *Overtures* to his operas and oratorios are not really programmatic, but he frequently introduces descriptive and imitative effects in his instrumental interludes. For instance, the lively music at the beginning of the third act of *Solomon* is probably a tone picture of the arrival of the Queen of Sheba. *Belshazzar* has a rather programmatic *Overture* and contains also a *Sinfonia Postilione* (or "Postilions," as printed by the Handel Society), following the words "Call all my wise men, sorcerers, Chaldeans, astrologers," indicating the departure posthaste of servants to carry out the command.

The famous *Dead March* from *Saul* must be considered program music and has actually been sung to words. A practical interpretive text for the main theme is suggested herewith:

Also legitimately included in the great program music of the world is the *Pastoral Symphony* in Handel's *Messiah,* which beautifully conveys a picture of the "shepherds in the fields on the night of the nativity." Words are hardly needed to interpret these melodies:

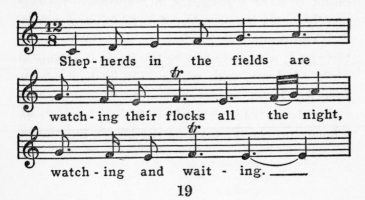

"I sing a loud song, and a heart-y, proud song, keep-ing time with ham-mer strokes that ech-o far and near." "Black-smith, black-smith, you have found the an-swer, You're quite a man, sir, and you bring us good cheer.

Johann Sebastian Bach (1685–1750) also showed his genius in dramatic and realistic musical expression through instrumental passages in his great choral works. A fine example is the wailing introduction to the opening chorus of the *Passion According to St Matthew*, "Come, ye daughters, weep with me." Contrastingly, the *Christmas Oratorio* opens with an instrumental suggestion of wild rejoicing. This composition also contains a *Pastoral Symphony* which affords an interesting comparison with Handel's, with a consistent figure that suggests the rocking of a cradle:

When Bach breaks through the restraints of the fugal and polyphonic style he is consistently dramatic and often intensely realistic, as when he depicts the rending of the veil of the temple in the *St Matthew Passion* or, in the same work, calls upon man to lament his many sins. There is drama in the *Sinfonia* that opens the *Easter Oratorio* and in the long instrumental introduction to the *Magnificat*.

But the one Bach piece that is generally recognized as program music (even though not at all well known today) is the *Capriccio on the Departure of His Favorite Brother*. (The German title contents itself with the word *lieb,* meaning "dear," but the Italian uses the superlative, *"dilettissimo,"* which could be translated "best loved" or "favorite.")

The actual brother was Johann Jacob, who left home to take a job as oboe player with the Swedish Guard. Sebastian Bach was only nineteen at the time, and his affection for Jacob must have been intensified by the cruel treatment he had suffered from his eldest brother, Johann Christoph.

The *Capriccio* is in six movements, and Bach made every detail of the program clear by definite, printed explanations. The first movement, *Arioso,* is described as "Cajolery of friends, trying to dissuade him from his journey." The music of the upper voices clearly represents these pleadings and cajolings, while the bass part must be interpreted as the firm and persistent resolve of the brother to stick to his intentions. Some such wording as this would seem legitimate:

Do not go, Ja-cob dear, we shall

I must be off!

miss you so! Will you stay if we hug and

Fare - well, I must be

kiss you so? You'll not find friends like

go - ing, I must say good-

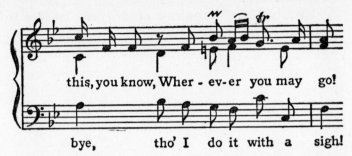

this, you know, Wher - ev- er you may go!

bye, tho' I do it with a sigh!

The second movement, *Con Moto,* "is a representation of various casualties that might befall him in a strange place," with the additional note "to be played half humorously, half in earnest," with "the theme always sharply emphasized."

Have you thought of all that might

eas - i - ly be - fall If you

Have you thought of all that might

go far a-way from your friends here?

eas-i - ly be - fall a-way from

Have you thought of

(The contrapuntal music above requires four voices for its overlapping melodies.)

Next comes a beautiful *Adagio,* described by the composer as "a general lament of the friends." Its chief theme can be worded thus:

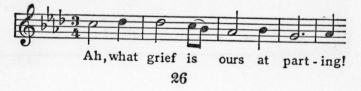

The fourth movement is called *Recitativo*, with the superscription, "Here finally the friends come and take their leave, as they see that after all it cannot be otherwise." The voices again overlap ("as though speaking all mixed up") and the short section is lively and realistic, with this thematic material:

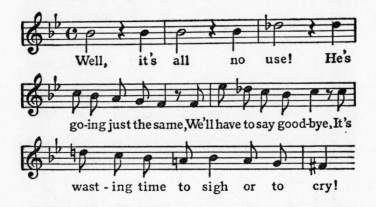

Number five is the *Aria of the Postilion*, in which the horn is definitely imitated in octave jumps. The chief tune goes like this:

Finally there is a *Fugue* "in imitation of the trumpet of the Postilion." The octave jumps appear again, but the fugal subject is really this:

Crack! get a - long you good for noth - ing nags, Get a - way from all those feed - ing bags, We must be on our way! Get a - long, get a - long! Can't you hear what I say? Ta - ra - ra!

It all ends quite cheerfully as the beloved brother takes his departure.

Several of Bach's contemporaries wrote program music of a sort, most of which is now completely forgotten. Christoph Graupner in 1733 produced four suites for clavier with the title *The Four Seasons*. J. J. Fux, best known for his famous treatise, *Gradus ad Parnassum,* wrote an orchestral suite containing a *Spring Overture* and movements superscribed "To the Nightingale," "To the Quail" and "To the Cuckoo."

More important is the work of Georg Philipp Telemann (1681–1767), who composed two programmatic orchestral suites, one called *Water Music* and the other *Don Quixote*. The *Overture* of the *Water Music* clearly describes a calm sea, with a breeze gradually stirring up rippling waves. This is followed by "the sleeping Thetis," "the wakening Thetis," "the amorous Neptune," "the playful Naiads," "the sportive Tritons," "the stormy Aeolus," "the pleasant Zephyr," "ebb and flood" and "the merry mariners."

Don Quixote, after a general introduction, gives tonal pictures of "the dream of Quixote," "his attack upon the windmills," "the amorous sighs for the Princess Aline," "Sancho Panza blanketed," "the gallop of Rosinante" and "that of Sancho's donkey." It is all carried out musically with spirit and considerable success.

The Italian, Antonio Vivaldi (1680–1743), whose music strongly influenced Bach, composed his full share of programmatic material. Three concertos (Opus 10) bear the titles *Storm on the Sea, The Night* and *The Goldfinch,* with some detailed superscriptions over the individual movements.

Vivaldi called his Opus 8 *The Trial of Harmony and Invention*, with the first four concertos

definitely labeled *The Four Seasons.* The titles
are amplified with four sonnets, whose contents
are then summarized in direct connection with the
music. Here are Vivaldi's summaries exactly as
he wrote them:

"Spring: (a) Spring is come; (b) The festive
birds salute it with their merry songs; (c) The
fountains run with a soft murmur under the
breath of the zephyrs; (d) The sky becomes over-
cast, and thunder and lightning ensue; (e) When
calm is restored the birds recommence their singing; (f) On the flowery meadow, amid the rustling of leaves and plants, sleeps the goatherd
with his faithful dog by his side; (g) Pastoral
dance to the sound of the rustic bagpipe.

"Summer: (a) The heat of the sun makes man
and flock languid; (b) The cuckoo sings; (c) The
dove and the goldfinch; (d) First zephyrs, then
suddenly Boreas; (e) Lament of the fearful vil-
lager; (f) Fear of lightning and thunder and
swarms of flies disturb his repose; (g) The
heavens thunder and lighten, and the hail destroys
the ears of corn.

"Autumn: (a) The villagers celebrate the harvest festival with dance and song; (b) Bacchus
seduces many; (c) Sleep concludes their enjoyment; (d) Dance and song cease and all are
wrapped in sweet slumber; (e) The hunters set
out at dawn with horns, guns and dogs; (f) The
fleeing quarry is followed; (g) Stunned and tired

by the noise of shots and barks, it is wounded; (h) It dies fleeing.

"Winter: (a) Shivering with cold; (b) A terrible wind; (c) Running and stamping from cold; (d) The teeth chatter; (e) Feeling quiet and contented by the fireside, while outside the rain pours down; (f) Walking on the ice; (g) Walking cautiously and timidly; (h) Walking boldly, slipping and falling; (i) Running boldly on the ice; (j) The ice breaks up and melts; (k) The sirocco; (l) Boreas and all the winds at war."

At the close of this elaborate composition spring returns once more, "bringing with it joy."

Mention should also be made of a strange piece called *The Enchanted Forest,* by Francesco Geminiani (1680–1762), "An instrumental composition expressive of the same ideas as the poem of Tasso of that title." The ideas are chiefly that trees can be brought to life, to the extent of indulging in conversation. In the thirteenth canto of Tasso's *Jerusalem Delivered* the trees are represented as objecting to being made into battering-rams and other engines of destruction for the siege of Jerusalem. Geminiani's music, however, does not go much beyond the mere idea and is programmatic in name only.

The next truly great composer to be credited with real program music is Christoph Willibald von Gluck (1714–1787). His operatic reforms included the treatment of *Overtures,* so as to relate them as closely as possible to the dramatic action that was to follow. Yet the earlier Gluck *Overtures* do not carry out these intentions. It is only with the *Overture* to *Iphigenia in Aulis* (1774) that Gluck becomes definitely programmatic.

Wagner later described this *Overture* in the following terms: "1. A motive of invocation from painful, gnawing heart sorrow. 2. A motive of force, of an imperious, overwhelming demand. 3. A motive of grace and maidenly tenderness. 4. A motive of painful, tormenting sympathy."

On the other hand, the better-known *Overture* to *Orpheus and Eurydice* (1762) is little more than a lively curtain raiser, whose chief themes require no more than a general association with the opera.

The best program music in *Orpheus* occurs in the instrumental interludes, of which the ballet of the *Elysian Fields* is the most popular:

Come, bless-ed spir - its fly - ing,

Where mor-tal men are sigh-ing, Or-pheus has

need of your coun-sel and your aid.

The succeeding melody, of similar calm and spirituality, is often heard as a violin solo, although originally carried by the flute:

There are also three contrastingly dramatic *Dances of the Furies* whose music scarcely needs words to make its meaning clear.[3]

The rest of Gluck's program music requires only a brief summary without quotations. The *Overture* to *Alceste* (1767) may be interpreted as picturing the sadness of the heroine, Alcestis. In the music preliminary to the opera of *Paris and Helen* (1769) there is pomp and passion, to represent the hero, a suggestion of the doubts and regrets of Helen and a mood of festive rejoicing.

The *Overture* to *Armide* (1777) had already been used by Gluck for two other operas, *Telemachus* and *The Festivals of Apollo,* and cannot therefore be granted any definite program. But for that of *Iphigenia in Tauris* (1779) the composer supplied notes to indicate that the music is descriptive of "calm, a distant storm, the nearer approach of the storm, rain and hail," and finally "the storm ceases."

C. P. E. Bach (1714–1788), most distinguished

---

[3]Berlioz pointed out that the second chorus of the Furies contains in its instrumental accompaniment a direct imitation of the howling of Cerberus, the watchdog of Hades.

of the musical sons of the giant, Johann Sebastian, wrote much program music in the smaller forms, but most of it is forgotten today. He often gave titles to his short instrumental pieces in the manner of the French school of Couperin and Rameau (*La Complaisante, La Capricieuse,* etc.), and a trio for two violins and bass contains an elaborate dialogue between *Sanguinicus* and *Melancholicus,* representing the eternal argument of optimism and pessimism. The younger Bach mentions no less than forty-two points in this lengthy debate, which evidently ends in a draw.

A *Sonata in F minor,* by C. P. E. Bach, was marked with a red pencil, "The April day drawn from nature," which may have been the composer's own description. It is worth noting also that the poet Gerstenberg wrote two sets of words to a *Fantasia,* "Socrates drinking the poison cup" and "Hamlet's monologue," thereby setting a precedent for the treatment of program music in this book.

While Franz Joseph Haydn (1732–1809) is considered primarily a composer of absolute music, he must be credited with his full share of programmatic effects, within the limits of the orchestral medium at his command. *The Creation* has an instrumental introduction which represents Chaos. His other oratorio, *The Seasons,* offers four introductory sections, also instrumental, described by the composer as "Transition from winter to spring," "Dawn," "The peasants' joyous feelings at the rich harvest" and "The thick mist with which winter begins."

Frederick Niecks finds in *The Creation* definite imitations or suggestions of "the picturing of light ("Let there be *light*") ; of the throng of hell's black spirits sinking to the deep abyss; of lightning, thunder, rain and wind; of the billowing sea, the flowing river and the gliding, purling brook; of the roaring lion, the flexible tiger and the noble steed; of the peaceful herds and flocks; of the eagle soaring on mighty pens, the cooing dove, the merry lark and the tuneful nightingale; of the flashing shoal of fish and the immense leviathan; of the buzzing host of insects; of the sinuous serpent," etc.

In the music of *The Seasons* the same historian hears "the picture of fleeing winter and his howling ruffian winds, the torrents of melting snow, the tepid air of spring and zephyr's breath; of the morning light on the mountaintops, the rising sun, dusky night and gloomy caves; of the whispering foliage and murmuring streamlet; of thrilling nerves; of the ill-omened lich owl, shrill-voiced cock, bounding lambkins, sporting fish, twittering birds, chirping cricket, croaking frogs, bright-colored insects and barking dogs; of the whirring spinning wheel; of the shepherd's pipe, the merry fife and drum, the loud hunting horns, the spaniel roving in search of scent, the fleeing stag and the pursuing men, horses and dogs." This is program music indeed, and it would be cruel to quote the actual measures that presumably fit these picturesque details. There is, to be sure, a thunderstorm in *The Seasons* that is quite realistic.

Haydn's outstanding piece of program music is probably *The Seven Last Words of Our Saviour on the Cross,* written in 1785 for the Cathedral of Cadiz on Good Friday. It was originally called *Passione Instrumentale* and written for orchestra but soon rearranged for string quartet and eventually fitted with words as a cantata. The work is a series of seven *Adagios,* representing the sentences traditionally spoken by Christ on the Cross and ending with a *Presto* called *The Earthquake.*

Many of the symphonies of Haydn have definite titles, but these do not necessarily indicate a program. One symphony was called *Maria Theresa* merely because it was played before the Austrian empress; another, *La Reine de France,* bears perhaps a similar relationship to Marie Antoinette; and the *Oxford Symphony* gets its name from the fact that England's university gave the composer an honorary degree of doctor of music.

The familiar *Surprise Symphony* has a second movement in which the theme is interrupted by a

36

crashing chord, variously interpreted as "to wake up the audience" or "to make the ladies scream." In the *Clock Symphony* there is a definite tick-tock in the *Andante*. The *Military Symphony* has its suggestions of band music.[4]

The *Roxelane Symphony* of Haydn is supposed to refer to the French romance of that name in its *Andante,* and the symphonies called *L'Ours* (The Bear) and *La Chasse* justify their titles in the *Finales*. *La Poule* (The Hen) contains definite suggestions of cackling, but there is no particular reason, so far as known, for such symphonic titles as *The Schoolmaster, Lamentations, Il Distratto* and *The Philosopher*. Three early symphonies of Haydn have the descriptive names *Le Midi* (Midday), *Le Matin* (Morning) and *Le Soir* (Evening), but again there is no indication of a detailed program, although they are very good absolute music.

The famous *Farewell Symphony* was written as a hint to Prince Esterhazy that the orchestra deserved a vacation, with its program mostly in the last movement, *Adagio*. This *Finale* employed the effective trick of having the men gradually blow out their candles, until the last two violinists brought the symphony to a close and left the stage in darkness. (The prince took the

[4] Analyses of these symphonies, with words set to their chief melodies, will be found in the author's *Great Symphonies: How to Recognize and Remember Them,* Garden City Publishing Co., New York, pp. 3–36.

hint.) Here is the theme of this *Adagio*, transposed from G to the more comfortable key of F, with interpretive words:

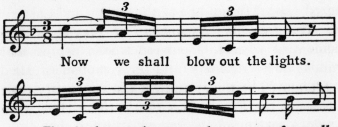

Now we shall blow out the lights.

That is the way that an or-ches-tra says fare-well.

Two of Haydn's biographers, Griesinger and Carpani, refer to a symphony in which the composer portrayed a dialogue between God and a hardened sinner, "shadowing forth in it the parable of the Prodigal Son." But it is not made clear just which symphony this was. Carpani also describes Haydn as "weaving a kind of romance or program on which to hang the musical ideas and colors."

For another symphony, also unfortunately not identified, this biographer works out an elaborate program, presumably with Haydn's consent, describing "a friend, rich in a large family and poor in worldly goods, setting out for America to improve his circumstances, succeeding in his project and returning in safety." He gives the following detailed analysis of the music: "Embarcation of the adventurer; departure of the ves-

sel with a favorable wind and the lamentation of
the family and the good wishes of the friends on
shore; a prosperous voyage; arrival in strange
lands; barbarous sounds, dances and voices are
heard (about the middle of the symphony); after
an advantageous exchange of merchandise the
homeward voyage is entered upon; propitious
winds blow (return of the first motive of the
symphony), then a terrible storm supervenes (a
confusion of tones and chords); cries of the pas-
sengers, roaring of the sea, whistling of the wind
(the melody passes from the chromatic to the
pathetic); fear and anxiety of the wretched
voyagers (augmented and diminished chords and
semitone modulations); the elements become
calm again; the wished-for country is reached;
joyful reception by family and friends; general
happiness." "In this way," writes Carpani, "were
produced other symphonies to which, without
saying why, Haydn assigned names that without
the explanation now given would appear unin-
telligible and ridiculous." Perhaps the modern
estimate of Haydn as a composer of rather formal, pure music is all wrong after all.

An almost forgotten composer, Carl Ditters
von Dittersdorf (1739–1799), created some of
the most interesting program music of the eighteenth century in his twelve symphonies based on
Ovid's *Metamorphoses*. The titles are as follows:
1. *The Four Ages of the World;* 2. *The Fall of*

Phaeton; 3. The Transformation of Actaeon into a Stag; 4. The Rescue of Andromeda; 5. The Lycian Peasants Transformed into Frogs; 6. The Turning into Stone of Phineus and His Friends; 7. Jason Carries off the Golden Fleece; 8. The Siege of Megara; 9. Hercules Is Translated to Olympus among the Gods; 10. Orpheus and Eurydice; 11. Midas as Judge between Pan and Apollo; 12. Ajax and Ulysses Contend for the Armour of Achilles.

These symphonies all follow the classic form, in four movements, generally with a direct quotation from Ovid prefacing each movement. The tone painting is excellent, and there is little of the obvious imitation so often found in program music. An exception is the musical expression of the barking of dogs in the Actaeon episode. Even here, however, there is no straining after effect.

Beethoven's *Pastoral Symphony* was almost literally foretold in a *Musical Portrait of Nature* by Justin Heinrich Knecht (1752–1817), published in 1784. While Knecht's music is vastly inferior to Beethoven's the two programs are almost identical, as may be gathered from Knecht's own descriptions of his symphony:

"1. A beautiful country, where the sun shines, gentle zephyrs frolic, brooks cross the valley, birds twitter, a torrent falls from the mountain, the shepherd pipes, the lambs gambol and the sweet-voiced shepherdess sings.

"2. Suddenly the sky darkens; an oppressive closeness pervades the air; black clouds gather; the wind rises; distant thunder is heard, and the storm slowly approaches.

"3. The tempest bursts in all its fury; the wind howls and the rain beats; the trees groan, and the streams rush furiously.

"4. The storm gradually passes; the clouds disperse, and the sky clears.

"5. Nature raises her joyful voice to heaven in songs of gratitude to the Creator."

Knecht's thunderstorm is unconvincing, and most of his music is dull and uninspired. But Beethoven's indebtedness to his original idea cannot be denied.

A complete enthusiast for program music was J. F. Lesueur (1760–1837), who had the distinction of teaching Berlioz to master the art. Lesueur published (in 1787) a book which declared that the object of music must always be imitation. "Music can imitate all the inflections of nature. All the sentiments are also within its domain."

But Lesueur applied these theories mostly to choral and operatic music and wrote no independent orchestral compositions. His intentions were better than his music, as when he describes an instrumental passage in the Psalm, *Super Flumina,* as "the chorus of the Hebrews recalling their captivity at Babylon, when they mingled

their tears with the murmuring of Euphrates."
He then points out that the interpretation
"should furnish not only the imitation of Euphrates, but also the imitative image of the dull
noise of the contrary winds and the distant roaring of the cataracts of the river, which seemed
coming to join the lamentations of the Hebrews,
their dolorous chants, and the plaintive accents
of the musical instruments with which they accompanied their chorus."

A famous piece of program music was *The
Battle of Prague,* by Franz Kotzwara, who committed suicide in 1791. But it is today little more
than a reminder of how easy and generally in-
effective it is to make music imitate the sounds of
war.

Johann Ludwig Dussek (1760–1812) also
wrote bad battle pieces, including a trio called
Combat Naval and orchestral works with the following elaborate titles:

*The Naval Battle and Total Defeat of the
Dutch Fleet by Admiral Duncan, October 11,
1797; A Complete and Exact Delineation of the
Ceremony from St James's to St Paul's on Tues-
day, the 19th December, 1797, on Which Day
Their Majesties, Together with Both Houses of
Parliament, Went in Solemn Procession to Re-
turn Thanks for the Several Naval Victories Ob-
tained by the British Fleet over Those of France,
Spain, and Holland; and The Sufferings of the*

Queen of France: A Musical Composition Expressing the Feelings of the Unfortunate Marie Antoinette during Her Imprisonment, Trial, etc., Op. 23.

Dussek gives this detailed program of *The Sufferings of the Queen of France,* unfortunately also a very bad composition:

"1. The Queen's imprisonment. 2. She reflects on her former greatness. 3. They separate her from her children—the farewell of her children. 4. They pronounce the sentence. 5. Her resignation to her fate. 6. The situation and reflections on the night before her execution—the guards come to conduct her to the place of execution. 7. March. 8. The savage tumult of the rabble. 9. The Queen's invocation to the Almighty just before her death—the guillotine drops (crashing chord with quickly descending diatonic scale). 10. Apotheosis."

In the same class is the program music of Daniel Steibelt (1765–1823), who wrote *The Battle of Neerwinden,* consisting of cheap imitations of bugles, bells and shots (with the modern trick of bringing the palms of both hands down on the keyboard). Steibelt's most elaborate and futile program was supplied for his *Public Christening on the Neva at St Petersburg,* as follows:

"The Bells announce the ceremony. Firing the guns. The joy of the people. The emperor sets out from the palace. The throng of the people. Chorus in *Iphigenia* by Gluck. March of the troops. Acclamation of the people. His Majesty's arrival at the place where the ceremony is performed. The divine service. *Te Deum.* Chorus. *Let us pray,* sung by the Patriarch. Departure of His Majesty. The joy of the people. Firing of the guns. The people thronging from the place. Air in *Alceste* with three variations."

The Abbé Vogler, immortalized by Browning in a very fanciful poem and generally considered a charlatan by his contemporaries, naturally turned to program music for ideas which he was unable to express in the absolute style. (He had the distinction of teaching both Weber and Meyerbeer and was at least a good scholar and theorist, though totally uninspired.)

Vogler wrote a quintet called *The Matrimonial Quarrel* and was credited with improvising on the organ a musical description of storms and the fall of Jericho. Among his more elaborate programs the following seem worth quoting:

"*Naval Battle:* 1. Beating of the drums. 2. Martial music and marches. 3. Movement of the ships. 4. Crossing of the waves. 5. Cannon shots. 6. Cries of the wounded. 7. Shouts of victory of the triumphant fleet.

"*Musical Imitation of Rubens's Last Judg-*

ment: 1. Magnificent introduction. 2. The trumpet resounds through the graves; they open. 3. The wrathful Judge pronounces the terrible judgment on the reprobates; their fall into the abyss; wailing and gnashing of teeth. 4. The just are received by God into eternal blessedness; their bliss. 5. The voices of the blessed unite with the choirs of angels.

"Death of Prince Leopold of Brunswick: 1. The quiet course of the river; the winds that chase it into greater rapidity; the gradual rise of the water; the complete inundation. 2. The general terror and lamentation of the unfortunate who foresee their misery; their shuddering, complaints, tears and sobs. 3. The arrival of the prince, who resolves to help them; the representations and prayers of his officers, who wish to keep him back; his voice in opposition to them, which at last stifles all lamentation. 4. The boat sets out; its reeling through the waves; the howling of the wind; the boat capsizes; the prince sinks. 5. A touching piece with the feeling that suits the occasion."

Early Italian program music might include the *Devil's Trill,* a popular violin sonata by Giuseppe Tartini (1692–1770), supposedly representing music that the composer, in a dream, heard the devil play. Actually there is nothing very devilish about the music, which still serves

concert violinists for the display of technique and
style. There is a series of sustained trills in
the second movement, against a countermelody,
thus:

Dev - il's trill, Dev - il's thrill, Real-
- ly Tar - tin - i's skill!

Luigi Boccherini (1743–1805), remembered
today chiefly by a popular *Minuet* (definitely of
the absolute type), is credited with one piece of
real program music, a quintet called *The Aviary*.
His biographer, Picquot, says that in this piece
the composer "intended to depict a rural scene,
where the song of birds unites with the sound of
the hunting horn, the shepherd's bagpipe and the
dance of the villagers." Certainly this quintet
contains plenty of bird songs, both at the start
and at the finish.

Wolfgang Amadeus Mozart (1756–1791) put
most of his realistic and dramatic music into
his operas. His purely instrumental works must
be considered absolute music of the highest
quality.

Even the *Overtures* to the Mozart operas are

not strictly programmatic, although they generally express the mood and sometimes a suggestion of the content of the drama that is to follow.
The *Overture* to *Don Giovanni* is actually given
a complete program by E. T. A. Hoffmann in
his *Fantasie Pieces* (No. 4), but it is enough to
quote here only the main theme, with a general
reference to the musical story of the world's
greatest lover. ("Oh, Giovanni, oh!" as Alec
Templeton would put it.) The words below are a
bit optimistic, for Don Juan really went to his
doom without any sign of repentance or con-
science. But maybe he was sorry later.

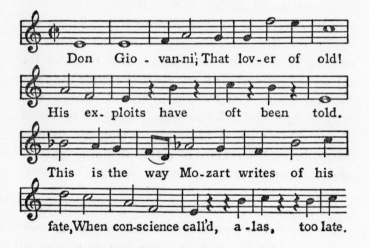

Don   Gio - van-ni, That lov-er of   old!

His ex- ploits have   oft been told.

This is the   way Mo-zart writes of his

fate,When con-science call'd, a -las, too late.

The most famous melody within the opera
itself is the *Minuet,* danced in the final scene of
the first act. Its music contains no hint of the

tragedy that is to be enacted, and it needs no
words except by way of reminder.

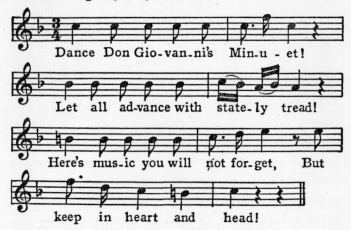

Dance Don Gio-van-ni's Min-u-et!

Let all ad-vance with state-ly tread!

Here's mus-ic you will not for-get, But

keep in heart and head!

The *Overture* to *The Magic Flute* refers directly to the Masonic ritual of the opera in
solemn calls of the trombones. But most of its
music is light and airy, suggesting rather the fantastic characters of Papageno and Papagena, the
birdcatcher and his bewitched lady. The chief
theme of this great *Overture,* which the violins
carry through a variety of clever designs, may be
remembered by not too serious words:

Pa - pa - ge - no, Pa - pa - ge - na,

What a grand Ma-son-ic sce - na,

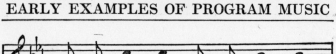

In - tro - duced by fid - dles cute, The

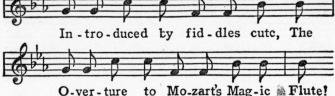

O - ver - ture to Mo - zart's Mag - ic Flute!

For *The Marriage of Figaro* Mozart wrote a very lively *Overture,* suggesting the pomp of an actual wedding ceremony, although this does not appear until the very end of the opera, whose plot concerns mostly the machinations of the Count Almaviva to keep Figaro, his valet (the former Barber of Seville), from marrying Susanna, the maid. The first real theme is built mostly on chord tones, with the effect of a fanfare:

Sound the wed - ding mu - sic, Bar - ber's

wed ding mu - sic loud!

This is imitated in a second theme, with change of key. (Both melodies are here transposed to a convenient vocal register. The first melody was originally in the key of D major and the second in A major.)

49

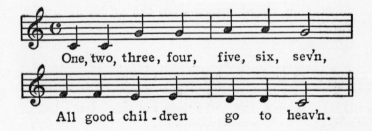

Mozart is often credited with the little tune to which children still sing their ABCs, as well as the familiar couplet:

One other Mozart piece may be called program music, and that is the *March* in rondo form generally known as *Alla Turca* or *Turkish*. It carries out the tradition of the time that Turkish music must make frequent use of the cymbals, bass drum and triangle, and its chief themes easily lend themselves to simple words emphasizing this formula. (The keys are made practical for singing, as usual.)

Cym - bals clang, Bass drums

bang, With the tri - an-gle's ting-a-ling-a-

lang! This was known as Turk - ish

mu - sic in the days when Mo - zart sang.

This is march - ing al - la

Tur - ca, to the sound of ring - ing

brass; Tink - ling cym - bals not too

nois - y help the march - ing sol - diers pass.

This final strain might be called the *Trio* of the *Turkish March:*

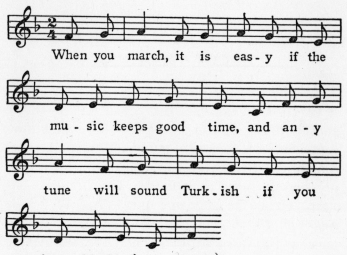

When you march, it is eas-y if the

mu-sic keeps good time, and an-y

tune will sound Turk-ish if you

have this kind of rhyme.

Mozart had far too much dramatic sense to restrict himself entirely to absolute music, although he is remembered today chiefly for the perfection of his tonal patterns. It would be a serious mistake to deny Mozart an important place in any history of program music.

BEETHOVEN'S MASTERY OF PROGRAM MUSIC

WITH Ludwig van Beethoven (1770–1827) another musical giant is found making a genuine contribution to program music. As the first great romanticist Beethoven turns naturally to the expression of more than merely formal tonal designs. He wrote only one opera, *Fidelio,* which was not too successful, but his instrumental music is full of descriptive, narrative, suggestive and even imitative passages.

Of the nine Beethoven symphonies four are given definite programs by the composer. The fifth, in C minor, represents the battle between man and Fate, and Beethoven himself said of the opening four notes, "Thus Fate knocks upon the door."[1]

The contents of the sixth or *Pastoral Symphony* are described in far greater detail by Beethoven.[2]

[1]See the analysis and verbal interpretation of this and other Beethoven symphonies in the author's *Great Symphonies: How to Recognize and Remember Them,* Garden City Publishing Company, New York.

[2]See *Great Symphonies: How to Recognize and Remember Them,* pp. 101–107.

In the ninth he actually introduces words in the *Finale,* from Schiller's *Ode to Joy.* The seventh was called by Wagner "the apotheosis of the dance," and the eighth contains a movement (the second) built on a personal compliment to Maelzel, inventor of the metronome.

The third has the title *Eroica,* originally dedicated to Napoleon Bonaparte, with a famous Funeral March for its slow movement.[3]

Probably the worst composition ever written by Beethoven was the so-called *Battle Symphony,* also known as *Wellington's Victory,* a typical piece of claptrap, fit to be classed with all the other musical glorifications of war. The commercially minded Maelzel inspired this monstrosity in order to get some cheap and sensational music for his panharmonicon, an early form of automatic player. It eventually led to a lawsuit between Maelzel and Beethoven.[4]

The composer himself called his *Battle Symphony* "Eine Dummheit" (a foolishness). But, considered merely as blatant program music, it has its points, notably in the clarity of its contents. There are two parts, *The Battle* and *Triumphal Symphony.*

The English army is represented by *Rule,*

[3] See *Great Symphonies: How to Recognize and Remember Them,* pp. 77–85. (Garden City Publishing Co., New York.)

[4] See the author's *Stories behind the World's Great Music,* pp. 78–82. (Garden City Publishing Co., New York.)

Britannia, played as a march, with the French soldiers using the old *Malbrough* as a theme. When the French are defeated Beethoven simply puts a few measures of *Malbrough* into minor key. The second part of the symphony makes considerable use of *God Save the King,* and it may be assumed that all these melodies are too familiar to require quotation.[5]

Beethoven's truly great program music is in his *Overtures,* including the four that he wrote for his one opera, *Fidelio.* Opinions vary as to the reasons for this prodigality, but it seems fairly well established that the *Overture* known as *Leonore No. 1* was played at rehearsals of the opera but discarded by the composer as unsatisfactory. Actually it is far below the level of the other three, and it was not published during Beethoven's lifetime, appearing posthumously as Opus 138.

The one theme that is common to all three of the *Overtures* called *Leonore* (but not appearing in the one called *Fidelio,* which is printed in the score of the opera) is the slow melody sung by the hero, Florestan, in the first scene of the second Act, when he recalls in prison the happy days of his youth. Here is its basic form as it finally appears in the third *Overture:*

[5]*Malbrough* is known by the modern words, "We won't go home until morning," and "For he's a jolly good fellow."

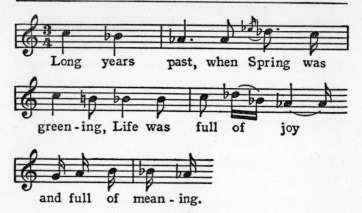

Long years past, when Spring was green-ing, Life was full of joy and full of mean-ing.

The second and third *Leonore Overtures* both start with a descending scale passage which clearly describes the halting steps of Leonora herself, as she goes down into the dungeon where her husband, Florestan, is imprisoned.

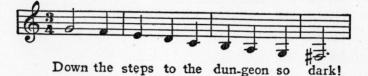

Down the steps to the dun-geon so dark!

She realizes that the cruel Pizarro intends to murder Florestan, already close to death by starvation, and she intends to foil the villain if possible. Disguised as a young man, using the name Fidelio, she has won the confidence of Rocco, the old jailer, and now helps him dig the grave in which her husband is to be buried.

A fast, syncopated theme, also common to both the second and third *Overtures,* clearly depicts the bravery of Leonora, as she prepares to defend Florestan until help arrives in the person of Don Fernando. This exciting melody forms a large part of the material of both *Overtures,* and is given a great variety of treatment by Beethoven.

Brave Le - o - nor - a, what a no-ble wife!

Brave Le - o - nor - a saved her hus-band's life.

Another broad and somewhat slower melody seems to express hope and confidence, with a close musical relationship to Florestan's theme of youth in springtime. It occurs in both *Overtures* but is treated at greater length in the second.

Hope still____ must a - bide and Fi-

del-i-ty be her guide. No e-vil shall

foil her, No slan-der can soil her.

The climax of the third *Leonore Overture* and the feature which makes it stand out clearly above the others is the distant trumpet call, played off stage, announcing the approach of Don Fernando, repeated shortly after and obviously much closer. This effect is quoted literally from the opera itself, and Beethoven was severely criticized for introducing such a revolutionary idea into a classic *Overture*. But it really makes the whole piece and justifies the rapturous comment of Wagner that this music "is no longer an *Overture;* it is the most grandiose drama in itself." Since this passage is an outright imitation of a trumpet no words are necessary for its interpretation:

It is followed immediately (in the third *Overture*) by a slow theme that definitely expresses relief and the calm expectation of a happy ending, with the rhythm of the trumpet call still heard in the subdued accompaniment. (The story of the policeman who arrested the off-stage trumpeter for disturbing a concert is not true.)

Ah, at last we're saved, the trum - pet's call means help at hand and vil - lain's fall.

Both the second and the third *Leonore Over-tures* introduce their final sections with a brilliant display of passage work by the strings, at lightning speed. Only the opening measures need be given here, naturally without words:

With such an ecstatic finish to the *Overture* there can be no question as to the happy ending of the opera itself. Strictly speaking, both of these *Overtures* are far too significant to act as mere introductions to a rather conventional music drama. The third, in particular, is as Wagner said, a complete drama in itself, and its overwhelming popularity as a concert piece is fully justified. It is often played as a special introduction to the third Act, with the real *Fidelio Overture* used at the start.

This final *Overture* was written for a revival of *Fidelio* in 1814, after Beethoven had revised the entire score for the third time. By this time he must have realized that both the *Leonore Overtures* overshadowed his drama and actually constituted a handicap to a work already burdened by too many weaknesses. He therefore wrote a perfectly conventional, cheerful prelude of the type that might introduce almost any gay and entertaining opera, much shorter than the earlier *Overtures* and far better suited to its purpose.

This *Fidelio Overture* practically ignores the darker side of the story and stresses only its lively excitement. It contains no direct quotations from the opera itself and in this respect differs completely from the other three *Overtures*. But modest as it is in its pretensions, the *Fidelio Overture* is a little masterpiece, an ideal introduction for the opera and an effective concert piece in its own right.

The chief thematic material is announced immediately, as though the callboy were knocking on the doors of the dressing-rooms, warning the actors that the curtain is about to rise. But the lively opening is followed immediately by plaintive harmonies, as though to remind the hearer that everything may not be so joyous after all.

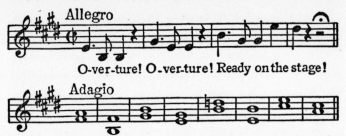

O-ver-ture! O-ver-ture! Ready on the stage!

Sad - ness, glad - ness, slave - ry, brave - ry!

This introductory material is developed into a complete melody later but still with the suggestion that we are merely being told that the opera is about to begin:

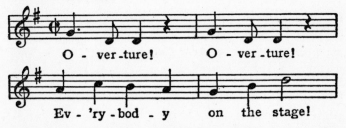

O - ver -ture! O - ver -ture!

Ev - 'ry - bod - y on the stage!

When the plaintive harmonies return, near the end of the *Fidelio Overture,* they are accompanied by the soft voices of the wood wind, in a figure that reappears some years later in the slow movement of Schubert's *Unfinished Symphony:*

From here to the close everything is happy and gay, with the little three-note pattern that spells "Overture" insistently heard to the very end. In writing a rather unsuccessful opera Beethoven managed to produce at least three outstanding pieces of program music.

Beethoven wrote two other *Overtures* that stand high in the program music of the world. The one called *Coriolanus,* Opus 62, was published in 1808, as a prelude to the drama of an obscure poet, Heinrich von Collin. It is fair to say, however, that Beethoven was inspired by Shakespeare and actual history rather than the play for which this *Overture* was written. It is a tremendously dramatic work, expressing the energy and will power of Coriolanus, the imploring entreaties of his wife and mother, the terrific struggle of conflicting emotions, with the eventual collapse and death of the hero.

According to Plutarch (with Shakespeare and Von Collin generally agreeing), Coriolanus was banished from Rome by the plebeians and took vengeance by leading the Volscian army to the very gates of the city, only to yield to the pleading of the Roman women, led by his own family. After withdrawing his army, Coriolanus, according to different versions of the story, either committed suicide or was put to death by the Volscians.

Beethoven's *Overture* opens with a fortissimo

unison of strings followed by a blasting chord from the full orchestra, depicting the proud character of Coriolanus himself. (This occurs three times.) The first theme expresses agitation and might be interpreted thus:

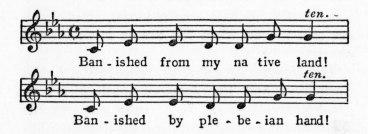

Ban - ished from my na tive land!
Ban - ished by ple - be - ian hand!

The second theme is definitely imploring and clearly depicts the scene in which the women, led by the mother and wife of Coriolanus, plead with him to withdraw from his attack upon Rome:

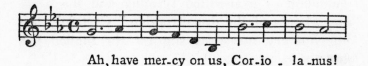

Ah, have mer-cy on us, Cor-io - la -nus!

The restless, agitated figure of the first theme supplies most of the material for the development section. In the recapitulation the imploring theme returns in a new key (C major) and the *Overture* ends with the tearing unisons and chords of the start, leading dramatically to the death of Coriolanus, which is emphasized by

63

gradually diminishing volume, closing with very soft pizzicato octaves in the strings.

Beethoven's Opus 84, written in 1810, is the incidental music to Goethe's tragedy, *Egmont,* of which only the *Overture* is generally heard today. (It originally included also four entr'actes, two songs and three instrumental pieces, all of which are still played when the drama is performed abroad.)

The *Egmont Overture* deserves to stand with *Coriolanus* and the *Leonore* masterpieces as great program music. It is really a symphonic poem, and it concentrates upon the historical significance of the drama rather than the human relationships.

There are three parts to the *Overture,* representing in turn oppression, conflict and victory. The first part has been described as "the stern command of iron-willed tyranny and the wails and plaints of the downtrodden." Certainly the introductory measures suggest the mailed fist and the iron hand.

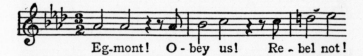

The second strain of the introduction might represent wailings, but is also easily associated with Clara, the brave young girl who loves Egmont and is beloved by him.

Love is en-dur-ing, as-sur-ing.

The main theme of the *Overture* unquestionably expresses the gathering discontent of the Netherlanders, finally breaking out in open revolt against Spanish tyranny, under the leadership of Count Egmont:

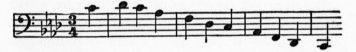

The final section represents a "symphony of victory" with the ultimate triumph of liberty and the death of Egmont. The introductory theme changes to a complete melody, with strong suggestions of the later material of the ninth symphony.

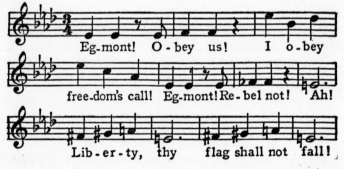

Eg-mont! O-bey us! I o-bey

free-dom's call! Eg-mont! Re-bel not! Ah!

Lib-er-ty, thy flag shall not fall!

At the close a terrific fanfare of brass echoes the actual trumpets ordered by the Duke of Alva to drown out the farewell speech of Egmont. No matter how it is interpreted, this is a climax such as no composer before Beethoven had been able to write.

Beethoven's earliest *Overture*, numbered as Opus 43 and dated 1801, was composed for the *Prometheus Ballet*, a work which gained him great popularity in Vienna. It is a naïvely simple piece as compared with his later inspirations in this form, but its introductory theme is worth quoting, if only because it strongly suggests the slow melody of Beethoven's second symphony. His opening chords are a similar reminder of the start of the first symphony, and the Adagio strain that follows is definitely reminiscent of the tune best known today as a hymn. (The tune is generally called *Alsace*, with words by Isaac Watts beginning, "Kingdoms and thrones to God belong.")

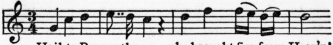

Hail to Pro-me-the-us, who brought fire from Heav'n!

Beethoven wrote several other *Overtures*, none of them particularly important. Two of them belong to the year 1811, contributing to the incidental music for two of Kotzebue's dramas, *King Stephen* and *The Ruins of Athens*. The former is given a Hungarian flavor (Stephen

66

was Hungary's first benefactor) by closing with a brilliant czardas. The latter has the distinction of being the shortest and least pretentious of all the Beethoven *Overtures.*

In 1814 Beethoven contributed an *Overture* to the celebration of the Emperor's "Name Day" (*Zur Namensfeier*) and thereby created the type of concert *Overture* later perfected by Mendelssohn and other composers. He specifically called it an *"Overture* for any occasion or for use in the concert hall," and it therefore escapes the legitimate title of program music.

Eight years later, in 1822, Beethoven wrote his final *Overture, Die Weihe des Hauses* (*The Consecration of the House*), to inaugurate the new Josephstädter Theatre in Vienna. It suggests the style of Gluck and Handel, yet curiously contains something of the rare spirit that went into the *Missa Solemnis* and the ninth symphony. Its opus number is 124, and it therefore belongs among the most mature compositions of the master.

Far more obvious and popular is the incidental music to *The Ruins of Athens,* best known today by the familiar *Turkish March.* This little tune, largely built upon a two-tone pattern, deserves to be quoted if only because of its wide vogue among amateur pianists. It suggests the traditional drums, cymbals and triangle, with the effect of a passing parade.

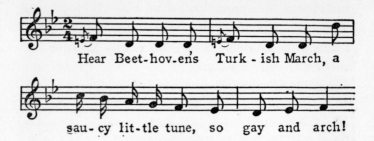

Hear Beet-hov-en's Turk-ish March, a
sau-cy lit-tle tune, so gay and arch!

Also ranking among the more obvious pieces of program music by Beethoven is the *Rondo* for piano, Opus 129, whose manuscript bears the title, "Fury over the lost penny, vented in a capriccio." It is rather a pleasant fury, unquestionably expressed with the composer's tongue in his cheek. The chief theme goes like this:

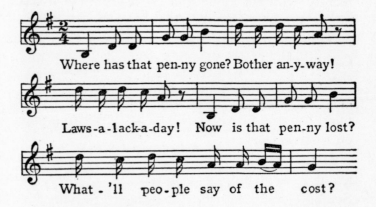

Where has that pen-ny gone? Bother an-y-way!
Laws-a-lack-a-day! Now is that pen-ny lost?
What-'ll peo-ple say of the cost?

Among the Beethoven piano sonatas two are given definite programs by the composer. The title *Pathétique*, applied to Opus 13, is his own,

thoven *Farewell, Absence* and *Return*. It is only fair therefore to give its leading themes a suggestion of these meanings.

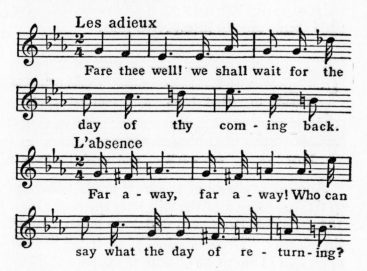

The "return" theme is a galloping affair that scarcely needs or permits words.

It is generally accepted that these sentiments applied to Beethoven's pupil, the Archduke Rudolph, who left Vienna at the approach of the French. But it is entirely possible that the sonata refers to one of the ladies who influenced so much of Beethoven's life and music.

In one of his last string quartets (Opus 132) Beethoven gives the second movement the title, "Thanksgiving Song in the Lydian Mode, Offered to the Divinity by a Convalescent." Its chief theme may be interpreted thus:

Thanks to God from a mor-tal soul,

Now re - cov - er'd and made whole.

Another evidence of program music turns up in the last section of the still later quartet, Opus 135, in which Beethoven definitely labels two of the phrases, "Muss es sein [Must it be]?" "Es muss sein [It must be]," with the superscription, "Der schwergefasste Entschluss [The Resolution Formed with Difficulty]." Here are the actual phrases in question, the first appearing in the cello part, and the second announced by the first violin:

Must it be?   It must be!   It must be!

This about completes the program music of Beethoven, and the list is admittedly impressive. There is a story that when Schindler asked Beethoven the meaning of two of his sonatas (Opus 31, No. 2, and Opus 57) he answered gruffly, "Read Shakespeare's *Tempest*." Of the sonata in E minor, Opus 90, dedicated to Count Moritz Lichnowsky, Schindler reported that Beethoven "remarked that he had intended to picture in his music the love story of the count and his wife; adding that if a superscription was required that of the first movement might be 'Struggle between head and heart,' and that of the second, 'Conversation with the loved one.' " (The reference is to the love of Count Lichnowsky for an opera singer, whom he eventually married.) Beethoven also told his friend Amenda that when he composed the Adagio of the string quartet in F, Opus 18, No. 1, "he thought of Romeo and Juliet in the tomb scene." These are interesting bits of gossip, but they add little to the estimate of Beethoven as a creator of program music, based upon his truly great *Overtures* and *Symphonies*. Judged by these masterpieces, he becomes one of the outstanding dramatic composers of all time, with a convincing realism that is challenged only by Wagner himself.[6]

[6]It may be worth noting that the final melody of the *Eroica* symphony was used twice before by Beethoven, once in the *Prometheus* music and once as a *Contredanse* (sometimes called *Country Dance*), No. 7 in the series. The first of the *Country Dances* has been turned into a lively mixed chorus, published by the E. B. Marks Music Corporation, with words by this author, under the title *On Time*. The popular *Minuet in G* has also been supplied with words.

EARLY ROMANTICISTS

A YOUNGER contemporary of Beethoven, the successful operatic composer, Carl Maria von Weber (1786–1826), well deserves a high place among the creators of real program music. One of his most popular instrumental pieces is a set of waltzes known as *Invitation to the Dance,* which has been used as accompaniment to the ballet, *Spectre de la Rose,* with Fokine's choreography.

The composer himself, however, supplied a complete and totally different program when he played these waltzes to his wife in 1819, two years before their publication. She reported his commentary as follows: "First approach of the dancer (measures 1–5); the lady's evasive reply (5–9); his pressing invitation (9–13); her consent (13–16); they enter into conversation; he begins (17–19); she replies (19–21); he speaks with greater warmth (21–29); she sympathetically agrees (23–25). Now for the dance! He addresses her with regard to it (25–27); her answer (27–29); they draw together (29–31), take their places, are waiting for the commencement of the dance (31–35). The dance. Conclusion: his thanks, her reply, their retirement. Silence."

This is surely a detailed program, even though the dance itself is left entirely to the imagination of the hearer. But the mood of this captivating waltz music is unmistakable. Niecks says, "We may read in it a whole story of youthful joyousness, coquetry, courtship and love."

For the first thirty-five measures of the *Invitation to the Dance* it is possible to follow Weber's program quite closely. The opening conversation, for instance, could run about as follows:

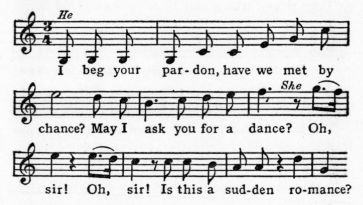

He

I beg your par-don, have we met by chance? May I ask you for a dance? Oh, *She* sir! Oh, sir! Is this a sud-den ro-mance?

(All the music is here transposed from five flats into the easy key of C major, but even then the vocal range is a bit extreme in both directions.) The next eight measures are an elaboration of the same idea, with the lady finally saying, in effect, "Oh, I might as well consent!"

Their actual "conversation" might start like this (as it generally does):

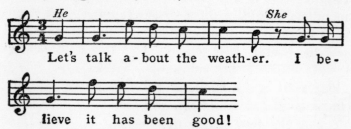

Let's talk a-bout the weath-er. I be-

lieve it has been good!

When he "speaks with greater warmth" and she "sympathetically agrees" an extension of the same music might fit the words, "Now at last we are together." "Oh, alackaday, I'm being wooed!"

The introduction can then be concluded thus:

It's time for danc-ing! Shall we be-

gin? I must give in! You win! Let's take our

plac-es, com-pose our fac-es, No one will

no-tice, if we mere-ly dance, The hap-py

chance that has brought us ro - mance!

Most of the actual waltzes neither admit nor require words. The first is very lively with tremendous jumps into the upper register, and this is followed by a quieter strain but still with widely spaced intervals:

The next melody may be considered the chief waltz of the series, and this deserves a rudimentary text, although really too high for singing:

Now   we're   danc - ing!

How   en - tranc - ing!

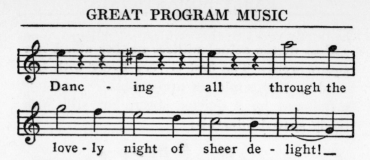

Danc - ing   all   through the

love - ly   night of   sheer de - light!__

One more waltz strain is worth quoting, again in a lively mood and purely instrumental:

Beyond this there are fast scale passages for connecting links and various repetitions and re-capitulations, with occasional changes of key. When the dance is finished the music of the in-troduction returns, and it may be left to the imagination of the hearer to supply the words of "his thanks" and "her reply." The charming com-position ends very softly with three major chords.

A still more elaborate program was supplied by Weber for his celebrated *Concertstück* (Con-cert Piece), Opus 79, although it is often looked upon as absolute music. When he first planned this composition in 1815 he called it a *Concerto in F minor,* and in a letter to his friend Rochlitz he briefly revealed this program: "Allegro, separation; Adagio, lament; Finale, profoundest sorrow, consolation, meeting again and jubilation."

Weber later decided to conceal this program from the public, fearing to be accused of charlatanism. But in 1821, when he had finished the work, Weber played it for his wife and his pupil, Julius Benedict, and gave them the complete story in these words: "The lady sits in her tower; she gazes sadly into the distance. Her knight has been for years in the Holy Land; shall she never see him again? Battles have been fought, but there is no news of him who is so dear to her. In vain have been her prayers and her longing. A dreadful vision rises in her mind: her knight is lying on the battlefield, deserted by his companions; his heart's blood is ebbing fast away. Could she but be at his side! Could she but die with him! She falls down exhausted and senseless. But hark! What is that distant sound? What glimmers in the sunlight from the wood? What are those forms approaching? Knights and squires with the cross of the Crusaders, banners waving, acclamations of the people, and there! It is he! She sinks into his arms. What a commotion of love! What an infinite, indescribable happiness! The very woods and waters sing the song of true love; a thousand voices proclaim its victory."

While it is difficult to follow this program in detail throughout the music it is definitely there in spirit and sentiment. A literal translation of some of the themes is therefore justified, in accordance with the composer's intentions. The opening, in the wood wind (here transposed down a fourth) may well represent the mournful sighs of the bereaved lady:

The strings then enter with an explanatory theme:

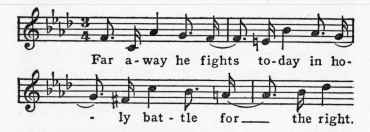

The piano starts with brilliant arpeggios and soon plays the opening theme, repeating it in imitation against the strings. The solo instrument proceeds through more and more dazzling technical displays, with rapid chromatic scale passages, all giving the effect of extreme emotional excitement.

A quieter melody is eventually introduced by the solo flute, in competition with the piano:

Sigh   no   long - er,   Hope

grows stronger, Ne'er___ feel de - spair!

(As written, the flute plays this an octave higher.) The same material is then treated by other instruments, and finally the clarinets and trumpets announce the stirring march which heralds the hero's return:

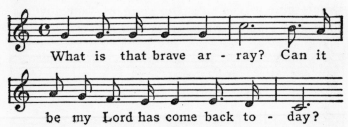

What   is   that brave ar - ray? Can it

be my Lord has come back to - day?

From this point to the end the mood of the *Concert Piece* is one of pure joy. The piano runs wild in rapid scale passages, to start the section marked *Presto giojoso,* and then organizes its ecstasy in the following terms, reminiscent of the

81

Presto of Beethoven's seventh symphony, written only a few years earlier:

A tender touch, marked *dolce* (sweetly), varies this unrestrained enthusiasm, first in the strings, then in the wood wind:

Finally the full orchestra expresses, still in a fast six-eight time, the sentiments of Weber's closing lines. ("What a commotion of love! What an infinite, indescribable happiness! The very woods and waves sing the song of true love; a thousand voices proclaim its victory.")

Na - ture is sing - ing,
Wel - kin is ring - ing! What _ a com-
mo - tion! Lov - er's e - mo - tion!

One realizes at the end of the *Concert Piece* that Weber did not exaggerate the dramatic significance of his self-confessed program.

Weber's three well-known *Overtures,* to the operas *Der Freischütz* (The Free Shooter), *Euryanthe* and *Oberon,* all rank high as program music. Each of them makes some quotations from the opera which it preceded, but in general they reflect the mood and atmosphere of the entire work rather than serving as mere medleys of the outstanding tunes.

The *Freischütz Overture* begins in a spirit of peaceful calm, glorified by the quartet of horns, whose music has often been used as a hymn tune:

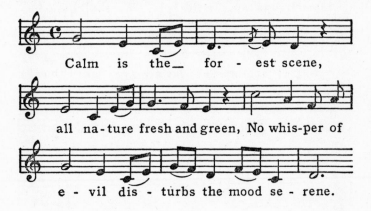

Calm is the for-est scene, all na-ture fresh and green, No whis-per of e - vil dis - turbs the mood se - rene.

The subjection of the hero, Max (or Rodolpho or Giulio, as he is variously known), to the evil Samiel is suggested in the *Allegro* portion of the *Overture,* which quotes directly from Max's aria,

"What evil power is closing round me?" and from the scene in the Wolf's Glen, with its thunderstorm and flames starting from the earth. Another quotation from the music of the hero ("No ray will shine upon my darkness") leads to the jubilant song of the heroine, Agatha (also called Agnes and Reseda), representing the redeeming motive which finally triumphs over evil:

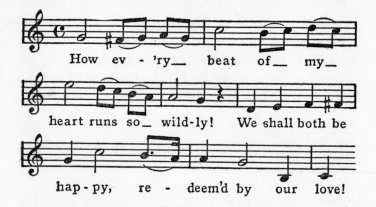

The *Overture* to *Euryanthe* breathes the spirit of chivalry. The brilliant opening is followed by quotations from the music of Adolar, the hero:

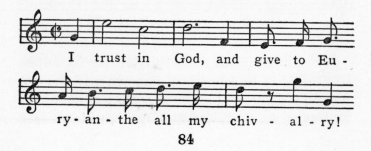

84

Before the development of these subjects there is a slow section apparently representing the ghostly apparition of Emma. But chivalry finally triumphs, as indicated by the recapitulation of the earlier themes.

O bliss, thy joy I can-not fa - thom!

In the *Oberon Overture* Weber comes closest to writing a potpourri of the tunes in the opera, and it may be on this account that it has become the most popular of the three. Yet this great *Overture* is also a sustained and consistent picture of the dream world, peopled by the characters of fairyland and of a romantic realm of the imagination.

At the start the horn of Oberon is heard, with an echo in the muted strings.

O - ber - on!   O - ber - on!____

Delicate passages in the wood wind (taken from the opening scene of the opera) carry on the suggestion of fairyland and lead to a soft fanfare of elfin trumpets. Then comes the first

85

real melody, of sustained beauty, summing up the entire mood of charming fantasy:

Fair land of dreams, Re - mov'd from mor-tal ken, Faint star-ry gleams re-mind us of a world un-known to grop-ing men. Hark!

The final note is actually a crashing chord, which introduces the main body of the *Overture,* in fast time (derived from the accompaniment to the quartet in the second act).

Then comes one of the most familiar melodies of the opera, originally written for Oberon himself but later given to the hero, Huon of Bordeaux, and sung by him in the first act:

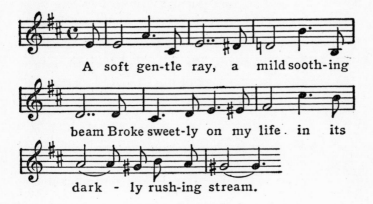

A soft gen-tle ray, a mild sooth-ing beam Broke sweet-ly on my life in its dark - ly rush-ing stream.

The remaining melodic material is based mostly on Rezia's air, the peroration to "Ocean, thou mighty Monster," when she believes that help is at hand. After a development in sonata form this same exciting music provides the lively conclusion of the *Overture:*

My hus-band, my love, we are sav'd, we are saved!

Franz Schubert (1797–1828) wrote his program music mostly in the form of actual songs. But a few of his instrumental pieces may also be credited with a definite meaning, and his romantic tendencies seldom permitted him to write in a purely formal style.

The best-known Schubert piece with a descriptive title is probably the *Marche Militaire,* and this straightforward example of lively rhythm is not difficult to interpret:

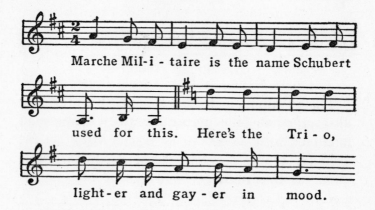

Marche Mil-i - taire is the name Schubert used for this. Here's the Tri - o, light-er and gay - er in mood.

There is also some delightful ballet music in the opera *Rosamunde* which, with one of the *Entr'actes,* has become permanently popular. The second *Entr'acte* contains one of the loveliest melodies in all music, and it is worth quoting here in its entirety, needing no words to interpret its message of pure beauty:

The first *Ballet* in *Rosamunde* strongly suggests the familiar *Moment Musical,* which has also served as dance music for many a tulle-clad amateur, with imitations of Greek flutes, in the Isadora Duncan style. A short quotation is enough for a reminder:

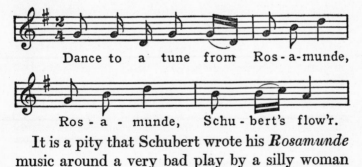

Dance to a tune from Ros - a - munde,

Ros - a - munde, Schu - bert's flow'r.

It is a pity that Schubert wrote his *Rosamunde* music around a very bad play by a silly woman named Helmina von Chezy, who also ruined the *Euryanthe* of Weber by her libretto. But the spirit of gay, rather wistful charm triumphs over all absurdities of text, and this mood alone is enough to place the *Rosamunde* melodies among the outstanding programmatic compositions of the world.[1]

Between Schubert and those other great romanticists, Mendelssohn, Schumann and Chopin, several minor composers produced program music of an interesting character if not a particularly high quality. Ludwig Spohr (1784–1859) is perhaps the most important, although his works are today mostly catalogued as "worthy but uninspired."

Spohr's programmatic ideas, like those of many another limited composer, were far beyond his ability to carry them out. Yet he was something of a pioneer in his field and therefore deserves at least respectful attention.

Three of Spohr's symphonies have definite titles and detailed programs. The first he called *The Consecration of Sounds* (1832), based upon a poem of the same name by Karl Pfeiffer which, according to the composer, "must be printed and

[1]Schubert's symphonies must all be considered absolute music, even though a theme from the *Unfinished Symphony* was turned into the *Song of Love* by Sigmund Romberg, in his Schubert-biographical *Blossom Time*. Three of the symphonies are analyzed in the author's *Great Symphonies*, pp. 133–50. Schubert's familiar *Serenade* and *Ave Maria* are often played as instrumental pieces, but of course these were originally songs.

distributed or recited aloud before the performance."

Pfeiffer's poem ran about as follows: "The earth was lying solitary in the flowery splendor of spring. Amid the silent forms man walked in darkness, following only wild instinct, not the gentle promptings of the heart. Love had no tones, nature no speech. Eternal goodness determined to manifest itself and breathed into the human breast sound and caused Love to find a language that penetrated blissfully to the heart." After taking up the various sounds of nature the poet concentrated on the application of music to different phases of life.

Spohr's own outline of his symphony showed four divisions. The first has two parts: *"Largo—* The unbroken silence of nature before the generation of sound; *Allegro*—Subsequent active life. Sounds of nature. Uproar of the elements." The second division covers three subjects: "Cradle Song; Dance; Serenade." The third contains the subheads, "Martial Music; Departure for the Battle; The Feelings of Those Remaining Behind; Return of the Victors; Thanksgiving." Finally the fourth division presents "Funeral Music" and "Comfort in Tears."

Another Spohr symphony, *The Earthly and the Divine in Human Life* (1841), is written for two orchestras, the full band representing the earthly, while the divine is interpreted by eleven solo stringed instruments, certainly a novel and decidedly clever idea. The first movement depicts childhood, the second "the time of the passions," and the third "the final victory of the divine."

To these two program pieces Spohr added a symphony called *The Seasons* (1850), with only two movements, the first including winter and spring and the second summer and autumn.

Spohr's *Overture* to his opera, *Faust,* should also be classed as program music, and he likewise wrote a "Travel Sonata" for violin and piano, with the detailed title, *Echoes of a Journey to Dresden and Saxon Switzerland,* a concert *Overture* based on Raupach's *Daughter of the Air,* and a set of "Duettinos" for violin and piano, with the general title *Elegiac and Humorous.*

Even less important are a series of piano pieces by Frederic Kalkbrenner (1788–1849) with fanciful titles or the descriptive works of Carl Czerny (1791–1857), who tried to present a conflagration on the piano and also wrote four four-handed pieces "inspired by the romances of Walter Scott."

Another pianist-composer, Ignaz Moscheles (1794–1870), produced a number of programmatic pieces, including an *Overture* to Schiller's *Maid of Orleans* and twelve *Characteristic Studies,* called *Anger, Reconciliation, Contradiction, Juno, Fairy Tale for Children, Bacchanal, Tenderness, Popular Festival Scenes, Moonlight on the Seashore, Terpsichore, Dream* and *Fear.*

That master of the ballad, J. K. G. Loewe (1796–1869), also tried his hand at instrumental pieces with definite programs but without success. His titles included *Mazeppa, Spring, Alpine Fantasia, Biblical Pictures, Scotch Pictures* and *Gipsy Sonata.*

Giacomo Meyerbeer (1791–1864) showed his command of program music in the instrumental portions of his operas, with an outstanding example in the popular *Coronation March* from *The Prophet.* The chief theme might be interpreted thus:

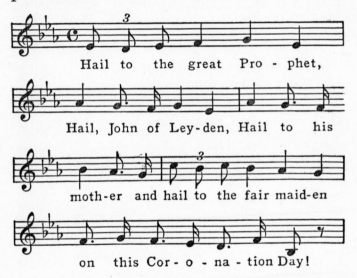

(All of these characters figure prominently in the opera.)

There is a second theme, of lighter character, which may have influenced Verdi's *Triumphal March* in *Aïda* some years later and which really needs no words to establish its mood of pomp and circumstance:

A far more important man in the operatic field was Gioacchino Rossini (1792–1868), whose *Overtures* contain some excellent program music. The best known, of course, is that of *William Tell*, whose chief themes may be worth interpreting in words.

William Tell was written under the influence of Beethoven, with a rather bad libretto supplied by four French hack-writers, based on the Schiller drama of the same name. The *Overture* is far superior to the opera as a whole and constitutes one of the ideal pieces of all program music in its vivid dramatization of Alpine life.

The introduction represents dawn in the Alps, opening with the solo voice of a cello, to which three more are soon added to form a quartet that is practically unique in operatic literature. Here is the broad melody announced by the cello quartet:

Dawn breaks on snow-y Al-pine height, All of the world shows its calm and de-light.

The second section of the *William Tell Overture* describes an Alpine storm, with a similar passage in Beethoven's *Pastoral Symphony* as a model. Rapid passages in the strings represent the wind and the rain, with lightning flashes in the cymbals and thunder in the roll of the drums.

Calm after the storm, with the shepherds' thanksgiving (again reminiscent of Beethoven's symphonic program), may be considered successfully suggested by the familiar slow melody sung by the English horn, soon joined by the flute in a livelier tune, with brilliant embellishments.

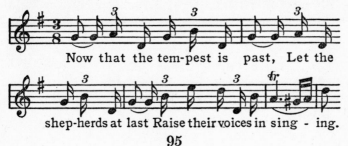

Now that the tem-pest is past, Let the shep-herds at last Raise their voices in sing - ing.

In the final section there occurs the immensely popular quickstep (long a stand-by of the movies and vaudeville music), representing the march of the Swiss troops, which brings the *Overture* to a spectacular conclusion:

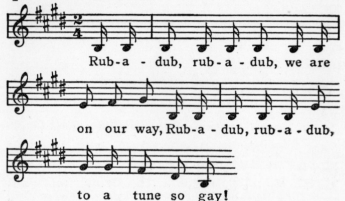

Rossini's *Overture* to *The Barber of Seville* has nothing to do with the opera and is merely a lively introduction that would serve as a prelude to any comedy. Actually it had previously been used as an *Overture* to *Elisabetta,* for which it was borrowed from the still-earlier opera, *Aureliano.* Here is the best-known theme in a slangy interpretation:

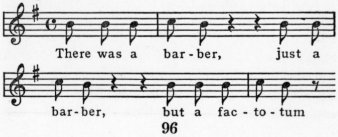

who smote 'em   in   old Se - ville.

Rossini's *Overture* to *Semiramide* also deserves mention as program music, completing the trio still heard frequently on the concert stage and over the air. The opening theme is reminiscent of Mozart and Haydn:

Here's   Se - mi - ra - mi - de,

this   brings   on   the   O - ver - ture,

Felix Mendelssohn-Bartholdy (1809–1847) not only wrote great program music but had definite ideas on the subject, which he expressed very well. He once remarked that since Beethoven had written the *Pastoral Symphony* it was "impossible for composers to keep clear of program music."

In 1842 he wrote to a friend: "If you ask me what were my thoughts when composing the *Songs without Words* I say, 'Just the songs as they stand.' And though in one or the other I had in my mind a definite word or definite words, yet I do not like to communicate them to anyone, because words have not the same meaning for one

97

as they have for another. . . . Resignation, melancholy, praise of God, the hunt—these words do not call up the same thoughts in everybody; to one resignation is what melancholy is to another, and a third is unable to form a vivid idea of either. Nay, to him who is by nature a keen hunter the hunt and the praise of God might come pretty much to the same thing, and for him the sound of horns would really and truly be also the right praise of God. We should hear in it nothing but the hunt, and however much we disputed the matter with him we should never get further. The word remains ambiguous, and yet we should both of us understand the music aright." In the same letter Mendelssohn uttered this significant thought: "A piece of music that I love expresses to me thoughts not too indefinite to be put into words but too definite."

In conversation with another friend he referred to his "luck" in connection with the *Overture* to *A Midsummer Night's Dream,* written when he was only seventeen years old. The friend replied, "Luck? I should think such an *Overture* is created not by luck but by the genius of the artist."

"Of course it requires talent," answered Mendelssohn modestly. "But I call it luck to have been inspired with such a subject, a subject that was capable of furnishing me with such musical ideas and forms as generally appeal to the larger public. What I could do as a composer I could do before writing the *Overture*. But I had not yet had before my imagination such a subject. That was an inspiration, and the inspiration was a lucky one."

Unquestionably the *Midsummer Night's Dream Overture* is Mendelssohn's most important piece of program music. It is a complete instrumental summary of the Shakespearean play—a miracle of achievement for a boy in his teens.

The *Overture* begins with sustained chords, played by the wind instruments, representing a magic formula which opens the doors of fairyland to the listener.

There is no mistaking the dainty tripping of the fairies in the rapid passages of the violins that follow. They are a veritable evocation of moonlight and magic and a miniature world of dreams.

Then comes a broader theme, of dignity and real splendor, to suggest Duke Theseus and his retinue.

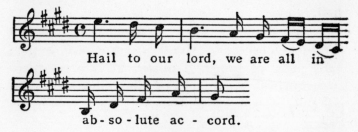

Hail to our lord, we are all in ab-so-lute ac-cord.

A romantic double melody introduces the two pairs of lovers, Hermia and Lysander and Helena and Demetrius:

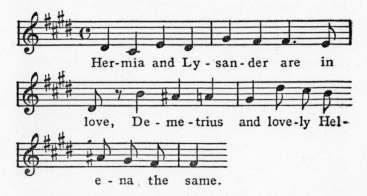

Her-mia and Ly-san-der are in love, De-me-trius and love-ly Hel-e-na the same.

This is suddenly interrupted by a clownish passage that clearly depicts the efforts of Nick Bottom and his rural companions in the direction of a summer theater. The bass strings grind out a vigorous accompaniment in the style of a bagpipe while the uncouth tune throws in sudden imitations of the braying of an ass, unmistakably portraying the ambitious weaver, Nick Bottom himself, after the magic spell has been cast upon him:

Come a - long, come a - long, with a dance and a song, hee haw, hee haw.

There is a musical development of all this material, full of bustle and fun and lively excitement. After a recapitulation comes a quiet ending, with the Theseus theme heard once more, quite softly and slowly, to indicate the elves' blessing on his home. Echoes of the dancing fairy feet also return as a final reminder, and the chords of the magic formula dissolve the dream which they had originally brought to life.

Close to the perfection of this *Overture* and even finer as a piece of pure musical form is the one variously known as *Fingal's Cave* and *The Hebrides*. Mendelssohn got his inspiration for this work on a trip to Scotland when he saw, at Staffa, the historic cave whose pillars of basalt look like "the interior of a gigantic organ, for the winds and tumultuous waves to play upon." He wrote immediately to his beloved sister Fanny,

101

the anxiety caused by it. The waving motion is indicative of her grace and at the same time reminds us of the element with which she was connected. Near the end we may recognize her cries on being discovered by her husband. The rest is like the vanishing of a beautiful reality into a beautiful memory."[3]

The *Ruy Blas Overture* may also be considered program music, although it has nothing whatever to do with the Victor Hugo play for which it was written. Mendelssohn considered the dramatic material "detestable and more utterly beneath contempt than you could believe," possibly because he knew it only through a very bad German translation. But he gave in to the solicitations of the Theatrical Pension Fund of Leipzig to provide a curtain raiser for a performance of *Ruy Blas* and in three days turned out an *Overture* of rollicking, carefree character that has now achieved a permanent popularity.

At least one of its tunes has become widely known:

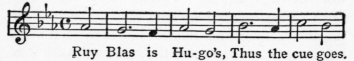

Ruy Blas is Hu-go's, Thus the cue goes.

Mendelssohn gave titles to three of his symphonies, calling them respectively *Scotch, Italian* and *Reformation,* the last marked by the use of

[3]This is the interpretation of Frederick Niecks.

Luther's Reformation Hymn, *A Mighty Fortress Is Our God,* which Bach had previously turned into a cantata.[4]

The remaining incidental music to *A Midsummer Night's Dream,* written many years after the *Overture,* has its programmatic significance also. The dainty *Scherzo* again captures the spirit of fairyland and is played between the first and second acts of the comedy. Here is its leading theme:

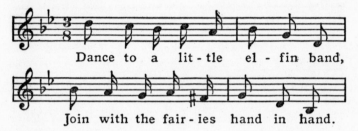

Dance to a lit - tle el - fin band,

Join with the fair - ies hand in hand.

There is a lovely *Intermezzo,* usually played at the end of the second act, representing Hermia's fruitless search for Lysander, with the violins answered by flute and clarinet, followed immediately by the *Clown's March,* which introduces Nick Bottom and his companions:

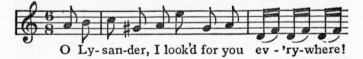

O Ly- san-der, I look'd for you ev - 'ry-where!

[4] All three of these symphonies are discussed in *Stories behind the World's Great Music,* and the first two are analyzed and given detailed programs in *Great Symphonies,* pp. 174-84.

A beautiful *Nocturne* serves as an interlude between the third and fourth acts, while the four lovers are asleep in the forest, with Puck appearing to straighten out the mischief that his charms have caused. The French horn figures prominently in the opening theme:

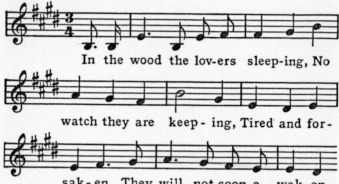

In the wood the lov-ers sleep-ing, No watch they are keep- ing, Tired and for-sak-en, They will not soon a - wak-en.

Finally there is the familiar *Wedding March,* regularly used at the close of the marriage service and written by Mendelssohn to introduce the last act of *A Midsummer Night's Dream,* with its double wedding, presided over by the happy couple, Theseus and Hippolyta, and blessed by the monarchs of fairyland, Oberon and Titania. The first theme is usually enough to bring the bride and groom up the aisle and break up the congregation:

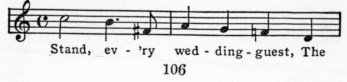

Stand, ev - 'ry wed - ding - guest, The

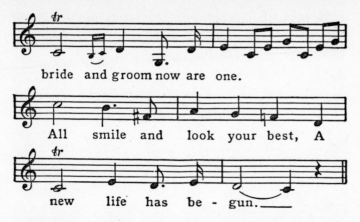

bride and groom now are one.

All   smile and   look your best, A

new   life has be - gun.___

Aside from his orchestral works, Mendelssohn's little piano pieces, the popular *Songs without Words,* may well claim to be successful program music. They are mostly sentimental and often insignificant, but they express their moods and occasional titles with obvious felicity. Best known of the series is the familiar *Spring Song,* whose melody was borrowed by Irving Berlin for his ragtime hit, *That Meddlesome Mendelssohn Tune.* It has been played to death, but its charm is undeniable, and it deserves a fairly extended quotation here:

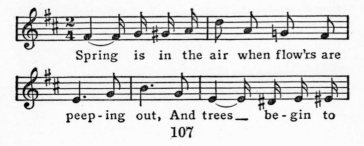

Spring   is in the air when flow'rs are

peep - ing out, And trees__ be - gin to

burst in col-ors pink and green and

yel - low. For Spring__ will nev-er

leave our minds in an - y doubt, when

Ap- ril show'rs have turn'd to sun-shine mel-low.

Of the rest of the *Songs without Words* the most popular are probably the two called *Confidence* and *Consolation*. The first has a melody which is a robust version of the slow theme of Beethoven's second symphony, known as a hymn tune:

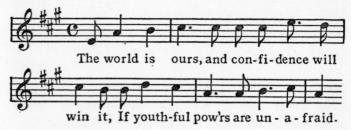

The world is ours, and con-fi-dence will

win it, If youth-ful pow'rs are un - a - fraid.

Consolation has itself appeared in the hymnals of several denominations and lends itself easily to words:

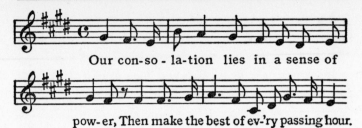

Our con-so - la-tion lies in a sense of

pow- er, Then make the best of ev-'ry passing hour.

There is also a familiar *Spinning Song* by Mendelssohn, with its simple, straightforward tune accompanied by a rapid figure that clearly imitates the monotonous turning of the wheel itself:

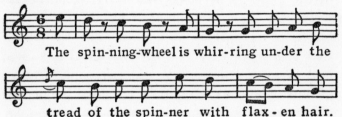

The spin-ning-wheel is whir-ring un-der the

tread of the spin-ner with flax - en hair.

It is impossible to dismiss this outstanding composer of program music without mentioning three rather obscure *Caprices,* for piano, which he dedicated individually to the three Taylor sisters, at whose home (in Coed-du, near Holly-well, North Wales) he stayed in 1829. The eldest sister, Anne, describes how Mendelssohn entered into the beauty of the hills and woods with his whole artistic being.

"His way of representing them was not with the pencil, but in the evening his improvised music would show what he had observed or felt in the past day. The piece called *The Rivulet,* which he wrote at that time for my sister Susan, will show what I mean. It was a recollection of a real, actual rivulet. We observed how natural objects seemed to suggest music to him. There was in my sister Honora's garden a pretty creeping plant, new at that time, covered with little trumpetlike flowers. He was struck with it and played for her the music which, he said, the fairies might play on these trumpets. When he wrote out the piece he drew a branch of that flower all up the margin of the paper. The piece which Mr Mendelssohn wrote for me was suggested by the sight of a bunch of carnations and roses. The carnations that year were very fine with us. He liked them best of all the flowers, would have one often in his buttonhole. We found he intended the arpeggio passages in that composition as a reminder of the sweet scent of the flower rising up."

Such a firsthand account should silence any possible arguments as to the nature and legitimacy of program music in general.

The archromanticist of them all, Robert Schumann (1810–1856), wrote his full share of program music but seems to have had conflicting ideas on the subject. It is in his piano pieces, and particularly the miniatures that have become so widely popular, that Schumann expresses his most definite ideas, pictures, stories and even imitations.

For a consistent and unmistakable set of programs one has only to examine the *Scenes from Childhood* (Opus 15, 1839), every one of which has a definite title. It should be understood that these charming pieces were not meant to be played by children. They are, in the words of the composer, "reminiscences of an older person for older ones." The titles speak for themselves: *Of Foreign Lands and People, Curious Story, Blind Man's Buff, Entreating Child, Happiness Enough, Important Event, Dreaming, At the Fireside, The Knight of the Hobby Horse, Almost Too Serious, Frightening, Child Falling Asleep* and *The Poet Speaks.*

The critic Rellstab took all this very hard and demanded to know whether Schumann was in earnest or joking. "When we see a piece of music," he wrote, "superscribed *Of Foreign Lands and People* we feel our pulse to find out if we are not in fever dreams. To where has Art strayed through some false fundamental principles? (*The capital A is Rellstab's.*) To what irrational solutions do these irrational roots and equations lead?"

Schumann, who was himself a pretty good music critic, was annoyed with this review and expressed himself in his usual forceful fashion: "Anything more inept and narrow-minded than what Rellstab has written about my *Scenes from Childhood* I have never met with. He seems to think that I place a crying child before me and then seek for tones to imitate it. The reverse is the case. However, I do not deny that while composing some children's heads were hovering before me; but of course the superscriptions came into existence afterward and are indeed nothing else but more delicate directions for the rendering and comprehension of the music."

Yet on another occasion Schumann wrote with equal sincerity, "We confess we have a prejudice against this kind of creation (program music) and share this perhaps with a hundred learned heads who, it is true, have often strange notions of composing and refer always to Mozart, who is supposed never to have thought of *anything* in composing. As I said, not a few may have that prejudice; and if a composer holds up a program to us before the music I say: 'First of all let us hear that you make beautiful music; afterward we shall be glad of your program.' "

One more quotation completes the paradox: "As regards the difficult question, how far instrumental music may go in the representation of thoughts and occurrences, many are far too timid. People are certainly mistaken if they believe that composers prepare pen and paper with the miserable intention of expressing, describing and painting this and that. But chance influences and impressions from without should not be underestimated. Along with the musical imagination an idea is unconsciously operative, along with the ear, the eye; and this, the ever-active organ, in the midst of the sounds and tone, then holds fast certain outlines which, with the advancing music, may condense and develop into distinct figures."

Regardless of Schumann's opinions, his program music is mostly worth quoting, and it includes some of his best-known and most popular compositions. The *Scenes from Childhood* are little gems of musical expressiveness, each carrying out its expressed intention convincingly.

The first piece, *Of Foreign Lands and People,* far from suggesting the "fever dreams" of Rellstab, is a simple and rather wistful melody indicating, perhaps, a mere wanderlust rather than actual travel abroad.

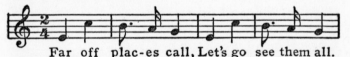

Far off plac-es call, Let's go see them all.

Curious Story is livelier and definitely catches the attention, in the manner of an actual storyteller.

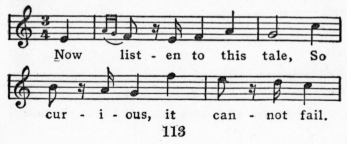

Now list - en to this tale, So cur - i - ous, it can - not fail.

113

Blind Man's Buff is a rapid combination of scales and chord tones with a strong suggestion of chasing and being chased. *Entreating Child* presents the contrast of another slow melody, somewhat similar to that of the opening piece.

Sad is this en - treat-ing child.

There is animation once more in *Happiness Enough* and a sturdy confidence in the page called *Important Event,* which might mean anything from a birthday to the winning of a prize in school. Then comes the universally loved *Träumerei,* which could be translated as *Dreaming* or *Revery,* a perfect melody which has survived all kinds of mistreatment.

The hour__ of twi-light is a dream,

When the world is all at peace and

things are what they seem, And mu - sic

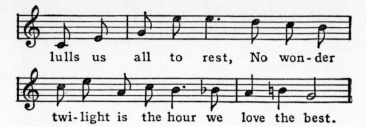

lulls us all to rest, No won-der

twi-light is the hour we love the best.

By the Fireside offers another lovely theme, which has the advantage, like so many of these *Kinderscenen,* of being very easy to play.

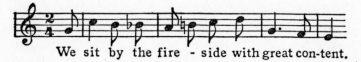

We sit by the fire - side with great con-tent.

Knight of the Hobby Horse has a spirited waltz melody, with a syncopated accompaniment, preserving a rocking motion throughout.

There is syncopation also in the somewhat longer piece called *Almost Too Serious,* while the *Frightening* episode rather naïvely alternates a quiet little tune with faster passages carrying the melody in the left hand and presumably making faces. In *Child Falling Asleep* there is again an overlapping of melodic phrases, almost with the effect of nodding, and finally *The Poet Speaks* in one of the tenderest, most haunting themes ever written by Schumann or any other composer.

115

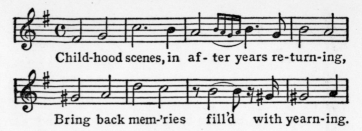

Child-hood scenes, in af - ter years re-turn-ing,
Bring back mem-'ries fill'd with yearn-ing.

The *Album for the Young* differs from these *Scenes from Childhood* in being written for performance by actual children, for by 1848 Schumann was happily married and had children of his own. The pieces in this series are simpler and more obvious, representing a juvenile rather than an adult point of view. There are forty-three little piano compositions in the *Album for the Young,* of which only a few require quotation.

The opening *Melody* is little more than a child's keyboard exercise, followed by a gay *Soldiers' March,* whose theme echoes the *Scherzo* of one of Beethoven's violin sonatas:

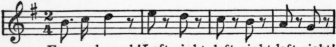

For-ward march! Left, right, left, right, left, right!

The next seven pieces demand little attention, although they admirably carry out such descriptive titles as *Choral, Poor Little Orphan, Little Hunting Song, Wild Rider,* etc. But then comes *The Happy Farmer,* which every child that ever took piano lessons must have played at some time.

The hap - py farm-er leads a pleas-
loves the land and ev - 'ry liv -

ant life, With pigs and cows and hay
ing thing, From dog and cat to bird

in. mows and one fine wife. He
and bat, in snow or spring. He

ploughs and sows, He cuts the crop in
plain to see How hap - py he must

rows, And then he sits and smokes a
be, Yet I con - fess, in spite of

corn-cob pipe, And chews his cud as
all its charm, I'd rath - er fare most

cat - tle would on ap - ples ripe. It's
an - y - where than on a farm.

The author has recently written the foregoing set of words to this popular tune, for school use, which are quoted here by special permission of their publisher.[5]

The next piece of general interest is the *Little Romance,* often played as a companion to the *Träumerei* and with a melody quite worthy to stand beside it:

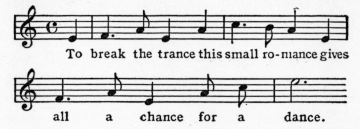

To break the trance this small ro-mance gives all a chance for a dance.

One of the last of the series is the *Northern Song,* dedicated to Niels Gade, the Norwegian composer, with a theme that spells out the last name and turns it into a sturdy and effective folk song:

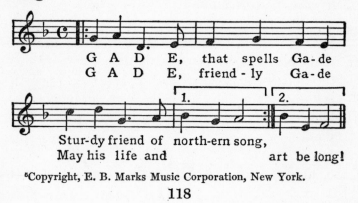

G A D E, that spells Ga-de
G A D E, friend-ly Ga-de
Stur-dy friend of north-ern song,
May his life and art be long!

Both the *Album for the Young* and *Scenes from Childhood* may have been written for or about children, but they have a high standing in the world's program music nevertheless. In his more elaborate piano compositions Schumann went far beyond these charming but fairly obvious pieces. Both the *Papillons* and the *Carnaval* are definitely programmatic throughout, with the *Davidsbündlertänze, Kreisleriana* and *Novelettes* not far behind.

Papillons is one of Schumann's earliest works, written when he was only nineteen. The "butterflies" are not insects but real people, taking part in a masked ball. He traces the program back to the *Flegeljahre* (Apprentice Years) of Jean Paul Friedrich Richter, a fantastic writer who was very popular at the time. In the last chapter he says, "All is to be found in black and white."

Schumann even wrote to Rellstab (this was before his anger over the misconception of his *Scenes from Childhood*): "You remember the last scene in the *Flegeljahre*—the masked ball, Walt, Vult, masks, confessions, anger, revelations, hasty departure, concluding scene and then the departing brother. Often I turned over the last page, for the end seemed to me a new beginning—almost unconsciously I was at the pianoforte and thus came into existence one *Papillon* after another."

There are twelve of these little pieces, and they

form a miniature carnival in themselves. After a brief introduction, in octaves, the first waltz is heard, with its melody also played in octaves:

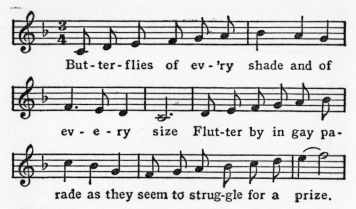

But-ter-flies of ev-'ry shade and of
ev-e-ry size Flut-ter by in gay parade as they seem to strug-gle for a prize.

The second piece is very short and fast, with a skipping motion in duple time, suggesting eccentric dancers. Then comes another octave passage, in minor key, later changing to major, with never more than a skeleton accompaniment:

The car-ni-val spir-it is
reign-ing to-night, Ex-cuse us if
we are not al-ways po-lite.

The fourth waltz is another fast melody, again played in octaves, which Schumann seems to favor all through the *Papillons*. The main tune is interrupted by some more musical pokes, digs and nudges of a most realistic type. The waltz goes like this:

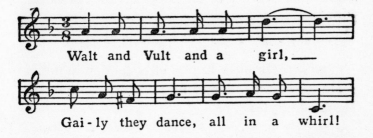

The next section gets away from the waltz movement, although still in triple time, with a gracefully flowing theme, followed by dramatic shrieks and realistic giggles.

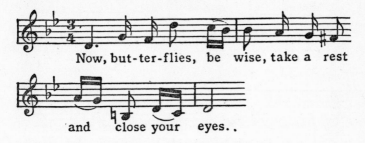

There is drama in the next section, too, crashing chords contrasting with a dainty descent over the tones of the common major harmonies and

121

then a gently flowing melody of a new type and mood:

Not quite so ve - he - ment,

car - ni - val mer - ri - ment

The seventh piece has an introduction in minor scale passages, followed by a smooth tune in the barcarole style:

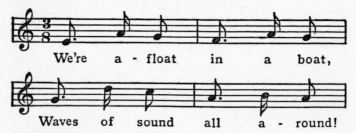

We're a - float in a boat,

Waves of sound all a - round!

Dramatic chords in minor key are again prominent in number eight, developing into a major melody of fresh beauty:

But - ter - flies still flut - ter by, with

time for - got - ten ut - ter - ly.

Another fantastic little dance follows, with a round or canon in the bass clef. Number ten gets its effects from its harmonies rather than the melodic line, which is largely on one note (G), soon going into a fortissimo repetition of the theme that had previously been heard pianissimo (on the major chord tones). This is followed by a really sustained waltz melody of the lyric type:

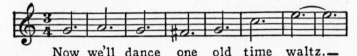

Now we'll dance one old time waltz.—

The eleventh movement is like a Polonaise, quite elaborate and dramatic, with more skipping effects for contrast. Finally comes the old *Grandfather's Dance,* which was always played at country weddings, hinting that the party was over.[6]

Und als der Gross - va - ter die

Gross-mut-ter nahm, Da ward der Gross-

va - ter ein Bräu - ti - gam.

[6]An account of this traditional dance will be found in *Stories behind the World's Great Music,* pp. 123–24. The literal translation would be: "And when Grandfather took Grandmother, Grandfather became a bridegroom." Above are the original words.

The *Grandfather's Dance* is followed by a sprightly little tune, as if the old man himself were stumping about, sending people home to bed:

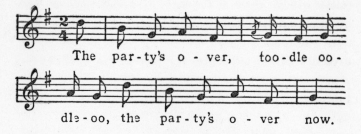

The par-ty's o-ver, too-dle oo-dle-oo, the par-ty's o-ver now.

But just as a reminder back comes the first waltz, in octaves as before, then syncopated as a countermelody to the *Grandfather's Dance,* played in the left hand. This neat little musical trick is interrupted by the sound of the church clock striking six (A.M.!) and the composer's own superscription says, "The noise of the carnival night dies away." The three tones of the major triad are sustained against soft chords, and a final breath of harmony vanishes over three soft farewell notes in the bass, *presto, quasi niente* (quick, like nothing).

Schumann's *Carnaval* is a more mature and elaborate *Papillons,* composed in 1834 and 1835, and published as Opus 9. The composer wrote this explanation to his friend Moscheles: "The *Carnaval* came into existence incidentally and is built for the most part on the notes ASCH, the name of a little Bohemian town, where I have a musical lady friend, but which, strange to say, are also the only musical letters in my name.[7] The superscriptions I placed over them afterward. Is not music itself always enough and sufficiently expressive? *Estrella* is a name such as is placed under portraits to fix the picture better in one's memory; *Reconnaissance,* a scene of recognition; *Aveu,* an avowal of love; *Promenade,* a walk, such as one takes at a German ball, arm in arm with one's partner. The whole has no artistic value whatever; the manifold states of the soul alone seem to me to be interesting."

Schumann is too modest in this appraisal and too reticent as to his programs. The *Carnaval* is an important piece of music and one of the most provocative as to its details of meaning. There are twenty-one sections, each with a definite title. Many of them do not require explanation or interpretation. There can be no argument about such superscriptions as *Valse Noble, Pierrot, Arlequin, Pantalon et Colombine, Coquette, Chopin* and *Paganini.*

Florestan and *Eusebius* represent the dual nature of Schumann's own personality, possibly influenced again by Richter's Walt and Vult. Florestan is a wild, impetuous, fantastic character; Eusebius is tender and mild, a typical dreamer.

---

[7]The letter H represents B in the German scale, while S (Es) stands for E flat.

The *Replique* seems a mocking reply to the *Coquette*. The *Papillon* is this time a real butterfly. *Chiarina* is of course Clara Wieck, Schumann's real love, whom he eventually married. *Estrella* is Ernestine von Fricken, who lived in Asch and was for a time actually engaged to the composer. (Today we would call her a stooge.)

During the next to the last piece, called *Pause,* there is a great bustle, with everyone apparently getting ready for a fight. The reason then becomes evident in the final *March of the Davidsbündler against the Philistines,* representing the champions of progress and idealism in their eternal battle with the reactionaries, "the upholders of tradition and the commonplace."

The Philistines are represented by the traditional *Grandfather's Dance,* which had already figured in *Papillons.* They put up a good fight, but are finally defeated by the exuberance and courage of the *Davidsbündler.* This was the name used by Schumann for an imaginary organization of progressive thinkers (literally the League of David), in which he himself was the leader and practically the whole membership. He elected or appointed his friends to the club, according to his whim, and built up an elaborate activity, in his writings and his music, entirely from his own imagination. It was all a little mad, but it produced some great compositions.

mine. The story is a whole wedding eve. You can picture to yourself beginning and end. If I was ever happy at the pianoforte it was when I composed them."

Schumann gave this description of the Davidsbund: "The society was more than a secret one, since it existed only in the head of the founder. The Davidsbund is a spiritual, romantic one. . . . Mozart was as great a Bündler as Berlioz is now."

There are eighteen numbers in this series, preceded by an old rhyme and opening with a musical motto by Clara herself which has been described as "the sign of the prompter":

Da - vids - bünd - ler, Da - vids - bünd - ler!

Florestan and Eusebius alternate and sometimes combine in signing the various pieces in the *Davidsbündler* series.

There are programs also in the *Fantasiestücke* (*Fantasy Pieces*), several of which have become deservedly popular. *Des Abends* (In the Evening) has a quiet, dreamy melody:

Eve-ning comes steal-ing, Qui-et re - veal - ing.

129

Aufschwung (Soaring) is full of passion and impatience:

In cou - ra-geous flight on up-ward soar-ing!

Of them all, the best known is probably the simple *Warum* (Why?):

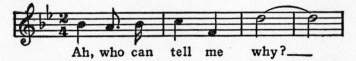

Ah, who can tell me why?——

Other programmatic titles in this series are *Whims, In the Night, Fable, Dream Visions* and *End of the Song.*

The *Fantasie,* Opus 17 (1836–38), must be credited with a program, since Schumann superscribed its three movements in three different ways: "Ruins, Trophies, Palms; Ruins, Triumphal Arch, Crown of Stars; Ruin, Triumphal Arch, Constellation." Schumann later added a motto by Schlegel: "Through all the tones that sound in earth's much-mingled dream a gentle tone is heard by him who listens with quiet attention."

To Clara the composer wrote that the first movement "is a profound lament about you." She herself answered in 1839 (a year before their marriage) : "Many pictures rise before me, too, when I play your *Fantasia;* they are sure to be very much in agreement with yours. The *March* makes upon me the impression of a triumphal march of warriors returning from battle; and at the A flat major I always think of young village girls, all clad in white, each with a wreath in her hand, crowning the kneeling warriors, and a great deal more that you know already."

Here are the opening and the march theme:

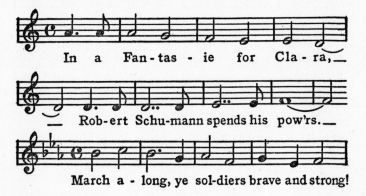

In a Fan-tas-ie for Cla-ra,

Rob-ert Schu-mann spends his pow'rs.

March a-long, ye sol-diers brave and strong!

Kreisleriana is another programmatic composition by Schumann, with its title derived from E. T. A. Hoffmann's account of the eccentric and clever Kapellmeister (Conductor) Johannes Kreisler. This character Schumann again identifies with his own. According to Niecks, "No one acquainted with Schumann's work can for a moment doubt that he describes here his own and

131

not Kreisler's joys and sorrows. In fact, *Schumanniana* would be a more correct title than *Kreisleriana*."

But it is Clara who once more serves as the inspiration. To her Schumann writes: "Oh, this music in me! And always such beautiful melodies! Imagine, since my last letter I have finished again a whole book of new things. *Kreisleriana* I will call them, in which you and a thought of you play the principal role, and I will dedicate it to you—yes, to you and to no one else. How sweetly you will smile when you recognize yourself. Do play sometimes my *Kreisleriana!* In some parts of it there lies a veritable wild love and your life and mine and many a look of yours."

Clara also deserves credit for the *Novelettes,* concerning which Schumann thus expressed himself to her: "I have composed an appalling amount for you during the last few weeks—drolleries, Egmont stories, family scenes with fathers, a wedding—in short, charming things. The whole I call *Novelettes,* because your name is Clara and Wieckettes would not sound well." (There is here a play on the name of Clara Novello.) Later he added the dictum: "They are for the most part cheerful and superficial, except for something here and there where I touch the bottom."

The opening theme of the *Novelettes* is another

of those sturdy marches that Schumann could
write so well:

One more march, no re-grets, we'll
call this mu - sic Nov - el - ettes!

Of the remaining piano pieces by Schumann
many carry programmatic titles, but only a few
need be quoted. The familiar *Abendlied* (Evening Song), now heard mostly as a violin solo or
an orchestral number, was originally written as
a piano duet.

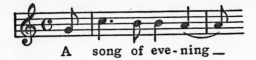

A song of eve - ning —

There is also a *Slumber Song,* reminiscent of
Chopin in its flowing melody and also quite familiar to piano students:

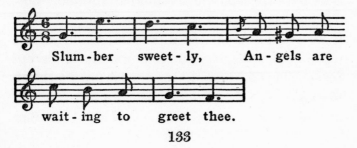

Slum - ber sweet - ly, An - gels are
wait - ing to greet thee.

A set of *Nachtstücke* (Night Pieces) likewise contains one very popular slow tune, often sung as a hymn:

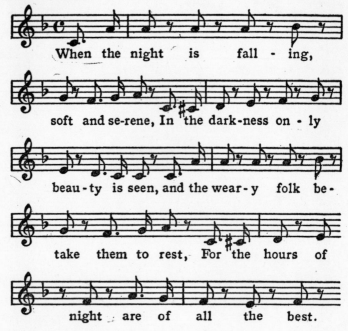

When the night is fall - ing,
soft and se-rene, In the dark-ness on - ly
beau - ty is seen, and the wear - y folk be -
take them to rest, For the hours of
night are of all the best.

There are besides three *Romances*, without specific programs, a series of *Pictures from the East,* with considerable Oriental atmosphere, several more descriptive duets (including such titles as *Bear Dance, At the Fountain, Ghost Story* and *Birthday March*) and some charming *Forest Scenes,* one of which is that almost unique bit of tone painting, *Vogel als Prophet* (The Bird as Prophet).

134

Schumann's larger works, and particularly those written for orchestra, must generally be considered absolute music, although his sonatas are of a very personal and emotional character. He gave his first symphony the title of *Spring*, and the last is commonly called *Rhenish*, because of the unquestioned influence of the Rhineland.[8]

Of the Schumann *Overtures* only *Manfred* is generally played today, and this is actually one of his finest pieces of program music. It was written as a prelude to Byron's poem of the same name (along with other incidental music), and it may be called a successful attempt to paint in music the soul of a man. The mood is completely somber, relieved only by the "surging agitation of despair" and the "tender, longing, regretful recollection of Astarte." The opening theme, played by the solo oboe with the second violins, might be interpreted in the light of Manfred's own dying words to the abbot:

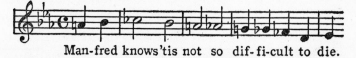

Man-fred knows 'tis not so dif-fi-cult to die.

[8]All four of the Schumann symphonies are analyzed and supplied with programs in the author's *Great Symphonies: How to Recognize and Remember Them*, pp. 151–73.

Schumann may not have been the greatest composer of program music, but he was certainly the most prolific. He has rightly been called "the most romantic of the romanticists." It seems to have been almost impossible for him to compose mere formal patterns of notes without a definite and often obvious meaning.

Now comes the problem of Frédéric Chopin (1809–1849), another highly poetic, deeply emotional soul, of whom one would say offhand that every note of his music must have played a part in some program. If the testimony of George Sand (Mme Dudevant) is to be accepted, then Chopin was an outstanding composer of program music. His editors, publishers, critics and listeners have attached definite names to many of his piano pieces.

Yet there are comparatively few cases in which Chopin himself announced a specific program for any of his music. The titles given to so many of his compositions are generally not his own. Nor did he often refer to a poem or play or story or to any definite place or experience when creating the flawless combinations of sound that have enchanted music lovers ever since.

The famous *Funeral March,* in the B flat minor piano sonata, is certainly the clearest and best example of program music from the pen of Chopin. It was written independently and later inserted in the sonata as a slow movement. The main theme is so familiar that it hardly requires quotation:

Peace to the dead, Peace to the dead,

Peace to the soul that from mortal life has fled.

Unfortunately the lunch-time singers of our service clubs have acquired the habit of giving Chopin's *Funeral March* the words, "Where will we all be a hundred years from now?" answering their own question with, "*Push*ing up the daisies." The tune has also been used occasionally by gallery whistlers at a boxing match that was not lively enough to suit the customers. The second melody of the march is not so well known as the minor strain and almost too cheerful for its program:

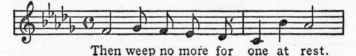

Then weep no more for one at rest.

The *Finale* of this piano sonata has generally been interpreted as representing "the wind over the graves." But Chopin himself wrote to his friend Fontana, in 1839, that in this short movement "the left and right hand *unisono* are gossiping after the march." Take your choice, if you can play it at all.

Beyond this one morbidly jocular comment Chopin gives very few hints as to the meanings hidden in his compositions. When he was in love with Constantia Gladkowska, a pupil at the Warsaw Conservatory, in 1829, he wrote: "Whilst my thoughts were with her I composed the *Adagio* of my concerto." (This was the one in F minor, Opus 21.) A year later he described the slow movement of his other piano concerto, in E minor, as "of a romantic, calm and partly melancholy character. It is intended to convey the impression which one receives when the eye rests on a beloved landscape that calls up in one's soul beautiful memories—for instance, on a fine moonlight night."

Outside of these three direct and personal explanations the programs attached to Chopin's music are all a matter of hearsay or secondhand information. The so-called *Revolutionary Étude* (Opus 10, No. 12), "full of fuming rage and passionate ejaculations," was presumably inspired by the news of the capture of Warsaw by the Russians, September 8, 1831.

On the lighter side there is the story of the

138

Waltz "of the little dog chasing his tail," also called the *Minute Waltz* (because it is said to be playable in exactly one minute).[9] The dog belonged to George Sand, and she is doubtless responsible for the tale. At least the opening strain has a convincingly whirling motion:

The middle melody was eventually turned into the fox trot, *Castle of Dreams,* in the musical comedy *Irene:*

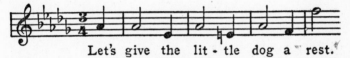

Let's give the lit - tle dog a rest.

The *Waltz in A flat,* Opus 69, No. 1, published posthumously, is said to have been improvised on Chopin's departure from Marie Wodzinska, in Dresden, when she gave him a flower, later found pressed in a bundle of her letters, tied with a ribbon and marked, "My Pain."

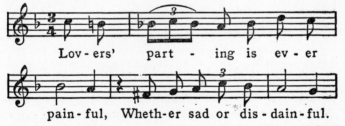

Lov - ers' part - ing is ev - er

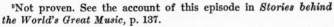

pain - ful, Wheth-er sad or dis - dain - ful.

[9]Not proven. See the account of this episode in *Stories behind the World's Great Music,* p. 137.

They were engaged for a while, and it was when Marie broke it off that Chopin, in a frenzy of disillusionment, wrote his great *Ballade* in G minor, Opus 23, which Schumann called "one of the bitterest and most personal of his works."

The association with George Sand produced some highly dramatic music, much of which has been interpreted by that literary lady herself. Their voyage to Majorca produced the beautiful *Nocturne,* Opus 37, No. 2, really a barcarole, with shimmering harmonies to represent the rippling water, perhaps inspired by their actual sailing on the Malloquin on a moonlight night. The second melody is definitely a boatman's song, and some accounts insist that it was heard by Chopin when he was left alone on board a ship at anchor.

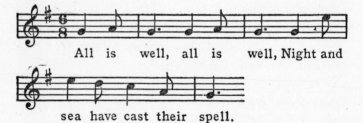

Another *Nocturne,* No. 1 of the same series, contains a religious melody supposedly inspired by a vision Chopin had in the old monastery of Valdemosa. He thought he saw a procession of monks and heard them chanting, "Santo Dio," and these words do fit the melody:

San-to   Di - o,   San-to   Di - o.

Of the *Nocturne* in B, Opus 32, No. 1, Chopin is said to have declared that he got his idea from Browning's *In a Gondola*. Asked for the meaning of the one in G minor, Opus 15, No. 3, he is quoted as saying, "After Hamlet," but adding hastily, "Let them guess for themselves." Kullak took this advice literally and supplied an entire program for the *Nocturne,* with the lost Lenore as a heroine. James Huneker thought it was "more like Poe's *Ulalume.*"

The *Nocturne* in C sharp minor, Opus 27, No. 1, has been described as "a calm night in Venice where, after a scene of murder, the sea closes over a corpse and continues to mirror the moonlight." (No comments are necessary!) Opus 62, No. 1, is often called the *Tuberose Nocturne,* with its suggestion of actual flowers climbing up a trellis and something like a real fragrance in the music.

There may be truth in the legend that the E flat *Nocturne,* Opus 9, No. 2, was Chopin's answer to a lady's remark that it was "a pity the piano could never sound like a violin." In any case, this *Nocturne* is now played by violinists more often than by pianists.

Sus - tain'd — and le - ga - to, we hear vi - o - lin-ists' warm vi - bra - to.

Of the *Étude* in E, Opus 10, No. 3, Chopin supposedly said to his pupil, Gutmann, "I have never in my life written another such melody," and exclaimed on hearing it played, "O ma patrie!"

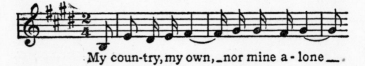

My coun-try, my own, — nor mine a-lone —

The fifth in this series of *Études* is always given the title "On the Black Keys," although this is not strictly true and was certainly not suggested by the composer. There is more reason for calling Opus 25, No. 7, the *Cello Étude,* because of the melody in the bass. It has actually been arranged for string quartet, with the cello carrying this theme. Hans von Bülow called it "a *Nocturne* for cello and flute."

Number nine of Opus 25 is the popular *Butterfly Étude,* also a fanciful title but somewhat justified by the character of the music. (It might equally well refer to lambs or goats or kittens.)

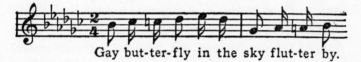

Gay but-ter-fly in the sky flut-ter by.

George Sand's most elaborate story of a Chopin program concerns the sixth *Prelude* of Opus 28 in B minor. She and her son had gone to Palma and were delayed in their return by a terrific storm. During their absence, "in calm despair" and "bathed in tears," he composed this *Prelude,* with its insistent sound of rhythmically falling rain. When they finally entered the old monastery which they had made their home Chopin exclaimed, "with a wild look and in a strange tone": "Ah! I knew well that you were dead."

He had seen their entire experience in a dream and believed himself dead when finally lulled to sleep by his own piano playing. "He saw himself drowned in a lake; heavy, ice-cold drops of water

143

fell at regular intervals upon his breast, and when I drew his attention to those drops of water which were actually falling at regular intervals upon the roof he denied having heard them. He was even vexed at what I translated by the term imitative harmony. He protested with all his might, and he was right, against the puerility of these imitations for the ear. His genius was full of mysterious harmonies of nature, translated by sublime equivalents into his musical thought and not by a servile repetition of external sounds. His composition of this evening was indeed full of the drops of rain which resounded on the sonorous tiles of the monastery, but they were transformed in his imagination and his music into tears falling from heaven on his heart." These final, highly imaginative words may be permitted to supply the interpretation of this familiar "raindrop" *Prelude*:

(The melody is obviously in the bass.)

Another *Prelude,* number fifteen in this series, is also generally given the title of *Raindrop,* because of the steady tapping of the A flat in the left hand. In fact, one is tempted to give programs to practically all of the Chopin *Preludes,* and many of them seem to cry out for words. Alfred Cortot, the great French pianist, when recording the complete set, actually supplied names or descriptive sentences for every one of the twenty-four, and some of his interpretations are most interesting.

Mr Cortot calls the sixth *Prelude,* so elaborately dramatized by George Sand, merely "Homesickness." The brief number seven, which has been played by every amateur, receives from him the superscription, "Delicious recollections float like perfume through the memory," and is described as "a dainty minuet."

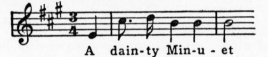

A dain-ty Min-u - et

The fifteenth *Prelude,* generally associated with rain, is given a highly original story by M. Cortot: "A young mother rocking her child. She herself is half asleep. A frightful dream shows her the scaffold that is the destiny of her son. The dream is banished by a sudden return to consciousness, but the mother is still disquieted." (Referred to the Department of Understatement!)

Most familiar of all the Chopin *Preludes* is

number twenty, in C minor, which Cortot calls "A Funeral Procession," but also quoting the more conventional description: "Twelve measures of the loveliest chords ever written." He refers to the "inexorable finality" of this music, thereby seeming to agree with the author's interpretation in a choral version called *Fate*.[10]

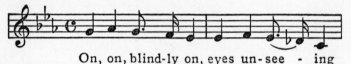

On, on, blind-ly on, eyes un-see - ing

All this amounts to mere guesswork—a nice exercise of the imagination but not important in any serious discussion of program music. One continues to sense a definite meaning in the romantic music of Chopin, but it is too elusive to be put into words.

His great *Scherzos* are perhaps the most dramatic of all his works, but they resist any literal translation, and certainly they have nothing to do with the cheerful, lively strains ordinarily associated with such a title. The *Ballades* sound like actual narratives, but it would be presumptuous to try to interpret them in detail. The tremendous *Fantasie in F minor* expresses all the things that a mere piano can possibly be expected to utter, but what they are is the composer's own secret.

It is perhaps legitimate to translate the *Berceuse* literally as a slumber song:

[10]Published by the H. W. Gray Co., 1934.

Sleep soft-ly with an-gels their watch

o'er you keep-ing.

The title of the famous *Barcarolle* may also be
accepted as definitely suggesting boat music, in
the conventionally rocking rhythm:[11]

In his actual dances, of course, Chopin suggests colorful pictures and plenty of action. The
Waltzes are mostly too fast and elaborate for
dancing, but the *Mazurkas* need only the accompaniment of stamping Polish boots and flashing costumes to become as vivid as if they were
part of a real ballet (as they often are). Most
picturesque of all are the *Polonaises,* again literal
expressions of the spirited yet dignified Polish
court dance, which is really a march in triple time.
The *Polonaise* in A major is generally known as
Military and was called by Rubinstein "a picture
of Poland's greatness."

[11]The French name for a boat song will be found sometimes
with one l, sometimes with two.

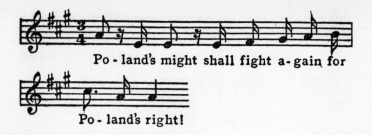

Po - land's might shall fight a-gain for

Po - land's right!

Perhaps the final answer to Chopin's program music is that he painted moods, emotions and spiritual processes in tones but practically never descended to mere imitation, or even musical description or narration. This, after all, is program music in its highest form. It becomes absolute in its musical values but still convinces the listener of its programmatic content. It has little or nothing in common with the billboard school of tone painting, which came later, with the development of realistic orchestration. It is not even closely related to the naïve musical pictures and stories of Schumann. But it paved the way toward the subtleties of Debussy and laid the foundation for all the romantic phases of modernism. It was a completely individual form of expression, within the limits of a single instrument, and it has never been duplicated or paralleled in the entire history of music.

THE TRIUMPH OF PROGRAM MUSIC

THERE is dramatic irony in the fact that immediately after Chopin had demonstrated the subtleties and the subjective qualities of program music in its least obvious phases the megalomaniacs of music seized upon the style and, in a succession of blitzkriegs, placed it in the dominating and dictatorial position which it still occupies.

Three men were chiefly responsible for this complete triumph over absolute music: Hector Berlioz (1803–1869), Franz Liszt (1811–1886) and Richard Wagner (1813–1883). Of the three only Wagner had the genius to carry out his announced programs with a full realization of his ideals. But Wagner could express anything in music and scarcely needed words to enhance the tone painting of his music dramas. Actually his orchestra tells the whole story, and through his command of this medium, plus the superhuman rightness of his ideas and conceptions, he became the greatest dramatic composer of all time.

Berlioz deserves credit for being the pioneer in this mechanization of the materials of program music. He was revolutionary in his use of the orchestra and made possible by his innovations the later work of Liszt, Wagner, Richard Strauss and the moderns. His orchestral music is almost entirely programmatic, in spite of the fact that he often argued violently against the abuse of this form of composition.

He objected to Gluck's ideas on the operatic *Overture* (that it should prepare the spectator for the action, present the argument, perhaps even "indicate the subject"). According to Berlioz: "Musical expression cannot go so far as that. It certainly can reproduce joy, sorrow, gravity, playfulness; it can mark a striking difference between a queen's grief and village girl's vexation, between calm, serious meditation and the ardent reveries that precede an outburst of passion. Again, borrowing from different nations the musical style that is proper to them, it can make a distinction between the serenade of a brigand of the Abruzzi and that of a Tyrolese or Scotch hunter, between the evening march of pilgrims impregnated with mysticism and that of a troop of cattle dealers returning from the fair; it can contrast extreme brutality, triviality and the grotesque with angelic purity, nobility and candor. But if it tries to overstep the bounds of this immense circle music must necessarily have recourse to words—sung, recited or read—to fill the gaps left by its expressional means in a work

150

that addresses itself at the same time to the intellect and to the imagination."

Unfortunately Berlioz did not always have the inspiration to express musically the ideas that he wished to impart to his listeners. His megalomania produced huge works, very difficult to perform and therefore seldom heard. One of his symphonies requires two orchestras and a chorus. For his *Requiem* he demands "four orchestras of brass instruments, separated one from the other and dialoguing at a distance, placed around the grand orchestra and the mass of the voices."

Berlioz wrote proudly of the "strangely gigantic physiognomy" and the "colossal aspect" of these works (cf. Hollywood), adding that "the enormous size of this form is another reason why people either understand nothing at all or are overwhelmed by a terrible emotion."

This strangely contradictory composer of program music dealt largely in exaggerated language, with emphatic adjectives and extreme figures of speech. He was a volcano in constant eruption. "Shakespeare, falling upon me unexpectedly, struck me like a thunderbolt; his lightning, in opening the heaven of art with a sublime crash, illuminated to me the most distant profundities. I recognized true grandeur, true beauty, true dramatic truth. I saw, comprehended, felt that I was alive and must rise and march."

Berlioz wrote of his "infernal passion" for the actress, Henrietta Smithson, whom he unhappily married. "She reproached me with not loving her. Thereupon, tired of all this, I answered her by poisoning myself before her eyes. Terrible cries of Henrietta. Sublime despair! Atrocious laughter on my part. Desire to revive on seeing her terrible protestations of love. Emetic!"

Such a man could not help writing program music, and all his attitudes, arguments and paradoxes mean nothing more than the habits of a superexhibitionist. Even in the act of suicide he thought of his audience!

It is a pity that the actual music of Berlioz so often falls short of his intentions. He was far from a Wagner and not even close to a Liszt. Yet he influenced them both, even though they treated him with contempt. As a master of the obvious on a gigantic scale, Berlioz becomes a fascinating subject for analysis and interpretation.

Strictly speaking, the significant program music of Hector Berlioz may be limited to his *Overtures*, the *Symphonie Fantastique*, with its sequel, *Lélio*, another symphony called *Harold in Italy* and the instrumental portions of the elaborate *Romeo and Juliet* symphony and of the oratorio or "dramatic legend," *The Damnation of Faust*.

The last shall be first. It is an uneven and often dull work, but *The Damnation of Faust* contains three orchestral numbers that must be included in the great program music of the world. They are the *Ballet of the Sylphs,* the *Dance of the Will-o'-the-Wisps* and the *Rakoczy March.*

The *March* was really the creation of a gypsy violinist, Michael Barna, court musician to Prince Franz Rakoczy, later revised by another gypsy named Ruzsitka and recognized as an established piece of folk music by the time Berlioz decided to orchestrate it. He inserted it in *The Damnation of Faust* (merely calling it *Hungarian March*) by letting Faust watch the departure of some Hungarian troops for the battlefield. It was first played in Budapest, where the *March* threw the audience into absolute hysteria and a frenzy of patriotism. The opening notes are a sufficient reminder:

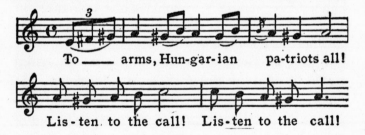

The *Ballet of the Sylphs* occurs near the end of the second part of the Berlioz *Faust,* after Mephistopheles has shown Faust a vision of Marguerite and then lulled him to sleep with the help of a chorus of sprites. The charming melody combines the mood of a lullaby with the tempo of a graceful waltz:

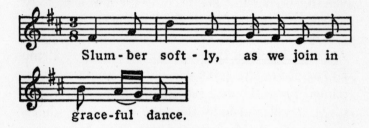

Slum - ber soft - ly, as we join in

grace - ful dance.

The *Dance of the Will-o'-the-Wisps,* in the third part, is used by Mephisto to bring Marguerite under his control, leading to her love scene with Faust. Its tune is purely instrumental:

The most complete and explicit program announced by Berlioz for any of his instrumental works is that of the *Fantastic Symphony.* He gave no less than three different versions of this program, but they agree in essential details and were finally summed up as follows: "A young musician of a morbid sensibility and an ardent imagination poisons himself with opium. The dose of the narcotic, too weak to kill him, plunges him into a heavy sleep, accompanied by strange visions, during which his sensations, sentiments

154

and recollections are translated in his sick mind into musical thoughts and pictures. The beloved woman, she herself, has become for him a melody and, as it were, an *idée fixe,* which he finds and hears everywhere."

In the first version of the program Berlioz elaborates this idea: "Strangely enough, the image of her he loves never presents itself without the accompaniment of a musical thought in which he finds a character of grace and nobleness similar to that which he attributes to the loved object. This double *idée fixe* pursues him incessantly; this is the reason of the constant appearance, in all the divisions of the symphony, of the principal melody of the first *Allegro.*"

Here is the theme representing this "fixed idea":

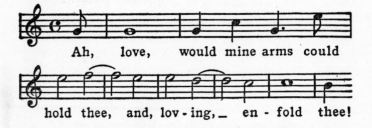

Ah, love, would mine arms could hold thee, and, lov-ing,＿ en-fold thee!

Berlioz continues: "After a thousand agitations he conceives some hope; he believes himself loved. Being one day alone in the country, he hears from afar two shepherds dialoguing a *ranz des vaches;* this pastoral plunges him into a delicious reverie.

The melody reappears for a moment across the motives of the *Adagio*."

"He is present at a ball; the tumult of the fete cannot divert him; his *idée fixe* finds him out, and the cherished melody makes his heart beat during a brilliant waltz":

"In a fit of despair he poisons himself with opium, but instead of killing him the narcotic produces in him a horrible vision. While it lasts he believes himself to have killed her whom he loves, to be condemned to death and to be present at his own execution. March to the execution; an immense procession of executioners, soldiers and people. At the end the melody appears again, like a last thought of love, interrupted by the fatal stroke."

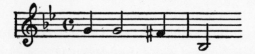

"Next he sees himself surrounded by a hateful crowd of sorcerers and devils, gathered to celebrate the Witches' Sabbath. They call to each other in the distance. At last arrives the melody, which hitherto had appeared only in its graceful form but which now has become a vulgar, ignoble tavern air; it is the beloved object who comes to the Witches' Sabbath to be present at the funeral of her victim. She is no better than a courtesan, worthy to figure in such orgies." (This cruel sentence was omitted after the renewal of his love for Miss Smithson.)

"Then commences the ceremony. The bells ring; the infernal crew prostrate themselves; a choir sings the prose of the dead, the plain chant, *Dies Irae;* two other choirs repeat it, parodying it in a burlesque manner. After that the round of the Witches' Sabbath whirls and whirls, and when it has reached the extreme degree of violence combines with the *Dies Irae* and the vision ends."

Of this well-named *Fantastic Symphony* Wagner wrote: "An immense inner wealth, a heroically vigorous imagination forces out, as from a crater, a pool of passions; what we see are colossally formed smoke clouds, parted only by lightning and streaks of fire and modeled into fugitive shapes. Everything is prodigious, daring, but infinitely painful."

Gounod called it a real event in the musical world, whose importance might be gauged by the fanatical admiration and the violent opposition it aroused. Regardless of how successfully Berlioz carried out his magniloquent intentions, the *Symphonie Fantastique* is a milestone in the history of program music.

Its sequel, *Lélio, or The Return to Life,* is far weaker and utterly unworthy of its creator or the school that he represented. Berlioz gave this fanciful name to the morbid hero of the *Fantastic Symphony* and added to his orchestra (with piano, played four-handed) an invisible chorus and solo voices, writing the words as well as the music himself.

Lélio's first words are, "God! Am I still alive?" which may be considered a keynote speech. There are six episodes in this artificial, sentimental, posturing work, labeled *The Fisher* (after a ballad by Goethe), *Chorus of the Shades, Song of the Brigands, Song of Happiness, The Aeolian Harp: Souvenirs* and a *Fantasy* on Shakespeare's *Tempest*. The composition is not worth quoting or discussing further.

Harold in Italy, however, is a very different matter. Here is a real piece of program music and at the same time an excellent symphony, with narrative and descriptive significance as well as emotional effect.

The program is given in the subtitles of the

four movements: (1) *Harold in the Mountains: Scenes of Melancholy, Happiness and Joy;* (2) *March of Pilgrims Singing the Evening Prayer;* (3) *Serenade of a Mountaineer of the Abruzzi to His Mistress;* (4) *Orgy of Brigands.*

This symphony was composed in 1834 for orchestra and viola solo at the suggestion of Paganini, who had a beautiful viola which he wanted to demonstrate in public. The composer first considered the subject of Mary Stuart but finally decided on Byron's *Childe Harold.* Paganini himself never played the viola part, possibly because, as Berlioz admitted, "the viola has not been treated sufficiently in the concerto style."

The Harold of Byron's poem is Byron himself; similarly the Harold of Berlioz becomes identified with the composer. The scenes and events described in the symphony have nothing to do with Byron's story. The character and personality of the hero are summed up in the introductory theme, which runs through all four of the movements:

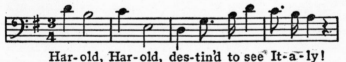

Har-old, Har-old, des-tin'd to see It-a-ly!

The *Romeo and Juliet* symphony of Berlioz is a jumble of instrumental and choral music, mostly programmatic, with a few episodes of rare beauty. The *Introduction,* superscribed "The

159

Combats, Tumult and Intervention of the Prince," is not very promising, particularly when it allows the prince to speak in a recitative of trombones and other brass instruments. Nor is the *Finale* much more satisfactory in its attempts to describe "Romeo in the Tomb of the Capulets; Invocation; Awakening of Juliet; Delirious Joy, Despair, Last Anguish and Death of the Two Lovers." Berlioz here tried for too much in the way of detail, even to reproducing the convulsions of the poisoned lovers (according to Garrick's ending of the tragedy).

But the finer portions of the *Romeo and Juliet* symphony more than make up for these defects. The section marked, "Romeo alone, sadness; concert and ball: grand festival at the house of Capulet," is effective in its dreamy beginning and brilliant close. There is true tone painting in the "Love scene: a serene night, the silent and deserted garden of Capulet." But the gem of the whole symphony is the *Scherzo,* "Queen Mab, or the Dream Fairy," based on the famous speech of Mercutio. Saint-Saëns considered this superior even to the fairy music of Mendelssohn's *Midsummer Night's Dream Overture.* A brief quotation is enough to supply the material for comparison:

In addition to his colossal symphonic works Berlioz wrote eight *Overtures,* all of which can be called program music, although they are of decidedly unequal value. The most popular is the one called *Carnaval Romain,* eventually introduced into the opera *Benvenuto Cellini.* Among its lively themes is a *Saltarello,* danced in the Piazza Colonna in the second act of the opera:

The original *Overture* to *Benvenuto Cellini* is also an admirable composition, although most listeners prefer its more brilliant successor. Another good *Overture* by Berlioz is that written for *King Lear* (1831), demonstrating once more the powerful influence of Shakespeare on the composer. He wrote, after passing some time as an invalid in Florence: "On the banks of the Arno, in a delightful wood a mile from the town, I passed whole days in reading Shakespeare. It was there I read for the first time *King Lear,* and this work of genius made me utter exclamations of admiration. I thought I would burst with enthusiasm; I rolled about in the grass, rolled about convulsively to satisfy my transports."

A rather commonplace *Overture to Waverley* (Opus 2) is headed by a quotation from the

161

poem, *Mirkwood Mere,* in the fifth chapter of Sir Walter Scott's book:

> *Dreams of love and lady's charms*
> *Give place to honour and to arms.*

Opus 3 is the *Overture des Francs-Juges* (1828), still youthful and crude, but powerful. The Francs-Juges were judges of the Vehmic Tribunal, and the *Overture* supposedly describes the sensations of a prisoner brought before them, with vehement denials of his appeals for mercy.

The composer's own hysterical comments on this *Overture* are more worth quoting than the music itself: "Nothing is so terribly frightful as my *Overture des Francs-Juges.* . . . It is a hymn to despair, but the most desperate despair, the most desperate despair imaginable, horrible and tender. . . . In short it is frightful! All that the human heart can contain of rage and tenderness is in the *Overture.*" When he heard it played he exclaimed, "How monstrous, colossal and horrible it is!"

Of the remaining *Overtures* by Berlioz one was inspired by *The Corsair* of Byron, one by Scott's *Rob Roy* (subsequently burned by the composer) and one by Shakespeare's *Much Ado about Nothing,* a title which adequately covers all three.

In spite of all his shortcomings and obvious absurdities Hector Berlioz remains a significant figure in the development of program music, of the greatest importance in his influence on the modern orchestra.

Of the triumphant triumvirate of program music Franz Liszt (1811–1886) was the most persistent, musically far better equipped than Berlioz and often approaching the inspirations of Wagner himself. (He is said to have supplied many actual themes as well as general ideas to his more gifted son-in-law.)

Liszt seems to have been practically unable to write a piece of music without giving it at least a descriptive title. Even his *Études* were mostly tagged with a definite meaning. Unfortunately the program was often more important than the music.

Like Berlioz, also, Liszt expressed himself strongly and definitely on the subject of program music, without making any great effort to live up to his theories. (This will be found characteristic of most programmatic composers.)

In spite of his persistent attempts at tonal painting and narration Liszt wrote with apparent sincerity: "It is obvious that things insofar as they are objective are not at all within the department of music, and that the merest tyro in landscape painting can with one stroke of his pencil produce a scene more faithfully than a consummate musician with all the resources of the cleverest orchestra. But the same things, insofar as they affect the soul, these things made subjective and turned into reverie, meditation, *élan,* have they not a singular affinity with music? And could not music translate them into its mysterious language? Supposing the imitation of the quail and cuckoo in the *Pastoral Symphony* to be open to the charge of puerility, must we conclude from this fact that Beethoven was wrong in seeking to affect the soul as would the view of a smiling landscape, of a happy country, of a village festival suddenly interrupted by an unexpected thunderstorm? Does not Berlioz in the *Harold Symphony* strongly recall to the mind mountain scenes and the religious effects of bells that lose themselves in the windings of steep paths? In regard to poetical music, do you think that some stupid burden of a romance or some declamatory libretto is indispensable for the expression of the human passions—such as love, despair and anger?"

Elsewhere Liszt makes clear distinctions between absolute and program music. Composers of the latter type he calls "poetizing symphonists." The creator of absolute music, he says, "transports his hearers with him to ideal regions, which he leaves the imagination of every individual free to conceive and adorn."

Liszt defines program music as "any foreword in intelligible language added to a piece of pure instrumental music, by which the composer intends to guard the hearer against an arbitrary poetical interpretation and to direct his attention in advance to the poetical idea of the whole, to a particular point of it." "The program," he adds, "has no other object than to indicate preparatively the spiritual moments which impelled the composer to create his work, the thoughts which he tried to incorporate in it."

In spite of these dicta the music of Liszt is full of direct imitation, as well as attempted description and narration, plus the suggestion of moods and emotions which can be considered the highest form of program music. It is in his piano pieces that he achieves his most obvious effects and also some of his best.

Only an occasional quotation is necessary from this mass of programmatic material. In many cases it is enough to list the titles alone.

Youthful travels in Switzerland and Italy inspired the three sets of piano compositions which he called *Years of Pilgrimage*. Included in the Swiss series were such titles as *The Chapel of William Tell, On the Lake of Wallenstadt, Beside a Spring, Storm, Obermann Valley* and *The Bells of Geneva*. Recollections of Italy figured in such pieces as *Il Penseroso, Canzonetta of Salvator Rosa, Three Sonnets by Petrarch, After a Reading from Dante, Angelus* and the *Cypresses* and *Fountains of the Villa d'Este*. A special group, *Venice and Naples*, included a *Gondo-*

liera and a *Tarantella,* both fairly well known.

Spain suggested to Liszt a *Rhapsodie Espagnole, Folies d'Espagne* and a *Jota Aragonesa.* His religious feeling and love of nature combined to produce the popular *Legends, St Francis of Assisi Preaching to the Birds* and *St Francis of Paula Walking on the Waves.* The latter must have been suggested by a drawing of Steinle, standing on Liszt's writing-table, which he described thus in his testament: "St Francis of Paula walks on the waves, his mantle spread out under his feet, holding a glowing coal in one of his hands, raising the other, either to conjure the storm or to bless the threatened sailors, looking heavenward, where in a glory appears the word *Charitas.*"

The best-known piece of program music by Franz Liszt is unquestionably the *Liebestraum* (Dream of Love), one of a set of three *Nocturnes,* often supplied with words. The sentimental melody carries out satisfactorily the implications of the title, and a rather spiritual interpretation may do no harm:

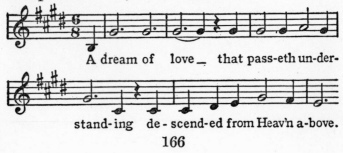

A dream of love — that pass-eth un-der-
stand-ing de - scend-ed from Heav'n a-bove.

Two of his *Concert Études* are also popular, the *Waldesrauschen* (Forest Murmurs) and *Gnomenreigen* (Dance of the Gnomes). The melody of the first might be interpreted thus:

Wal-des-rau-schen means the rust-ling of the for-est, as this E-tude lets us hear it and feel that we are near it.

The *Dance of the Gnomes* is very fast and light, purely pianistic and unsuited to words.

Another familiar *Étude* is generally given the title *Un Soupir* (A Sigh). It has an excellent melody which has been imitated by other composers, including Wagner:

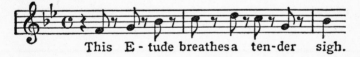

This E-tude breathes a ten-der sigh.

The Liszt *Lorelei* is a good, straightforward piece of program music, whose meaning is indicated not only by the title (immortalized in the folklike song of Silcher, which everybody knows) but by the fact that Liszt himself fitted it with

Heine's familiar words for a vocal version. The chief theme goes like this:

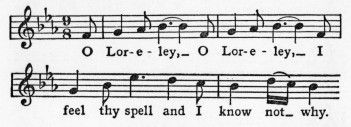

Liszt wrote several *Mephisto* waltzes, of which one has become quite popular with concert pianists. But the public still responds most enthusiastically to his fifteen *Hungarian Rhapsodies,* based on authentic folk tunes but actually very personal and individual compositions. They may all be considered programmatic in a sense, especially as the themes mostly had actual words in their original versions. They follow the Magyar tradition of a slow strain (*Lassan* or *Lassu*), leading to a fast and brilliant *Finale* (*Friska*), and this arrangement of material adds to the dramatic effect.

The general favorite among the *Hungarian Rhapsodies* is of course the second, and it is an excellent representative of the entire series. Here is the slow theme of the first part:

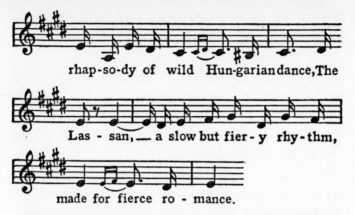

rhap-so-dy of wild Hun-garian dance, The

Las - san, — a slow but fier - y rhy - thm,

made for fierce ro - mance.

The *Friska,* or lively part of the national *Czardas,* begins with this melody, played quite softly:

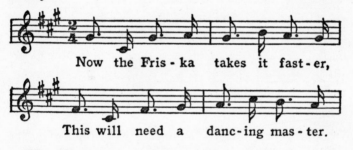

Now the Fris - ka takes it fast - er,

This will need a danc-ing mas - ter.

The climax is reached in this well-known fast tune, long established as vaudeville and movie music:

From there to the end the second *Hungarian Rhapsody* continues to introduce spectacular

169

effects of great melodic and rhythmic variety, finishing with a *Cadenza, Prestissimo,* which never fails to draw the desired applause.

Of the other *Hungarian Rhapsodies* the sixth and the twelfth are perhaps the most frequently played. The fifteenth contains Liszt's version of the *Rakoczy March,* and the fourteenth makes use of the most famous of Hungarian folk songs, *The Heron,* which appears also as the chief theme of the *Hungarian Fantasie,* with orchestra. It is a simple scale tune, made effective by syncopation and heavy chords:

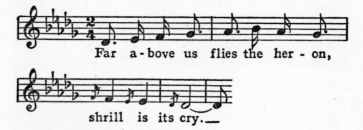

Far a - bove us flies the her - on,
shrill is its cry.___

Before turning to the orchestral works of Liszt there should perhaps be mentioned the brilliant piano transcription of *La Campanella* (The Little Bell), whose theme was supplied by a violin study of Paganini. Liszt treats the unpretentious tune with a dazzling display of technique, and the *Campanella* has become one of the pet show-pieces of virtuoso pianists. It is legitimate program music, even in its overdecorated form:

170

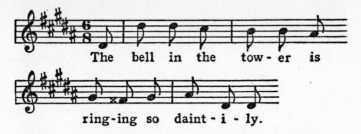

Franz Liszt's great contribution to orchestral music, and to program music in general, was the *Symphonic Poem.* This was his own invention, although some of the earlier concert *Overtures* amounted to practically the same thing. His idea was to write orchestral pieces of symphonic proportions, but shorter than the conventional symphony, and in one continuous movement. Almost necessarily these *Symphonic Poems* were programmatic, achieving unity through a central dramatic subject, treated with symphonic technique.

Liszt wrote twelve such orchestral works, all with definite titles. The first he called *What One Hears on the Mountain,* basing it upon the fifth of Victor Hugo's *Autumn Leaves.* The entire poem is prefixed to the score and thus serves as its complete program. It deals with a mystic dialogue of two voices, representing Nature and Humanity and arriving at rather sophomoric arguments on destiny, the soul, God and the universe.

The second of the *Symphonic Poems* bears the title *Tasso: Lamento e Trionfo.* It was written in

171

1849 to celebrate the centenary of Goethe's birth, but the subject matter was taken from Byron's poem, *The Lament of Tasso,* rather than from the drama of the German poet.

In his preface to the composition Liszt writes: "Tasso loved and suffered in Ferrara; he was revenged in Rome, and he lives still today in the folk songs of Venice. These three moments are inseparable from his imperishable fame. To render them musically we called up first his great shade as it still haunts the Venetian lagoons; we then saw his proud, sad face pass through the festivities of Ferrara, where he gave birth to his masterpieces; finally we followed him to Rome, the Eternal City, which, in bestowing on him her crown, glorified in him the martyr and poet."

Liszt specifically states that the principal theme of his *Tasso* is a melody to which he heard the Venetian gondoliers sing the opening stanzas of the poet's *Jerusalem Delivered.*

The most popular of the Liszt *Symphonic Poems* is unquestionably *Les Preludes,* the third of the series. This melodious composition was inspired by one of Lamartine's *Poetic Meditations,* whose content was thus interpreted by Liszt: "What is our life but a series of preludes to that unknown song, the first solemn note of which is sounded by death? Love forms the enchanted daybreak of every life; but what is the destiny where the first delights of happiness are not interrupted by some storm, whose fatal breath dissipates its fair illusions, whose fell lightning consumes its altar? And what wounded spirit, when one of its tempests is over, does not seek to rest its memories in the sweet calm of country life? Yet man does not resign himself long to enjoy the beneficent tepidity which first charmed him on nature's bosom; and when the 'trumpet's loud clangor has called him to arms' he rushes to the post of danger, whatever may be the war that calls him to the ranks, to find in battle the full consciousness of himself and the complete possession of his strength."

Regardless of inner meanings, *Les Preludes* is a most effective concert piece. There are three important themes which sum up the program:

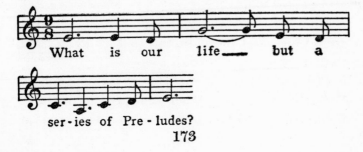

Sweet is the calm of the
coun - try, where na - ture is
seen at her best.
When the trum-pet's loud clan - gor has
called "To arms!"

The fourth *Symphonic Poem* is *Orpheus,* whose title alone is enough to establish the program. Its basic ideas, according to the composer, were suggested by a combination of Gluck's opera and an Etruscan vase in the Louvre. "Today as of old and always," said Liszt, "Orpheus, that is Art, should pour forth his melodious waves and vibrating chords like a soft and irresistible light over the contrary elements that tear each other and bleed in the soul of every individual, as in the bowels of society."

Number five is *Prometheus,* a favorite subject with composers, to which full justice has never been done musically. Liszt wrote his version as an introduction to some dramatic scenes by Herder, *Prometheus Unbound,* performed in Weimar in 1850 for the dedication of a statue of the poet.

Mazeppa is the sixth *Symphonic Poem,* originally a piano *Étude,* with its story taken from one of the poems in Victor Hugo's *Les Orientales.* The entire poem is prefixed to the score, but the music is mostly a series of galloping rhythms, with some intensely realistic touches, when the horse is evidently trying to scrape off Mazeppa, unwillingly tied to its back. This is probably the most imitative of all the program music of Liszt.

Festklänge (Festal Sounds), the seventh in the series (1851), was to have been Liszt's own wedding music when it seemed that his marriage to the Princess Wittgenstein would be a possibility. Neither the wedding nor the music came off.

Another vague and wordy preface introduces the *Heroide Funèbre,* eighth of the *Symphonic Poems,* but without saving the music from comparative oblivion. The ninth is called *Hungaria,* obviously with a patriotic program, and the tenth is *Hamlet,* whose indebtedness to Shakespeare is equally obvious. The emphasis is on the brooding tendencies of the Danish prince, not the story of the play.

Number eleven, *The Battle of the Huns,* was inspired by Kaulbach's fresco in the Berlin Museum, showing Attila's men and the Romans continuing their fight in the sky after being killed on the Catalaunian Plain. The final *Symphonic Poem* is *Die Ideale* (Ideals), based on Schiller's poem of the same name. There are nine separate quotations from the poem, prefixed to different sections of the music, which divides naturally into three main parts, labeled *Aspiration, Disillusion* and *Activity,* preceded by an *Introduction* and followed by *Apotheosis.*

In addition to the *Symphonic Poems* both of Liszt's actual symphonies have programs, with Dante and Faust as their heroes. The latter uses a male chorus in the *Finale,* quoting Goethe's famous words on "the eternal feminine." The first movement deals with Faust himself, the second with Marguerite and the third with Mephistopheles. The themes are mostly personal and developed very much in the manner of the *Leitmotif,* or "leading motive," which Wagner later made famous.

Faust, for example, is immediately introduced with a brooding theme, which then progresses through a number of transformations. It appears thus in the *Introduction:*

Faust — would solve life's mys-ter-y,

u-nique in his-tor-y! ——

Several other themes represent the hero of the symphony at various points, all traceable to some extent to the basic melodic material. The mood of "brooding inquiry" is followed by that of "struggling aspiration," then "passionate appealing," "love longing" and "triumphant enthusiasm." (The descriptive phrases are supplied by Niecks.) This impressive musicianship, added to highly dramatic conceptions, successfully expressed, would seem to place the *Faust Symphony* at the head of all the works of Franz Liszt.

The second symphony has as its full title *A Symphony to Dante's Divina Commedia,* for "grand orchestra and soprano and alto chorus" (1855). There are only two movements, *L'Inferno* and *Il Purgatorio.* Liszt intended to add the logical *Paradiso,* but Wagner dissuaded him, arguing that no one was equal to the task of expressing Paradise musically.

A long interpretative introduction to the *Dante Symphony,* by Richard Pohl, presumably expresses the ideas of the composer as to its program. Trombones and tuba introduce the *Inferno:* "Through me you pass into the city of woe. Through me you pass into eternal pain." Trumpets and horns follow with the oft-quoted announcement: "Abandon hope, all ye who enter here."

The music proceeds to illustrate the "madness, hopelessness, fury and curses of the damned" in

a "demoniac turmoil," from which the only relief
is afforded by the beautiful episode of Paolo and
Francesca. "There is no greater grief than to remember days of joy when misery is at hand."

The *Purgatory* section of the symphony expresses Dante's own feelings after leaving the
Inferno: "Infinite longing for godliness, a growing feeling of unworthiness and weakness, of
humility, contrition and repentance, of redemption by prayer."

The *Dante Symphony* ends with a *Coda,* which
has as its climax a real *Magnificat,* "joining itself
to the whole universe, to the general hallelujahs
and hosannas." With this chant, sung by women's
or boys' voices, it closes "ecstatically."

Three more pieces of orchestral program music
by Franz Liszt deserve mention. In 1858–1859 he
composed two *Episodes from Lenau's Faust,*
with the individual titles *The Nocturnal Procession* and *The Dance in the Village Inn.* These
have little to do with the conventional Faust
story, although in the second Mephistopheles
takes the instrument of a village fiddler and plays
a diabolically seductive waltz. There is also a
Dance of Death, based on the *Dies Irae,* for
piano and orchestra, inspired by the Orcagna
fresco, The Triumph of Death, in the Campo
Santo at Pisa. Liszt hesitated to publish "such a
monstrosity" but was persuaded to do so by his
temporary son-in-law, Hans von Bülow. It has

been called "a gruesome treatment of a gruesome subject."

Franz Liszt was the necessary link between Berlioz and Wagner. He had an imagination equal to that of the former but better disciplined, and his musical technique, as such, was superior to Wagner's. What he lacked was the creative genius that made the Wagnerian music rise above any announced program. Liszt could not hope to do more than carry out the intentions proclaimed by his voluminous titles. The resulting music seldom if ever transcended its subject matter.

Yet Franz Liszt made a definite and important contribution to the development of the *Leitmotif,* and for this he deserves a high place in the history of program music. For these musical labels, these tags of identification called "leading motives," suggested by both Berlioz and Liszt and perfected by Wagner, represent the most direct and obvious way of carrying a program through a musical composition and certainly the most convenient trick of technique ever invented for such a purpose.

The *Leitmotif,* consisting generally of only a few notes in a specific and easily remembered pattern, not only makes it easy to follow a story or a picture through music but provides a species of musical form worthy to stand beside the conventional sonata form of symphonic composition. Just as a symphony is easily followed by the listener who is acquainted with its thematic materials, so any piece of program music becomes simple and intelligible if its leading melody designs are tagged with definite meanings and repeated without too much alteration.

But the greatness of Richard Wagner (1813–1883) does not rest merely upon his perfecting of the *Leitmotif* technique. He uses it as a key to his musical thoughts, but what he writes is far more than a catalogue of tonal merchandise. His orchestral inspirations use the *Leitmotif* merely as a starting-point (and only in the later, more elaborate works). To anyone with a truly perceptive ear these index cards are entirely unnecessary. Even the words of Wagner's music dramas could often be omitted entirely, for it is the orchestra that tells the story.

Wagner wisely wrote his own librettos in such a way that the singers could never get in the way of the instrumental accompaniment. When he wanted to express such an emotional climax as the love scenes of *Tristan und Isolde* he contented himself with mere exclamations, which might just as well have been meaningless syllables. Inevitably most of the details of the Wagnerian text are lost in actual performance, even when the greatest and most experienced singers are on the stage.

Thus broadly considered, all of Wagner's music dramas are program music in the highest

180

sense. They have proved this repeatedly by their effectiveness in concert performance. The effects of scenery, costume and staging unquestionably add to the appeal of Wagner's music to the average listener, yet they are not strictly necessary, and occasionally there is more than a slight danger of permitting these stage appurtenances to turn the sublime into the ridiculous. This author is still waiting impatiently for the time when Wagner will be played upon the screen with no singing at all and a minimum of dialogue, but using people and scenes that really look like what he had in mind and leaving it to his gorgeous orchestral music to tell the rest of the story.

Like Berlioz, Liszt and other composers of program music Wagner had the habit of writing voluminously on the subject and then completely contradicting himself by his actions. Theoretically he disapproved of instrumental program music, yet what he actually composed was consistently programmatic, with or without words.

Wagner's endless arguments on art, music, mankind and the universe were so full of sophistry, so specious and false and contradictory and often sophomoric, that they cannot be taken very seriously. He wrote page after page of dull prose to prove the significance of his musical and dramatic creations but could not thereby alter the simple fact that they are so full of genius and instinctive rightness that no arguments or explanations are needed.

Against his will and his own protestations, therefore, he must be placed automatically among the greatest composers of program music. Actually every piece of instrumental music that he ever wrote had some programmatic significance, with the possible exception of one early piano sonata and one symphony in C major, both now completely forgotten.

Early *Overtures* by Wagner, now also forgotten, include such titles as *King Enzio* (to a tragedy by Raupach), *Polonia* (referring to the current Polish insurrection), *Rule, Britannia* (requiring no explanation) and *Columbus* (evidently modeled after the *Overtures* of Beethoven, whom Wagner greatly admired). The instrumental preludes to his first two operas, *Die Feen* (The Fairies) and *Das Liebesverbot* (The Forbiddance of Love), are likewise of no importance today.

But in his *Rienzi Overture,* which is still successfully performed, Wagner wrote an excellent piece of program music, in the style of Meyerbeer, and from then on all of his creative work belongs definitely in the programmatic category. The opera of *Rienzi* is an old-fashioned absurdity, at least in comparison with Wagner's later inspirations, but its *Overture* makes pleasant concert music and contains some fine tunes. Here is the one by which the *Overture* is most easily identified:

Bold   Rien-zi,   Ro-man   trib-une,
last of his kind.

Far more important is the *Overture* to *The Flying Dutchman* (1843), which is today a very popular concert number and perhaps the first example of Wagner's use of the *Leitmotif*. For this *Overture* Wagner himself wrote a "Programmatic Elucidation" which is worth quoting in part: "The Flying Dutchman's dreadful ship is driven along by the storm; it makes for the land . . . where its master hopes to find salvation and redemption. We hear the pitying strains of this annunciation of salvation, which sounds to us like a prayer and a lament. . . . How often has the unhappy man gone through the same experience! How often has he steered his ship through the ocean billows to the inhabited shore, where once every seven years it is permitted him to land! How often did he imagine that he had reached the end of his torments! And, ah, how often, woefully disappointed, had he to set out again and recommence his frantic ranging of the

183

ocean. From the depth of his misery he calls for redemption. In the horrible solitude of his existence only a woman can bring him salvation. Where, in what land, does the deliverer dwell? Where is the feeling heart that beats for sufferings such as his? Where is she who does not flee from him with fear and trembling, like those cowardly men who, terrified, cross themselves at his approach? A ray of light breaks through the night. It pierces his tormented soul like lightning. It is extinguished. It flashes again. The seaman keeps his eye fixed on a star and stoutly steers toward it through flood and wave. What so powerfully draws him is a woman's look, full of sublime pity and divine sympathy. A heart has unlocked its unfathomable depth to the immense suffering of the cursed man. It must sacrifice itself for him, break with compassion, in order to annihilate at the same time itself and his sufferings. At the sight of this divine apparition the unhappy man breaks down, dashed in pieces like his ship. But while the latter is engulfed by the sea he rises from the waves, healed and holy, led by her who victoriously saved him to the dawn of sublimest love." (Wagner was always fascinated by the subject of sacrifices made by others, particularly women, but he never made any sacrifices himself.)

The chief theme of the *Flying Dutchman Overture,* which is used practically as a *Leitmotif,* is this, introduced by the horns and bassoons:

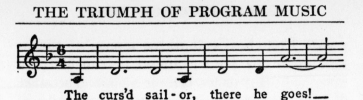

The curs'd sail-or, there he goes!__

It represents the accursed sailor himself and is heard through an orchestral portrayal of a very realistic storm at sea. The second and more melodious theme is taken from the ballad of Senta, the heroine, and expresses the combined ideas of womanly love, sacrifice and redemption:

Sen - ta   is   here, re - deem - ing by

love, with nev - er a   sign__ of fear.

Wagner's "Programmatic Elucidation" of the *Flying Dutchman Overture* was a fanciful and rather wordy exposition of its general meaning, including that of the opera as a whole. In writing a similar prose introduction to the familiar *Tannhäuser Overture* (1845) he stated a definite program which follows the music in detail: "At the beginning the orchestra lets us hear the song of the pilgrims; it approaches, swells into a mighty outburst and at last passes away. Evening twilight: dying sounds of the song. It is nightfall, and magic lights and sounds steal on our senses;

a rosy mist rises; voluptuous sounds of jubilation reach our ears; confused movements of a weirdly lustful dance become visible. These are the seductive spells of the Venusberg, which at dead of night manifest themselves to those in whose breast burns the fire of sensual desire. Attracted by the alluring vision, a tall, manly form approaches: it is Tannhäuser, the minstrel. He intones his proud, jubilant love song, joyous and challenging, as if to draw to himself the voluptuous enchantment by compulsion. Wild shouts of joy answer him; the rosy cloud grows more dense around him; entrancing perfumes envelop him and intoxicate his senses. Now he perceives before him, reclining in seductive twilight, an inexpressibly lovely female form. He hears the voice which, sweetly thrilling, hails him with the siren call that promises the darer the satisfaction of his wildest wishes. It is Venus herself who has appeared to him. Then heart and senses burn; a glowing, consuming longing inflames the blood in his veins; he is impelled with irresistible force to approach, and before the goddess herself he now in the utmost ecstasy intones his jubilant love song in her praise.

"As it were by this magic call, the wonders of the Venusberg open before him in all their brilliance: tumultuous jubilation and wild, voluptuous cries arise on all sides; in drunken exultation the Bacchantes come noisily rushing up and, tearing Tannhäuser along with them in their furious dance, lead him into the arms of Venus, who embraces him and carries him along with her into unapproachable distances, into the realm of no-more-being. A hubbub passes like the Wild Hunt, and soon after the storm subsides. Only a voluptuous wailing is still whirring in the air, and a weird whispering, like the breath of unblessed sensual love, hovers over the place where the entrancing, unholy enchantment manifested itself and over which night now again spreads her wings.

"But morning already begins to dawn; from afar is heard once more the approaching pilgrims' song. As this song comes nearer and nearer, as advancing day dispels night, the whirring and whispering in the air, which before sounded like the woeful lamentation of the damned, rises to a more and more joyful billowing, until at last, when the sun appears in his splendor and the pilgrims' song with mighty enthusiasm proclaims salvation to all the world and all that is and lives, the billowing swells into a blissful rustling of sublime ecstasy. It is the jubilation of the Venusberg itself, redeemed from the curse of unholiness, which we hear in the song. Thus move and leap all the pulses of life to the song of redemption; and the two divided elements, spirit and sense, God and Nature, embrace each other in the holy, uniting kiss of love."

It will be noticed that all this has very little to

do with the plot of the opera and does not even mention the sainted Elizabeth, who is the real cause of the regeneration of Tannhäuser. It makes the *Overture* practically an independent piece of program music, and this is emphasized by the fact that Wagner later built up the ballet music, for the benefit of his Paris audience, making of the combination an elaborate and effective concert piece.

The *Pilgrims' Chorus* is so well known as hardly to require quotation, but a reminder of its real meaning may be in order:

With joy-ful song to our home sounds our greet-ing, Thy love-ly fields we re-joice once more at meet-ing. Now soon shall cease our wan-d'rings far, Since God knows right well how faith-ful we are.

The music of the Venusberg is introduced by the violas and forms the basis of the instrumental *Bacchanale:*

And here is the triumphant song of Tann-häuser himself, when he succumbs temporarily to the goddess:

Thanks for_ thy_ grace and what thou would'st be giv - ing! What joy shall be his that_ knows such_ trans - ports_ liv - ing! En - vied_ of_ men shall be thy chos-en con - sort, Not man but_ di - vine, by a god - dess_ glor - i - fied.

189

The *Prelude* to *Lohengrin* is one of Wagner's
finest pieces of program music, and once more he
himself provides a full and detailed explanation:
"To the entranced gaze of highest supermundane
love longing the serenest blue celestial ether
seems at first to condense itself into a wonderful
vision, hardly visible and yet magically captivating the eye. In infinitely tender lines, gradually
growing in distinctness, the miracle-ministering
host of angels appears, descending imperceptibly
from on high with the Holy Grail in their midst.
As the vision becomes more and more distinct
and moves more and more visibly toward the
earth, intoxicatingly sweet perfumes are exhaled
from it; entrancing vapors flow down in golden
clouds, captivate the beholder's senses and fill his
thrilling heart to its inmost depths with a won-
drous devotional emotion. . . . And when at last
the Holy Grail itself in its miraculous reality is
presented to the sight of those deemed worthy,
when the vessel sends forth far and wide the sun-
rays of sublime love, like the effulgence of a
heavenly fire, so that all hearts within the radi-
ance of the eternal glow tremble—then the gaz-
er's senses fail him; he sinks down in adoring an-
nihilation. But upon him, lost in the blissfulness
of love, the Grail now pours its blessing, with
which it consecrates him as its knight. The shin-
ing flames become subdued to a milder glory
which now spreads over the earthly valley like a

breath of unspeakable delight and tender emotion and fills the adorer's breast with never-divined blissfulness. In chaste joy the host of angels, looking down smilingly, soar upward again: the fountain of love, dried up on earth, they have brought anew to the world; the Grail they have left behind in the keeping of pure men, into whose hearts its contents had poured themselves as a blessing; and the noble host disappear in the brightest light of the celestial ether, whence they had descended."

Again this *Prelude* makes no attempt to tell the story of the opera. It is in effect a musical expression of pure mysticism, developed mainly from the delicate opening theme which represents the angels descending from heaven with the Holy Grail, to whose service the celestial knight, Lohengrin, was pledged:

Ho - ly Grail, sac - red chal - ice, ben - e - dic - tion from Heav - en we hum - bly pray.

Liszt described this *Prelude* as "a sort of magic formula which, like a mysterious initiation, prepares our souls for the sight of unaccustomed things and of a higher signification than that of our terrestrial life."

There is also an instrumental *Prelude* to the third Act of *Lohengrin* which has become one of the war horses of radio and the records. It describes a torchlight procession, preceding the familiar *Wedding March,* and its introduction and main theme make a lusty effect, with emphasis on the trombones:

Up with the torch, let cym - bals ring! Pre - pare for the bride and groom that we crown them queen and king.

Here is where the sounding brass and far more than tinkling cymbals create their most exciting effects, against an agitated background of strings:

Up with the torch! Let its light shine in process - ion! Up with the torch, and with
no sign of de - press - ion! Keep it a -
blaze — and let its rays — to ev'- ry
gaze be — clear, The time for the
brid - al is draw - ing — near! —

The *Wedding March* itself, regularly played as the entrance music for every marriage ceremony, has words in the opera and therefore does not need them here.

The *Prelude* to *Die Meistersinger* (The Mastersingers), representing the maturity of Wagner's workmanship, and his only composition in lighter vein, may be called a perfect piece of program music. Here he definitely outlines the plot of the great musical comedy that is to follow, and all of the themes are borrowed from the drama itself.

This *Overture* opens with the pompous march theme representing the Mastersingers themselves:

It soon gives way to the love music of Walter and Eva, which is in turn interrupted by the real march of the Mastersingers (borrowed directly from the medieval "long tone"), stately and dignified, but also a bit pompous:

The next melody to be heard is that of Walter's *Prize Song,* which is given a variety of treatment:

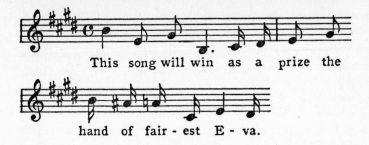

A caricature of the march breaks in, with staccato bassoons, suggesting the absurdities of Beckmesser and of the critics at whom the opera was aimed. A climax is reached when Wagner combines all of the themes in an amazing exhibition of counterpoint, a gesture of scholarship that is as musically effective as it is technically impressive. With a blare of brass the *Prelude* ends with the theme of the Mastersingers with which it opened.

The great music dramas of the cycle of the *Nibelungen Ring* are full of program music, much of which is directly imitative. One has only to listen to Siegfried's horn, the voice of the Forest Bird, the Fire Music, the Ride of the Valkyries, the yawning of the dragon, the little hammer of Mime compared with the forging of the sword, the storm and the forest murmurs to realize that Wagner's music is often far more than suggestive.

But its real programmatic significance lies in

its use of the *Leitmotif,* and since every one of these musical labels has a definite meaning it is entirely fair to supply them with words for their quick and easy differentiation. Here are the most important "leading motives" running through the cycle of the *Ring* operas:

THE RHEINGOLD

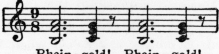

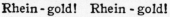

Rhein - gold!   Rhein - gold!

THE RING

This   ring   is   no   bond   of   joy!

VALHALLA

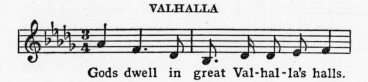

Gods dwell   in   great   Val-hal-la's halls.

FIRE MUSIC

MIME'S FORGE

Tap, lit-tle Mi-me your ham-mer so small.

THE SWORD NOTUNG

Hail No - tung, thou fier - y sword.

RIDE OF THE VALKYRIES

THE VALKYRIES' CRY

Ho - yo - to - ho! —

FATE

This is fate!

SIEGFRIED, THE HERO

Hail to Sieg - fried, he - ro so bold,

want-ing no gold! —

There are significant instrumental passages throughout the *Ring* operas also, including *Preludes* of varying length and importance. The introductory work, *Das Rheingold,* is preceded by a long orchestral description of the Rhine itself, built upon a sustained low E flat, representing the steady current of the river, with the gradual addition of more and more tones of the major chord. (Wagner claimed that this effect had come to him in a dream.) The closing *Entrance of the Gods into Valhalla* is an imposing orchestral climax, definitely suggesting the glory of the rainbow and of the heroic figures crossing this magic bridge to their new abode.

The *Prelude* to *Die Walküre* is a realistic musical storm which directly introduces the opening scene. (The distinction is sometimes made that a *Prelude* technically leads right into the action of an opera, whereas an *Overture* is an independent piece of music, complete in itself.)

198

This drama contains the instrumental presentation of the *Ride of the Valkyries,* as well as their *Battle-cry* and, near the close, the famous *Fire Music,* marking the beginning of Brünnhilde's long sleep.

Siegfried is introduced by a fairly long orchestral description of the dwarf Mime, musing over the problem of his superhuman foster-child, making considerable use of the dainty motif of the silversmith and leading immediately into the scene with Mime at the forge. Later in the opera occurs the beautiful instrumental passage known as *Forest Murmurs* (*Waldweben*), which contains independent material in addition to various *Leitmotifs,* featuring the song of the Forest Bird:

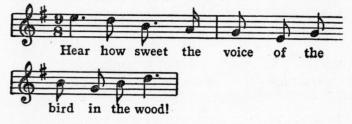

The final music drama of the cycle, *Götterdämmerung* (Twilight of the Gods), has a very short instrumental introduction, leading right into the scene of the Norns, which is itself the real *Prelude* to the opera. Orchestrally the climax of this great work is the *Funeral March,* after Siegfried's death, in which most of the leading motives are heard once more but with a realistic basis

which makes it one of the outstanding compositions of its kind.

Closely connected with the *Ring* cycle and em-
ploying one of the loveliest of the *Leitmotifs* is
the *Siegfried Idyl,* which Wagner composed as a
Christmas and birthday gift for his wife, Cosima,
in honor of their son Siegfried. It was played as
a surprise on the steps of their home, Triebschen,
early on Christmas morning of the year 1870.
Its chief theme is built upon the *Peace* motif from
Siegfried, which is itself derived from the tonal
pattern of Siegfried's horn, turning its defiant
notes into the tenderest and most appealing of
melodies:

Peace,— our Sieg - fried's a - sleep.

Wagner also made use of a folk song in the
Siegfried Idyl, "Schlaf', Kindchen, balde," re-
taining its original character of a lullaby:

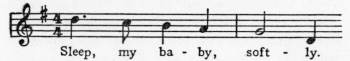

Sleep, my ba - by, soft - ly.

The *Prelude* to *Tristan und Isolde* is generally
considered music's perfect expression of sensuous

love. To call it anything but program music would be absurd.

Wagner's own description of it includes these sentences: "World, power, fame, splendor, chivalry, fidelity, friendship, all are gone; only one thing still remains: longing, longing unquenchable, ever anew self-begetting desire—languishing and thirsting; the sole redemption—death, extinction, never-awakening . . . As the theme could not possibly be exhausted, the composer lets the insatiable desire swell out . . . in a long articulated train from the bashful confession, the most tender devotion, through timid sighing, hoping and fearing, lamenting and wishing, rapture and torments, to the most violent efforts, in order to find . . . the way into the ocean of infinite love bliss. In vain! Fainting, the heart droops, to languish in longing, in longing without attaining, as every attaining produces only new longing, until . . . the presentiment of the highest bliss of attainment dawns upon the dying eye: it is the bliss of dying, of being no more, of the last redemption, the passing into that wonderful realm from which we swerve farthest when most violently striving to enter it. Shall we call it death? Or is it the nocturnal wonder world out of which, as the legend has it, the ivy and the vine grow up in close embrace on the grave of Tristan and Isolde?"

The *Prelude* is built mostly upon the opening theme, which is in the form of a question and an answer, clearly representing the two ill-fated lovers themselves:

Ah, Tris - tan! Ah,— I - sol - de!—

The *Love Death* (*Liebestod*) is often played orchestrally with the *Prelude* in concert, but in the music drama itself, which it brings to a close, there are words to this dramatic passage, which thus falls outside the category of program music in the technical sense. But the title could be applied to the introduction to the third act, which establishes the mood of pity and yearning long before the curtain rises. There is also the extended solo by the English horn, representing, in fact, directly imitating, the shepherd's pipe.

In contrast to the *Prelude* to *Tristan und Isolde* the *Parsifal Vorspiel* treats of divine rather than human love. Its themes are taken from the scene of the Love Feast of the Knights of the Grail.

There are two outstanding motifs, which Wagner called Love and Faith, connected by the Grail motif, which is based upon the *Dresden Amen*. The first he associates with the words of the ceremony, "Take my blood, for our love's sake," and, "Take my body, that you may remember me," both sung by angelic voices.

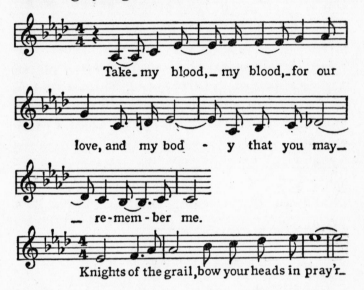

Take my blood, my blood, for our love, and my bod - y that you may re-mem-ber me.

Knights of the grail, bow your heads in pray'r

The second (strictly the third) motif expresses the promise of redemption through faith. In the words of Wagner, "Now once more the plaint of loving compassion rises from out the awe of solitude. The fear, the holy agony of the Mount of Olives, the divine sorrow of Golgotha—the body grows pale, the blood flows forth; and now begins to shine the heavenly blissful glow in the cup, pouring out over all that lives and suffers the

joy of the divine grace of the redemption by love.
. . . Once more we hear the promise and—hope."

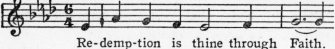

Re-demp-tion is thine through Faith.

The so-called *Good Friday Spell* is a beautiful orchestral passage in *Parsifal* which must definitely be recognized as program music. It gives a musical picture of early spring with the beauty of the awakening meadows, combining various motifs of the opera with a special *Good Friday* melody:

All na - ture feels the spell of

peace - ful Good Fri - day.

Wagner's program music also includes a *Faust Overture,* originally designed for a symphony of the same title, and a *Centennial March* (not very good), commemorating America's Declaration of Independence, for which the city of Philadelphia paid him five thousand dollars.

Regardless of his paradoxical statements and the exaggerated sentimentalities of his wordy descriptions and arguments, Wagner's dramatic compositions, at their best, set a standard that has not yet been equalled and is not likely to be surpassed. He gave a new significance to program music by his use of the *Leitmotif,* and he proved that words need not be considered either a necessity or a handicap to the expression of a completely definite and highly emotional train of thought. The triumph of program music reached its climax in the compositions of Richard Wagner.

MISCELLANEOUS EXAMPLES OF PROGRAM MUSIC

A VAST AMOUNT of program music has been written since Wagner's day. In modern music it is the rule rather than the exception. There are instances of minor composers turning out one or two striking pieces of programmatic character and thereby making a reputation out of all proportion to their consistent ability. There are other cases where acknowledged masters of music, devoted to the absolute style, have unbent a few times to the extent of composing something definitely programmatic, generally to the decided advantage of their popularity.

Only the really important works can be given attention here, and of these only a few need to be treated in any detail. Many charming and successful pieces may only be named in passing, and some worthy program music may be omitted altogether.

Johannes Brahms (1833–1897) stands out as a composer primarily of absolute music, combining the best elements of both the classic and the romantic schools, who nevertheless produced far more program music than is generally realized.

Only three of his works bear definitely programmatic titles: the *Edward Ballade,* for piano, Opus 10, No. 1, and the *Tragic* and *Academic Festival Overtures.* But even in what seems outwardly absolute music of the purest type there are often hidden programs, and Brahms was too much a romanticist to let the form consistently overwhelm the content of his music.

In his very first piano sonata, Opus 1, Brahms wrote above the theme of the second movement, "after an old German *Minnelied,*" and quoted the words of the song. In his third sonata, Opus 5, he again gave the second movement a superscription, this time three lines from a poem by Sternau, and above the *Intermezzo* he wrote the word "Rückblick [Retrospect]." Brahms also told a friend that in the *Finale* of his first sonata he had in mind the song *My Heart's in the Highlands* and that the *Andante* of the second sonata, Opus 2, was inspired by the *Winter Song* of the Minnesinger Kraft von Toggenburg.

The piano *Concerto* in D minor has been called "a monument to Schumann," and Joachim insisted that its somber opening was suggested by Schumann's attempted suicide. The smaller piano pieces, *Ballades, Rhapsodies, Waltzes, Intermezzos* and *Capriccios,* might all have programs, but as the composer gave no hint of them their interpretation would be mere guesswork.

One important symphonic theme Brahms himself traced to the sound of an Alpine horn. It is in the *Finale* of the first symphony, and its melody has often been related to the Westminster Chime, whose notes it duplicates. But Brahms wrote to Clara Schumann the day he heard this brief melody in the Alps and put down the words that fitted it: "Hoch über'm Berg, tief im Tal [High above the mountain, deep in the valley]."

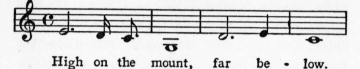

High on the mount, far be - low.

His third symphony has a motto consisting of three notes, F, A flat and the F an octave above. Brahms said that these three letters (FAF) stood for the words, "Frei aber froh [Free but happy]," his own improvement on Joachim's motto, "Frei aber einsam [Free but lonely]."[1]

Of the three *Ballades* in Opus 10 only the first has a definite title. Brahms marked it "after the Scotch ballad *Edward*," and referred to Herder's collection, *Stimmen der Völker* (Voices of the Peoples). Hermann Deiters wrote of this group of *Ballades:* "Brahms tries even in this early work to build a bridge as it were between instrumental and vocal art, or rather to declare that music without words perfectly suffices him for the ex-

[1] See the discussion of this and the other three Brahms symphonies in the author's *Great Symphonies: How to Recognize and Remember Them*, pp. 185-215.

pression of what impels him to composition, that to him it expresses the same."

Certainly the *Edward Ballade* fits perfectly the content of the famous folk tale of the young man who killed his father, first hiding the truth, explaining that the blood was that of his hawk, then of his horse, and finally cursing his mother for impelling him to commit the crime. The music has a definite suggestion of question and answer, as in the original ballad, and the repetition of the name, "Edward, Edward," at the end of the first line of each stanza is clearly imitated by Brahms. Some of the traditional Scotch words can almost be fitted to the notes:

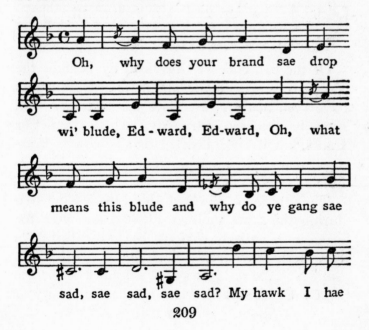

kill'd him, I hae kill'd my hawk, Oh, mith-

er, I kill'd him, and I had nae mair.

Your hawk's blude was ne'er sae red, my

dear - est son, your hawk's blude was

ne'er sae red, my dear - est son.

Of the two concert *Overtures* by Brahms the *Tragic* is programmatic only in its title. Attempts have been made to associate the *Overture* with some definite hero of tragedy, such as Hamlet or Faust, but Brahms insisted that he was expressing tragedy itself, not portraying any tragic person or event.

The *Academic Festival Overture* was written during the same summer (1880), and here the program is entirely obvious. Brahms called it "a very jolly *potpourri* of students' songs à la Suppé." It was his way of acknowledging the Ph.D. degree awarded him by the University of

Breslau. Since all the tunes of this *Overture* originally had words it is enough to adapt or quote them directly. Certainly there is nothing difficult or abstruse about the sunny, exuberant *Academic Festival Overture*.

After a brief introduction, slightly reminiscent of the *Rakoczy March,* the first student song is played by the brass: *Wir hatten gebauet ein stattliches Haus* (We had built a stately house).

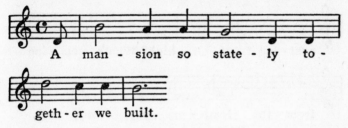

Then comes the beautiful *Landesvater* (Country Father), introduced by the second violins:

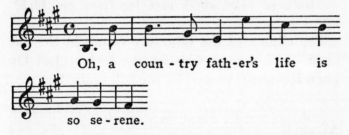

The familiar *Freshman Song* (*Fuchslied*) receives a comic treatment from the bassoons. Its world-famous tune is basically the same as our *Farmer in the Dell.* The original words are nonsensical, starting with the question, "Was kommt dort von der Höh'?" and answering it with the Herr Papa, the Frau Mamma and other members of the family, all modified by the adjective *ledern* (leathern).

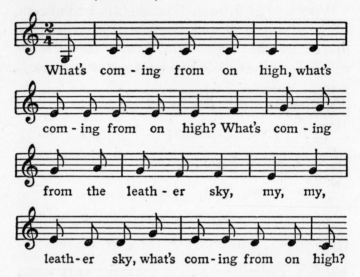

The climax of the *Overture* comes in the old Latin student song, *Gaudeamus Igitur* (Let Us Then Rejoice), played by the full orchestra:

212

Most of the other German and Austrian composers of the nineteenth century wrote program music, but little of it is worth quoting until the modern Richard Strauss is reached, and he is too important to be passed over lightly at this point. The waltzes of Johann Strauss (1825–1899) are all programmatic, as witness such titles as *The Beautiful Blue Danube, Tales of the Vienna Woods, Artists' Life, Wine, Women and Song, Viennese Blood, The Thousand and One Nights, Roses of the South*, etc. No help is needed to make these melodies easily remembered.

The Hungarian, Carl Goldmark (1830–1915), is remembered for his *Rustic Wedding Symphony*, whose five movements bear the titles *Wedding March, Bridal Song, Serenade, In the Garden* and *Dance*, and for the *Overtures, Sakuntala, In Spring, Penthesilea, Prometheus Bound* and *Sappho*, all respectable program music. Otto Nicolai (1810–1849) is known today only by his *Overture* to *The Merry Wives of Windsor*, but this is an excellent piece, containing one tune which is a definite ancestor of the *Marcheta* of modern popular music:

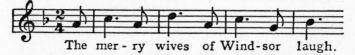

The mer-ry wives of Wind-sor laugh.

Joachim Raff (1822–1882) had the distinction of acting as assistant to Liszt and actually supplied many details of technique and instrumentation to the master's works. Raff's own music was largely programmatic. Of his eleven symphonies nine have titles, including the two best known, *Im Walde* (In the Forest) and *Lenore*. He also wrote a cycle of twelve piano pieces under the title *Angele's Last Day in the Convent,* another dozen called *Messengers of Spring,* an eclogue, *From Switzerland,* etc. A violin solo, *La Fée d'Amour* (The Love Fairy) was popularized by Sarasate. Raff even gave a title to a string quartet, his seventh, called *Die schöne Müllerin* (The Beautiful Maid of the Mill), and he wrote four *Overtures* on Shakespearean subjects: *Romeo and Juliet, Othello, Macbeth* and *The Tempest.*

Adolf Jensen (1837–1879) was a follower of Schumann and gave titles to many of his piano pieces, such as *Romantic Studies, Inner Voices, Travel Pictures, Idyls, Carnival Scenes, Wedding Music, Recollections* and *Erotikon.* The last series contains seven numbers, called *Cassandra, The Sorceress, Galatea, Electra, Lament for Adonis, Eros* and *Cypris.*

Czechoslovakia has contributed two important composers of program music, Friedrich Smetana (1824–1884) and Antonin Dvořák (1841–1904). Smetana survives not only in the gay and charming *Overture* to his opera, *The Bartered Bride,* but in an autobiographical string quartet called *Aus meinem Leben* (From my Life) and in the fine orchestral composition, *My Fatherland*. This piece is in six parts, of which the most popular is the second, *Ultava*, representing the river Moldau. Here is its chief theme:

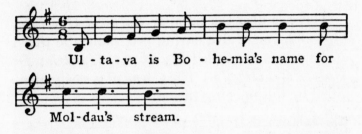

Ul - ta-va is Bo - he-mia's name for Mol-dau's stream.

Dvořák is far better known than Smetana, chiefly through his symphony, *From the New World*, which has some programmatic significance. At least it contains themes of Negro origin, one of which directly echoes the spiritual, *Swing Low, Sweet Chariot*. The famous *Largo* has been treated to several sets of words, leading to the mistaken notion that this also is Negro material. The *Finale* contains a definite echo of "Yankee Doodle" in the development of the main theme.[2]

Dvořák has written more obvious program music in his smaller works. The *Slavonic Dances*, originally piano duets, might easily lend some of their familiar melodies to words.

[2]This symphony is fully discussed and interpreted on pp. 258–67 of the author's *Great Symphonies: How to Recognize and Remember Them.*

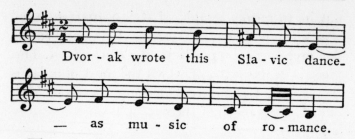

Dvor - ak wrote this Sla - vic dance —

— as mu - sic of ro - mance.

There is also the popular *Carnival Overture,*
Opus 92, one of five having programmatic titles.
(The others are called *My Home, Husitzka, In
Nature* and *Othello.*) The *Carnival* is easily iden-
tified by this opening theme:

Dvořák's five *Symphonic Poems* all have titles,
mostly with detailed programs added. The most
elaborate is that of *The Wild Dove,* a rather
gruesome story of the peasant woman who poisons her husband and marries another, only to kill
herself eventually in a fit of remorse brought on
by the cooing of the wild dove over her husband's
grave.

The other stories are equally horrible, or even
more so, under such disarming titles as *The
Water-Fay* (which includes drowning and in-
fanticide), *The Mid-day Witch* (another baby

killed) and *The Golden Spinning Wheel* (with murder and mutilation nicely combined). Only the *Heldenlied* (Heroic Song) gets along without a detailed program and presumably with a cheerful background.

Dvořák's piano pieces include such titles as *Silhouettes, From the Bohemian Forest* and *Poetic Mood Pictures.* He wrote eight *Humoresques,* of which the seventh is the familiar one. Among his string quartets is one generally known as *American,* containing themes of Negro character, as well as ragtime effects.

A minor Czech composer, Zdenko Fibich (1850–1900), turned out a number of *Symphonic Poems* and other program music but is remembered chiefly by his *Poème* for violin, whose melody became the popular song, *My Moonlight Madonna*—a fairly adequate interpretation.

Niels W. Gade (1817–1890) was the first Scandinavian composer to achieve prominence,[3] and much of his music was programmatic. His very first work was an *Overture* called *Echoes from Ossian* (1841), and four later *Overtures* had the titles *In the Highlands, Hamlet, Michelangelo* and *A Mountain Excursion in the North.*

A set of five smaller orchestral pieces, under the general heading of *A Summer Day in the Country,* covers such subjects as *Stormy, Forest*

[3]See Schumann's musical tribute, p. 118.

Solitude and *Evening: Merry Life of the People.*
Gade's piano pieces have some programmatic
titles like *Aquarelles* and *Northern Tone Pictures.*

Of the minor Scandinavian composers Johann
Svendsen produced four *Norwegian Rhapsodies,*
an *Overture* to *Romeo and Juliet* and other orchestral pieces with such titles as *Carnival in
Paris* and *Wedding Feast.* Christian Sinding,
who taught for a time at the Eastman School of
Music in Rochester, is best known in America by
his descriptive piano piece, *Frühlingsrauschen*
(Rustle of Spring), much played by students
who have acquired the necessary technique:

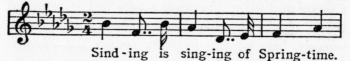

Sind-ing is sing-ing of Spring-time.

But the prince of program music in Norway
(and for that matter the whole Scandinavian
peninsula) was Edvard Grieg (1843–1907). His
strong feeling for folk music made it difficult for
him to write in the absolute style, although he has
excellent sonatas, chamber music and an outstanding piano concerto to his credit. Grieg, however, will probably be remembered most enthusiastically for his songs and his programmatic
instrumental pieces.

His incidental music to Ibsen's drama of *Peer
Gynt* appears on concert programs in the form of

two *Suites,* containing much familiar and deservedly popular material. The four best-known numbers are *Morning, Asa's Death, Anitra's Dance* and *In the Hall of the Mountain King.* The first is merely a bit of nature painting in tones, thematically limited but consistently charming.

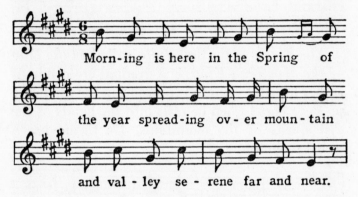

Morn-ing is here in the Spring of the year spread-ing ov-er moun-tain and val-ley se-rene far and near.

Asa (pronounced Osa) is Peer Gynt's mother, and her death is portrayed in powerful chords of solemn dignity:

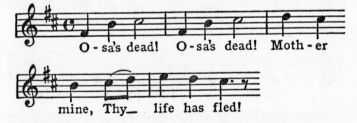

O-sa's dead! O-sa's dead! Moth-er mine, Thy_ life has fled!

Anitra is a desert maiden with whom the scapegrace hero falls in love during his fantastic travels. Her dance music has something of the Oriental quality:

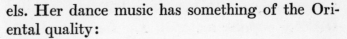

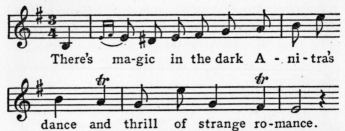

There's ma-gic in the dark A - ni-tra's dance and thrill of strange ro-mance.

The *Finale* of the first *Suite,* called *In the Hall of the Mountain King,* is a gradual crescendo of rather horrible sounds, representing the torturing of Peer Gynt when he falls into the hands of the evil spirits of the mountains. Its theme has a weird monotony:

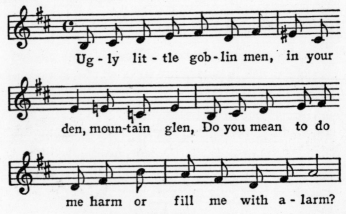

Ug - ly lit - tle gob - lin men, in your den, moun-tain glen, Do you mean to do me harm or fill me with a - larm?

Two *Elegiac Melodies* for string orchestra by Grieg have become very popular, and both are good examples of program music requiring only

a title to convey its meaning. The first is called
Heart Wounds:

Of pain we know that in time it

must go, But what of the pain of our

heart wounds?

The second has the title *The Last Spring:*

When all the world is at peace, mak-

ing wars to cease, 'twill be Spring time

Grieg's small compositions for the piano
mostly have definite titles and their popularity is
enormous. Best known, perhaps, are his *Papillon*
(Butterfly), *Norwegian Bridal Procession, To
Spring, Sailor's Song, Erotik, Berceuse, Wedding Day at Troldhaugen* and *March of the
Dwarfs.* Their principal melodies follow:

PAPILLON

NORWEGIAN BRIDAL PROCESSION

TO SPRING

Ev' - ry thing joins the song to Spring

EROTIK

BERCEUSE

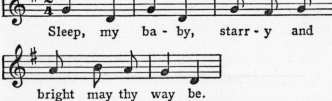

Sleep, my ba - by, starr - y and

bright may thy way be.

MARCH OF THE DWARFS

WEDDING DAY AT TROLDHAUGEN

There's a wed-ding at Trold-hau-gen and we're

222

all going to go, Ev-'ry fel-low has

his girl and ev-'ry girl has her beau.

SAILOR'S SONG[4]

Yo heave ho! The salt spray flies

and the trade winds blow.

Among the French composers of program music three men stand out prominently: Georges Bizet (1838–1875), Camille Saint-Saëns (1835–1921) and Claude Debussy (1862–1918). The last named is really the founder of the modern school of music and should therefore be saved for consideration with that group. Bizet wrote magnificent program music in the *Overture* and instrumental interludes of his popular opera, *Carmen*. It clearly paints the bull ring at the start and then suggests various phases of the familiar story of the gypsy cigarette girl and her lovers.

But more important as program music are the

[4]A complete arrangement of the *Sailor's Song,* for male chorus is published by Sprague-Coleman, New York.

two *Suites* of incidental compositions for Daudet's play, *L'Arlesienne* (1872). The first begins with an *Overture* based upon an old Provençal Christmas carol, *The March of the Three Kings*, suiting the Christmas atmosphere of the play.

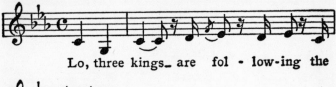

Lo, three kings⸺ are fol - low-ing the

star.⸺

The second movement is a *Minuet,* also suggestive of folk music, with a *Trio* of the *Musette* type, implying a bagpipe accompaniment:

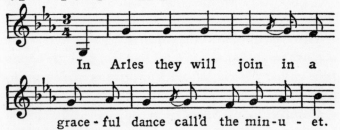

In Arles they will join in a

grace - ful dance call'd the min-u - et.

Next comes a *Romanza Adagietto* depicting the love scene of an aged shepherd with the sweetheart of his youth. It takes the form of a tender duet between wood wind and strings.

The first *L'Arlesienne Suite* ends with a *Carillon,* representing the bells of Christmas Eve. Three tones are repeated against a dance theme in the strings, with a pastoral section for contrast.

The second *Suite* contains an *Intermezzo,* whose melody is often sung as an *Agnus Dei:*

Ag - nus De - i, qui tol - lis pe -

ca - ta mun-di.

The most popular movement of the second *Suite* is the *Farandole,* a lively Spanish dance.

(This tune is preceded by *The March of the Three Kings.*)

Bizet wrote two other *Suites, Roma* and *Jeux d'Enfance* (Games of Childhood), and an *Overture* called *Patrie,* all with programmatic significance.

Camille Saint-Saëns is perhaps the most satisfactory of the French romanticists, for his programs are always definite and picturesque. His four *Symphonic Poems* are a significant link between those of Liszt and the modern masterpieces of Richard Strauss.

The first is called *The Spinning Wheel of Omphale* (*Le Rouet d'Omphale*), originally written as a *Rondo* for piano. The composer gives this description of the work: "The subject of this symphonic poem is feminine seductiveness, the triumphant contest of feebleness against strength. The spinning wheel is merely a pretext, chosen only for the sake of the rhythm and the general turn of the piece. Those interested in the examination of details will see . . . Hercules groaning in the bonds which he cannot break and . . . Omphale mocking at the vain efforts of the hero."

For his second *Symphonic Poem* Saint-Saëns chose the subject of *Phaeton,* for which he wrote this introduction: "Phaeton got permission to drive in heaven the chariot of the sun, his father. But his unskilled hands made the horses go astray. The flamboyant chariot, thrown out of its course, approached the terrestrial regions. The whole universe is about to be set on fire when Jupiter strikes the imprudent Phaeton with his thunderbolt."

From the standpoint of the listener the *Danse Macabre* of Saint-Saëns is the perfect *Symphonic Poem,* and it therefore deserves a detailed analysis and interpretation.

Here is one of the clearest and most exciting pieces of program music in the entire literature of the art. It is predominantly narrative, as the music illustrates a definite sequence of events. But it also has a strong descriptive quality and more of actual imitation than would ever be permitted in absolute music.

The title is generally translated as *Dance of Death* but could equally well mean *Ghost Dance* or *Dance of the Skeletons.* It is an honestly macabre piece of music but with a curiously morbid humor and touches of actual burlesque.

Saint-Saëns' music was directly inspired by a poem of Henri Cazalis, with the same title, which he quotes in full. It could be freely translated thus:

Zig, zig, zig, Death in grim rhythm
Beats with a bony hand upon the graves.
Death at the hour of midnight plays a waltz,
Zig, zig, zig, upon his weirdly tuned fiddle.
The night is dark, and the wintry winds are
    sighing;
Moans of the dead are heard through the linden
    trees.
Through the darkness the white skeletons dart,
Leaping and dancing in their spectral shrouds.
Zig, zig, zig, each ghost is gaily dancing;
The bones are cracking rhythmically on the tomb-
    stones.
Then suddenly the dance is at an end.
The cock has crowed! Dawn interrupts the dance
    of Death.

This vivid program is faithfully followed by the composer. At the start of the *Symphonic Poem* the twelve strokes of the clock are heard upon the harp with a background of soft chords.

Whispered octaves in the bass suggest the opening of the graves. Then suddenly Death is heard tuning his fiddle, with the E string half a tone flat. The "zig, zig" of the original poem would seem to fit this weird tuning:

Zig, zig, zig, zig, zig, zig,
zig - a - zig zig, zig - a - zig zig,
zig - a - zig zig zig.

Two abrupt pizzicato (plucked) chords in the strings introduce the first waltz melody, a lively tune in minor key, featuring the flute and then taken up by the violins:

Dance up - on the grave, all ye tim - id
spir - its, It is Death him - self play - ing
you a tune; Be a lit - tle brave, all

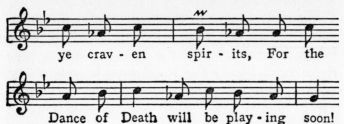

ye crav - en spir - its, For the

Dance of Death will be play - ing soon!

This leads to a second theme by the solo violin, also in minor key, the chief melody of the piece. It has been called a parody of the Latin *Dies Irae*, and it is possible that Saint-Saëns had this famous melody in mind, although his broad tune is far more attractive:

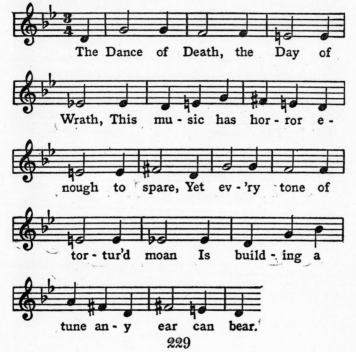

The Dance of Death, the Day of

Wrath, This mu - sic has hor - ror e -

nough to spare, Yet ev - 'ry tone of

tor - tur'd moan Is build - ing a

tune an - y ear can bear.

These two themes alternate, with occasional interruptions of the tuning violin, working up to a fugal effect in the lower strings and then a melodious imitation by the wood wind in major key, with flowing accompaniment. The solo violin of Death enters once more with a new note of pathos, which is taken up by the whole orchestra. This leads into chromatic runs that suggest the whistling of the wind through the trees, after which the composer gives himself up unreservedly to a development of the two leading themes in counterpoint, arriving at a series of effective chords, played by alternating strings and wind instruments.

Chromatic runs again suggest the sighing of the wind or perhaps the shrieks of the spirits, and the tuning violin develops a new melodic idea:

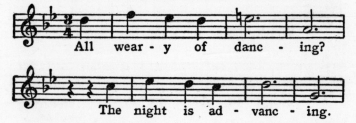

There is a recapitulation of both melodies, in harmony with each other, and a long *Coda* starts with a surprising variation of the main theme. The dance has reached its climax, with the xylophone realistically imitating the actual sound of bones on tombstones. A series of fortissimo chords

breaks off suddenly as the sound of a crowing
rooster is heard, represented by the oboe:

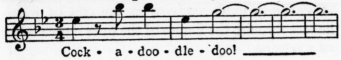

Cock · a · doo · dle · doo! _____

Soft *agitato* chords indicate the scurrying of
the ghosts back into their graves. Once more the
solo violin is heard, this time quite sadly, as
though Death regretted the whole disturbance:

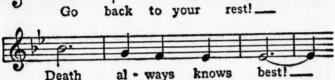

Go   back   to your   rest! ___

Death   al · ways   knows   best! ___

Under a long trill, dying away, the violas timidly suggest the opening waltz, echoed by the
second violins and then still more hesitatingly by
the top strings, with a tentative pizzicato by the
bass viols. Two soft, abrupt chords, and the
Danse Macabre is ended.

A similarly detailed analysis may be made of
any piece of program music if the listener is thor-
oughly familiar with the thematic materials.
Saint-Saëns wrote one more *Symphonic Poem,*
which he called *The Youth of Hercules,* with this
program: "Legend: Mythology states that on
entering life Hercules saw opening before him
two paths—the path of pleasure and the path of

virtue. Unmoved by the seductions of the Nymphs and Bacchantes, the hero enters the road of struggles and combats, at the end of which he sees through the flames of the pyre immortality as a reward."

There is both humor and realism in the Saint-Saëns *Suite, Carnival of the Animals,* which contains the popular melody, *The Swan,* originally written as a cello solo and since transcribed in many ways:

Float-ing like mist in the ear - ly dawn,

White on the wa - ter glides a grace-ful swan.

Among the other animals described in this charming *Suite* are lions, fishes, turtles and even critics. The program music of Saint-Saëns also includes a *Suite Algérienne,* a *Rhapsodie d'Auvergne,* a *Fantasia* for piano and orchestra called *Africa* and various short pieces with descriptive titles, *Songs without Words,* etc.

César Franck (1822–1890) contributed some significant works to program music, although he was essentially a composer of the absolute type. The first of three *Symphonic Poems* was called *Les Eolides* (The Daughters of Aeolus), inspired by some poetic lines of Lecomte de Lisle. The music, like the poetry, has a delicate, airy quality, suggesting the offspring of the god of the winds.

Le Chasseur Maudit (The Wild Huntsman), second of the *Symphonic Poems* of César Franck, is based on Bürger's ballad of the same name (*Der Wilde Jäger*), imitated also by Sir Walter Scott. The composer sums up the program in four sections: "It was Sunday morning; from afar sounded the joyous ringing of the bells and the glad songs of the people. . . . Sacrilege! The wild count of the Rhine has wound his horn.

"The chase dashes through cornfields, brakes and meadows. Stop, Count, I pray, hear the pious songs! No! And the horsemen rush onward like the whirlwind.

"Suddenly the count is alone; his horse will go no further; he blows his horn and the horn sounds no longer. . . . A lugubrious, implacable voice curses him: 'Sacrilege!' it says, 'thou shalt be forever hunted through Hell.'

"Then flames dart from everywhere. The count, maddened by terror, flees, faster and faster, pursued by a pack of devils."

Les Djinns (evil spirits of Arabian mythology) is César Franck's third *Symphonic Poem,* using the piano along with the orchestra. Its program is to be found in Victor Hugo's poem of the same name in *Les Orientales.* The Djinns are depicted as a hideous army of vampires and dragons, driven by the north wind, filling the air with infernal howls and groans.

César Franck is best known by his popular symphony in D minor, which has no program. But he wrote another symphony, called *Psyche,* for chorus and orchestra, and its instrumental parts are definitely program music. These include a *Prelude* (*The Sleep of Psyche*), *The Abduction of Psyche by the Zephyrs, Joy of Nature in the Gardens of Eros, Love Scene, Suffering of Psyche* and *Psyche after Her Pardon.*

The *Prelude* to Franck's *Redemption* also has a program that is almost too ambitious: "The centuries pass. Joy of the world, which transforms itself and expands under the word of Christ. In vain the era of persecutions opens. Faith triumphs over all obstacles. But the modern hour has struck. Belief is lost; man, once more a prey to the fierce desire for pleasure, for sterile agitations, has found the passions of another age."

Among other French composers of program music Edouard Lalo (1823–1892) is remembered for his fine *Overture* to *Le Roi d'Ys* and the violin concerto known as *Symphonie Espagnole,* which uses a folk tune, *The Silversmith,* in its *Finale.* He also wrote a *Norwegian Fantasie,* a *Russian Concerto* and a *Norwegian Rhapsodie,* as well as some descriptive piano pieces.

Emanuel Chabrier (1841–1894) rests his reputation on one highly effective piece of program music, the *Spanish Rhapsody* (*España*) whose chief theme was contributed by Waldteufel, later borrowed, along with one of Lalo's themes, for the nonsensical *Ti-pi-tin* of Tin Pan Alley. Chabrier's typically Spanish tunes are the following:

Lis - ten how mus - ic gets the

bold rhy - thm of cas - ta - nets.

Ti - pi - tin tin tin, _ ti-pi - tin tin tin. _

Just be - gin, ti - pi - tin,

it comes right in ti - pi - tin.

Ti - pi - ti - pi tin, ti - pi - tin,

ti - pi - ti - pi tin, ti - pi - tin.

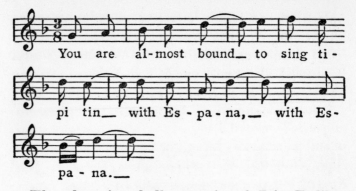

The charming ballet music of Léo Delibes (1836–1891) should not be overlooked. His *Coppélia* and *Sylvia* both contain material of legitimate popularity, and the waltz from *Naila* has become familiar in piano transcriptions.

Jules Massenet (1842–1912) is primarily an operatic composer, with the *Meditation* from *Thais* indelibly impressed on all music lovers' memories as a hackneyed violin solo:

But Massenet wrote a lot of real program music, too, including the *Symphonic Poem, Visions,* the *Fantasia, Pompeia,* the *Overture, Phèdre,* and *Suites* with such titles as *Les Erynnies (The Fates), Scènes Pittoresques, Scènes Dramatiques, Hungarian,* etc.

Benjamin Godard (1849–1895) is responsible not only for the familiar *Berceuse* from *Jocelyn* (known in every variety of instrumental arrangement) but for three symphonies named respectively *Legendary, Gothic* and *Oriental,* a *Tasso* for orchestra and chorus and a *Suite* of *Scènes Poétiques.*

Truly important as a composer of program music is Vincent d'Indy (1851–1931), whose symphonic variations, *Istar,* tell in music a complete story from the Babylonian epic, *Izdabar.* His *Symphony on a French Mountain Theme, Overture* to *Anthony and Cleopatra,* symphonic trilogy, *Wallenstein,* and other works are significant contributions to tonal narration and description.

Gustave Charpentier and Charles Gounod might also be mentioned among the French composers of program music, the former for his orchestral *Suite, Impressions of Italy,* and the latter for the popular little *Funeral March of a Marionette.*

Cécile Chaminade, one of the world's few feminine composers of prominence, has to her credit a number of minor works of programmatic significance, including the popular *Scarf Dance, The Flatterer, Autumn, Pas des Amphores,* etc.[5]

Italy has not contributed much to recent program music, being still occupied chiefly with operatic traditions. Verdi, of course, has programmatic passages in the instrumental portions

[5]Debussy, Ravel and Paul Dukas will be found among the modern composers, pp. 292–307.

of his operas, and so has Puccini. Ponchielli's *Dance of the Hours* is an effective and colorful piece, justly popular. The most famous individual number is unquestionably the *Intermezzo* from Mascagni's *Cavalleria Rusticana,* which presents, with its peaceful melody, a dramatic contrast to the brutal passions of the two acts of that realistic opera. There are two melodies in the *Intermezzo:*

England has done far more for program music, after a long silence, dating back to the days of Henry Purcell. William Sterndale Bennett (1816–1875) was greatly admired by Schumann for his programmatic *Overtures, Parisina, The Naiads, The Wood Nymph* and *Paradise and the Peri.* This last piece has its meaning emphasized by excerpts from the poem of Thomas Moore. Bennett also wrote piano pieces with programs, such as the *Three Musical Sketches* bearing the titles *Lake, Mill-Stream* and *Fountain* and the sonata called *The Maid of Orleans,* each movement of which has a quotation from Schiller's play prefixed to it.

Sir Charles Villiers Stanford (1852–1924), of Irish birth, wrote five symphonies, of which four have programmatic titles: *Elegiac, Irish, Thro' Youth to Strife, Thro' Death to Life* and *L'Allegro ed Il Pensieroso*. His *Overture, Queen of the Seas,* was composed for the Armada Tercentenary.

Sir Arthur Sullivan (1842–1900) not only indicated the programs of his Gilbertian operas in their *Overtures,* which are generally medleys of the outstanding tunes, but also wrote an *Irish Symphony,* an *Overture* called *In Memoriam,* inspired by his father's death, as well as the *Overtures* to *Marmion, Macbeth,* etc., and incidental music for *The Tempest, The Merchant of Venice, The Merry Wives of Windsor, Henry VIII, Macbeth* and *King Arthur.*

Granville Bantock is considered an extremist of program music and has been accused of going too far in the direction of realism. His greatest works are choral, but he has managed to express many definite ideas through such instrumental music as *The Witch of Atlas, The Great God Pan,* the *Overtures, Eugene Aram, Cain* and *Belshazzar* and the tone poems, *Thalaba, the Destroyer, Dante, Fifine at the Fair, Hudibras* and *Lalla Rookh.*

Another distinguished English composer of program music is Frederick Delius (1863–1932), whose most popular orchestral piece has the intriguing title, *On Hearing the First Cuckoo in Spring*.

But it is Sir Edward Elgar (1857–1934) who stands out among the musicians of Great Britain for his creative works in general and particularly for those of programmatic content. Most famous are his *Enigma Variations,* whose theme is "a counterpoint on some well-known melody, which is never heard (and remains unrevealed by the composer). The variations are the theme seen through the personalities of friends." Fanciful names, like Ysobel, Troyte, Dorabella and Nimrod, are used to designate these friends, often merely initials.

There is good program music also in Elgar's *Overtures, Cockaigne (In London Town), Froissart* (inspired by a passage in Scott's *Old Mortality*) and *In the South* (containing impressions of Italy, especially "on a glorious afternoon in the Vale of Andora, with streams, flowers and hills, the distant snow mountains in one direction and the blue Mediterranean in the other").

Elgar's most popular piece, however, is unquestionably the *March* known as *Pomp and Circumstance,* one of two bearing the same title, written for the Coronation of King Edward VII. The quotation is from Shakespeare's *Othello* (Act III, Scene 3): "Pride, pomp and circumstance of glorious war!" At the head of the score the composer placed this verse:

Like a proud music that draws men to die,
Madly upon the spears in martial ecstasy,
A measure that sets heaven in all their veins
And iron in their hands.

This march is best known by the stately melody of the *Trio,* which is often sung to words and has acquired in England almost the significance of a national anthem.

America's outstanding composer, specializing likewise in program music, is Edward Macdowell (1861–1908). His four piano sonatas have the titles *Tragic, Heroic, Norse* and *Keltic.* To the second of these the composer prefixed the motto *Flos regum Arthuris* and wrote: "While not exactly program music, I had in mind the Arthurian legend when writing this work. The first movement typifies the coming of Arthur. The *Scherzo* was suggested by a picture of Doré's showing a knight in the woods surrounded by elves. The third movement was suggested by my idea of Guinevere. That following represents the passing of Arthur."

The *Norse Sonata* is preceded by verses which include these lines:

Rang out a Skald's strong voice, with tales of
battles won,
Of Gudrun's love and Sigurd, Siegmund's son.

Similarly the *Keltic Sonata* has a poetic superscription:

Who minds now Keltic tales of yore,
Dark Druid rhymes that thrall,
Deidré's song and wizard lore
Of great Cuchullin's fall?

Two orchestral *Suites* by Macdowell are decidedly programmatic. The first has its four movements titled *In a Haunted Forest, Summer Idyl, The Shepherdess' Song* and *Forest Spirits.* The second is called *Indian* and has the individual titles *Legend, Love Song, In War Time, Dirge* and *Village Festival,* with some use of actual Indian themes.

Other programmatic orchestral pieces by Macdowell are *The Saracens, The Lovely Aldá* (after the *Song of Roland*), *Hamlet, Ophelia* and a *Symphonic Poem* called *Lancelot and Elaine.* Of the last work Macdowell said, "I would never have insisted that this *Symphonic Poem* need mean Lancelot and Elaine to everyone. It did to me, however, and in the hope that my artistic enjoyment might be shared by others I added the title to my music." (This is a significant hint as to the way in which a great deal of program music has come to life.)

The popularity of Edward Macdowell, however, rests largely upon his little piano pieces, all fitted with descriptive or suggestive titles and all, therefore, to some extent programmatic. These pieces appear in groups, with each group under a general name, like *Forest Idyls, Little Poems, Les Orientales, Marionettes, Moon Pictures* (after Hans Christian Andersen) and *Fireside Tales*. The best-known volumes are the *Woodland Sketches, Sea Pieces* and *New England Idyls*.

The most popular of them all is, of course, the simple, tender nature study *To a Wild Rose,* played by countless piano students:

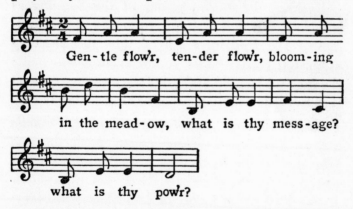

Gen-tle flow'r, ten-der flow'r, bloom-ing

in the mead-ow, what is thy mess-age?

what is thy pow'r?

This is the first of the *Woodland Sketches* and is followed by *Will-o'-the-Wisp, At an Old Trysting Place, In Autumn* and *From an Indian*

Lodge. Then comes another great favorite, *To a Water-Lily,* whose melody is slow and serene, suggesting the calmly floating flower:

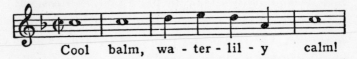

Cool   balm, wa - ter - lil - y   calm!

The set of *Sea Pieces* begins with *To the Sea,* with the superscription: "Ocean, thou mighty monster." The second is *From a Wandering Iceberg,* preceded by the lines:

An errant princess of the north, a virgin, snowy white,
Sails adown the summer seas to realms of burning light.

Perhaps the most popular of the *Sea Pieces* is the one called *A.D. 1620,* referring to the landing of the Pilgrim Fathers. The introductory quotation reads: "The yellow setting sun melts the lazy sea to gold and gilds the swaying galleon that towards a land of promise lunges hugely on." The opening theme seems to express this thought:

Gold sway - ing galle - on lung - ing

huge - ly on.

In the second part of *A.D. 1620* the melody definitely suggests that of *God Save the King,* which later became *America,* and Mrs Macdowell herself has assured the author that her husband actually had this connection in mind. The tune is given a stately march rhythm, with only a slight change in the melodic line:

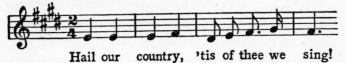

Hail our country, 'tis of thee we sing!

The fourth *Sea Piece* is called *Starlight,* with this inscription: "The stars are but the cherubs that sing about the throne of gray old Ocean's spouse, fair Moon's pale majesty."

Next comes another favorite, designated merely as *Song,* with a superscription that exactly fits the opening phrases of the music:

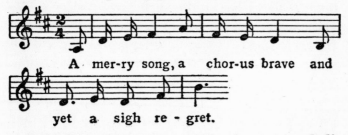

A mer-ry song, a chor-us brave and yet a sigh re - gret.

(The first eight notes of this piece are melodically duplicated in the *Autumn* of Chaminade, Bizet's *Habanera* from *Carmen* and Victor Herbert's *Beatrice Barefacts,* a solid argument against the absurd claims of plagiarism that pester the modern composer, particularly of popular music, since these identities are obviously accidental.)

The remaining *Sea Pieces* are *From the Depths* ("And who shall sound the mystery of the sea?"), *Nautilus* ("A fairy sail and a fairy boat") and *In Mid-Ocean* ("Inexorable! Thou straight line of eternal fate, that ringst the world whilst on thy moaning breast we play our puny parts and reckon us immortal").

Since Macdowell's death much important program music has been written in the United States, and contemporary composers in general seem to have a leaning toward that form of expression. Charles Martin Loeffler, a transplanted Alsatian, set a high standard with his *Pagan Poem* and *The Death of Tintagiles.* Charles T. Griffes died at the very outset of a promising career but already had to his credit such fine works as *The Pleasure Dome of Kubla Khan* and *The White Peacock.* John Alden Carpenter wrote a piece of program music, *Adventures in a Perambulator,* whose preface is almost as fascinating as the music itself. It views the world from the standpoint of a baby, and a Chicago baby at that. A few random quotations can hardly be resisted: "Out is wonderful! It is always different, though one seems to have been there before. . . . It is confusing, but it is Life! For instance, the Policeman—an Unprecedented Man! Round like a ball;

taller than my Father. Blue—fearful—fascinating! I feel him before he comes. I see him after he goes. I try to analyze his appeal. It is not buttons alone, nor belt, nor baton. I suspect it is his eye and the way he walks. He walks like Doom. My nurse feels it too. She becomes less firm, less powerful. My perambulator hurries, hesitates and stops. They converse. They ask each other questions—some with answers, some without. I listen with discretion. When I feel that they have gone far enough I signal to my nurse, a private signal, and the Policeman resumes his enormous blue march. He is gone, but I feel him after he goes.

"Then suddenly there is something else. I think it is a sound. We approach it. My ear is tickled to excess. I find that the absorbing noise comes from a box—something like my music box, only much larger and on wheels. A dark man is turning the music out of the box with a handle, just as I do with mine. A dark lady, richly dressed, turns when the man gets tired. They both smile. I smile, too, with restraint, for music is the most insidious form of noise. And such music! So gay! I tug at the strap over my stomach. I have a wild thought of dancing with my nurse and my perambulator —all three of us together. Suddenly, at the climax of our excitement, I feel the approach of a phenomenon that I remember. It is the Policeman. He has stopped the music. He has frightened away the dark man and the lady with their music box. He seeks the admiration of my nurse for his act. He walks away; his buttons shine; but far off I hear again the forbidden music. Delightful, forbidden music!"

In these notes, both literary and musical, Carpenter proved that program music need not be limited to bird songs and battle sounds, nor even to the conventional descriptions of nature. He went even further in the direction of satirical comedy with his *Krazy Kat* ballet and showed the serious possibilities of his tone painting in *Skyscrapers* and *The Birthday of the Infanta.*

Douglas Moore has also introduced effective comedy into his *P. T. Barnum Suite.* There is real charm in Deems Taylor's *Through the Looking Glass.* Henry Hadley's *Overture, In Bohemia,* is perhaps his most popular composition. Aaron Copland found a new public when he wrote his *Outdoor Overture* and *El Salon Mexico,* eventually winning success also with motion-picture scores.

Robert Russell Bennett has written an *Abraham Lincoln Symphony,* a *Charleston Rhapsody* and a *Hollywood Scherzo.* Robert Delaney has a *Don Quixote Symphony,* Charles Ives a *Concord Sonata,* Seth Bingham a *Wall Street Fantasy* and George Antheil an *Airplane Sonata.* Other American program music includes Marc Blitzstein's *Jigg-saw,* Ernst Bloch's *Schelomo* and *American Symphony*, Howard Hanson's *Pan and the Priest* and *Nordic Symphony*, John Powell's *Banjo Picker* and *In Old Virginia*, Abram Chasins' *Parade* and *Chinese Pieces*, Emerson Whithorne's *New York Days and Nights*, Ferde Grofé's *Mississippi* and *Grand Canyon Suites*, Roger Sessions' *Black Maskers*, Stillman-Kelley's *New England Symphony* and incidental music to *Ben Hur*, Ernest Schelling's *Victory Ball*, Daniel Gregory Mason's *Chanticleer*, Rubin Goldmark's *Samson*, Henry F. Gilbert's *Dance in the Place Congo* and Charles Wakefield Cadman's *Dark Dancers of the Mardi Gras*.

The greatest popularity along these lines was attained by George Gershwin, whose *Rhapsody in Blue* proved epoch-making in its adaptation of the jazz idiom to serious music. It is hardly definite enough to be called program music, but his later orchestral piece, *An American in Paris*, fully lives up to the requirements of the style. An opening theme suggests the sights and sounds of Paris, interrupted by the horns of taxicabs:

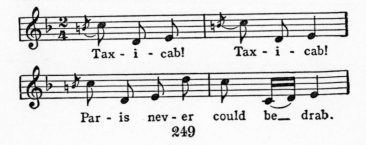

Later comes a blue strain that is typical Gershwin, representing the homesickness of the American in Paris:

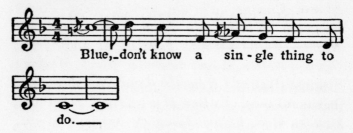

Blue,_don't know a sin-gle thing to do._

In the end the atmosphere of Paris seems to win the argument.

RUSSIAN COMPOSERS OF
PROGRAM MUSIC

RUSSIA has produced so much program music
that it deserves a chapter of its own. It all goes
back to the almost legendary Michael Glinka
(1804–1857), who was largely responsible for
the revived interest in Russian folk music and a
national idiom. Such music lent itself naturally to
a programmatic style. The *Overtures* to Glinka's
operas, *Russlan and Ludmilla* and *A Life for
the Czar,* are often played in concert.

Perhaps even more important as program
music are the incidental pieces written by Glinka
for Koukolnik's drama, Prince Kholmsky, which
have been compared favorably with Beethoven's
work. There is real Russian folk music in
Glinka's *Kamarinskaia,* and he pays a similar
tribute to Spain in his *Jota Aragonesa* and *A
Night in Madrid.*

Glinka's ideas were carried still further in the
direction of realism by Alexander Dargomijsky
(1813–1869), who wrote three programmatic
orchestral pieces, *Kazachok, Baba-Yaga* and a
Dance of Mummers. He was the direct inspiration of the group of five composers who per-

manently established Russian nationalism in music. These five were Balakireff, César Cui, Moussorgsky, Borodin and Rimsky-Korsakoff.

Mily Balakireff (1836–1910), the real founder of the group, exerted an enormous influence throughout musical Russia, although he never fully developed his own extraordinary talents. His best-known work is the *Symphonic Poem, Tamara,* based on a poem by Lermontoff. It tells the story of the beautiful but bloodthirsty queen who entertained her lovers in a high tower on the banks of the Terek River and had their corpses thrown into the water at dawn. Balakireff's other *Symphonic Poem* is called *Russia,* written for the one thousandth anniversary of his native land and based on three national melodies representing different periods of Russian history. He also composed an *Overture* and *Entr'actes* to *King Lear,* an *Overture* on the theme of a *Spanish March* and an *Oriental Fantasia, Islamey,* considered the most difficult music ever written for the piano.

The most interesting and exciting character in this Russian group of five nationalistic composers was Modest Moussorgsky (1839–1881). Often crude in his workmanship, he nevertheless managed to express the soul of the people more convincingly than any of his colleagues. There are instrumental passages in his great opera,

Boris Godounoff, including imitations of the clanging bells of the Kremlin, that create a dramatic realism such as no other Russian composer achieved.

Moussorgsky summed up his own feeling about program music in these words: "To seek assiduously the most delicate and subtle features of human nature, of the human crowd, to follow them into unknown regions, to make them our own; this seems to me the true vocation of the artist. . . . To feed upon humanity as a healthy diet that has been neglected—in this lies the whole problem of art."

The program music of Moussorgsky includes the popular orchestral piece, *A Night on Bald Mountain* (which has even been filmed in a fantastic fashion), a *Turkish March,* various Russian folk dances and the *Pictures from an Exhibition,* a set of ten piano pieces with such titles as *Children's Fun, The Seamstress, In the Village, A Tear,* etc.

Alexander Borodin (1834–1887), like the others in the group, started his musical career as an amateur and never really arrived at a thorough command of technique. But he wrote a fine piece of program music in the symphonic sketch, *On the Steppes of Central Asia.* For this he provided the following explanation: "In the monotonous steppe of Central Asia there are heard the hitherto unknown tones of a peaceful Russian song. From afar comes the trampling of horses and camels and the peculiar sound of an Oriental melody. A native caravan approaches. Protected by Russian arms, it proceeds safe and fearless on its way through the immeasurable desert. Further and further it goes. The song of the Russians and the melody of the Asiatics combine in a common harmony, the echo of which gradually dies away in the air of the steppe."

Some of Borodin's most effective program music occurs in the incidental dances of the opera *Prince Igor,* which are today far better known than the opera as a whole.

César Cui (1835–1918) was primarily a composer of operas, songs and absolute music. His popularity today rests largely upon one small piece of program music called *Orientale,* which has been arranged in a variety of instrumental combinations. Its chief melody is based upon the same Russian folk tune that Tschaikowsky used for his *Marche Slav.*[1]

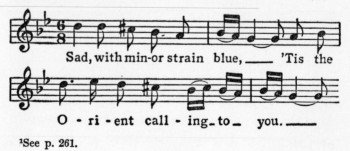

Sad, with min-or strain blue, ____ 'Tis the

O - ri - ent call - ing_ to_ you. ____

[1]See p. 261.

The real scholar and technician of the "five" was Nikolai Rimsky-Korsakoff (1844–1908). Although he created much absolute music he was essentially a master of the programmatic style. His *Symphonic Poems, Sadko* and *Antar,* are both fine examples of program music. The first tells the story of the Russian Orpheus, Sadko, a minstrel, who was thrown overboard during a storm, as a tribute to the king of the seas, but so charmed the king with his music that eventually the entire ocean broke into a dance, which destroyed the ship and did not cease until Sadko tore the strings from his lyre. The hero of *Antar* is an Arab chief and poet of the sixth century who passed through various adventures in pursuit of his love for Abla.

There is also the *Suite* called *Czar Saltan,* in three movements, preceded by quotations from Pushkin. With a *Serbian Fantasia, Russian Easter,* the familiar *Flight of the Bumblebee* and a *Fairy Tale* the program music of Rimsky-Korsakoff includes an effective *Spanish Caprice,* often heard on orchestral programs and one of the best demonstrations of the possibilities of individual instruments.

It is hard to tell whether the tunes of this *Spanish Caprice* are actual folk music or merely clever imitations. The first is an *Alborado* or *Aubade* (Morning Serenade). Then comes a set of variations on a Spanish folk song. The next theme is a typical gypsy song, and the *Caprice* ends in a *Fandango of the Asturias.*

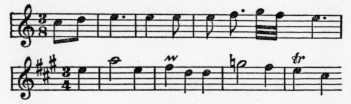

But Rimsky's masterpiece of program music is of course the *Symphonic Suite, Scheherazade,* which gives a vivid musical picture of the *Arabian Nights,* featuring the story of *Sinbad the Sailor.*[2]

A pupil of Rimsky-Korsakoff, Michael Ippolitoff-Ivanoff (1859–1935), won an honored place in the history of program music with his *Caucasian Sketches,* which are played by all the symphony orchestras today. The most popular melody in the *Suite* is probably that of the *March of the Sardar* (Caucasian Chief) whose opening bears a curious resemblance to the verse of Foster's *Old Black Joe:*

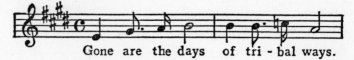

Gone are the days of tri - bal ways.

Another minor Russian composer, Alexander Glazounoff (1865–1936), wrote a quantity of pro-

[2]A complete analysis of this popular work will be found in the author's *Great Symphonies: How to Recognize and Remember Them,* pp. 248-57.

gram music, of which the ballet of *The Seasons* is the best known, chiefly because the great Pavlowa made a feature of the *Autumn Bac-chanale*.

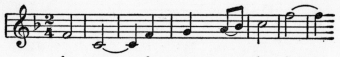

Au - tumn,_when grapes are_glow-ing._

Glazounoff also has to his credit a *Symphonic Poem, Stenka Razin,* two *Fantasias, The Forest* and *The Ocean, Through Night to Light, The Kreml, In Memory of a Hero, Spring,* a *Rhapsodie Orientale* and a *Mediaeval Suite.*

Least Russian and most cosmopolitan in their music were Anton Rubinstein and Tschaikowsky, but both were responsible for some vivid tonal programs. Rubinstein (1830–1894) wrote much absolute music, too, as well as songs and operas. His little *Melody in F* is known to all the world, but it has no definite program. Almost as popular is the piano piece called *Kamenoi-Ostrow,* whose name designates a small, rocky island in the Neva River, below Leningrad, a favorite summer resort. This piece, No. 22 in a series of twenty-four written on the island, is reputedly a portrait of Mme Anna de Friedebourg, to whom it is dedicated. There is the sound of a bell, presumably from the Greek chapel on the island, and a fragment of ancient Hebrew

257

music. The opening melody represents the personality of the lady who inspired it, and a good tune it is:

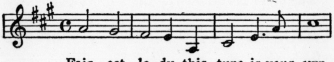

Fair - est la - dy, this tune is your own.

Rubinstein's familiar *Romance* might also be classed as program music, though it scarcely needs quoting.

In Peter Ilitch Tschaikowsky (1840–1893) the climax of Russian music is reached, and much of his work is programmatic. One of his earliest and best compositions is the popular *Fantasie-Overture, Romeo and Juliet,* whose themes had been intended for an actual opera and appeared in a vocal duet representing the second balcony scene.[3]

Tschaikowsky's *Romeo and Juliet* begins with somber music, perhaps suggesting the cell of Friar Laurence. There is a syncopated tumult, to represent the feud between the houses of Montague and Capulet. Then comes the love music, chiefly expressed in two themes. One is delicate and fragile, a mere whisper of youthful sentiment:

[3]This duet is published, with English words by the author, in Kurt Schindler's collection of Russian songs, G. Schirmer, New York.

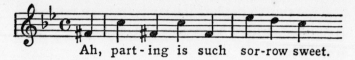

Ah, part - ing is such sor-row sweet.

The other is full of passion, a glorious melody, unfortunately now all too familiar in the fox-trot version of *Our Love:*

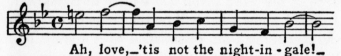

Ah, love,—'tis not the night-in - gale!—

One of Tschaikowsky's first attempts at composition was an *Overture* to the drama of Ostrowsky, *The Thunderstorm,* for which he wrote out a complete and detailed program. Later he composed a *Fantasia* on Shakespeare's *Tempest,* again giving the program in detail.

An important work is the Tschaikowsky *Francesca da Rimini,* perhaps influenced by Liszt's *Dante Symphony,* but based directly on the Italian poem and the Doré pictures. Less significant are a *Hamlet Overture* and the symphonic ballad, *Le Voyevode.*

Like Schumann and other composers Tschaikowsky also tried his luck with *Manfred,* which he called "a symphony in four pictures after the dramatic poem of Byron." Again there is a detailed program, the first movement showing Manfred wandering in the Alps, the second introducing the Witch of the Alps, under the rainbow of the torrent; the third is a simple pastoral, and the fourth depicts the subterranean palace of Arimanes, where he evokes the shade of Astarte and dies.

Tschaikowsky wrote of this work: "After some hesitation I have decided to write *Manfred,* for I feel that I shall have no rest until I have redeemed my word given last winter to Balakireff. I do not know what will be the outcome of it. In the meantime I am dissatisfied with myself. No, it is a thousand times more agreeable to compose without a program. When I write a program symphony I have continually the feeling that I cheat the public and deceive them, that I do not pay with ready money but with worthless paper rags." (Like most composers of program music Tschaikowsky allowed his words and actions to be completely contradictory.)

Of his *Overture 1812,* today one of his most popular pieces, he wrote: "The *Overture* will be very banging and noisy. I wrote it without much love, on which account it is probably without much artistic value." The *Overture* represents Napoleon's attack upon Moscow and uses the tunes of the *Marseillaise* and the Czarist anthem in a musical battle, in which the Russian melody finally triumphs. According to the orchestral directions the noise of drums may be supplemented by actual cannon shots, and this is often done, particularly in outdoor performances of the *Overture.*

Another popular programmatic piece by Tschaikowsky is the *Marche Slav,* whose chief theme is a real Russian folk song, also used by César Cui for his *Orientale.*[4]

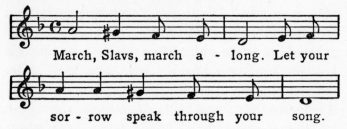

March, Slavs, march a - long. Let your
sor - row speak through your song.

This march likewise introduces the old Russian anthem at the close.

But for program music at its best one has only to listen to the beloved *Nutcracker Suite.* Here is a complete story in music for adults as well as children. It was written originally as a ballet but is now regularly heard as an orchestral concert number, with a great popularity on records and the radio.

Tschaikowsky based this charming music on the Dumas translation of E. T. A. Hoffmann's story, *The Nutcracker and the Mouse King.* The program begins with a Christmas Eve party at the home of little Marie, whose favorite present is a silver nutcracker. But when the boys get to playing rough games the nutcracker is broken, and Marie goes to bed completely upset by the tragedy.

[4]See p. 254.

She cannot sleep for worry over the nutcracker and finally steals downstairs to check up. To her surprise she finds that the Christmas tree has grown much larger and all the toys have come to life. A terrific battle is going on between the toys and the mice, who have attacked the candies and cakes. The brave nutcracker finally leads the tin soldiers in a successful defense, with Marie herself settling the issue by throwing her slipper at the Mouse King and killing him instantly.

The nutcracker immediately turns into a handsome prince, who thanks little Marie and invites her to visit the land of the Sugar-Plum Fairy. They fly through the air with the greatest of ease and are eventually entertained by the dances of various dolls and fairies. These dances supply most of the music of the *Nutcracker Suite.*

It begins with an *Overture Miniature,* in which the atmosphere of Christmas and toys and fairyland is quickly established. Violins and flutes carry the silvery theme, and the lower strings are not used at all.

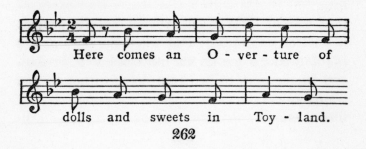

Here comes an O - ver - ture of dolls and sweets in Toy - land.

An *Arabian Dance* follows, with characteristic Oriental touches and clever use of the bassoon and English horn. Next comes the *Dance of the Sugar-Plum Fairy,* with everything in miniature, the tones of the celesta contrasting with those of the bass clarinet.

A *Russian Dance (Trepak),* strikes a more serious note than the others and pays tribute to the native folk music. Then comes a *March* of the toys, gay and fantastic, with fascinating instrumental combinations.

A *Chinese Dance* employs the unusual instrumentation of flute, piccolo and bassoon, and this is followed by one of the most popular sections, the *Dance of the Mirlitons* or toy pipes. Here Tschaikowsky achieves realism by using a trio of flutes against pizzicato strings, with embellish-

with his later inspirations in the symphonic form.

All three of the great symphonies have definite programs indicated by Tschaikowsky, with a consistent emphasis on Fate, probably inspired by Beethoven's success with the same idea. For his fourth symphony Tschaikowsky wrote out an elaborate program for his friend and benefactress, Nadejda von Meck.[6]

The fifth symphony makes similar use of a "fate motto," heard first in a portentous minor key and eventually transformed into the triumphant major melody of the *Finale*. No title or written explanation is needed to emphasize the program of this popular work.

The sixth is the famous *Pathétique,* whose title was supplied by Tschaikowsky's brother Modeste. The composer originally meant to call it merely *Program Symphony.* Its *Finale* is perhaps the most melancholy music ever written, and the preceding march of triumph has been called "sheer bravado." Certainly the pessimistic program of the *Pathétique Symphony* is an obvious one.

Tschaikowsky's ideas on program music are worth quoting in part. To Mme von Meck he wrote: "What really is program music? As for us two, for me and for you, a mere play with

[6] This program, with those of the fifth and sixth symphonies, is given in full on pp. 234–36 of the author's *Stories behind the World's Great Music,* and analyzed on pp. 224–48 of *Great Symphonies: How to Recognize and Remember Them.*

sounds is a long way from being music; every kind of music is program music from our standpoint. But in the narrower sense this expression signifies such symphonic music or such instrumental music generally as illustrates a definite subject placed before the public in a program and bearing the title of this subject. . . . From my point of view both kinds of music have a right to exist, and I do not understand the people who will admit the legitimacy of only one of them. Of course not every subject is suitable for a symphony, just as not every one is suitable for an opera; nevertheless, there can and must be program music."

To his friend Taneieff he added these significant comments: "As to your remark that my symphony sounds like program music I agree with you. Only I do not see why that should be a fault. I am afraid of the contrary; that is to say, I should be sorry if symphonic works were to flow from my pen which express nothing but consist merely of chords and a play of rhythms and modulations. Of course my symphony is program music. . . . Moreover, I must confess to you that in my simplicity I had believed that the thought of this symphony was so clear that its meaning, at least in outline, would be intelligible even without a program. . . . At bottom my symphony is an imitation of Beethoven's *Fifth Symphony;* that is to say, I imitated not its musi-

The immediate results were not very important. A *Symphonic Fantasia* named *Aus Italien* (From Italy) was called by Strauss "the connecting link between the old and the new method." It had four movements: *In the Campagna, Amid the Ruins of Rome, By Sorrento's Strand* and *Scenes of Popular Life in Naples.* (Unfortunately it quoted Luigi Denza's *Funiculi, Funicula,* under the impression that it was an Italian folk song.)

The first of the *Symphonic Poems* to be written, although not published until four years later (1891), was *Macbeth,* fittingly dedicated to Alexander Ritter. It is an attempt to sum up the character and soul struggles of Shakespeare's thane, and the only hint of a program beyond the title is a quotation from Lady Macbeth's lines: "Hie thee hither, that I may pour my spirits in thine ear, and chastise with the valour of my tongue all that impedes thee from the golden round, which fate and metaphysical aid doth seem to have thee crown'd withal."

But with *Don Juan,* composed in 1888, Richard Strauss became suddenly one of the most important of the composers of program music, and each succeeding tone poem added to that importance. *Don Juan* is based on a poem by Niklaus Lenau and has little to do with the conventional character of the great lover who finally kept his infernal date with a statue. Lenau's *Don*

Juan is a man who looks eternally for the perfect woman and fails to find her.

The opening of this dramatic composition is magnificent in its arrogant sensuousness. Three women of different types appear in turn, and Don Juan fights a duel with the father of the third. The fatal sword thrust which kills the protagonist is suggested by a high, dissonant note on the trumpet. Here are the important themes of *Don Juan:*

The next *Symphonic Poem* composed by Strauss, *Tod und Verklärung* (Death and Transfiguration), has a far more elaborate program and is on the whole a more obvious piece of music. The poem prefixed to the score has been translated thus: "In a poor little room, dimly lighted and awfully and ominously silent, except

The first of the Eulenspiegel motives appears at the start of the *Rondo* in its "apotheosis" form, as a gentle, sweet melody:

Till Eu - len-spieg-el's dead, So for-give him for the life he led.

Later these notes are given a diabolically mischievous ring in a recurrent pattern whose connection with the opening (and closing) theme has not always been realized:

The second Eulenspiegel theme is introduced by the French horn and is also full of mischief:

Till Eu - len - spieg - el, Till Eu-len - spieg - el!

This sums up the chief melodic material of the entire piece. At one point there is a lively dance in the manner of a folk tune, perhaps indicating Till's bravado as he sees himself getting into more and more trouble:

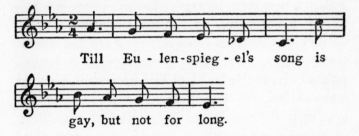

The actual hanging is almost cruelly realistic. After a masterly development of the chief Eulenspiegel motive, with elaborate and complicated orchestration, there is a sudden, portentous interruption in the manner of a dead march. The threat of the scaffold is unmistakable. Till's nonchalant little melodic label continues to be heard, but the funereal tones become ever stronger and more insistent.

Suddenly Till seems to realize that he is about to die. A wailing theme is heard (marked "kläglich"), growing more and more desperate. Finally the rogue is on the gallows, the rope around his neck. His own motive carries him aloft to a high, sustained note. There is a sickening struggle, growing weaker and finally descending to soft, staccato chords as the breath of life is exhausted.

Then comes a touch of genius in the return of

the opening theme, the apotheosis of the Eulenspiegel motive, carried out this time as a complete
and charming melody. The second motive also
returns, in a transfigured, ethereal form, the two
finally alternating, as though uncertain of the
verdict on this most fascinating of rogues. Eventually sadness vanishes. Eulenspiegel is triumphant even in death. "Let him be remembered as
a gay fellow, albeit a nuisance." Till's mischievous
grin appears once more in the closing measures,
untouched by regret or repentance. The final
chords are shouts of laughter.

Actually Strauss later changed his mind and
gave out a score with penciled annotations, re-
vealing the *Till Eulenspiegel* program in considerable detail: "Prologue. 'Once upon a time
there was a rogue—of the name of Till Eulenspiegel.' That was a mischievous sprite. Away for
new pranks. Wait! You hypocrite! Hop! On
horseback through the midst of the market
women! With seven-league boots he makes off.
Hidden in a mousehole. Disguised as a pastor, he
overflows with unction and morality. But the
rogue peeps out from the great toe. Before the
end, however, a secret horror takes hold of him on
account of the mockery of religion. Till, as a
cavalier, exchanging tender persiflage with pretty
girls. With one of them he has really fallen in
love. He proposes to her. A polite refusal is still
a refusal. He turns away in a rage. Swears to

take vengeance on the whole human race. Philistine motive. After proposing to the Philistines a couple of monstrous theses he abandons the dumbfounded ones to their fate. Great grimace from afar. Till's street song (*Gassenhauer*). He is collared by the bailiff. The judgment. He whistles to himself with indifference. Up the ladder! There he is swinging; his breath has gone out—a last quiver. All that is mortal of Till is ended. Epilogue. What is immortal, his humor, remains."

After all, such details are not needed for the enjoyment of *Till Eulenspiegel and His Merry Pranks*. The important point is that this *Rondo* is a superb piece of orchestral music, full of life and vigor and imagination. As such it will continue to please audiences, even if they are entirely unaware of its program.

The next *Symphonic Poem* of Richard Strauss was deeply philosophical, with the title, *Thus Spake Zarathustra*. Its inspiration came from Friedrich Nietzsche, and the composer himself gave this explanation of the program: "I did not intend to write philosophical music or portray Nietzsche's great work musically. I meant to convey musically an idea of the development of the human race from its origin, through the various phases of development, religious as well as scientific, up to Nietzsche's idea of the Superman. The whole *Symphonic Poem* is intended as my homage to Nietzsche's genius, which found its greatest exemplification in his book, *Thus Spake Zarathustra."*

The Zarathustra of Nietzsche is not the legendary Zoroaster of Persia but a Superman who preaches the gospel of the Superman. Actually it is Nietzsche himself, expounding his views on life and death. The Strauss program published before the first performance of the tone poem read as follows: "First movement: Sunrise; man feels the power of God. *Andante religioso.* But man still longs. He plunges into passion (second movement) and finds no peace. He turns toward science and tries in vain to solve life's problem in a fugue (third movement). Then agreeable dance tunes sound and he becomes an individual, and his soul soars upward while the world sinks far beneath him."

Strauss's opening is impressive, with a solemn trumpet motive leading to a great climax for orchestra and organ on the C major chord. There is a heading, "Of the Dwellers in the Back World," meaning those who had looked for a solution in religion, of whom Zarathustra himself had been one. The horns intone a solemn Gregorian *Credo.*

The next superscription is, "Of the Great Yearning," with cellos and bassoons answered by the other wood wind. Then comes a pathetic passage in C minor, with the heading, "Of Joys and

Passions." The oboe sings the "Grave Song" (*Grablied*) tenderly above the Yearning motive played by cellos and bassoons. "Of Science" is the fugal section, technically involved, with the responses to the subject coming in always a fifth higher. "The Convalescent" is the next title, and then comes a "Dance Song," beginning with laughter in the wood wind. ("The Superman has thrown off the burdens of the common man.") The final section is a "Night Song," also called by Nietzsche "The Drunken Song," following a fortissimo stroke of the bell, which sounds twelve times and then dies away softly. ("Eternity of all things is sought by all delight.") The tone poem ends in two keys, with the wood wind and violins high up in B major while the basses play pizzicato in C. "The theme of the Ideal sways aloft in the higher regions in B major; the trombones insist on the unresolved chord of C,E,F sharp; and in the double basses is repeated CGC, the world riddle." It remains unsolved, by Strauss as well as Nietzsche.

Richard Strauss went furthest in the direction of realism and direct musical imitation in his *Don Quixote,* which he subtitled *Fantastic Variations on a Theme of Chivalrous Character.* Actually it includes an *Introduction* and *Finale,* and in spite of its extreme programmatic style it might easily be accepted as a piece of absolute music. Strauss himself added only two superscriptions to the program indicated by the title. Over the first half of the theme he wrote "Don Quixote, the Knight of the Rueful Countenance," and over the second half "Sancho Panza."

In spite of this reticence on the part of the composer, *Don Quixote* has been given more elaborate analyses and programmatic explanations than have fallen to the lot of any of the other Strauss tone poems. Arthur Hahn has written a twenty-seven-page pamphlet of "elucidation," which contains some surprising statements. He even tells us that certain strange harmonies in the *Introduction* "characterize admirably the well-known tendency of Don Quixote toward false conclusions."

Max Steinitzer, an official biographer of Strauss, worked out a detailed program, probably with the composer's approval, and this may be accepted as sufficiently authentic. Quotations from these sources and from Thomas Shelton's translation of the Cervantes novel provide a reasonably connected story.

The *Introduction* begins with a version of the hero's motive, and pictures "with constantly increasing liveliness by other themes of knightly and gallant character life as it is mirrored in writings from the beginning of the seventeenth century." Don Quixote, busied in reading romances of chivalry, loses his reason and determines to go through the world as a wandering knight. According to Cervantes, "through his little sleep and much reading he dried up his brains in such sort, as he lost wholly his judgment. His fantasy was filled with those things that he read, of enchantments, quarrels, battles, challenges, wounds, wooings, loves, tempests and other impossible follies."

The Strauss music implies the growing madness of the knight by the fantastic harmonies already mentioned. The oboe sings to him of the Ideal Woman, and the trumpets announce that a giant has attacked her and she is being rescued by a knight. "In this part of the *Introduction* the use of mutes on all the instruments, including the tuba, here so treated for the first time, creates an indescribable effect of vagueness and confusion, indicating that they are mere phantasms with which the knight is concerned, which cloud his brain. . . . An augmented version of the first section of the theme, followed by a harp glissando, leads to shrill discord: the knight is mad."

The complete theme of Don Quixote is introduced by the cello and always thereafter associated with that instrument, which makes the tone poem in a sense a cello concerto, for which a distinguished soloist is generally used.

The Sancho Panza theme is first played by bass clarinet and tenor tuba, but later becomes regularly a viola solo.

There are ten *Variations* on this combined theme. The first represents the adventure with the windmills, and there is a realistic portrayal (with heavy drumbeats) of the knight's downfall as he attacks them.

The second *Variation* describes the more successful attack on a flock of sheep, which Don Quixote believes to be the army of the great Emperor Alifanfaron. The bleating of the sheep is directly imitated by muted brass.

In the third *Variation* the knight and his squire argue about the value of a life of chivalry. Don Quixote speaks nobly of honor, glory and ideals. Sancho Panza prefers the easy, comfortable realities of life. Eventually the knight loses his temper and tells Sancho to hold his tongue.

Variation four covers the episode of the pilgrims who are carrying a covered image, which the knight takes for the abduction of a great lady. He attacks the pilgrims, who knock him senseless and continue on their way with prayers and sacred songs. Sancho watches over his unconscious master until he shows signs of life, then lies down beside him and goes to sleep, to suggestive sounds of the bass tuba and double bassoon.

In *Variation five* Don Quixote holds watch over his armor. A vision of Dulcinea, the Ideal Woman, appears to him, and a cadenza for harp and violins leads to a musical expression of his rapture.

Sancho points out a common country wench as Dulcinea, and the knight is convinced that this transformation has been worked by an evil spell and vows vengeance. This is the sixth *Variation*.

In the seventh the two companions sit blindfolded on a wooden horse, imagining that they are being carried through the air. Here Strauss makes use of a regular wind machine for effects of realism which have been criticized as illegitimate even in program music. Actually, of course, a wind machine is not a musical instrument.

The eighth *Variation* is the "Journey in the Enchanted Bark." Don Quixote sees an empty boat and is sure it has been sent by some mysterious power that he may do a glorious deed. They embark, and his theme becomes a barcarolle. The boat upsets, but they swim back to shore and give thanks for their safety.

In the ninth *Variation* the knight, once more astride his faithful mare, Rosinante, meets two peaceful monks, riding along on donkeys. He is convinced that they are the magicians who have been working against him and immediately charges and puts them to flight.

The tenth and last *Variation* describes the battle between Don Quixote and the Knight of the White Moon, who wins easily and persuades the rueful hero to go back home and forget about chivalry. A pastoral theme (previously connected with the sheep) indicates that Don Quixote consents to become a quiet shepherd.

The *Finale* deals with the death of Don Quixote. The strange harmonies of the *Introduction* have now become conventional and commonplace. The knight has acquired wisdom through experience and is now his natural self, "of a mild and affable disposition and of a kind and pleasing conversation." The Cervantes description of the knight's death demands at least a partial quotation: "He had no sooner ended his discourse and signed and sealed his will and testament but, a swooning and faintness surprising him, he stretched himself the full length of his bed. All the company were much distracted and moved thereat and ran presently to help him; and during the space of three days that he lived after he had made his will he did swoon and fall into trances almost every hour. All the house was in a confusion and uproar; all which notwithstanding the niece ceased not to feed very devoutly, the maidservant to drink profoundly and Sancho to live merrily. For, when a man is in hope to inherit anything, that hope doth deface or at least moderate in the mind of the inheritor the remembrance or feeling of sorrow and grief which of reason he should have by the testator's death. To conclude, the last day of Don Quixote came, after he had received all the sacraments and had by many and godly reasons made demonstration to abhor all the books of errant chivalry. The notary was present at his death and reporteth how he had never read or found in any book of chivalry that any errant knight died in his bed so mildly, so quietly and so Christianly as did Don Quixote. Amidst the wailful plaints and blubbering tears of the bystanders he yielded up the ghost; that is to say, he died."

The tone poem *Ein Heldenleben* (A Hero's Life) is generally considered autobiographical, and Strauss practically admitted this, both in conversation and in the direct quotations from his earlier works that appear in the score. Like *Don Quixote,* this orchestral piece has been subjected to a wide range of detailed interpretation, including a thick volume by Friedrich Rösch containing no less than seventy thematic illustrations and a descriptive poem by Eberhard König.

Strauss himself said to Romain Rolland, "There is no need of a program. It is enough to know that there is a hero fighting his enemies." But he is also quoted as adding that he wrote his *Heldenleben* as a companion piece to *Don Quixote* and that he presents in it "not a single poetical or historical figure, but rather a more

285

general and free ideal of great and manly heroism—not the heroism to which one can apply an everyday standard of valor, with its material and exterior rewards, but that heroism which describes the inward battle of life and which aspires through effort and renouncement toward the elevation of the soul."

The *Hero's Life* starts with the arrogant, self-confident theme which represents the hero himself, "his pride, emotional nature, iron will, richness of imagination, inflexible and well-directed determination instead of low-spirited and sullen obstinacy." It is brilliantly developed in the first section of the tone poem.

The second section deals with the hero's enemies, who are painted as petty, backbiting, snarling, vicious figures, trying to tear down the greatness of a man whom they envy. This jealous gabbling (which may include the comments of music critics) is vividly dramatized in the wood wind, particularly through the dialogue of flute and oboe.

Next comes "The Hero's Helpmate," represented by a tender, sentimental theme, introduced by the solo violin. In this section all is peace and beauty, with no interruptions from the outside world.

But a flourish of trumpets announces the call to battle. With dramatic realism and striking originality Strauss pictures the hero in a triumphant struggle with his enemies. It is a real fight, but there is no doubt as to the eventual winner.

The next section covers "The Hero's Works of Peace," and here it becomes quite evident that Richard Strauss is himself the protagonist. It has been claimed that there are as many as twenty-three direct quotations from earlier Strauss works, some introduced simultaneously, "and the hearer who has not been warned cannot at the time notice the slightest disturbance in the development." Perhaps the most obvious echo is from the song, *Traum durch die Dämmerung* (Dream through the Twilight), but it is not difficult to find also snatches of *Macbeth, Guntram, Till Eulenspiegel, Don Quixote, Zarathustra, Death and Transfiguration* and *Don Juan.*

In the final section of the *Heldenleben* Strauss celebrates "The Hero's Renouncement of the World," with a conclusion which represents Perfection in contemplative contentment. Resignation takes possession of the hero's soul. The blustering storm reminds him of his triumphs in battle. The theme of his beloved helpmate brings domestic peace and tranquillity. The hero's own theme rises once more to a sonorous climax. At the end the music is solemn, almost funereal, perhaps anticipating the death that is inevitable.

Ein Heldenleben may be considered the last really significant example of program music produced by Richard Strauss. His *Domestic Symphony* was a practical joke, deliberately descending from the sublime to the ridiculous. It presents a day in the life of the Strauss family, with the clock striking 7 P.M. and 7 A.M. to indicate the passage of time. There are themes for the husband, the wife and the child, and at one point the baby's bath is realistically portrayed in music. Unfortunately this program does not demand serious consideration for itself alone, and the music as such has little importance beyond its obvious connection with the program.

Strauss also wrote an *Alpine Symphony*, which is not particularly significant either as absolute or as program music. His ballets, *Joseph and His Brethren* and *Schlagobers* (Whipped Cream) are interesting experiments and seem to have been effective in actual performance, where the music does not carry too much responsibility.

But there are instrumental passages in *Elektra* and *Der Rosenkavalier* that represent program music at its best. (The music of the rose is positively silver in its color, and the hatchet strokes and other morbid details of *Elektra* are unmistakable.) *Salome* also contains some instrumental realism, even though the famous *Dance*

288

of the Seven Veils leaves the imagination somewhat unsatisfied.

Strauss has sufficiently established his genius in his operas, his songs and his tone poems for orchestra. It is his privilege to doze in the twilight of his life, surrounded by elements that have proved themselves destructive to all art, culture and ideals.

PROGRAM MUSIC AMONG
THE MODERNISTS

IT HAS ALREADY been made clear that the modern tendency is more and more toward program music. While some composers are still trying to write in the pure, classic style, the current distortions of rhythm, melody, harmony, tone color and form lend themselves far more easily to an announced program than to a distinguishable pattern or logical design of tonal significance.

Since much of this modern music is meaningless to the average listener (and often to the trained musician as well) it is a simple matter for contemporary composers to claim whatever meaning they choose to bestow upon their music, often stating their programs in abstract terms which are as confusing as the music itself. Some are obviously sincere, if not always equal to carrying out their intentions. Others are either deceiving themselves or practicing deliberate tricks on the public and the critics.

The habit of giving at least a definite title to a piece of music has become so common that it would be literally impossible even to list the names of recent compositions that claim to be program music. Much of this material is bound to be forgotten soon, if it is ever remembered at all. But some of it has already established its permanence, and this must be given serious consideration, even when a detailed analysis would be difficult if not impossible.

It is also obvious that modern music is less and less inclined to stand on its own feet, whether programmatic or of the absolute type. More and more it has become the handmaiden of other arts, often with a distinctly utilitarian purpose. Music is today most effective when combined with the color and motion of the ballet, the action, scenery and dialogue of the screen, the highly specialized technique of radio, the amazing possibilities of new electrical instruments. Often it makes use of words and action and backgrounds of various kinds, but not in the conventional manner of opera or the established schools of song. The new technique employs novel stagecraft and showmanship. Possibly a new art is in the process of development, combining the best features of all the old ones. In any case, the independence of music, like that of many other products of human thought, becomes more and more open to question.

It will be enough to consider here the modern music that has definitely proved its artistic value, within the limits of what can honestly be called program music, as judged by the standards and definitions of the past. From this standpoint the composer who deserves the greatest respect and the most careful consideration is Claude Debussy (1862–1918), rightly considered the founder of the whole modern school.

The word most commonly applied to Debussy's music is "impressionism," and it happens to be right, as well as convenient and practical. The impressionists of painting and literature created a recognizable style of art, in which outlines were blurred, clear and definite statements avoided, backgrounds hazily suggested, ideas presented mystically and by implication rather than directly, straightforwardly or obviously. A single picture by Monet or almost any example of Debussy's later style makes the term "impressionism" entirely intelligible.

Music offers a better field for the impressionistic style than any of the other arts, and Debussy was the first to prove this. His innovations have been so generally adopted that modern listeners are likely to forget the enormous importance of what he accomplished.

The impressionism of Debussy resulted in program music which seldom tried to tell a story or paint a picture in tones. He was satisfied to create a mood, generally indicated by a mere title, and he did this with complete success.

Debussy's *Prelude to the Afternoon of a*

Faun, which he called an "orchestral eclogue after the poem by Stéphane Mallarmé," written only a short time after he had emerged from weak imitations of Massenet, was a declaration to the musical world of a new type of program music. It remains a perfect thing of its kind.

"Just as Mallarmé's lines are an idealess evocation of summer warmth and a faun daydreaming of the only delights he can know, Debussy's shimmering score is a musical gloss on this Theocritan afternoon. There is no real programmatic connection between the two works; this is mood music and pretends to nothing more."[1]

The Mallarmé poem has been interpreted by Edmund Gosse in the following words: "A faun, a simple, sensuous, passionate being, wakens in the forest at daybreak and tries to recall his experience of the previous afternoon. Was he the fortunate recipient of an actual visit from nymphs, white and golden goddesses, divinely tender and indulgent? Or is the memory he seems to retain nothing but the shadow of a vision, no more substantial than the arid rain of notes from his own flute? He cannot tell. Yet surely there was, surely there is, an animal whiteness among the brown reeds of the lake that shines out yonder. Were they, are they, swans? No! But Naiads plunging? Perhaps! Vaguer and vaguer grows

[1]From *Men of Music,* by Wallace Brockway and Herbert Weinstock, Simon & Schuster, New York.

that impression of this delicious experience. He would resign his woodland godship to retain it. A garden of lilies, golden-headed, white-stalked, behind the trellis of red roses? Ah, the effort is too great for his poor brain. Perhaps if he selects one lily from the garth of lilies, one benign and beneficent yielder of her cup to thirsty lips, the memory, the ever-receding memory, may be forced back. So when he has glutted upon a bunch of grapes he is wont to toss the empty skins in the air and blow them out in a visionary greediness. But no, the delicious hour grows vaguer; experience or dream, he will never know which it was. The sun is warm, the grasses yielding, and he curls himself up again after worshiping the efficacious star of wine, that he may pursue the dubious ecstasy into the more hopeful boskages of sleep."

The chief theme of the *Afternoon of a Faun* is announced immediately by the flute, in imitation of the faun's own primitive pipe:

Louis Laloy, in his life of Debussy, describes the development thus: "One is immediately transported into a better world; all that is leering and savage in the snub-nosed face of the faun disappears; desire still speaks, but there is a veil of tenderness and melancholy. The chords of the wood wind, the distant call of the horns, the limpid flood of harp tones accentuate this impression. The call is louder, more urgent, but it almost immediately dies away, to let the flute sing again its song. And now the theme is developed: the oboe enters in; the clarinet has its say; a lively dialogue follows, and a clarinet phrase leads to a new theme which speaks of desire satisfied, or it expresses the rapture of mutual emotion rather than the ferocity of victory. The first theme returns, more languorous, and the croaking of muted horns darkens the horizon. The theme comes and goes; fresh chords unfold themselves; at last a solo violoncello joins itself to the flute; and then everything vanishes, as a mist that rises in the air and scatters itself in flakes."

Debussy did not care for the way Nijinsky danced this tone poem. He made it too definite and realistic. Audiences were shocked at the finish, when he took vicarious pleasure from the veil of the nymph who had been tempting him. The composer's comment: "It is ugly: Dalcrozian, in fact." Actually the *Prelude to the Afternoon of a Faun* needs no action, no words, no program. It accomplishes something unique in music and comes as close as is humanly possible to the ideal of expressing the abstract in concrete terms.

Debussy repeated this miracle in his three *Nocturnes, Nuages, Fêtes* and *Sirènes*. Although the composer adds women's voices to the orchestration of *Sirènes* these voices do not sing any actual words and hence the composition may be classified as program music. Debussy himself supplied a program for these three impressionistic tone poems: "The title *Nocturnes* is intended to have here a more general and, above all, a more decorative meaning. We, then, are not concerned with the form of the *Nocturne* but with everything that this word includes in the way of diversified impression and special lights."

"*Clouds:* the unchangeable appearance of the sky, with the slow and solemn march of clouds dissolving in a gray agony tinted with white."

"*Festivals:* movement, rhythm dancing in the atmosphere, with bursts of brusque light. There is also the episode of a procession (a dazzling and wholly idealistic vision) passing through the festival and blended with it; but the main idea and substance obstinately remain—always the festival and its blended music—luminous dust participating in the universal rhythm of all things."

"*Sirens:* the sea and its innumerable rhythm; then amid the billows silvered by the moon the mysterious song of the Sirens is heard; it laughs and passes."

The three symphonic sketches under the title of *La Mer* (The Sea) are generally considered Debussy's greatest program music. They are frankly impressionistic and leave much to the imagination of the listener. For those who like the ocean they are a perfect expression of its moods. To those who are not interested the music may sound like a hopelessly involved conglomeration of sounds.

Debussy himself loved the ocean. In 1905 he wrote from Eastbourne: "The sea rolls with a wholly British correctness. There is a lawn, combed and brushed, on which little bits of important and imperialistic English frolic. But what a place to work! No noise, no pianos, except the delicious mechanical pianos, no musicians talking about painting, no painters discussing music. In short, a pretty place to cultivate egoism."

Near Dieppe, in 1906, Debussy added these observations: "Here I am again with my old friend the sea, always innumerable and beautiful. It is truly the one thing in nature that puts you in your place; only one does not sufficiently respect the sea. To bathe in it bodies deformed by the daily life should not be allowed; truly these arms and legs which move in ridiculous rhythms —it is enough to make the fishes weep. There should be only Sirens in the sea, but could you wish that these estimable persons would be willing to return to waters so badly frequented?"

Debussy's sea is something quite different from Mendelssohn's. According to Philip Hale, "Debussy knows a wilder ocean, many-faced, now exulting in Aeschylean laughter, now spasmodic, sinister, terrible, and never so terrible as when calm or inviting mortals to sport with it, and smiling—as though it were forgetful of rotting ships and sunken treasure and the drowned far down that were for a time regarded curiously by monsters of the deep."

The titles of the three sketches are *From Dawn till Noon on the Ocean, Play of the Waves* and *Dialogue of Wind and Sea.* Actually this music has no detailed program. Quoting once more from Brockway and Weinstock: "When Erik Satie wisecracked about the first movement, that he liked 'the part at quarter past eleven,' he was attacking Debussy's sometimes too-specific titles rather than implying that the music was realistic. For *La Mer* is an imaginative response to thoughts about the sea and its moods, not a wave-by-wave description of it. As Debussy conceived poetically of the sea, *La Mer* is necessarily a large and masculine work. Without sacrificing the sensuous delicacy of his perceptions or the subtly tapering color of the *Faun* or *Nocturnes* he had widened his scope to include big orchestral effects he had never before needed. The shattering climaxes of *La Mer* are unique to that composition only because Debussy never again felt called upon to use them. . . . The more one hears this great poem of the sea the more one realizes that *La Mer* is Debussy's masterpiece precisely because it adds to his decorative and mood-evocative qualities a powerful and satisfying emotional impact."

One more orchestral piece by Debussy demands attention as program music. It is called *Iberia,* the second of a set of *Images* for orchestra. Philip Hale says of these *Images:* "They are impressionistic, but there is a sense of form; there is also the finest proportion. This music is conspicuous for exquisite effects of color. There are combinations of timbres and also contrasts that were hitherto unknown. There are hints of Spanish melodies, melodies not too openly exposed; there are intoxicating rhythms, sharply defined, or elusive, and then they are the more madding.

"The music is pleasingly remote from photographic realism. The title might be *Impressions of Spain.* There is the suggestion of street life and wild strains heard on bleak plains or savage mountains; of the music of the people; of summer nights, warm and odorous; of the awakening of life with the break of day; of endless jotas, tangos, *seguidillas,* fandangos; of gypsies with their spells brought from the East; of women with Moorish blood. *Iberia* defies analysis and beggars description."[2]

A critic (M Boutarel) wrote after the first performance of *Iberia:* "Debussy appears in this work to have exaggerated his tendency to treat music with means of expression analogous to those of the impressionistic painters. Nevertheless, the rhythm remains well defined and frank in *Iberia.* Do not look for any melodic design nor any carefully woven harmonic web. The composer of *Images* attaches importance only to tonal color."

The rest of Debussy's program music is found mostly in his piano pieces. He wrote a *Sacred and Profane Dance* for harp and strings and some other instrumental music that may be given a program. But his compositions for the piano are unique in their advance over Chopin and Schumann in the creation of definite moods, pictures, even stories in tone. They are impressionistic for the most part, but there is never any doubt as to their meaning, even with no more than a title for guidance.

Two comparatively insignificant works for the piano have become perhaps the most popular of all of Debussy's music. One is the trifle called *Reverie,* which became a fox-trot hit of Tin Pan

[2]Philip Hale's *Boston Symphony Programme Notes,* Doubleday, Doran & Co., New York.

Alley by the simple process of prefixing the personal possessive pronoun "my":

Dream - ing___ in the spell of a
rev - er - y sweet.___

The other is the honestly appealing *Clair de Lune* (Moonlight), which is now heard orchestrally as well as in its original keyboard form:

Pale moon - light_ ev'- ry - where_

But there is far better program music than this in Debussy's pianoforte literature. *Gardens in the Rain* draws on two old French folk songs but translates them into something ethereal and at the same time realistic. The goldfish of *Poissons d'Or* are lacquered on a Japanese plate, but the music makes them alive. *Reflections in the Water* might have been painted by any of the impressionists. It is a true picture in tones. *The Girl with the Flaxen Hair* is even more vivid, in spite of the delicacy of her musical portraiture.

It is only in the *Children's Corner* that Debussy's program music becomes obvious, and even then it is effective. He wrote these little piano pieces for his daughter "Chouchou," and even though children can seldom play them they remain among the classics of juvenile music.

For some reason Debussy gave them English titles. They begin with a beautiful parody of all piano exercises in the *Doctor Gradus ad Parnassum*. Next comes *Jimbo's Lullaby,* in which Debussy quite naturally mispronounced the name of Barnum's big elephant. Then there is a *Serenade for the Doll* and *The Little Shepherd,* whose theme is worth quoting:

The Snow Is Dancing is an exquisite miniature, and the series ends with the familiar *Golliwog's Cake-Walk,* which pays its tribute to American ragtime. Just what a Golliwog is no one seems to know, but there is general agreement as to the charm of the syncopated tune that Debussy attached to the name:

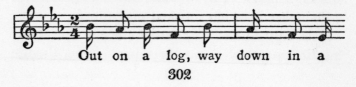

Out on a log, way down in a

bog there dan - ces a Gol - li - wog.

Debussy's piano music includes many other subjects: a *Dance of Puck, General Lavine* (also in ragtime), *Homage to S. Pickwick, Esq., In Black and White* (for two pianos) and such *Preludes* as *The Submerged Cathedral,* with its realistic suggestion of muffled bell tones. During the World War he went so far as to compose a *Berceuse Héroïque* in honor of King Albert of Belgium.

Debussy was an instinctive painter in tones, even when he made use of words, as in his unique songs and the equally unique opera, *Pelléas and Mélisande.* He invented the technique of creating a background of tone color, over which his melodies or his rhythmic patterns or his words stood out. He came as near as any composer legitimately can to expressing the abstract in musical terms, and that really has been the ideal of every modern musician.

Maurice Ravel (1875–1937) has often been compared with Debussy, and to many listeners their styles are the same. But a study of their works reveals many points of difference, and each has an individuality that defies comparisons.

It is a pity that Ravel should be best known by his *Bolero,* which is purely a trick piece, though a clever one. The trick is to keep one rhythmic pattern and one melody going through the entire composition, getting variety entirely by the instrumentation and gradations of volume. There have been so many arguments about the *Bolero* rhythm that it may as well be given here. There are two alternating measures throughout, as follows:

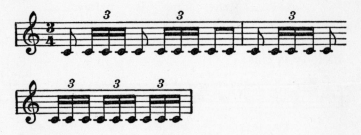

It will be noticed that this represents a fundamental beat in triple time but with an elaborate pattern of triplets within this general outline. The melodic pattern starts like this:

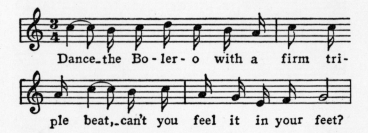

Next to the *Bolero* Ravel's best-known tune is probably the *Pavane for a Dead Infanta,* chiefly

because part of it was borrowed for a popular
song called *The Lamp Is Low:*[3]

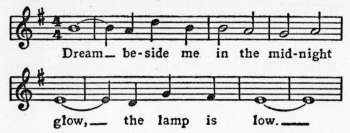

Dream— be-side me in the mid-night
glow,— the lamp is low.—

The first and most important part of the
melody is this:

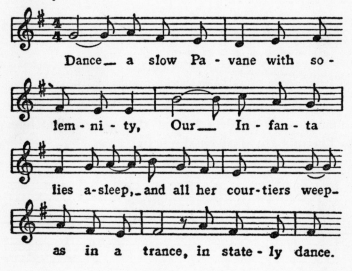

Dance— a slow Pa - vane with so -
lem - ni - ty, Our— In - fan - ta
lies a-sleep,— and all her cour-tiers weep—
as in a trance, in state - ly dance.

Far more important than these pieces are
Ravel's *Daphnis and Chloë* ballet and *La Valse,*

[3]Copyright, 1939, Robbins Music Corporation, New York. Words
by Mitchell Parish.

both for orchestra. The former was written for the
Russian Ballet, with Nijinsky and Karsavina as
the leading dancers and Fokine and Diaghileff
fighting over the choreography. The argument
printed with the score is typical of the artifi-
cialities of conventional ballet pantomime but
cannot destroy the beauty of the music.

A more obvious and attractive program is attached to Ravel's *Mother Goose,* a set of five
children's pieces, representing some of his cleverest orchestrations (originally written as a piano
duet). It begins with a *Pavane of the Sleeping
Beauty,* with *Hop o' My Thumb* for the second
movement. The third is called *Laideronnette,
Empress of the Pagodas* (grotesque figures with
movable heads). In this movement there is an
imitation of the "pagodes and pagodines" playing on "theorbos made of walnut shells" and
"viols made of almond shells," since they "were
obliged to proportion the instruments to their
figure."

The fourth movement of Ravel's *Mother Goose*
consists of *Conversations between Beauty and
the Beast.* Part of the conversation is quoted
thus:

"When I think how goodhearted you are you
do not seem to me so ugly."

"Yes, I have, indeed, a kind heart; but I am a
monster."

"There are many men more monstrous than you."

"If I had wit I would invent a fine compliment to thank you, but I am only a beast."

Beauty finally consents to marry the beast, who thereupon turns into a beautiful prince, full of gratitude for the delivery from his enchantment.

Among the programmatic piano pieces of Ravel *Jeux d'Eau* (The Fountain) deserves special mention. It is a perfect tonal description of sparkling water, created by simply breaking chords into their component notes and letting them splash all over the keyboard.

In the French "Group of Six" Arthur Honegger stands out as a composer of program music through his *Pacific 231,* which is a direct imitation of the noise of a locomotive. He has denied this vehemently, like most other imitative composers (going all the way back to Beethoven's apologies for his *Pastoral Symphony*). Nevertheless and notwithstanding, *Pacific 231* is an imitation of a locomotive and an excellent imitation too.

One more classic of modern French program music deserves detailed discussion. It is *The Sorcerer's Apprentice,* by Paul Dukas (1865–1935). This is as complete and picturesque in its dramatic realism as any tone poem of Saint-Saëns or Richard Strauss.

The story goes back to a dialogue of Lucian, in which he tells of a magician named Pancrates whose disciple, Eucrates, tried one of his master's tricks during his absence. The trick consisted in bringing to life a broom or some other implement so that it would act as a servant. Eucrates learned the charm and made a broom fetch water for him. But then he found that he could not stop it. He tried cutting the broomstick in half, but this merely doubled the supply of water. The magician arrived just in time to prevent a flood. Goethe made a ballad of this story, and it was his poem (*Der Zauberlehrling*) that inspired the music of Dukas.

The theme which represents the coming to life of the broom contains a suggestion of the familiar "bums' march" and supplies most of the melodic material for *The Sorcerer's Apprentice*:[4]

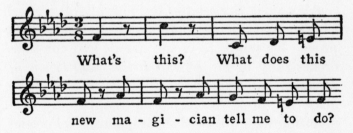

What's this? What does this new ma - gi - cian tell me to do?

Italy's most important contribution to modern program music has been through Ottorino Respighi, whose *Fountains of Rome* and *Pines of*

[4]A complete analysis of this composition will be found in *The Art of Enjoying Music*, pp. 335–36.

Rome are impressive examples of advanced orchestration and descriptive realism. The second piece has been credited with achieving the loudest climax known to musical literature. It also makes use of a phonograph record of the actual song of a nightingale, which is generally agreed to be less effective than a good musical imitation would have been. Alfredo Casella has added to the musical reputation of Italy with various clever programmatic works, including a successful ballet, *La Giara* (The Jar), performed at the Metropolitan Opera House.

Russia has maintained its reputation as a leader in program music with such men as Scriabin, Stravinsky and Prokofieff. Shostakovitch might be included if only by reason of the instrumental realism of one scene in his opera, *Lady Macbeth of Mzensk*.

Alexander Scriabin is the logical follower of Chopin and Debussy in his piano music. He proved his power to create moods and emotions orchestrally in his *Divine Poem* and *Poem of Ecstasy*. In *Prometheus: The Poem of Fire* he made use of a "color organ," supposedly harmonizing with the tonal shades, and thereby went beyond the limits of strict program music.

Igor Stravinsky has secured his best effects through the medium of the ballet, but it is significant that most of his music can stand on its own feet in concert performance. His most popular work is *Petrouschka,* which has been played even in a piano transcription.

The program of this ballet is fairly clear even without the stage presentation. Petrouschka is a puppet in a sideshow at a Russian carnival. He is in love with the ballerina but has a fatal rival in the Moor, also a puppet, who finally kills him. The climax of the drama comes when the showman, who had insisted that these were only dolls in spite of their wonderful feats, suddenly discovers that Petrouschka had a soul, as his spirit appears pathetically above the booth.

The carnival atmosphere is wonderfully sustained in this orchestral masterpiece, with clever use of a real Russian folk tune, known as *Down St Peter's Road,* here given in its original form.

Stravinsky has also made a deep impression on modern concert audiences with his *Fire-bird Suite,* from the ballet of the same name. This colorful program music includes an amazing *Dance of the Fire-bird,* a beautiful *Berceuse* and an *Infernal Dance of the Subjects of Katschei,* the terrible magician. The *Suite* is an excellent example of modern music in its most attractive form.

Stravinsky is less obvious in his *Rites of Spring,*

which caused considerable commotion when it was first performed in 1913. Alfred Capu wrote bitterly in the Paris *Figaro,* in connection with this ballet: "Bluffing the idle rich of Paris through appeals to their snobbery is a delightfully simple matter. . . . The process works out as follows: take the best society possible, composed of rich, simple-minded, idle people. Then submit them to an intense regime of publicity. By pamphlets, newspaper articles, lectures, personal visits and all other appeals to their snobbery persuade them that hitherto they have seen only vulgar spectacles and are at last to know what is art and beauty. Impress them with cabalistic formulae. They have not the slightest notion of music, literature, painting and dancing; still they have seen heretofore under these names only a rude imitation of the real thing. Finally assure them that they are about to see real dancing and hear real music. It will then be necessary to double the prices at the theater, so great will be the rush of shallow worshipers at this false shrine."

Carl Van Vechten, in his *Music after the Great War,* gives a vivid description of the opening night, which he attended: "A certain part of the audience, thrilled by what it considered a blasphemous attempt to destroy music as an art and swept away with wrath, began soon after the rise of the curtain to whistle, to make catcalls and to offer audible suggestions as to how the performance should proceed. Others of us, who liked the music and felt that the principles of free speech were at stake, bellowed defiance. It was war over art for the rest of the evening, and the orchestra played on unheard, except occasionally when a slight lull occurred. . . . A young man occupied the place behind me. He stood up during the course of the ballet to enable himself to see more clearly. The intense excitement under which he was laboring, thanks to the potent force of the music, betrayed itself presently when he began to beat rhythmically on the top of my head with his fists. My emotion was so great that I did not feel the blows for some time. They were perfectly synchronized with the beat of the music. When I did I turned around. His apology was sincere. We had both been carried beyond ourselves."

Actually this composition is a glorification of barbaric rhythms. Stravinsky divides it into two parts. The first is called *The Adoration of the Earth* and contains an *Introduction, Harbingers of Spring, Dance of the Adolescents, Abduction, Spring Rounds, Games of the Rival Cities, The Procession of the Wise Men, The Adoration of the Earth* and *Dance of the Earth.* The second part is called *The Sacrifice* and includes *Mysterious Circles of the Adolescents, Glorification of the Chosen One, Evocation of the Ancestors,*

Ritual of the Ancestors and *The Sacrificial Dance of the Chosen One.*

Stravinsky went even further in *Les Noces* (The Marriage), which has been described as "devitalizing his audiences." He has written a *Jazz Concerto* for piano and orchestra, a *Symphony of Psalms,* music for *Oedipus Rex, Apollo Musagetes, The Fairy's Kiss* and other programmatic material of unequal value, including even *The Card Party,* musically describing a poker game. It now seems fairly certain that, like Richard Strauss, he will contribute nothing more of importance to the art.

Serge Prokofieff has kept himself more alive with the concert public. His *Scythian Suite* and *Dance of Steel* are attuned to modern ears, and the pleasant little *March,* from the *Love of Three Oranges,* has become almost a popular hit. His gay and provocative musical fairy tale, *Peter and the Wolf,* has achieved great popularity and may fairly be considered program music, although the music is accompanied by a narrator who tells the story as the composition progresses. Prokofieff wrote it as a joke, to be sure that his listeners would understand, and they were sincerely delighted.

England has an important share in modern program music, with the *London Symphony* of Vaughan Williams, Gustav Holst's *Planets,* the

313

satirical works of Lord Berners and the genial creations of the Americanized Eugene Goossens. From Hungary the world has received a significant treatment of folk music by Bela Bartok and Zoltan Kodaly. France's Milhaud and Germany's Hindemith have done their bit, with America's Louis Gruenberg contributing new angles on the jazz idiom.

Above all other living composers towers the figure of Jean Sibelius, of Finland, whose symphonies are the last word in the modernization of the classic forms but who has also written some striking program music. The popularity of Sibelius rests largely on his orchestral tone poem, *Finlandia,* a timely summary of almost unique patriotism. Its chief melody has become practically a national anthem in Finland and is often sung to words:[5]

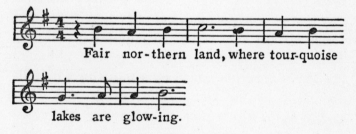

Far less important but almost equally popular is the little waltz known as *Valse Triste:*

[5]This is the version of Frederick H. Martens, published by G. Schirmer, New York. Chas. F. Manney makes it, "Dear land of home, our hearts to thee are holden." (B. F. Wood Music Co.)

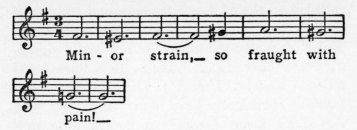

Min - or   strain,— so   fraught with

pain!—

Sibelius has to his credit a number of tone poems, all to be considered legitimate program music. Among them are *En Saga, The Swan of Tuonela, Lemminkainen's Homecoming, Pohjola's Daughter, Tapiola, Belshazzar's Feast* and *The Oceanides*. He belongs among the interpreters of moods and emotions rather than the tone painters whose programs demanded a definite story or picture to be reproduced in music.

CONCLUSION

Even this bird's-eye view of program music emphasizes certain points which may be worth remembering. The history and literature of the art actually show more music of the programmatic than of the absolute type. From the standpoint of popularity program music is far ahead of its classic rival.

The answer, as usual, is probably to be found in the line of least resistance. Music in general may be classified in several categories, ranging from the most to the least obvious, and the barometer of popularity seems to run parallel with these classifications.

First comes music that has the help of words, action, facial expression, costumes and scenery—in other words, opera. Next is the music that profits by words but without any of the other advantages of stagecraft. This includes song in general, oratorio, cantatas and choral works.

In the third class appears the music that has the co-operation of stage action, costumes and scenery but without words, namely, the ballet. When ballet music is played without the staging it becomes program music. This again may be divided into two classes. The first includes music for which a complete program is announced by the composer, usually through a poem or an elaborate outline. The second class contains those compositions that have their programs indicated only by a title. Narrative, descriptive and imitative music may be considered more obvious than the suggestive type, which seeks only to create a mood or an emotion, even with the help of a title or a program note.

Finally there is the music known as pure or absolute, into which no program enters and which contents itself with the beautiful arrangement of tones for their own sake. How far such absolute music may be influenced by definite ideas in the minds of its creators is a problem that has never been solved and never will be.

The surprising thing is that all the composers of music, regardless of the type they produced, were aiming at essentially the same ideals. They have all tried eventually to express the abstract in concrete terms. Specifically their task has been to transfer their own thoughts, moods and emotions to other human beings through the command of a common medium of expression. Their success has depended in part on the importance of these thoughts, moods and emotions and partly on the individual command of the medium. A man is not an artist merely because he has wonderful thoughts and feelings. He must be able to express them in a way that will be directly intelligible to others, whether his medium be music or pictures or the written word.

The chief weakness of modernism is that it fails to take into account this necessary communion of the artist with his audience. If he really has anything worth expressing, somehow, at some time or other, he will find an appreciative public. This appreciation has not always come during his lifetime, but generally there were unmistakable signs of it.

The greater the confidence of a creator in his art, the less he has felt called upon to announce his intentions and explain his meanings. Any programmatic title is in a sense an admission of weakness. Yet it would be absurd to expect a really dramatic piece of music, particularly of the narrative or descriptive type, to deliver its message automatically, without a hint of any kind to the listener. If it is really great music it will stand on its own feet, regardless of any announced program. If it is not great music no amount of explanation or interpretation will help it.

RECORDS OF GREAT PROGRAM MUSIC

THE LIST below includes the outstanding phonograph recordings issued by the leading American companies, Columbia, Decca and Victor. The makers are indicated by the initial just before each catalogue number.

COMPOSER AND COMPOSITION	INTERPRETER	RECORD NO.
ALBÉNIZ, ISAAC		
Fête-Dieu à Séville	Stokowski—Phila. Orch.	V. 7158
Granada (Serenata)	Harry Horlick	D. 18087
AUBER, DANIEL		
Fra Diavolo Overture	Harrison—Hastings Phil. Orch.	D. 25642
" " "	Bourdon—Victor Sym. Orch.	V. 22008
Overture, La Muette de Portici	Milan Sym. Orch.	C. 7268-M
BALAKIREFF, MILY		
Islamey	Hollywood Bowl Orch.	V. 6870
"	Simon Barer (piano)	V. 14023
BEETHOVEN, LUDWIG VAN		
Overtures:		
Consecration of the House	Weingartner—London Phil. Orch.	C. X-140
Coriolanus	Mengelberg—Concertgebouw	C. 68049-D
"	" "	D. 25275
"	Sir Adrian Boult—B.B.C. Sym. Orch.	V. 11909
"	Casals—London Sym. Orch.	V. 9279
"	Bruno Walter—London Sym. Orch.	V. 12535
Egmont	Weingartner—Vienna Phil. Orch.	C. 69195-D
"	Mengelberg—Concertgebouw	D. 25234
"	" Phil. Orch.	V. 7291
"	Victor Sym. Orch.	V. 35790
Fidelio	Raybould Orch.	C. DB-835
"	Weingartner—London Phil. Orch.	C. 69545-D
"	Boult—B.B.C. Sym. Orch.	V. 11809
Leonore No. 1	Mengelberg—Concertgebouw	C. 68055-D
" No. 2	Weingartner—London Sym. Orch.	C. X-96
" No. 3	Mengelberg—Concertgebouw	C. X-40
" " "	Weissmann—Phil. Orch.	D. 25811-2
" " "	Alfred Hertz—San Francisco Sym.	V. 6906-7
" " "	Bruno Walter—Vienna Phil.	V. M-359
Prometheus	Weingartner—Vienna Phil. Orch.	C. 68565-D
"	Weingartner—London Sym. Orch.	C. 68220-D
Piano Sonatas:		
Op. 13 ("Pathétique")	Karol Szreter	D. 25230-1
Op. 13 "	Wilhelm Bachaus	V. 6771-2
Op. 27, No. 2 ("Moonlight")	Egon Petri	C. X-77
" " " " "	Karol Szreter	D. 22015-6
" " " " "	Wilhelm Bachaus	V. 8735-6
" " " " "	Harold Bauer	V. 6591-2
" " " " "	Ignace Paderewski	V. M-349

319

COMPOSER AND COMPOSITION	INTERPRETER	RECORD NO.
BEETHOVEN, LUDWIG VAN—*Continued*		
Op. 23 ("Appassionata")	Walter Gieseking	C. M-365
" "	Harold Bauer	V. 6697–8
" " "	Edwin Fischer	V. M-279
" " "	Rudolf Serkin	V. M-583
Symphonies:		
No. 3, Op. 55 ("Eroica")	Weingartner—Vienna Phil. Orch.	C. M-285
" " " " "	Max von Schillings—Phil. Orch.	D. 25244–9
" " " " "	Koussevitzky—London Sym. Orch.	V. M-263
No. 6, Op. 68 ("Pastoral")	Paray—Concerts Colonne Orch.	C. M-285
" " " " "	Max von Schillings—Phil. Orch.	D. 25493–8
" " " " "	Toscanini—B.B.C. Orch.	V. M-417
" " " " "	Koussevitzky—Boston Sym. Orch.	V. M-50
BERLIOZ, HECTOR		
Overture, Beatrice & Benedict	Harty—London Phil. Orch.	C. 68342-D
" " " "	Goldman Band	V. 25757
BIZET, GEORGES		
L'Arlésienne Suite No. 1	Beecham—London Phil. Orch.	C. X-69
" " " "	Goossens—Royal Opera Orch.	V. 9112–3
L'Arlésienne Suite No. 2	Fiedler—Boston "Pops"	V. M-683
BORODIN, ALEXANDER		
In the Steppes of Central Asia	Pierné—Concerts Colonne Orch.	D. 25390
" " " " " "	Coates—London Sym. Orch.	V. 11169
BRAHMS, JOHANNES		
Academic Festival Overture	Mengelberg—Concertgebouw	C. X-42
" " "	Fritz Stiedry—Phil. Orch.	D. 25146
" " "	Gabrilowitsch—Detroit Sym. Orch.	V. 6833
" " "	Bruno Walter—Vienna Phil. Orch.	V. 12190
Tragic Overture	Beecham—London Phil. Orch.	C. X-85
" "	Boult—B.B.C. Sym. Orch.	V. 11533
" "	Toscanini—Phil. Sym. Orch.	V. M-507
Ballade in D Min. ("Edward")	Anatole Kitain (piano)	C. 69280-D
" " " " "	Wilhelm Bachaus (piano)	V. 7988
CARPENTER, JOHN ALDEN		
Adventures in a Perambulator	Ormandy—Minneapolis Sym. Orch.	V. M-238
Skyscrapers	Shilkret—Victor Sym. Orch.	V. M-130
CHAMINADE, CÉCILE		
Callirhoë (Ballet Suite)	Victor Olof—Salon Orch.	D. 25189
The Flatterer	Hans Barth (piano)	V. 20346
Scarf Dance	" "	V. 20346
CHOPIN, FRÉDÉRIC FRANÇOIS		
Ballade No. 1 G Min.	Léon Kartun	D. 25369
Ballade No. 3 A flat Maj.	Jean Dennery	D. 25314
Ballades	Alfred Cortot	V. M-399
Barcarolle	Alfred Höhn	D. 25117
Berceuse	Alfred Cortot	V. 6752
Étude No. 9 ("Butterfly")	Raoul Koczalski	D. 20426
" Op. 25, No. 11 ("Winter Wind")	Josef Lhevinne	V. 8868
Étude Op. 10, No. 2 ("Revolutionary")	Alfred Höhn	D. 25113
" " " " "	Ignace Paderewski	V. 1387

COMPOSER AND COMPOSITION	INTERPRETER	RECORD NO.
Fantasie Impromptu	Emil Sauer	D. 25110
" "	Harold Bauer	V. 6546
" "	Alfred Cortot	V. 8239
Fantasie F Min.	Alfred Cortot	V. 8250
Funeral March	H.M. Grenadier Guards Band	C. 7340-M
" "	Pryor's Band	V. 35800
" "	Mark Andrews (organ)	V. 35958
Prélude D flat Maj. ("Raindrop")	Josef Pembaur	D. 25132
CUI, CÉSAR		
Orientale	Emanuel Feuermann (cello)	C. 17158-D
"	Mischa Elman (violin)	V. 1354
DEBUSSY, CLAUDE		
L'Après-midi d'un Faune	Beecham—London Phil. Orch.	C. 69600-D
" " " "	G. Cloëz—Opera Comique Orch.	D. 25048
" " " "	Pierné—Concerts Colonne Orch.	D. 25392
" " " "	Stokowski—Phila. Orch.	V. 6696
La Cathédrale Engloutie	Walter Gieseking	C. 17077-D
" " "	Fray & Braggiotti	D. 23086
" " "	George Copeland	V. 7962
" " "	Alfred Cortot	V. 15049
" " "	Olga Samaroff Stokowski	V. 7304
" " "	Stokowski—Phila. Orch.	V. 7454
Children's Corner	Walter Gieseking	C. M-314
" "	Janine Weill	D. 25934
" "	Alfred Cortot	V. 7147
Clair de Lune	George Copeland	V. 7963
" " "	Harold Bauer	V. 7122
" " "	Stokowski—Phila. Orch.	V. 1812
Dancing Virgins of Delphi	Alfred Cortot	V. 1920
Fêtes	Inghelbrecht—Grand Orch.	C. P-69316-D
"	Josef & Rosina Lhevinne	V. 1741
"	Stokowski—Phila. Orch.	V. 1309
Feux d'Artifice	Marcel Ciampi	C. 69308-D
La Fille aux Cheveux de Lin	Grisha Golubov (violin)	C. 17078-D
" " " " " "	Marius Gaillard (piano)	D. 20090
" " " " " "	Fritz Kreisler (violin)	V. 1358
" " " " " "	Jascha Heifetz (violin)	V. 6622
General Lavine	George Copeland	V. 1644
Ibéria	Pierné—Concerts Colonne Orch.	D. 25558–60
"	Barbirolli—Philharmonic Sym.	V. M-460
Jardins dans la Pluie	Marius François Gaillard	D. 25365
La Mer	Coppola—Paris Conservatory Orch.	V. M-89
Minstrels	Marius Gaillard	D. 20091
Nocturnes	Inghelbrecht—Grand Orchestre	C. M-344
"	Pierné—Concerts Colonne Orch.	D. 25544–6
Pagodes	Marius Gaillard	D. 25427
Reflets dans l'Eau	Walter Gieseking	C. 68575-D
Rêverie	Walter Gieseking	C. 17138-D
Soirée dans Granade	Walter Gieseking	C. 68575-D
Suite Bergamasque	Walter Gieseking	C. X-8
" "	Marius Gaillard	D. 25021

COMPOSER AND COMPOSITION	INTERPRETER	RECORD NO.
DEBUSSY, CLAUDE—*Continued*		
Veils	George Copeland	V. 14904
"	Alfred Cortot	V. 1920
"	Ignace Paderewski	V. 1531
DE FALLA, MANUEL		
El Amor Brujo	Morales–Sym. Orch.	C. M-108
" " "	G. Cloëz—Grand Sym. Orch.	D. 20075-6
" " "	Léon Kartun (piano)	D. 25941
" " "	Boston "Pops" Orch.	V. 12160
Andaluza	Aline Van Bärentzen (piano)	V. 9705
Asturiana	Nathan Milstein (violin)	C. 17111-D
Nights in the Gardens of Spain	Orquestra Betica de Camera	C. M-156
" " " " " "	Coppola—Sym. Orch.	V. 9703-5
The Three-Cornered Hat	Arbos—Madrid Sym. Orch.	C. X-38
" " " "	Fiedler—Boston "Pops" Orch.	V. M-505
DELIBES, LÉO		
Coppélia Ballet	Kurtz—London Phil. Orch.	C. 69323-D
" "	G. Cloëz—Grand Sym. Paris	D. 20070-1
Lakmé Overture	G. Cloëz—Grand Sym. Paris	D. 20094
La Source	G. Cloëz—Grand Sym. Paris	D. 20112-3
" "	Ormandy—Minneapolis Sym. Orch.	V. M-220
Sylvia	Ormandy—Minneapolis Sym. Orch.	V. M-220
DELIUS, FREDERICK		
In a Summer Garden	Geoffrey Toye—London Sym. Orch.	V. 9731-2
On Hearing the First Cuckoo in Spring	" " " " "	V. 4270
DUKAS, PAUL		
The Sorcerer's Apprentice	Gaubert—Paris Conservatoire Orch.	C. 68959-D
" " "	Toscanini—Phil. Orch.	V. 7021
DVOŘÁK, ANTONIN		
Carnival Overture	Fiedler—Boston "Pops" Orch.	V. 12159
Symphony No. 5 (From the New World)	Harty—Halle Orch.	C. M-77
Symphony No. 5 (From the New World)	Szell—Czech Phil. Orch.	V. M-469
Symphony No. 5 (From the New World)	Stokowski—Phila. Orch.	V. M-273
ELGAR, EDWARD		
Pomp and Circumstance	H.M. Grenadier Guards Band	D. 25754
" " "	Chicago Sym. Orch.	V. 11885
" " "	Sir Edward Elgar—Royal Albert Hall	V. 9016
Enigma Variations	Harty—Halle Orch.	C. M-165
" "	Sir Henry Wood—Queen's Hall Orch.	D. 25739-42
" "	Boult—B.B.C. Sym. Orch.	V. M-475
GERSHWIN, GEORGE		
An American in Paris	Gershwin—Victor Sym. Orch.	V. 35963-4
GLAZOUNOFF, ALEXANDER		
From the Middle Ages	De Sabata—E.I.A.R. Sym. Orch.	D. 25824
The Seasons	Glazounoff—Orch.	C. M-284
" "	Järnefelt—Phil. Orch.	D. 25423-5
" "	Barbirolli—Royal Opera Orch.	V. 11442

COMPOSER AND COMPOSITION	INTERPRETER	RECORD NO.
GLINKA, MICHAEL I.		
The Enchanted Lake	Järnefelt—Stor Sym.	D. 25499
GLUCK, CHRISTOPH WILLIBALD		
Alceste Overture	Mengelberg—Concertgebouw	D. 25571
" "	Boult—B.B.C. Sym. Orch.	V. 12041
Iphigenia in Aulis	Barlow—Columbia B.C. Sym. Orch.	C. X-138
" "	Weissmann—Phil. Orch.	D. 25339
Orpheus and Eurydice (Ballet)	G. Cloëz—Phil. Orch.	D. 20065
GOUNOD, CHARLES		
Faust Ballet Music	Weissmann—Phil. Orch.	D. 25323
Funeral March of a Marionette	Ormandy—Minn. Sym.	V. 8661
GRIEG, EDVARD		
Heart Wounds	Järnefelt—Stor Sym. Orch.	D. 25286
Norwegian Bridal Procession	Bowers—Columbia Sym. Orch.	C. 7345-M
" " "	Clothilde Kleeberg (piano)	D. 20230
" " "	Bourdon—Victor Concert Orch.	V. 20805
Papillon	Marthe Rennesson (piano)	D. 20615
Peer Gynt Suite No. 1	Weissmann—Phil. Orch	D. 25254-5
" " " No. 2	" " "	D. 25462
" " " No. 1	Inghelbrecht—Grand Orch. Phil.	C. X-110
To Spring	Marthe Rennesson (piano)	D. 20616
" "	Myrtle Eaver (piano)	V. 22153
" "	Marek Weber's Orch.	V. 25777
Wedding Day at Troldhaugen	Walter Gieseking	D. 25283
GRIFFES, CHARLES T.		
The Pleasure Dome of Kubla Khan	Ormandy—Minneapolis Sym. Orch.	V. 7957
The White Peacock	Barlow—Columbia Sym. Orch.	C. 17140-D
" " "	Olga Samaroff Stokowski	V. 7384
GROFÉ, FERDE		
Grand Canyon Suite	Paul Whiteman—Concert Orch.	V. C-18
Metropolis	" " "	V. 35933-4
Mississippi Suite	" " "	V. 35859
HANDEL, GEORGE FREDERICK		
Dead March from Saul	H.M. Grenadier Guards Band	C. 7340-M
Fireworks	Moore—British Light Orch.	C. 331-M
" "	American Soc. Ancient Instruments	V. 1716
The Harmonious Blacksmith	Wm. Murdoch (piano)	D. 25819-D
" " "	Walter Gieseking	C. 68595-D
" " "	Alfred Cortot	V. 6752
" " "	Wanda Landowska	V. 1193
HAYDN, FRANZ JOSEPH		
Symphony No. 4 ("The Clock")	Toscanini—Phil. Orch.	V. M-57
Symphony No. 6 ("Surprise")	Barlow—Columbia B.C. Orch.	C. M-363
" " " "	Hans Knappertsbusch—Phil. Orch.	D. 25406
" " " "	Koussevitzky—Boston Sym. Orch.	V. M-472
Symphony No. 45 ("Farewell")	Wood—London Sym. Orch.	C. M-205
Symphony No. 100 ("Military")	Hans Knappertsbusch—Phil. Orch.	D. 20038-41
" " " "	Walter—Vienna Phil. Orch.	V. M-472
HONEGGER, ARTHUR		
Pastorale d'Été	Honegger—Grand Sym. Paris	D. 25199

COMPOSER AND COMPOSITION	INTERPRETER	RECORD NO.
HONEGGER, ARTHUR—*Continued*		
Pacific 231	Honegger—Grand Sym. Paris	D. 25206
" "	Continental Sym. Orch.	V. 9276
Prelude to "The Tempest"	Honegger—Grand Sym. Paris	D. 20072
HUMPERDINCK, ENGELBERT		
Overture, Hänsel & Gretel	Paul Minssart—Paris Phil.	D. 25092
IBERT, JACQUES		
A Giddy Girl	Jean Dennery (piano)	D. 20625
Le Petit Âne Blanc	Marthe Rennesson (piano)	D. 20615
IPPOLITOFF–IVANOFF, MIKAIL		
Caucasian Sketches	Georges Boulanger Orch.	D. 20459
In the Mosque	Victor Sym. Orch.	V. 36017
In the Mountain Pass	Fiedler—Boston "Pops"	V. 12460
" " " "	Victor Sym. Orch.	V. 36017
In the Village	Stokowski—Phila. Orch.	V. 6514
JANSSEN, WERNER		
New Year's Eve in New York	Victor Sym. Orch.	V. 36157–8
LALO, EDOUARD		
Norwegian Rhapsody	Pierné—Concerts Colonne	D. 25331–2
LIADOFF, ANATOLE		
Enchanted Lake	Koussevitzky—Boston Sym. Orch.	V. 14078
Music Box	Walter—Bohemians	C. 252-M
" "	Coates—London Sym. Orch.	V. 9728
" "	Fiedler—Boston "Pops"	V. 4390
" "	Victor Woodwind Ensemble	V. 19923
LISZT, FRANZ		
Au Bord d'une Source	Louis Kentner	C. 69308-D
" " " "	Theophil Demetriescu	D. 20356
La Campanella	Ignaze Friedman	C. 7141-M
" "	Ignace Paderewski	V. 6825
Consolation No. 3	Nathan Milstein	C. 68479-D
" " "	Emil Sauer	C. 69688-D
Dance of the Gnomes	Rachmaninoff	V. 1184
" " " "	Emil Sauer	D. 25110
" " " "	Eileen Joyce	D. 20048
Gondoliera	Josef Hofmann	C. 7024-M
Jeux d'Eaux	Claudio Arrau	D. 25175
Liebestraum	Percy Grainger	C. 7134-M
"	Karol Szreter	D. 25130
"	Wilhelm Bachaus	V. 6582
"	Rudolph Ganz	V. 7290
"	Victor Sym. Orch.	V. 35820
Mazeppa	Knappertsbusch—Phil. Orch.	D. 20082–4
St. Francis Walking on the Water	Sigfrid Grundeis	D. 20359
" " " " " "	Alfred Cortot	V. 15245
Totentanz	Kilenyi—Sym. Orch.	C. X-122
"	Sanroma & Boston "Pops"	V. M-392
Venezia e Napoli	Louis Kentner	C. X-105
" " "	Josef Hofmann	C. 7024-M
" " "	Karol Szreter	D. 20031
Waldesrauschen	Wilhelm Bachaus	V. 7270

COMPOSER AND COMPOSITION	INTERPRETER	RECORD NO.
MacDOWELL, EDWARD		
A.D. 1620	Myra Hess	C. M-234
From an Indian Lodge	Victor Concert Orch.	V. 20342
Indian Suite	Barlow—Columbia Sym. Orch.	C. M-373
To a Water-Lily	Chicago Sym. Orch.	V. 1152
To a Wild Rose	Musical Art Quartet	C. 215-M
" " " "	Chicago Sym. Orch.	V. 1152
" " " "	Michael Gusikoff	V. 19892
Witches' Dance	Felix Dyck	D. 20229
" "	Hans Barth	V. 20396
MASSENET, JULES		
Meditation from Thais	Defosse—Paris Sym. Orch.	D. 25323
" " "	Edith Lorand (violin)	D. 25079
Overture, Manon	G. Cloëz—Grand Sym. Orch.	D. 20088
Overture, Phèdre	Andolfi—Grand Orch.	C. P-69395-D
" "	Hertz—San Francisco Orch.	V. 7154
Scènes Alsaciennes	G. Cloëz—Grand Sym.	D. 25500
MENDELSSOHN, FELIX (BARTHOLDY)		
Overture, Fingal's Cave	Beecham—London Sym. Orch.	C. 69400
" " "	Bodanzky—Phil. Orch.	D. 25791-2
" " "	Boult—B.B.C. Sym. Orch.	V. 11886
" Midsummer Night's Dream	Fiedler—Boston "Pops" Orch.	V. 11919-20
" Ruy Blas	Boult—B.B.C. Sym. Orch.	V. 11791
Songs Without Words 22 & 47	Wm. Murdoch (piano)	D. 25729
" " " " 25	Gregor Piatigorsky (cello)	D. 20066
" " " " 30	Marthe Rennesson (piano)	D. 20616
" " " " 9	Archer Gibson (organ)	V. 36222
" " " " 9	Symphonet—Curtis	V. 25845
" " " " Op. 109	Pablo Casals (cello)	V. 7193
" " " " E Maj.	Alfred Cortot	V. 15174
Spinning Song	Sergei Rachmaninoff	V. 1326
Spring Song	London Sym. Orch.	V. 11453
" "	Florentine Quartet	V. 20195
" "	Victor Concert Orch.	V. 21449
MOUSSORGSKY, MODESTE		
Night on Bald Mountain	Paray—Concerts Colonne	C. 68305
" " " "	G. Cloëz—Paris Phil. Orch.	D. 20499
" " " "	Coates—London Sym. Orch.	V. 11448
Pictures at an Exhibition	Koussevitzky—Boston Sym.	V. M-102
" " " "	Ormandy—Phila. Orch.	V. M-442
Prélude, Khovantchina	Harty—Halle Orch.	C. 67743-D
MOZART, WOLFGANG AMADEUS		
Overture, Magic Flute	Walter & Orch.	C. 67660-D
Overture, Marriage of Figaro	Milan Sym. Orch.	C. 67947-D
" " " "	Beecham—London Sym. Orch.	C. X-85
Rondo alla Turca	Heger—Phil. Orch.	D. 20453
Overture, Il Seraglio	Weissmann—Phil. Orch.	D. 25155
Overture, Titus	Walter—Vienna Phil. Orch.	V. 12526
Turkish March	Wanda Landowska	V. 1193

COMPOSER AND COMPOSITION	INTERPRETER	RECORD NO.
NEVIN, ETHELBERT		
A Day in Venice	Victor Salon Orch.	V. 9478
Narcissus	Dajos Bela Orch.	D. 25441
"	Victor Sym. Orch.	V. 9479
NICOLAI, OTTO		
Overture, Merry Wives of Windsor	Beecham—London Sym. Orch.	C. 68938-D
" " " " "	Szell—Phil. Orch.	D. 25142
PIERNÉ, GABRIEL		
Entrance of the Little Fauns	Damrosch—New York Sym. Orch.	C. 67345-D
" " " " "	Fiedler—Boston "Pops" Orch.	V. 4319
Impressions de Music-Hall	Pierné—Concerts Colonne Orch.	D. 25396-8
March of the Little Lead Soldiers	Victor Concert Orch.	V. 19730
PONCHIELLI, AMILCARE		
Dance of the Hours	Weissmann—Phil. Orch.	D. 25162
" " " "	Fiedler—Boston "Pops" Orch.	V. 11833
" " " "	Lew White (organ)	V. 36225
" " " "	Victor Sym. Orch.	V. 35833
PROKOFIEFF, SERGE		
Love of the Three Oranges, March	Gaston Poulet—Paris	D. 25123-5
" " " " " "	Coates—London Sym. Orch.	V. 9128
" " " " " "	Koussevitzky—Boston	V. 7197
" " " " " "	" "	V. 4950
Peter and the Wolf	Koussevitzky—Boston	V. M-566
" " " "	Smallens—Decca Sym. Orch.	D. 29064-6
RACHMANINOFF, SERGEI		
The Isle of the Dead	Rachmaninoff—Phila. Orch.	V. M-75
RAVEL, MAURICE		
Bolero	Mengelberg—Concertgebouw	C. 67890-1-D
"	Minssart—Paris Sym. Orch.	D. 20074
"	Koussevitzky—Boston Sym. Orch.	V. 7251-2
"	Fiedler—Boston "Pops" Orch.	V. 2174-5
"	Shilkret—Victor Orch.	V. 22571
"	Morton Gould (piano)	V. 24205
Daphnis et Chloë	Gaubert—Orch. des Concerts	C. X-32
" " "	Koussevitzky—Boston	V. 7143-4
" " "	Coppola—Paris Conservatoire	V. 11882
Dream of a Naughty Boy	Continental Sym. Orch.	V. 9306
Jeux d'Eau	Alfred Cortot	V. 7729
Mother Goose Suite	Damrosch—New York Sym.	C. M-74
" " "	Pierné—Paris Conservatoire	D. 25319-20
" " "	Koussevitzky—Boston Sym.	V. 7370-1
Pavane pour une Infante Défunte	Pierné—Concerts Colonne Orch.	D. 25416
" " " " "	Freitas—Branco Orch.	C. 68066-D
" " " " "	Continental Sym. Orch.	V. 9306
RESPIGHI, OTTORINO		
The Birds	Defauw—Brussels Royal Cons. Orch.	C. X-108
The Fountains of Rome	Molinari—Phil. Orch.	D. 25841-2
" " " "	Weissmann—Phil. Orch.	D. 25375-6
" " " "	Barbirolli—New York Phil. Orch.	V. M-576
" " " "	Coates—London Sym. Orch.	V. 9126-7

COMPOSER AND COMPOSITION	INTERPRETER	RECORD NO.
The Pines of Rome	Molajoli—Milan Sym. Orch.	C. 17060–2
" " " "	Panizzo—Milan Sym. Orch.	D. 20146–8
" " " "	Coppola—Paris Conservatoire Orch.	V. 11917–8
RIMSKY–KORSAKOFF, NIKOLAI		
Flight of the Bumble Bee	Harty—Halle Orch.	C. 67743-D
" " " " "	Joseph Szigeti (violin)	C. 7304-M
" " " " "	Anatole Kitain (piano)	C. 69272-D
" " " " "	Pablo Casals (cello)	V. 7193
" " " " "	Stock—Chicago Sym.	V. 6579
" " " " "	Vronsky-Babin (two pianos)	V. 4377
" " " " "	The Aeolians	V. 4376
" " " " "	Jascha Heifetz (violin)	V. 1645
Russian Easter	H.M. Grenadier Guards	D. 25649
" "	Stokowski—Phila. Orch.	V. 7018–9
Schéhérazade Suite	G. Cloëz—Grand Sym. Orch.	D. 25561–6
" "	Stokowski—Phila. Orch.	V. 8698–8703
" "	Dorati—London Phil. Orch.	V. M-509
The Snow Maiden	Coates—London Sym. Orch.	V. 11454
ROSSINI, GIOACCHINO		
Overture, Barber of Seville	Mascagni—Phil. Orch.	D. 25141
Boutique Fantasque	Goossens—London Sym. Orch.	V. M-415
Overture, Italians in Algiers	Toscanini—Phil. Orch.	V. 14161
" " " "	Victor Sym. Orch.	V. 24109
Overture, Semiramide	Weissmann—Phil. Orch.	D. 25005
" "	Toscanini—Phil. Orch.	V. M-408
" "	Victor Sym. Orch.	V. 22288
Overture, William Tell	Beecham—London Sym. Orch.	C. X-60
" " " "	Mascagni—Phil. Orch.	D. 25457–8
RUBINSTEIN, ANTON		
Kamennoi-Ostrow	Fiedler—Boston "Pops" Orch.	V. 12191
" "	Victor Sym. Orch.	V. 35820
SAINT–SAËNS, CAMILLE		
Bacchanale	Pierné—Concerts Colonne	D. 25334
Carnival of the Animals	Stokowski—Phila. Orch.	V. M-71
Le Cygne (The Swan)	Lorenzi & Torch (harp-organ)	C. 418-M
" " " "	Emanuel Feuermann (cello)	D. 25085
" " " "	Gregor Piatigorsky (cello)	D. 20043
Danse Macabre	G. Cloëz—Philharmonic Orch.	D. 25525
" "	Karol Szreter	D. 25232
" "	Stokowski—Phila. Orch.	V. 14162
Phaëton	G. Cloëz—Philharmonic Orch.	D. 20006
" "	Coppola—Société des Concerts de Conservatoire	V. 11431
Le Rouet d'Omphale	G. Cloëz—Grand Sym. Orch.	D. 25419–20
Suite Algérienne	G. Cloëz—Grand Sym. Orch.	D. 20079–81
" "	Continental Sym. Orch.	V. 9296
SCHUBERT, FRANZ		
Rosamunde Ballet	Heger—Philharmonic Orch.	D. 20551–2
" "	Koussevitzky—Boston Sym. Orch.	V. 14119
" "	Stokowski—Phila. Orch.	V. 1312

COMPOSER AND COMPOSITION	INTERPRETER	RECORD NO.
SCHUBERT, FRANZ—*Continued*		
Rosamunde Ballet	Bruno Walter—London Sym. Orch.	V. 12534
" "	Victor Salon Orch.	V. 9307
Rosamunde Overture	Sir Hamilton Harty—Halle Orch.	C. 68322-D
" "	Sargent—New Symphony Orch.	V. 9475
SCHUMANN, ROBERT		
Abendlied (Evening Song)	Vienna Trio	D. 23050
" " "	Gregor Piatigorsky (cello)	D. 25139
" " "	Albert Spalding (violin)	V. 1727
Carnaval	Goehr—London Phil. Orch.	C. 69461
"	Karol Szreter (piano)	D. 25289-91
"	Sergei Rachmaninoff (piano)	V. M-70
"	Goossens—London Sym. Orch.	V. M-513
"	Myra Hess (piano)	V. M-476
Frühlingsnacht	Josef Lhevinne	V. 8766
Manfred Overture	Max von Schillings—Philharmonic Orch.	D. 25474-5
" "	Sir Adrian Boult—B.B.C. Sym.	V. 11713-4
Nachtstück	Archer Gibson (organ)	V. 36166
"	Wilhelm Bachaus (piano)	V. 14978
Papillons	Alfred Cortot	V. 1819-20
The Prophet Bird	Ignace Paderewski	V. 1426
Träumerei	Efrem Zimbalist (violin)	C. 17105-D
"	Gregor Piatigorsky (cello)	D. 20019
"	Ormandy—Minneapolis Orch.	V. 8285
"	Mischa Elman (violin)	V. 1482
"	Elman—Casals	V. 1178
"	Elman—Victor String Ensemble	V. 19854
"	Edwin Lemare (organ)	V. 35843
"	Albert Spalding (violin)	V. 1727
SCRIABIN, ALEXANDER		
Poem of Ecstasy	Stokowski—Phila. Orch.	V. M-125
Prometheus: Poem of Fire	" " "	"
SIBELIUS, JEAN		
Finlandia	Beecham—London Phil. Orch.	C. 69180-D
"	Weissmann—Philharmonic Orch.	D. 25418
"	Reginald Foort (organ)	V. 26225
"	Royal Albert Hall Orch.	V. 9015
"	Stokowski—Phila. Orch.	V. 7412
"	Victor Sym. Orch.	V. 36227
Night Ride and Sunrise, The Oceanides	Sir Adrian Boult—B.B.C. Sym.	V. M-311
Pohjola's Daughter	Kajanus—London Sym. Orch.	V. M-333
"	Koussevitzky—Boston Sym. Orch.	V. M-474
The Swan of Tuonela	Stokowski—Phila. Sym. Orch.	V. 7380
Valse Triste	Sir Hamilton Harty—London Phil.	C. 7322-M
" "	Sir Henry Wood—Queen's Hall Orch.	D. 20220
" "	Dajos Bela Orch.	D. 25277
" "	Stock—Chicago Sym. Orch.	V. 6579
" "	Stokowski—Phila. Orch.	V. 14726
" "	Goossens—Symphony Orch.	V. 9926
" "	Victor Concert Orch.	V. 36228

COMPOSER AND COMPOSITION	INTERPRETER	RECORD NO.
SINDING, CHRISTIAN		
Rustle of Spring	The Bohemians	C. 410-M
" " "	Marthe Rennesson (piano)	D. 20616
" " "	Weissmann—Philharmonic Orch.	D. 20453
" " "	Hans Barth (piano)	V. 20121
SMETANA, FRIEDRICH		
Overture, The Bartered Bride	Hamilton Harty—London Phil. Orch.	C. 7314-M
" " " "	Stock—Chicago Sym. Orch.	V. 1555
From Bohemia's Meadows and Forests	Kubelik—Czech Phil. Orch.	V. M-523
The Moldau	Mörike—Philharmonic Orch.	D. 25203–4
" "	Blech—Berlin State Opera Orch.	V. 11434–5
" "	Kubelik—Czech Phil. Orch.	V. M-523
" "	Victor Sym. Orch.	V. 21748–9
STRAUSS, JOHANN		
Overture, Die Fledermaus	Walter—Berlin State Opera Orch.	C. 9080-M
" " "	Bodanzky—Phil. Orch.	D. 25081
" " "	Dajos Bela Orch.	D. 25154
" " "	Ormandy—Minneapolis Orch.	V. 8651
" " "	Victor Sym. Orch.	V. 35956
" " "	Marek Weber Orch.	V. 36226
Waltzes:		
Artist's Life	Walter—Orch. Raymonde	C. 368-M
" "	Fiedler—Boston "Pops" Orch.	V. 12194
" "	Dajos Bela Orch.	D. 25033
The Beautiful Blue Danube	Walter—Orch. Raymonde	C. 262-M
" " " "	Weingartner—Royal Phil. Orch.	C. 69275-D
" " " "	Mörike—Philharmonic Orch.	D. 25173
" " " "	Ormandy—Minneapolis Sym. Orch.	V. 8650
" " " "	Stokowski—Phila. Orch.	V. 15425
" " " "	Josef Lhevinne (piano)	V. 6840
" " " "	Vienna Choir Boys	V. 1908
" " " "	Marek Weber's Orch.	V. 25199
" " " "	Pryor's Band	V. 35799
" " " "	International Concert Orch.	V. 35927
" " " "	Ray Noble and his Orch.	V. 24806
" " " "	Tommy Dorsey and his Orch.	V. 25556
Roses from the South	Bruno Walter and Orch.	C. 69561-D
" " " "	Stock—Chicago Symphony Orch.	V. 6647
" " " "	Pryor's Band	V. 35799
" " " "	Anton's Paramount Theater Orch.	V. 26322
Tales from the Vienna Woods	Walter and Symphony Orch.	C. 69562-D
" " " " "	Edith Lorand and Viennese Orch.	D. 25327
" " " " "	Stokowski—Phila. Orch.	V. 15425
" " " " "	Ormandy—Minneapolis Orch.	V. 8652
" " " " "	Leo Reisman's Orch.	V. 25745
" " " " "	Marek Weber and his Orch.	V. 20915
Thousand and One Nights	Weingartner and Orch.	C. 69563-D
" " " "	Krauss—Vienna Phil. Orch.	V. 9990
Voices of Spring	Walter—Orch. Raymonde	C. 360-M
" " "	Weingartner and Orch.	C. 69564-D

COMPOSER AND COMPOSITION	INTERPRETER	RECORD NO.
STRAUSS, JOHANN—*Continued*		
Voices of Spring	Dajos Bela Orch.	D. 25153
" " "	Koussevitzky—Boston Sym. Orch.	V. 6903
" " "	Szell—Vienna Phil. Orch.	V. 8925
" " "	Fiedler—Boston "Pops" Orch.	V. 4387
Wienerblut	Dajos Bela Orch.	D. 25153
"	Boston Sym. Orch.	V. 6903
"	Fiedler—Boston "Pops" Orch.	V. 12193
Wine, Women and Song	Bodanzky—Phil. Sym. Orch.	D. 25388
" " " "	Fiedler—Boston "Pops" Orch.	V. 12192
" " " "	Stock—Chicago Orch.	V. 6647
STRAUSS, RICHARD		
Also Sprach Zarathustra	Koussevitzky—Boston Sym.	V. M-257
Dance of the Seven Veils	Walter—Berlin Phil. Orch.	C. 67814-D
Death and Transfiguration	Weissmann—Phil. Orch.	D. 25350-2
" " "	Stokowski—Phila. Orch.	V. M-217
Don Juan	Klemperer—Phil. Orch.	D. 25444-5
" "	Coates—Sym. Orch.	V. 9114-5
" "	Busch—London Phil. Orch.	V. M-351
Don Quixote	Beecham—New York Phil. Orch.	V. M-144
Ein Heldenleben	Mengelberg—New York Phil. Orch.	V. M-44
Symphonia Domestica	Ormandy—Phila. Orch.	V. M-520
Tales from the Orient	Marek Weber's Orch.	V. 36181
Till Eulenspiegel's Merry Pranks	Klemperer—Phil. Orch.	D. 25421-2
" " " "	Defauw—Brussels Orch.	C. 67478-9-D
" " " "	Busch—B.B.C. Sym. Orch.	V. 11724-5
STRAVINSKY, IGOR		
Apollon Musagete	Boyd Neel Orch.	D. 25700-3-D
" "	Stravinsky—Orch.	V. M-49
The Firebird	Stravinsky—Orch.	C. M-115
" "	Boyd Neel Orch.	D. 25541-3
" "	Stokowski—Phila. Orch.	V. M-291
Fireworks	Pierné—Concerts Colonne Orch.	D. 25509
Pastorale	Szigeti—Magalov	C. 7304-M
"	Dushkin—Wind Quartet	C. 17075-D
"	Stokowski—Phila. Orch.	V. 1998
Petrouschka (Suite)	Stravinsky—Orch.	C. M-109
" "	Pierné—Concerts Colonne Orch.	D. 25526-8
" "	Stokowski—Phila. Orch.	V. M-574
Le Sacre du Printemps	Stravinsky—Orch.	C. M-129
" " " "	Stokowski—Phila. Orch.	V. M-74
Suite de Pulcinella	Stravinsky—Orch.	C. X-36
TAYLOR, DEEMS		
Through the Looking Glass	Barlow—Columbia B.C. Orch.	C. M-350
TCHAIKOWSKY, PETER I.		
Aurora's Wedding	Kurtz—London Phil. Orch.	V. M-326
Chanson Triste	Dajos Bela Orch.	D. 25152
1812 Overture	Fiedler—Boston "Pops" Orch.	V. M-515
" "	Stokowski—Phila. Orch.	V. 7499-7500
Francesca da Rimini	Coates—London Sym. Orch.	V. 11091-2
Hamlet Overture	Coates—London Sym. Orch.	V. M-395

COMPOSER AND COMPOSITION	INTERPRETER	RECORD NO.
Humoresque	Fritz Kreisler	V. 1170
Marche Slav	Stokowski—Phila. Orch.	V. 6513
" "	Fiedler—Boston "Pops" Orch.	V. 12006
Nutcracker Suite	Heger—Philharmonic Orch.	D. 25182–4
" "	Smallens—Decca Sym. Orch.	D. 23071–3
" "	Stokowski—Phila. Orch.	V. M–265
Romeo and Juliet Fantasie Overture	Mengelberg—Concertgebouw	C. X–33
" " " " "	Stokowski—Phila. Orch.	V. M–46
" " " " "	Koussevitzky—Boston Orch.	V. M–347
Sleeping Beauty Ballet	Fiedler—Boston "Pops" Orch.	V. 11932
Song Without Words	Stokowski—Phila. Orch.	V. 7202
The Swan Lake	Dorati—London Phil. Orch.	C. M–349
" " "	Barbirolli—London Phil. Orch.	V. 11666–7
Symphony No. 4	Mengelberg—Concertgebouw	C. M–133
" " "	" "	D. 25432–6
" " "	Stokowski—Phila. Orch.	V. M–48
" " "	Koussevitzky—Boston Sym. Orch.	V. M–327
Symphony No. 6 ("Pathétique")	Gaubert—Paris Conservatoire Orch.	C. M–277
" " " "	Koussevitzky—Boston Orch.	V. M–85
" " " "	Ormandy—Phila. Orch.	V. M–337
Troïka	Sergei Rachmaninoff (piano)	V. 6857
WAGNER, RICHARD		
A Faust Overture	Beecham—London Phil. Orch.	C. X–63
" " "	Coates—London Sym. Orch.	V. 9734
Fire Music (Die Walküre)	Von Hösslin—Bayreuth Festival Orch.	C. M–338
" " " "	Coates—Sym. Orch.	V. 9006
Overture, Flying Dutchman	Beecham—London Phil. Orch.	C. X–107
" " "	Mörike—Phil. Orch.	D. 25100–1
" " "	New York Phil. Orch.	V. 6547
" " "	Berlin State Phil. Orch.	V. 9275
Götterdämmerung, Siegfried's Funeral March	Bruno Walter—Orch.	C. 68044-D
Götterdämmerung, Siegfried's Rhine Journey	Mörike—Philharm. Orch.	D. 25377
" " " "	Bruno Walter—Orch.	C. 68101-D
Lohengrin, Prelude to Act III	Beecham—London Phil. Orch.	C. 68594-D
" " " " "	Bodanzky—Philharm. Orch.	D. 25556
" " " " "	Toscanini—Phil. Sym. Orch.	V. 14007
" " " " "	Chicago Sym. Orch.	V. 7386
" " " " "	Coates—Sym. Orch.	V. 9005
" Prelude	Victor Herbert's Orch.	V. 55048
" "	Mengelberg—Concertgebouw Orch.	D. 25270
" "	Toscanini—Phil. Sym. Orch.	V. 14006
Prelude to Die Meistersinger	Stokowski—Philadelphia Orch.	V. 6791
" " " "	Beecham—London Phil. Orch.	C. 68854-D
" " " "	Bodanzky—Phil. Orch.	D. 25555
" " " "	Karl Muck—Berlin State Opera Orch.	V. 6858–9
	Stock—Chicago Sym. Orch.	V. 6651
Prelude to Parsifal	Columbia Orch.	C. 67572–3-D
" " "	Muck—Berlin State Opera Orch.	V. 6858–62
	Stokowski—Phila. Orch.	V. 14728–31

COMPOSER AND COMPOSITION	INTERPRETER	RECORD NO.
WAGNER, RICHARD—*Continued*		
Good Friday Spell	Bayreuth Festival Orch.	C. 67370–1–D
" " "	Stokowski—Phila. Sym. Orch.	V. 14732–5
Rheingold, Entrance of the Gods	Bayreuth Festival Orch.	C. 67373–D
" " " " "	Siegfried Wagner—Phil. Orch.	D. 25073
" " " " "	Stokowski—Phila. Orch.	V. 7801
" " " " "	Coates—Sym. Orch.	V. 9109
Rienzi Overture	Weissmann—Phil. Orch.	D. 25073
" "	Fiedler—Boston "Pops" Orch.	V. 12447–8
	Stokowski—Philadelphia Orch.	V. 6624–5
Siegfried, Forest Murmurs	Bayreuth Festival Orch.	C. 67371–D
" " "	Pierné—Concerts Colonne Orch.	D. 25504
" " "	Mengelberg—Phil. Orch.	V. 7192
Tannhäuser Overture	Mengelberg—Concertgebouw Orch.	C. 68082–3–D
" "	Beecham—London Phil. Orch.	C. 69413–4–D
" "	Mengelberg—Concertgebouw Orch.	D. 25108–9
" "	Stokowski—Phila. Orch.	V. 15310–4
" "	Coates—Sym. Orch.	V. 9059–60
Tristan und Isolde, Prelude	Elmendorf—Bayreuth Orch.	C. M-101
" " " "	Stokowski—Philadelphia Orch.	V. 15302–6
" " " "	Hertz—San Francisco Sym. Orch.	V. 6585
Ride of the Valkyries (Die Walküre)	Von Hösslin—Bayreuth Festival Orch.	C. M-338
" " " " " "	Sir Henry Wood—Queen's Hall Orch.	D. 25569
" " " " " "	Coates—Symphony Orch.	V. 9163
" " " " " "	Stokowski—Phila. Orch.	V. M-248
Siegfried Idyl	Bruno Walter—Orch.	C. X-26
" "	Meyrowitz—Grand Opera Orch.	C. X-73
" "	Weingartner—London Phil. Orch.	C. X-139
" "	Muck—Berlin State Opera Orch.	V. 7381–2
	Toscanini—Phil. Orch.	V. M-308
WEBER, CARL MARIA VON		
Overture, Euryanthe	Mengelberg—Concertgebouw	C. 68069–D
" "	Von Schillings—Phil. Orch.	D. 25098–9
" "	Blech—Berlin State Opera Orch.	V. 9398
	Sir Adrian Boult—B.B.C. Orch.	V. 12037
Overture, Der Freischütz	Beecham—London Phil. Orch.	C. 68986–D
" " "	Brecher—Phil. Orch.	D. 25349
" " "	Weissmann—Phil. Orch.	D. 25151
" " "	Fiedler—Boston "Pops" Orch.	V. 12040
	Hertz—San Francisco Orch.	V. 6705
Overture, Oberon	Beecham—London Phil. Orch.	C. 69410–D
" "	Mengelberg—Concertgebouw	C. X-34
" "	Mengelberg—Concertgebouw	D. 25522–3
" "	Coates—Symphony Orch.	V. 9122
	Fiedler—Boston "Pops" Orch.	V. 12043
WILLIAMS, VAUGHAN		
London Symphony	Sir Henry Wood—Queen's Hall Orch.	D. 25618–22

A special set of twenty-four orchestral records, issued by "Music You Enjoy," New York, selected by an advisory board consisting of Harold Bauer, André Kostelanetz, Lily Pons, Albert Spalding and Lawrence Tibbett, with the author as chairman, includes the following examples of program music:

Beethoven, *Country Dances;* Berlioz, *Rakoczy March;* Bizet, *Overture* and *Entr'actes* from *Carmen;* Brahms, *Academic Festival Overture;* Elgar, *Pomp and Circumstance;* Gounod, *Ballet Music* from *Faust;* Grieg, *Peer Gynt Suite;* Ippolitoff-Ivanoff, *March of the Sardar;* Liszt, *Second Hungarian Rhapsody;* Mendelssohn, *Overture* to *A Midsummer Night's Dream;* Meyerbeer, *Coronation March* from *The Prophet;* Moussorgsky, *Gopak;* Mozart, *Overture* to *The Magic Flute;* Ponchielli, *Dance of the Hours;* Rimsky-Korsakoff, *Spanish Caprice;* Rossini, *Overture* to *William Tell;* Saint-Saëns, *Danse Macabre;* Schubert, *Ballet Music* from *Rosamunde;* Schumann, *Träumerei, Evening Song* and *The Poet Speaks;* Sibelius, *Finlandia;* Strauss, *Blue Danube Waltz* and *Tales from the Vienna Woods;* Tschaikowsky, *Nutcracker Suite;* Verdi, *Triumphal March* from *Aïda;* Wagner, *Ride of the Valkyries* and *Prelude to Act III, Lohengrin;* Weber, *Overture* to *Oberon.*

INDEX

(Composers of Program Music and Their Works)

335

INDEX

INDEX

338

INDEX

342

INDEX